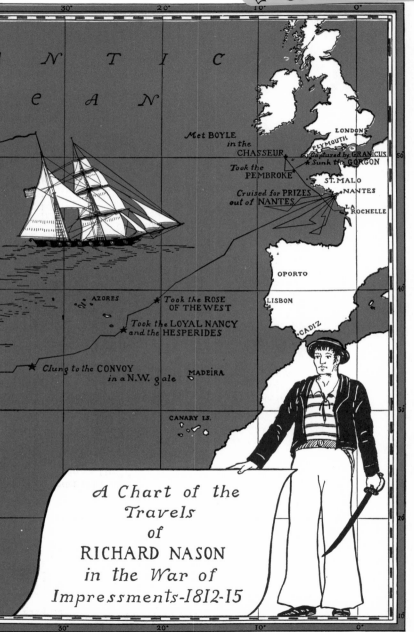

Met BOYLE
in the
CHASSEUR

Captured by GRANICUS

Took the
PEMBROKE

Sunk the GORGON

Cruised for PRIZES
out of NANTES

LONDON

PLYMOUTH

ST. MALO

NANTES

LA ROCHELLE

OPORTO

LISBON

CADIZ

AZORES

Took the ROSE
OF THE WEST

Took the LOYAL NANCY
and the HESPERIDES

Clung to the CONVOY
in a N.W. gale

MADEIRA

CANARY IS.

A Chart of the
Travels
of
RICHARD NASON
in the War of
Impressments-1812-15

THE LIVELY LADY

THE LIVELY LADY

KENNETH ROBERTS

DOUBLEDAY & COMPANY, INC.

Garden City, New York

TO
A. M. R.

THE LIVELY LADY

I

Our town of Arundel, at the mouth of the Arundel River in the Province of Maine, halfway between Portsmouth and Portland, is a small place; and those who live there think that nothing happens in it, ever. It is to escape from that dullness, no doubt, that so many of my townsmen have taken to the sea, knowing it and using it as landsmen know and use their front yards and back yards and farms and warehouses and highways.

Yet there is more curiosity among Arundel folk concerning the small things of life than concerning events commonly called great and romantic; and they are less interested in knowing how wars are won than in hearing how soup is cooked by the French and the English with whom Jeddy Tucker and I had so many dealings, some of them savory and some not so savory.

Therefore I shall put into this tale the small things that happened to me on the high seas and in various ports of this and other countries, and within the cruel bell-topped walls of Dartmoor Prison during our struggle with England's ships in the War of Impressments.

Jeddy Tucker, who was a school teacher and a scholar before he became a mariner, has said often that if he had the time, he could write more entertainingly than I of our adventures, putting in flowery language and noteworthy deeds and making a history out of it, whereas I can set down nothing but the simple truth and our own unimportant endeavors—though God knows they seemed important to us.

Yet, since he never had the time, being busy with conversation concerning his experiments with gambling games and the drinking of liquor, or concerning his uncle John Burbank, who was master at arms on the *Bonhomme Richard* under John Paul Jones, there was no way of getting it done unless I did it myself.

It seems strange that John Burbank, uncle to Jeddy Tucker, should have had an influence on me, considering that he died in 1793, which was three years after my birth. But it was because of him that Jeddy and I set out from Portland on a warm March day in 1812 and took the road down Bramhall's hill toward Arundel, and that journey profoundly affected my life.

This walk is a pleasant one under ordinary circumstances, what with the White Hills lying off to the northward, the vast flocks of ducks in the marshes near Dunstan's, and the sweet smells of young grass, moist earth and pine forests that blend with the fresh perfume of the sea between Biddeford and Arundel. Yet it is no walk for a man just ashore from a long cruise, lacking the feel of the land in his feet and legs; and if I had done as I wished I would have ridden home in state in a cushioned coach, for we were newly returned in our brig *Neutrality* from Cadiz in Spain and had not yet adjusted our clumsy sea legs to the hellish ruts and mire holes that are left in all our roads when the frost goes out of them in the spring.

But I couldn't ride; for when I went ashore from the *Neutrality* and turned into Fore Street with my small white dog, the one my father brought me from England when he last sailed there with my mother, I saw Jeddy waiting near the door of the Weather Rail Tavern. He came to me immediately with a serious expression on his face, which was small and innocent-looking, a little like a child's, but impudent.

I knew from the way he frowned and covered his lips with his hand that he had been splicing the main brace; for although this attitude gave him an air of thoughtfulness, it was only adopted to divert the smell of liquor from my nose. I wouldn't like to say Jeddy never spoke of his uncle John Burbank except when drunk; but it seemed to be a fact that whenever he devoted himself seriously to drinking, his uncle automatically entered the conversation—as a result of which there was immediate and overwhelming trouble. It seems that when his uncle was master at arms on the *Bonhomme Richard,* she had fought a desperate engagement with the *Serapis* and the *Countess of Scarborough;* and when the *Bonhomme Richard* was sinking, Jeddy's uncle had loosed the prisoners to let them escape with their lives. For doing it he was censured by John Paul Jones, who was a great captain, but hard. It was over this that the fighting began; for Jeddy, having stated his case, would at once offer to remove the hide from any man who would not admit that Paul Jones was a flint-hearted Scotch snake. Always, it seemed to me, there was someone to defend Paul Jones, which obliged Jeddy to fly at him without further formalities.

"Captain," Jeddy said, behind the shelter of his hand, "I'd think it a great favor if you'd take my bag to Arundel with you, seeing as how I might be delayed."

"Why might you?" I asked, mindful of his feelings. Men can do as they like for all of me, and I won't ask why they do it; but with Jeddy it was different. I didn't wish to lose sight of him, because he was quick to see the meaning in printed words and figures, which is a great help on shipboard to a new-made captain, young and forgetful of the many wordy problems in Bowditch's Navigator. Also, being skilled at card games, he was a pleasant companion on long voyages.

"Well, Captain," said Jeddy, moving quickly on his feet to keep from settling back on his heels, "it so happened I met two men, mariners from Halifax, looking for loads of potatoes for the British armies. They play piquet."

"So," I said, "you met two herring chokers, did you? Ten to one they're Scotch and hard losers."

"I'll make it as easy for 'em as I can," he said, drawing a deep breath and blowing it from the side of his mouth.

I saw there was nothing for it but to walk him to Arundel; for if

I left him with two Scotchmen, and he inflamed them by winning their money, they would fall on him together when he maligned Paul Jones, which was inevitable.

That was how we came to be plodding along the road together, with my small white dog Pinky running ahead of us, sniffling into every stone wall and ditch and old stump, and covering twenty miles for each one of ours. He was a good dog, this Pinky, called by that name because he was small and short, rising to a point at bow and stern, like the vessel known to us as a pink, a craft able to wriggle in and out of anything. When he came suddenly into a field he would behave like a pink in a choppy sea, leaping smoothly up and down, and seeing everything around him with a minimum of fuss and wild antics. He had small, high ears and black eyes, and important bristly white whiskers like those of Mr. Cutts the shipowner in Saco. He swaggered and rolled in his gait, his short tail bent upward, taut and jaunty; and he was high-and-mighty with other dogs, walking on his toes in their vicinity and seeming to fling oaths at them.

We traveled light, for I had given our dunnage, all but my mother's shawl, to Tommy Bickford, our cabin boy, the son of the Thomas Bickford who saved my father's life at the battle of Valcour Island; and Tommy, though only fourteen years old, would carry it safely to Arundel by coach, so that we needed to give it no further thought. The shawl, a white silk one embroidered with blue and pink flowers and bright green leaves, very rich and Spanish, was from Cadiz; and I had wrapped it around my waist under my jacket so I could give it to my mother on entering the house.

Between Dunstan's and Saco there is a dip in the road, with a meandering brook running through the meadow at the bottom. On the slopes are groves of birches, wild cherries and hawthorns, among which stand pines and tall elms. Even a man with half an eye would recognize it as the best of cover for partridges or woodcock.

When we came up from this dip we found a light coach standing by the side of the road, the driver asleep in the sun, and the body of the coach filled with expensive dunnage: hat boxes and coach robes and cloaks and small trunks, and atop the pile a man's beaver hat and an empty gun case.

While we stood looking at it, wondering whether to wake the driver, we heard a faint scream from a field nearby; then a ripple of laughter, soft and exciting laughter, unlike the sort I was accustomed to hear along the waterfronts of Havana and Lisbon. Close on the laughter came the sharp bark Pinky makes when waiting permission to accept food.

I left Jeddy, pushed through the shrubbery into the field and at once came on two women. They were on rising ground, a heavy stand of pines at their backs and the warm noonday sun shining down on them. One was an oldish woman, pleasant enough looking, but with an air of grayness about her, as if she had worn nothing but gray all her life and busied herself in colorless pursuits. The other was young and the opposite of her companion in appearance, for she had the look of never having worn gray and of never having done anything that didn't give her pleasure. She was kneeling on a robe, offering food to Pinky, who was sitting straight on his stub of a tail, as I had taught him when he was small; and her cloak, which had been placed around her shoulders, had fallen a little away, so I could see her dress was green, with ruffles on it, and her pretty arms bare below the elbow.

When Pinky looked around at me and barked, impatient to be allowed to accept the proffered food, the younger woman looked up. Her hair was the color of a copper rivet worn by rubbing, and her eyes seemed to mirror the greenness of her bonnet, though I could not make sure without staring overlong.

"Oh, la!" she said, prim and disdainful, "such a stubborn little wretch I never saw, never! Such a darling! Is he yours?" She turned from me at once, but I knew she had missed nothing of my clay-covered shoes, and the tie I had loosened at my throat, and the thickness at my waist where my mother's shawl was hid.

"Yes, ma'am," I said, wishing I had worn my varnished boots and my new baggy pantaloons and my blue silk shirt from Cadiz. "Take,

Pinky." With that Pinky leaped up and took the food from the lady's fingers. She screamed again, a faint, affected scream, and sank back on her robe, drawing her cloak around her. Pinky moved a little, so to be immediately before her, and, after glancing at me apologetically, threw himself upright once more; nor could I blame him, for if he was as empty as I he could have eaten a whole ox tongue and then looked around for something filling.

"You should feed your dog, sir!" she said to me severely.

It was then that Jeddy came up beside me and stood staring at the green-clad lady. When she held out more food to Pinky, Jeddy stepped forward and took it from her fingers.

"Is it fitten and proper for him to have such food as this?" he asked doubtfully. He held it out to me inquiringly; then popped it into his own mouth. He rolled his eyes upward, seemingly in contemplation. "You better taste it," he told me. "It might be bad for little dogs."

He burst into a rapid series of laughs, elevating his pale eyebrows until they almost vanished beneath his cap; and with that the lady in green, who had put on a dubious and distant look, glanced up at us and laughed herself. Her eyes, I then saw, were not green at all, but a sort of smoke color.

"La!" she said, rising to her knees to slice delicately at sausages and cheese that she took from a basket, "how thoughtless I am! I had it in mind you were on your way to your dinner, but perhaps you don't live hereabouts at all."

"No, ma'am," I said. "We live in Arundel, fifteen miles from here."

She looked at me blankly. "In a Rundle?" she asked, saying the name of our town as I had said it. "You live in a Rundle?" Then understanding seemed to come to her. "Lud!" she cried, "what a way to pronounce it! You should know it's Arun Del. We have an Arun Del in England, on the Arun River. You mustn't call it as you do, 'a Rundle'!"

"Well," I said, "there's no Arun River in Maine, and goodness knows what port you'll make if you go around asking for Arun Del."

She laughed lightly. "Small loss if we miss it! I remember the place too well!" She turned to her companion, the gray woman. "It was a Rundle where we stopped last night," she said, with an air of having suffered martyrdom. Then she turned back to me. "The food swam in grease, and we dared not rest in our beds. A terrible place! How do you stay there all winter without dying?"

"You'd say no such thing if you stopped with us!" I protested. "None of our food swims in grease! My aunt Cynthy's the best cook in the world, and I'd rather have our food than anything you can find in any country! Where do you live, ma'am?"

"I?" she asked, looking at me haughtily. "I live in London and at Ransome Hall, near Exeter and Plymouth in England."

"Those are terrible places," I told her. "London's a rabbit warren of filthy houses filled with drabs and slatterns and paupers, and Plymouth has fishwives and boozing kens enough to supply all America, I do believe."

"Ooh!" she said, tossing her head. "There was never such an untruth! Plymouth has the greenest hills and the fairest houses of all Devon; and there's no city anywhere with such fashionable people and lovely shops and entrancing routs as London!"

"Well, ma'am," I said, "I've been in London and Plymouth, and seen the things I tell you of."

"I don't care!" she cried, seizing Pinky in her arms and kissing the top of his head. "It isn't true! I've never seen such things in my life, and I've spent all of it in London or near Exeter."

"We've spent a good part of our lives in Arundel," Jeddy said, "and we don't recognize your description of the place."

The lady in green looked closely into Pinky's glazed eyes and ruffled his bristly whiskers with a small white hand, at which he sighed, throwing himself back voluptuously in her lap and raising his chin in the hope of having it scratched.

"Where is it you live in Arun Del?" she asked.

"I live in the garrison house at the mouth of the river. It was an inn when I left, and for all I know it's an inn still. If you'll come

there, my aunt Cynthy'll bake beans for you such as you'll get nowhere in England."

"Why did you leave it if you're so fond of it?"

"Because it's my trade to follow the sea."

"Oh, la!" she cried. "To follow the sea! What an expression! To
follow the sea! Where do you follow it to?"

"Why, to Spain," I told her, "or Portugal or Havana, or wherever
there's cargoes to be carried."

She rubbed Pinky's head idly. "Do sailors have sweethearts in every port?" She glanced at me from the corners of her eyes.

"As many as they want," I said, "and a nuisance it is, too, carrying
presents from each port to the next port for the sweethearts. Here's
what I mean." I unbuttoned my jacket and unrolled my mother's
Spanish shawl from around my waist, spreading it out in the bright
March sunshine so that its pinks and greens and blues flashed won-
derfully brilliant by contrast with the dead grasses and somber pines.

She squealed like a little girl, spilling Pinky from her lap and rising
quickly to her knees to get her hands on the shawl. I saw she was
younger than I had first thought, because of her hoity-toity air and
her fine lady's dress.

"There never was anything so lovely! How did you come by it?"
She jumped to her feet, letting her cloak fall from her shoulders and
pushing off her bonnet with a quick sweep of her hand. She took the
shawl from me, whipping it about her so that it bound her tightly,
making her beautifully smooth and slender.

"I got it in Spain."

She put her hands on her hips and flung me a look over her shoulder. "Is your sweetheart a fine lady?" I could see from the way she
asked the question that she had a slatternly wench in mind. "Do
you think she'll take the pleasure in this shawl that she ought, or will
she fold it away in a drawer and be afraid to touch it for fear of
soiling it?"

"How do I know?" I asked. "She suits me, and I've learned many
things from her; and if she hid it away in a drawer she'd probably

get as much pleasure from it as though she wore it at her work."

"At what does she work?" the lady inquired, smoothing the shawl over her hips.

"At anything that comes to hand." Then because there seemed to be a look of distaste about her small nose, I added quickly that she'd find few folk in New England who did no work, and that most of us worked because we liked to be busy.

"Oh, la!" the lady cried. "Teach your grandmother to suck eggs! You can't tell me anything about work, only I was thinking—I was thinking——"

"It's a difficult art!" Jeddy Tucker said with his best schoolmaster's air.

"I was thinking," she said, casting a scornful glance at Jeddy, "that your sweetheart might prefer another sort of present: a dress, or—or —or a sum of money. My husband, S'Roth, would pay well for this shawl."

That was how she called her husband—S'Roth; and it took me some time to realize it was her English way of saying Sir Arthur.

"Where is your husband?" I asked.

Instantly she was all smiles, so I could see she thought I would sell the shawl; nor, indeed, was I sure I wouldn't.

"He's gone into the fields," she said. "He saw some fine coverts and thought to shoot a few pheasant or woodcock." She seized the gray woman by the arm and shook her a little. "Give these good men a glass of wine, Annie," she added; and I knew she wished to keep us near at hand until the shawl was hers.

"Well," I said, while the gray woman rummaged for glasses and a bottle in the basket, "he'll get no pheasant, for we have no pheasant here, only partridges, which are better to eat and shoot than any pheasant; but it may be he'll find a woodcock, though it'll be luck if he does."

"Are they so hard to get?"

"No, but they're queer birds, vanishing like ghosts from where they were an hour before, and never to be seen in their flights, and shutting off their scent when they wish, so dogs can't smell them."

"Lud!" she said, laughing merrily, "you Americans can't be happy unless you're drawing the long bow! Shutting off their scent, indeed!"

"Why, so they do," I said. "There's no scent to them when they're nesting, and none when they're moulting, though a smart dog can track them by their footsteps."

She plumped herself down on her knees before me, wide eyed.

"What else do they do?" But there was no way of telling whether or not she was making game of me.

"Well," I said, when Jeddy and I had taken a glass of port from Annie's hands, and Jeddy had pledged all of us by raising his glass and saying, "Down the hatch!" as was his custom before drinking, "well, if they find there's too much passing near their nests, they take their chicks between their knees, one by one, and fly with them to a safer place."

"They never do!" she cried.

"Yes, they do! I've seen them."

"It's strange," she said, "that Sir Arthur has never told me of any such marvelous matters as these."

Pinky raised himself from where he had been drowsing with his head on my boot. He made a sound in his throat a little like a pump when it sucks, a malevolent sound to come from so small a dog. I looked around quickly to see what was amiss. Just this side of the young pines that screened us from the road stood a tall man with a fowling piece under his arm. He was a thin, glum-looking man with a pale face. There seemed to be an upward twist to his eyebrows and ears and hair, and a downward twist to his mouth, so that there was a flavor of old Diavolo about him that would have set me to growling like Pinky if I had been given to growling, even if the gentleman had not had a mislikable air of having listened to what we were saying.

II

Sɪʀ ᴀʀᴛʜᴜʀ ʀᴀɴsᴏᴍᴇ, I saw at once, would be forever free, where I was concerned, from any demonstration of devotion or affection; for when he joined us, he stooped over and brought out the bottle of port from the basket, held it against the light to see how much was gone, then looked coldly at the glasses Jeddy and I still held. It was in his face that if the giving had lain with him we would have tasted none of his wine.

It may be his wife was accustomed to finding a gray glumness in him, for she jumped to her feet, caught his arm, and swung herself close to him, looking gaily up into his face. "Look, Arthur!" she said, leaning back so he might see how she was encased in my shawl. "He bought it in Spain for his sweetheart, and I've asked him to sell it to us."

Sir Arthur examined her, back and front, as he might look at a chair he was minded to buy. "Not a bad shawl," he admitted. "Have one like it at Ransome Hall. Black though. How much did you pay for it?"

"Forty dollars," I told him.

"Ow! Did you now! That's rather high for a shawl! I'll take it off your hands for thirty."

"That's little short of princely!" Jeddy whispered.

Sir Arthur rounded on him. "Aren't you getting a bit above yourself, my man?"

I feared Jeddy would either cackle derisively or fly at the Englishman like a kingbird at an owl; and I knew whatever he did would prove disquieting to Lady Ransome, who had done nothing to deserve disquiet. Therefore I shouted his name, harsh and quick, as I might shout it on shipboard. "Set off up the road!" I said. "I've made this trip to keep you company, and I'll have no more delay."

When he looked at me uncertainly, I added that I'd catch up with him in five minutes. At this he made a pretense of pulling his forelock, saying in an obsequious voice, "Yes, sir, Captain, sir!"

He raised his eyebrows at Sir Arthur and laughed twice, glanced with broad and open admiration at Lady Ransome, and went strutting off through the brush like an impudent little gamecock. I half expected Sir Arthur to rebuke him again for his insulting laughter, but he only peered hard at me, as though he had forgotten Jeddy's very existence, which no doubt he had.

"Captain!" he exclaimed. "Surely you can't be a captain at your age: not of anything large enough to go out of sight of land!"

It has seemed to me that over-many Englishmen of my acquaintance pride themselves on what they call their frankness, and are seldom moved to be frank concerning the pleasant things that come to their notice, so that their frankness has much the flavor of rudeness. At such frankness Sir Arthur seemed a master.

"Well," I said, "it's true our brig's no great shakes in size, but she's a sweet sailer, and minds me as well as my dog Pinky. As for going out of sight of land, I've been in no Spanish harbor these two years past without seeing twenty Yankee craft for every Britisher; and eight out of ten of the Yankees were as small as our brig: yes, and smaller, too, though she tons only two hundred and sixteen."

"Haw!" Sir Arthur said. "Two hundred and sixteen! One must feel highly important, being captain of such a vessel!"

"There's no time aboard our brig to feel important," I told him. "Many people from Arundel follow the sea, but nobody does it to fatten his feelings."

"I see! You mean you do it for money!"

Now I have small love for folk who go up and down the land

squabbling and fighting for no reason except to coddle their own vanity. Yet every word this man spoke seemed somehow to exasperate me; and I would gladly have squabbled with him except that his lady, wrapped tight in my shawl, stood staring thoughtfully at him with one finger on her lower lip, which was as red as though newly wet with French wine.

"It's true," I said, "we must work for our living and, as you imply, have no leisure class like your own, which does nothing except for its own pleasure. This reminds me—I'm taking more leisure than I should; so if the lady'll return my shawl I'll be off on my business."

At this she clasped her hands before her and hopped a little on her toes, as children hop when teasing their mothers for cookies. "Arthur!" she cried, "you'll never let him go away without buying the shawl, Arthur!"

Sir Arthur said, "Ow!" again, as if he had forgotten about the shawl. Then he looked at me distantly. "I think the price was forty dollars," he said. "Of course, that's high, but I'll not argue. We'll take it at that price."

"The shawl's not for sale."

"My good man!" Sir Arthur said, "these trading tricks will do you no good, you know!"

I looked down at my knuckles, at a loss what to say to such a man; but while I still considered the matter I felt Lady Ransome's hand on my arm. "You wouldn't keep me from it, would you," she asked, "when you know how much I want it?"

I think it must have been Sir Arthur's talk of trading tricks that put an idea into my head as I looked at her standing straight and slender in the flowered shawl against the brown grass and the blue-green pines.

"No," I said, "I can't sell it to you, because it's for someone else; but if you'll stop to see her when you return from where you're going, she may exchange with you."

The lady laughed gaily. "La!" she cried, "I think I'll have no more chance of getting the shawl from your sweetheart than of getting the moon!"

"She thinks highly of me," I said.

Lady Ransome crowed with delight. "Such modesty!" she cried. "Or a skillful lover from having a sweetheart in every port! How shall I find this maid who's made you so trustful of her affections? Where does she live and what's her name?"

"She's my mother," I said. "Her name's the same as mine, and my name is Nason—Richard Nason."

"Oh," she said. She examined the flowers on the shawl. "It's beautifully worked," she added thoughtfully. "The shadings seem almost real." She whipped it off and handed it to me, turning to Sir Arthur as she did so. "He lives at an inn at the mouth of the river in Arun Del," she said. She clung to Sir Arthur's arm. "We could stop there on our way back from the Lygonia Patent."

Sir Arthur looked over my head contemptuously and ejaculated, "Tah!" or some word that sounded like it. "You must learn from experience, Emily! Do you really wish to return to Arun Del at the cost to ourselves of a meal of rancid pork, in company as unsavory? Do you know what these taverns are, my dear?"

"But the young man claims it's not so at his mother's inn," she persisted. "He spoke of some tasty dishes." She tossed her head at me impatiently. "What were they?"

"Lobster stew," I said quickly. "Corned beef hash moist in the middle and browned on both sides. Toasted brown bread spread with fresh butter, and with cream poured over it."

"Ow!" Sir Arthur said, rather more weakly than he had yet spoken. "Every traveler reports the inns of New England vile, with a few exceptions—which are viler."

Upon this, for a moment, I was near open profanity, but controlled myself by coughing and gave him a mild answer.

"Sir, you may have listened to the wrong travelers."

"I beg pardon?" Sir Arthur returned, looking at me from under drooping lids.

"Not all travelers say the inns of New England are vile," I said. "There was a French gentleman, Charles Maurice de Talleyrand-Périgord, who stopped more than once at our inn a few years ago. He was so taken with our chocolate custards that my aunt Cynthy had to teach him how to make them."

"Chocolate custards!" Lady Ransome exclaimed, clasping her hands at her throat and staring at me with eyes that seemed to glisten.

Sir Arthur favored her with a gesture of reproof. "What a pretty picture!" he exclaimed. "The great Talleyrand hovering over an oven in Arun Del!" He laughed an abrupt, unpleasant laugh, looking a little like a horse, and sounding somewhat like one. "You country folk are too credulous! I could tell you I was Talleyrand, and you'd believe me."

I thought of saying I would do no such thing, since all America knew Talleyrand to be a gentleman and a diplomat, whereas anyone could see Sir Arthur Ransome was neither; but I busied myself with my mother's shawl, adjusting it around my waist once more.

"I'm amazed," Sir Arthur continued in a thin and reedy voice, "that Talleyrand hasn't returned from France to Arun Del and brought the French emperor with him, if he found the cookery and the company so diverting! There'd have been a sight for sore eyes, my dear Emily —Boney eating with these fishermen! Highly congenial, I fancy!"

"Let me tell you something," I said. "Talleyrand never came back with the emperor, and that's the emperor's loss; but he did something almost as good. When Louis Philippe, Duke of Orleans, came to America three years after Talleyrand went home, he had been told by Talleyrand to come to our inn. Not only did Louis Philippe do this, but he brought with him his two brothers, the Duke of Montpensier and the Count of Beaujolais."

Seeing Sir Arthur again preparing to neigh like a horse, I raised my voice and hurried my speech. "They professed themselves well enough entertained. My mother says my father showed Louis Philippe and his brothers how to shoot an entire covey of partridges out of a tree, one by one, without frightening them away, and won fifteen dollars in so doing. There's no use saying they were impostors, for when Louis Philippe returned to Sicily he sent my mother ten silver skewers engraved with the royal crest."

Sir Arthur drew the fingers of his right hand across his forehead, as if to wipe a horrible vision from his mind. "Sitting!" he exclaimed, staring at me. "You shoot them sitting!" He raised his eyes to the sky with an appearance of helpless despair. "What a country!" he gasped. "What a country!"

"What gives him this trouble?" I asked Lady Ransome, who had crouched near me to pull Pinky's ears.

"The partridges," she said quickly. "You spoke of shooting them out of a tree, and it's not sporting to shoot a sitting bird. Everyone knows that."

"Oh," I objected, "there's some sport to it! It takes a good eye to find a partridge in a tree; and it only ceases to be sport when you hit one without killing it and then try to find it without the help of a dog."

"Dear me, dear me," Sir Arthur said, "they shoot sitting birds!"

"Well, we don't——"

"Tut, tut, young man!" the Englishman cut me off. "I had a grandfather, it happens, who purchased what was called the Lygonia Patent, and I'm on my way now to prove my ownership of all your province; but I think, though I might own it, I'd be pained to live in it if it's the habit here to shoot sitting birds."

"Well, sir," I said, "I've heard people in these parts speak of how your countrymen are forever trying to get away the Lygonia Patent from those who now live on it, and I can tell you you're wasting your time."

Sir Arthur looked at me icily, and turned to his wife. "Pick up this litter," he said. With that he stalked through the bushes toward his coach.

Lady Ransome jumped to her feet, knotting her bonnet strings beneath her chin. When I would have helped her with the rugs and luncheon basket, she pushed me away with a hand that looked a little like a child's, dimpled at the knuckles. "You should never be truthful with travelers," she said, "if you wish them to taste your chocolate custards."

I would have been glad to see her in Arundel if she could have come alone; but since I couldn't tell her this, I whistled to Pinky and set off after Jeddy Tucker, wondering how any woman could endure being the wife of an Englishman.

III

I F EVER there was a haven for a retired seafarer, it was our house at the mouth of the Arundel River; for it stood on a twenty-acre oblong of fertile ground, with the river running snug along the easterly end of it, a sheltered creek for its northern boundary, and the ocean and a long beach of hard gray sand bordering the side to the southwest. Within sight of its windows was everything a mariner could wish to occupy his attention. There were cows and hens, and fields of corn, beans, potatoes and pumpkins, large enough to keep our cellar stocked with food during the longest winters. In addition there were ducks, geese, wild pigeons and fish to be had for the taking; and best of all, from a seaman's viewpoint, there were eight shipyards between our house and the new toll bridge, all busily engaged in turning out the schooners, sloops and brigs that made our town of Arundel the busiest and the wealthiest in the province of Maine, next to Portland. It was the custom of large vessels to load the last of their cargoes while lying out beyond the bar that obstructed the river mouth, and never a day passed but what a brig or a snow or a ship entered the river at high water with a cargo from Spain or Portugal or Denmark or the Indies, or stood off and on, waiting for tide or wind.

There was a quickened thumping under the shawl that bound my waist when Jeddy Tucker and I came down the path between the tall pines, that evening, and saw our house, low and gray, against the ragged dunes and the darkening seas beyond. I could not blame

Pinky for the yapping he set up, nor for the dash he made across the narrow foot bridge and along the path to the house, scuttling into the dusk so rapidly that he might have been the ghost of a dog.

The front door opened; a stream of yellow light flooded out, and in the midst of it stood my mother. I had no more than kissed her when my aunt Cynthy, my sister Sarah and my older brother Nathan came at me with their greetings. Nathan's was brotherly but a little envious; for he had not followed the sea since the embargo, he being color blind and therefore unable to tell one flag from another—a dangerous affliction indeed in days when a mistake of that sort may result in a twelve-pound shot between wind and water.

We went at once into the large front room, which had changed during my absence. In place of the sanded floor and the trestle table there were braided rugs underfoot, brightly colored, and against the wall the long sofa inlaid with satinwood, and the tall secretary made for us by Benjamin Frothingham in Boston. Not only had my mother enriched the room with her carved chairs in the Chinese taste, bought when she sailed with my father to England, but she had covered the pine walls with wall paper depicting scenes in distant cities to which I had never been, so that to be in the room was as good as traveling to foreign parts.

"Quick!" said my mother, taking my arm and shaking me, "say how you like it!"

My mother was small and dark, with a back as flat as a board, though it was a mystery to me how she kept as straight as she did; for when I was young she had gone overboard in a gale to help my father, and had been pounded on a ledge by a heavy surf so that her lower half was somehow weakened. Above she was as strong as ever, and perhaps even stronger; as I was reminded when she thumped me on the chest to emphasize what she was saying.

I said at once that it was no sort of room for an inn, since Jeddy Tucker would use the sofa to heave at the head of any man who stood up for Paul Jones.

"Yes," my mother said, "that's what would happen if this house

should continue to be an inn. Our inn-keeping days are over, however, for I'm fond of my furniture; and things are going to be worse
instead of better, with all this talk of war, and our people ready to
throw chairs at any man who says a good word for the rights of
America."

"Well, and why not?" I asked her. "What rights do we have, and
what have we got to demand them with?"

My mother twisted her fingers in the string of cat's-eyes she had
worn at her throat since I was able to remember, and I knew I was
on the verge of hearing something that might not please me. Declaring hurriedly, therefore, that I was dying for lack of food, I unwrapped the shawl from my waist. "Look here," I said, tossing it
over her head so she was muffled in it, "I brought this from Spain,
and all I ask in return is that I sha'n't be talked to of war or anything
else till I've had supper."

It was on my mind, while eating, that I might have been overhasty
in speaking to Lady Ransome and her husband about our inn and
the food to be had there. After a time I asked my mother whether a
traveler could be accommodated as in the old days if there seemed
to be some special reason for it. When she was silent, I looked up
under my eyebrows at her, and saw her fingers at work again on her
cat's-eyes.

At length she nodded. "I think so," she said, "especially since she's
young and pretty and took such a fancy to my shawl."

I gave Jeddy Tucker a glance of some severity, but he, with un-
buckled belt, was busy on his third helping of corned beef and looked
entirely guiltless. Puzzled as to where my mother had her information, "She?" I inquired. "What 'She' took any fancy to your shawl?
She?"

My mother, exasperated at my stupidity, rolled her eyes toward
the ceiling. "There's the odor of a fine perfumery on the shawl," she
said. "Would it last all the way from Spain? I think not! It's been
somewhere, my son, and I think the where was young and pretty."

Perhaps I got a little red. "Maybe so. Maybe so; I admit it," I said, "but you might guess too much; for she was traveling with her maid and her husband——"

"Oh, her husband! And traveling? On foot, perhaps?"

"No, in their own coach."

"Ah! Then you thought the husband an unpleasant fellow, didn't you, and too old for her?"

"You've seen them!" I exclaimed. "They must have passed through here!"

My mother shook her head. "You must learn to draw conclusions, or you'll go through life not seeing half the things that lie before you. If the lady's young and pretty and traveling besides, it's quite certain she didn't marry a man younger than herself. And when a young lady marries an older man, he soon learns to be unpleasant toward the younger men who meet his wife; and to them he appears ancient and decrepit."

"If you're trying to accuse me of paying undue attention to the lady," I said, "you're making a mistake. There was some talk of the evils of our Arundel inns and our Arundel food, and her husband declared that all travelers invariably pronounced them vile."

"I see! And after that you were on such friendly terms that the lady tried on the shawl?"

"No," I said, conscious that my sister Sarah was casting sidewise glances at my brother Nathan, "the shawl came up in another way."

"Ah," my mother said, twisting her fingers in the string of cat's-eyes.

"The Englishman," I continued hurriedly, "wouldn't believe I was a captain, or that our brig was large enough to get out of sight of land; and he wished to buy your shawl for less than I paid for it. I told him it wasn't mine to sell; and since he had such a fine opinion of himself I added that if he'd visit our inn, it might be you'd trade him for it. I knew if you'd take the matter in hand he'd think twice before trading for Spanish shawls in New England again."

My mother lifted an eyebrow. "My son, I'm too old a bee to be caught with that sort of sugared water! Any traveler who wishes

hospitality in this house will always have it as long as I'm alive, unless he's the sort who doesn't deserve hospitality—and it seems to me
our country is producing more and more persons of this sort, thanks
to the preachments of that madman, Thomas Jefferson!"

Now one thing the sea had done for me was to give me relief from
the daily cursing of Thomas Jefferson that resounded through all our
province from morning until night, even though three years had
passed since James Madison had replaced him as president. So great
was my abhorrence of Jefferson that I preferred, for the benefit of
my digestion and my peace of mind, never to hear him mentioned.
Like nearly every other New Englander, I detested him for his petty
meannesses, his economies that proved to be dreadful extravagances,
his aping of the leaders of the French mob, his supplanting of our
fine navy with little gunboats that sank in a capful of wind and could
no more stand against a frigate than a jellyfish could fight a shark. I
couldn't endure his hatred of cities and city folk, and his desire to
rid the nation of manufacturers and artisans, so there might be nobody to cast votes except farmers; and I was fairly sickened by his
strange belief that all people are perfectly equal: not to be called by
any title whatever—a belief he could never have held if he had spent
less time examining the manners and customs of vegetables and
more time on a deep-water brig.

It was this last belief that most often turned the stomachs of our
seafaring people, who know disaster is bound to overtake any craft
on which the captain is not respected and instantly obeyed.

"What," I asked her, happy the conversation had at last turned
from Lady Ransome, "is this talk of war? Is it anything new, or is
it the same old war talk we've been hearing since I was knee-high
to a duck?"

My mother rapped her knuckles on the table to emphasize her
words. "It's new, because the crazy fools in Washington who've been
trying to sell their country's services to either England or France,
whichever would pay them best, haven't been smart enough to avoid
being cheated. They struck a bargain with Bonaparte, who's as great

a thief as a Barbary pirate. Bonaparte swindled them, and England's in a rage because we trafficked with him; so now there's nothing to be done but fight England. What wearies me is that if we had anybody in Washington but a pack of sawdust dolls, we'd have fought both of them a dozen years ago. We should have fought at once, as soon as they began telling us where we could trade and where we could sail our ships, as if they owned all the oceans of the earth, and taking our seamen from our own vessels as if we were black slaves in Africa."

"To be frank," I said, "I see no sense to this talk of war. We're making a living out of our brig; but if we fight England, we'll have no living at all, for we'll have to lay her up. You'll never get me into a war with England. England's the only nation that defends the world's freedom against Bonaparte."

My mother stood up, her hands on her hips and her new shawl clinging to her arms and her flat shoulders as if she had backed her topsail to give us a chance to come up with her.

"Yes, indeed!" she said ironically. "England's always been a great hand to defend freedom! She's as eager to defend freedom as to cut her own throat!" She made a derisive sound in her nose. "Can't you tell the difference between right and wrong? Can't you get in a rage when the British and French do things to us that they shouldn't?"

"They never did anything to me."

"Oh, my Land, Richard! The French never did anything to your grandfather, but he fought them at Louisburg! The English never did anything to your father, but he fought them at Quebec and Saratoga; and a good thing for you and all of us that he did!"

"There might be two ways of looking at that," I said. "Not even the English could have sent us worse governors than Jefferson and Madison with their damned embargoes and shilly-shallying. I can't see how my father gained much by his fighting if you now say we must fight again. How many people in this town want to fight England, anyway?"

"How many? How many? Probably four out of every four hundred.

The other three hundred and ninety-six are making a little money, and it blinds 'em. That's the way people are down here. You've caught it from 'em, Richard."

She came around the table to tap me on the chest. "Richard," she said, "you look a little like a sleepy pirate, with your gray eyes and your black side-whiskers. That's how your father and grandfather looked; so I have hopes that you, like them, may wake up at last."

IV

FRETTED by this talk of war, it seemed best to me, after a few days of our good Arundel food and feather beds, to get back to Portland and hasten the sale of our Spanish wine and hides, so we might be off to sea once more.

It was late afternoon when I set out to find Jeddy and let him hear my plans. I knew I would probably come across him at one of the taverns, hobnobbing with the men from the shipyards over their daily four o'clock rum.

Therefore I went to John Patten's inn on our own side of the river, but Patten had seen nothing of Jeddy for more than two hours. He had dropped in, Patten said, peaceful and elegant spoken, and taken a few glasses of rum with Job Averill; then left for Ward's shipyard to look at the new brig Ward was building.

I crossed the river to Ward's shipyard, where Dominicus Weeks, the rigger, told me he had seen Jeddy going toward Nathan Wildes' public house with Pelatiah Ham, Keziah Gooch, and Rowlandson Drown. I was not pleased to hear this. Rowlandson Drown was a chair maker, more quarrelsome than an old bull whale with a sore nose. Once, indeed, he had fallen out with his brother-in-law and tried his best to drown him in the river.

I hurried to Wildes' public house, fearful that Rowlandson Drown might take a sudden dislike to Jeddy; and even before I entered I could hear Jeddy and Keziah and several others saying their say against a war with England. I heard Drown whine that if there was a war there wouldn't be a chair made in Arundel in five years; while Keziah Gooch was bawling that not a man from Arundel would lift a finger against England; and Jeddy was shouting that he could use his time more profitably than in fighting.

I pushed open the door and went into Wildes' dark little front room, where you could either sit on kegs or stand up, as suited your convenience. No sooner had I set foot inside than Drown, a bull-necked man with a face all gray and blotched like the sides of a young sculpin, tossed off a glass of rum and complained that if we had a few seamen like Paul Jones there might be some sense in this talk of fighting England, but as it was we'd get nowhere.

There was a growl of assent from the caulkers and adze-men; but Jeddy came off his keg like a squirrel, peering into Drown's mottled face.

"Jones!" he exclaimed. "That piece of Scotch pudding! Why, we've got ten men that can sail rings around Jones!"

"Who are they?" growled Keziah Gooch, while Rowlandson Drown's face darkened as though the rum he had drunk were coming to the surface.

"Who?" Jeddy shouted. "Why, Bainbridge and Decatur and Hull and Perry and every man jack that helped lick the Pasha of Tripoli! Jones! He was a Scotchman, and there ain't a Scotchman on earth that can sail with our Yankee captains! Jones! Jones, hell! There's a dozen men in this town that can outsail Jones! Why, Richard Nason can outsail Jones! Why, my God, I can outsail Jones!"

Rowlandson Drown made a ripping sound between his tightly closed lips, whereupon Jeddy pushed closer to him, his spine so straight that he seemed to lean backward.

"Listen," he said, "I want to tell you about Jones! My uncle, John Burbank—John Burbank of Arundel—was master at arms under Paul Jones! Don't try to tell me about Paul Jones! I know all there is to know about Paul Jones! He was nothing but a big lucky bag of Scotch porridge, that's what he was! Master at arms under Jones, my uncle was! Don't you try to Jones me!"

Rowlandson Drown made a snarling sound, took Jeddy's small face suddenly in his tremendous hand, and pushed him backward over the keg. I started forward when I saw this; but before I could reach Rowlandson, Jeddy had slipped from beneath his hand, bounded upward as though shot from a mortar, and seized Drown by the ears. Drown's huge body seemed to float upward from the keg, and an instant later his head was driven against the top of the barrel with a hollow clang. Seeing that Keziah Gooch was making ready to kick Jeddy from behind, I hit him on the chin, knocking him between two kegs; and then, although Pelatiah Ham had made no move, I drove my fist into his stomach for fear he might take it into his head to leap at Jeddy. Pelatiah went down on top of Keziah and lay quiet, except for a slight choking sound; and Jeddy and I had a little space in which to move.

It was well we did; for Rowlandson, though his head was still being thumped against the keg top, had recovered from the first surprise of the attack and got his big hands under Jeddy's arms. I shouted to the little bantam to leave go and come away; but even as I did so Rowlandson heaved hard, and Jeddy turned a slow and majestic somersault over Rowlandson and the keg. Since he kept hold of Rowlandson's ears the keg was displaced and the two of them fell over on the floor, scuffling and panting.

By this time the adze-men and caulkers were shouting and milling around. It was plain they hadn't relished Jeddy's words about Paul Jones and hoped Jeddy would be killed. I jumped over to pull him away from Rowlandson, and I think we might have got out of it without further difficulty if Nathan Wildes had not come running in from the back of the house, a bung starter in his hand, shouting, "I'll get the little weasel!" Seeing this would never do, I took the bung starter from Wildes and hit him lightly with it on top of his head. Even as he fell, I saw, out of the tail of my eye, one of the caulkers coming for me. It is bad, in such a case, to wait for an attack; so I felled the caulker with the bung starter: then dropped it, for fear of spattering someone's brains on the floor, and went after

the rest of the caulker's friends with my fists. I felt two go down before me. Then the room was full of noise and confusion, and over my
left shoulder I saw a bottle coming hard at my head. The floor
seemed to fall out from under my feet, letting me drop miles into a
black pit.

*   *   *

We were lying outside in the dusk when my senses returned. My
skull seemed stuffed with sea urchins; and when I opened my eyes
they stung and smarted until I said to myself they must have been
knocked from their sockets. The smarting, I found, was caused by
brandy that had been poured on my head, whence it had run into
my eyes and over my clothes, so that I smelled like a distillery.
Keziah Gooch was standing over me, a brandy bottle in his hand;
and when he saw my eyes were open, he asked what should be done
about Jeddy's ear. "Drown got his teeth in it," he said, "and kind of
frayed it. Mebbe we ought to heat a poker and sear it off."

I sat up and looked at Jeddy. His left ear was torn in two or three
places, but there was nothing about it that couldn't be remedied
with stout thread and a sail maker's needle. None the less, he was so
still and white that he worried me.

"What happened to him?" I asked. "Is his back broken?"

"Not to speak of," Keziah said. "He was all right when they carried
Rowlandson home with his knee out of joint and four teeth missing.
Then we saw this ear and started to put brandy on it. He told us an
ear was no place for brandy, and before we could stop him he took
the bottle and drank the whole of it. That's his trouble."

I paid Keziah for two bottles of brandy, shoving the partly used
bottle into my trousers pocket; and after I had tied a handkerchief
around my head so no more blood could spatter on my shirt, I
picked Jeddy up, slung him over my shoulder, and went hunting for
a punt to carry us down river. It was dark by the time I found one,
and still darker when the punt grated on the sand at the river end of
our farm. I held Jeddy by the feet and dipped his head in the cold

river water; but since he seemed to derive no benefit from it I hung him over my shoulder once more and carried him through the potato patch to our house. When I kicked open the back door, there was nobody in the kitchen, which seemed strange to me; so I opened the door into our new big room, the one that was our gathering room in the old days. Every candle around the wall was lit, and as I staggered forward, carrying Jeddy toward my mother's sofa, there seemed to me to be a hundred people standing in the room, all of them blurred and indistinct in the brilliant light. My mother's face came out clear from the muddle, and then my sister's and my aunt Cynthy's. They were staring at me, and I could see horror in their eyes. With my left coat sleeve I wiped away the blood that was seeping through the bandage round my head; and then I saw, beyond Sir Arthur Ransome and, at the height of his shoulder, looking at me out of a haze, the startled face of his young wife.

I stared at her hard, not even shifting my gaze from her as I let Jeddy slip down upon the sofa. She was in brown, and not in green, as I had seen her in the field near Saco.

"You changed your dress," I said.

At that I heard my mother laugh. "Was it a good fight, Richard?" she asked as she put her arm about me and turned me toward the stairway.

*   *   *

By good fortune the next day was one of those fine unseasonable March days especially made for the loosening of the bands of ice that bind our Maine fields and streams. There was a sweet, warm, smoky breeze out of the northwest, a breeze that flattened the ocean near to shore, so that the waves were small and weak, dropping wearily on the sand as though they lacked the strength to press onward to the high-tide mark. I might have slept the clock around if my aunt Cynthy had not stood by my bed, smiling her gentle smile and holding in her hands a cup of clam broth to which she added a generous portion of horseradish juice—an excellent drink for relieving an aching head. When I told her about our fight at Wildes' public house, she clucked her tongue sympathetically and sat on the edge of my bed to wash the cut over my ear. It was a little tender, this cut, but nothing to think about unless a boom should swing against it.

While she stitched a neat band of old linen around my head, she told me how Sir Arthur had gone with Nathan to Batson's River to shoot teal, and how Lady Ransome was with my mother, asking a thousand questions concerning America.

When I came downstairs I found Lady Ransome beside my mother on our long sofa inlaid with satinwood. I thought she looked pale, though this may have been caused by the black dress she was wearing, a fetching dress that billowed out from her like a doll's dress, making her seem too small to be a grown woman and a wife. She was at work on a piece of needlework, a white thing on a round frame, entirely useless-looking, to my mind, more for appearance than anything else; and she was telling my mother about her father, who, if I correctly understood the little I heard, was a man who considered it demeaning to work, but wholly respectable to permit his wife and children to toil like Barbary galley slaves. She was so interested, seemingly, in what she was saying that she was oblivious to my entrance; and when she had finished she went at her needlework as if she intended never to look up from it.

My mother lifted an eyebrow at me but spoke to Lady Ransome. "My child, here's Richard himself come to tell you that you need distress yourself no more about him."

Lady Ransome dropped her hands in her lap. "Oh, lud!" she exclaimed, looking up at me as if in despair, "your mother calls me 'child' out of meanness, I do believe! I remembered you spoke of chocolate custards, and because I asked for them she calls me 'child'!"

"How many was it you ate?" my mother asked. "Five, it seems to me."

"I tell you that was *not* the reason I went early to bed!" Lady Ransome declared. "It was because I was weary!"

My mother's knitting needles clicked busily for a time, while Lady Ransome looked loftily from the window, wholly indifferent.

"Richard," my mother asked, "is it too early for woodcock to be nesting?"

Lady Ransome tossed her head a little. "La! I fear it's too warm for walking, and Sir Arthur will return shortly!"

"Do as you wish, my child," my mother said. "You spoke so much of them, I thought you wished to see one."

I could think of better ways to spend an afternoon than to walk in the woods with a girl who didn't know her own mind two minutes running; so I was turning away with no further words when Lady Ransome shot a quick glance at me without lifting her head from her sewing—a glance so fleeting I couldn't have sworn I saw it. Yet it left in my mind an impression of stifled hopefulness, such as I sometimes have from Pinky when I leave him lying in a corner of my cabin and he rolls an eye at me in the vain and momentary hope I may relent and invite him to come. Therefore I turned back and said that if her husband had never shot teal in our marshes he would be gone till sundown; for it would take him till then to learn he couldn't kill them as they came down on a northwest wind unless he led them, as our duck hunters say, from here to Scarborough. As for the woodcock, I told her, there was no way of telling whether they were nesting until we looked, and the place to look was an island of pines and birches in the marsh where they had always nested since I was able to find my way about. If there was none, I said, I could show her something in the marsh pools that she had never before seen—sticklebacks building round nests under water and slashing at each other out of cussedness with the rows of bayonets on their backs.

"I don't believe a word of it!" she said, proud and lofty. Then she dropped her needlework and hugged my mother's arm to her. "When can we go?" she asked. "Is it true, what he says? And shall we see bears and Indians?"

"You'll see no bears," my mother said, "because there are none hereabouts; and even if there were, they'd run for miles to escape a man or a woman, being timid creatures. Neither will you see an Indian unless you go around by Perkins' wharf, where there's an Abenaki working on Westbrook Hopping's sloop. You'll know him, if you see him, by the way he wears his shirt tails outside his trousers. You can't go walking in that dress, so you must change it: then you can go as soon as you like."

Lady Ransome jumped to her feet, smiled up at me as gaily as though she had never learned how to be stiff or haughty, and ran from the room. We could hear her calling to Annie that she wanted her green dress.

"She'd be better off to stay here," I said, "because she'll get her feet wet and turn up her nose at the things she thinks she wishes to see."

My mother shook her head and smiled her one-sided smile. "She's like a puppy taught to stay quietly in a house with old people and not bark or chew shoes. She wants to play but doesn't know how." Her knitting needles darted in and out of the stocking yarn. "Besides," she added, "her lot may be pleasanter if this husband of hers should find some man willing and able to throw her a kind word."

I went out in the sun to wait for her. A clean, soothing smell came from the hot sea sand. In the northwest wind the ocean was like ruffled dark blue velvet; and on the far side of Wells Bay the slopes of Mount Agamenticus rose sharp and smoothly curved. It came to me suddenly that there might be worse things than talk of war; and that, given the proper companions, another day or two on land could be mighty pleasant.

V

THERE is a wide-spreading beech tree with silvery bark in a clearing near the edge of the marsh that borders the tide creek on the northerly side of our farm; and when I set off with Lady Ransome we crossed the creek and struck in past this tree, which is covered with the initials of all the young folk who have kept company together since the earliest days of our town; for it stands in a pleasant spot, sweet with marsh odors and sheltered from the tang of unseasonable winds, and cursed only with mosquitoes, which are never troublesome to lovers.

She stared at this tree from every side, reading the initials and marveling at the hearts and arrows with which some of the initials were embellished, and asking about the people who carved them. I told her how a beech tree was always planted in every New England town by the first settlers in it, even before they planted corn, because without a beech tree the lovers would have no place to carve their initials and do their courting properly—and lacking this, there might be a dearth of marriages and consequently an insufficient increase in the size of the town. That was the trouble, I told her, with the earliest settlers in our province under the Lygonia Patent: they brought no beech trees with them from England, and therefore their settlements were not successful.

"You never tell me anything that isn't a wild tale for children," she complained. Then she begged for the loan of my knife so she could cut her own initials on the tree.

"You mustn't do that!" I told her.

She stamped her foot. "Indeed," she cried, "and why not? Give me your knife this minute, sir!"

"Well," I said, "you won't believe it, but this is the truth: when a person cuts his initials on that tree he can never be content to live in any place but Arundel."

She laughed lightly. "La!" she said. "I'd rather have your knife than hear about the strange weaknesses of your countrymen!"

Seeing she was bound to have her way I gave her the knife, and she went to hacking her initials in the bark, irregular and slovenly. I might have done it for her and carved an English crown over the letters, but she had been so hoity-toity about it that I said to myself she could make the whole tree into kindling wood without help from me. Nor was I sorry I had let her do it alone, for she was pleasing to look at as she stood pressed against the twisted trunk of the old beech, slim and straight in her bright green dress, cutting away at the bark with both her small hands clasped around the handle of my knife, and her bonnet fallen back from the copper-colored hair so that the braids in which it was twisted seemed like fillets of ruddy gold.

"There," she said, when she stepped back to look proudly at the malformed E. R. that had resulted from her labors, "when you tell your tales to other girls, don't forget to tell them Emily Ransome put her initials here and never came back again."

She seemed to wait for me to speak, but since I could think of nothing I took my knife from her and pocketed it. "Of course," she added, looking at me scornfully, "you'll be glad to tell them this."

"No," I said, "we don't talk of such things to other girls." With that, when I had shown her the path, which ran in and out of the pines and bayberry bushes at the edge of the marsh, I went ahead so she would pester me no more with her notions.

When we came to the brook that runs into the marsh, making a sort of bight in the pines, I showed her, close under the bank, one of the round pools cut in the marsh as though the earth had been removed by an enormous doughnut punch. It was near the brook, and I knew it must have been recently filled by the tides, so that sticklebacks would come up into it from the ocean. I told her to sit quietly on the bank and stare into the pool, and soon she would see sticklebacks fighting.

We sat together on the smooth carpet of pine needles, peering down into the clear water, and when we had sat a while, dark arrows began to shoot from the sides of the pool toward the center and return again to the banks like streaks of darkness. "Those," I told her, "are male sticklebacks driving the females from their nests."

She clutched my arm as two streaks of crimson rose to the surface and slashed at each other. They were giants among sticklebacks, three inches long and shaped like mackerel, and the belly of each was blood red because of the mating season. As they slashed and fought, we could see the stiff spines, erect and murderous, along their backs. When one of them turned and ran, the other caught him by the tail, brought him to the surface, and shook him as a dog shakes a rat, slapping him about on the water.

"Why," said Lady Ransome, as pleased as a small girl, "it's wonderful! What else do they do?"

"They weave nests the size of crab apples out of soft pieces of water plants. There's a hole at the bottom and top of each nest, and after the female lays her eggs, the male drives her away and stands guard beneath it, staring up at the eggs like a lovesick zany, and wriggling his fins to drive fresh water through the nest. When an egg falls out he picks it up in his mouth and blows it back, like a boy blowing a bean through an open window."

"Then what?" she asked, her eyes as round as my mother's blue beads.

"Then the eggs hatch out, and the faithful father eats all he can. When the marsh is flooded at the next spring tide he goes back to sea and forgets about them."

"Like a sailor?" she asked.

I had nothing to say to this, so she smiled at me pleasantly enough and said, "La! I didn't mean it! I'm sure no good sailor would eat little children!"

She leaned over and peered more intently into the pool. "Do you suppose you could find a nest?"

I lowered myself over the interlaced roots that held the bank intact, tossed my coat to her, and began to fumble among the growing things under water. I could feel the sticklebacks dashing themselves against my hands in a frenzy of rage, and soon I came across one of the loose nests. I passed my cap beneath it and drew it out; then turned back to Lady Ransome.

"Now," I said, "you can never again say I don't speak the truth." I seized a bush at the edge of the bank and sprang onto the tangle of roots. The bush pulled loose, and somehow my foot turned under me. As I pitched slowly backward I heard Lady Ransome scream and saw her reach for my arm. The thought came to me that I would land on the cut made by the bottle during last night's fight. Even as I thought it, the thing itself occurred. The little soreness in my head blazed into a mighty, all-pervading stab: then there was nothingness.

*   *   *

I was conscious, when consciousness returned, of a cold wetness, coming and going, on the side of my head. A voice, close to my ear, said often and often, "Richard, Richard, can you hear me, Richard?" Water, cold salt water from the feel of it, dripped on my head, which seemed to be solid, like a twelve-pound shot.

Lady Ransome was kneeling beside me. When I rolled over she held a wet cloth against the cut.

"I thought you'd lie there all night," she said. "Does it hurt?"

The air was cold, and there was a greenish pinkness in the west, so I knew the sun was down.

"No," I said. "I'm all right."

"I thought you'd bleed forever," she whispered.

I looked over the bank and saw a splotch of blood on a bit of driftwood near the pool. I wondered, considering her slenderness, that she had been able to drag me up over the tangled roots.

"I'm not as helpless as you may think," she said, answering my look. "If it hadn't been for the bleeding I believe I could have dragged you home."

My mind cleared. "You shouldn't be here at this hour," I told her. "Start back, and I'll follow as soon as I can. Your husband will be angry."

"Probably," she said. "I'll wait for you."

"Go home at once," I insisted.

She took the handkerchief from my head, and jumped down over the bank to wet it in the brook. When she returned, I rose to my feet, feeling as though my head had been beneath a log for days.

"Now we can tie this against the cut," she told me. "Bend down."

I bent down, and she fixed the pad in place. I could feel her soft arm against my cheek.

It was no great while before I was able to walk and disgusted to think of myself having fainting spells like a half-fed girl. By the time we reached the foot bridge across the creek Lady Ransome was clinging to my sleeve, trotting a little, every few steps, to keep up with me.

I had felt in my bones there'd be trouble when we reached our house, and so there was. It was dark when we came to the door. Lady Ransome ran into the front room before me and caught my mother by the arm. "He fell and struck his head again," she said, "but it's nothing."

I kept my eyes on Sir Arthur, who sat close beside the whale-oil lamp on our center table, reading or pretending to read some papers that filled his lap and his hands. He threw her one hard, cold look, I saw: then seemed to have no further interest in her.

When Lady Ransome had told my mother, she went to her husband and stood behind him, pressing her cheek to his.

"I'm sorry to be late, Arthur," she said, "but I couldn't leave Richard until he got his senses back. Did you shoot many ducks?"

He moved his shoulders petulantly under her hands. "I think you knew I'd finish shooting by mid-afternoon, and that we might need to press on at once."

"I thought I'd be back much earlier, Arthur."

He moved his head a little to one side, as if to avoid the touch of her cheek against his, and at that she stood straight. "I supposed you understood you weren't to leave, since there was a possibility we might move on. You're not to be trusted, I fear."

At this it may be I made some slight movement, for he eyed me frigidly.

"See here!" he said, "didn't you know better than to permit Lady Ransome to go gallivanting about, miles from any house? I can't afford to be detained in a place like this! I should think even an innkeeper's son would show more intelligence."

I looked from Lady Ransome to my mother, who gave me a warning glance and went hastily from the room; and at the same time my brother Nathan came in. I turned from Ransome and spoke to Nathan. "Did you have any luck with the teal?" But it was Sir Arthur who took it upon himself to reply.

"Ow!" he said, hitching himself petulantly in his chair, "I never saw such birds! Really, you know, it's fearful, they're so nervous, always on the go! I could scarcely see them, they'd go by so fast! And they'd never sit down for a moment!"

"We got thirty-two," my brother Nathan told me.

"Well, upon my word," Sir Arthur said in his thin, fretful voice, "I think you shot all of them! Very humiliating, I assure you!"

I must admit that although Sir Arthur was as disagreeable a man in his speech, almost, as any man I ever knew, he was just and fair according to his lights. I can only say he seemed detestable to me. It was plain to be seen he considered me in the light of a groom or a footman and thought I should keep myself in another part of the house, well removed from his sight.

When my mother returned, she brought with her two glasses of hot buttered rum, a drink favorably known in our province, where it is thought the blandness of the butter softens the action of the rum and produces a kindlier and more genial glow than does the raw liquor. Yet it is little used, not only because butter is dearer than rum, but because of a general belief that the mixture may so soften the drinker as to lead him into dangerous generosities.

"Drink this," she said to me, "so you won't catch cold from loss of blood." She held out the other to Sir Arthur. "It would never do," she told him, "for you to go back to England without tasting the great New England drink that made it possible for us to win our freedom from England."

Sir Arthur thanked her and tasted it. "Ow!" he exclaimed. "It's a trifle greasy, isn't it!" He tasted it again: then looked coolly at my mother. "I can't for the life of me see how Britain lost to such a rabble as your people must have been. Scarcely an officer in all your armies, I've heard it said, was trained to the profession of arms."

My mother looked up at the ceiling, as if trying to recall something about the war.

"I remember," she said, "that one of our officers before Quebec was a barber."

"Think of it!" Sir Arthur marvelled. He drank heartily of his buttered rum. "You were handsomely beaten at Quebec, I recall."

My mother nodded thoughtfully. "Yes, the English were unexpectedly helped by the French at Quebec, so they gave a tolerable account of themselves. The tale might have been different if we'd had food and clothes and dry powder."

Sir Arthur took another drink and eyed my mother warily.

"It was later at Saratoga," she added, "when we'd been able to get another barber or two, that we put an end to the nonsense and captured the entire British army, including your Hessian friends."

My mother sighed gently. Sir Arthur stared morosely into his glass, which was empty.

At length my mother took it from him. "I'll get you one more before supper."

Sir Arthur roused himself. "It's greasy," he admitted, "but not a bad drink."

"You seem almost like a New Englander," my mother said, "you're so quick to fall in with our ways of eating and drinking, and so hearty with your approval."

"Ow!" Sir Arthur said, somewhat uncertainly.

"We only learn these things about each other," my mother added, "as we become more intimate. When I know you understand our feelings, I realize you may at heart be as excitable and sentimental as we, in spite of your imperturbable exterior. About my shawl, for example. If you feel as strongly about my shawl as I do, it may be I've made a mistake in refusing to sell it to you. Of course, we have no great need of money, but we might be able to find some ground for exchange."

Sir Arthur almost glowed. "By all means!" he exclaimed immediately. "To be quite frank with you, my wife took a liking to your shawl when she first saw it. I'm sure we've a number of things in our boxes you'd be happy to possess—Ow! a great number of things."

My mother seemed surprised. "Oh," she said, "so it wasn't for yourself you wanted the shawl!"

"No, no!" Sir Arthur replied. "It's for my wife."

"I see!" my mother said, as though a new aspect of the situation had dawned on her. She looked down at the glass in her hand. "I must fill this," she added. She glanced up at me suddenly, "Don't stand there gawking!" she cried. "Go along upstairs; get a clean bandage on your head and make yourself proper for supper!"

I said to myself, as I climbed the steep stairs to my easterly room, that if I were fifty years old and the captain of a thousand-ton ship, there'd be times when my mother would still think of me as a small, stupid boy, and speak to me as if I were that, and make me feel so into the bargain.

When I came down again I found my mother had been up to her old tricks, she having been master of her own sloop for years, trading in Boston and Portsmouth and Portland, where a trader needs smartness if he hopes to come out of a trade without losing his breeches.

Beside her on the sofa sat Lady Ransome, wrapped tight in my

Spanish shawl. Across my mother's lap was the finest fowling piece
I had ever seen—a beautiful gun with two barrels and a raised ridge
between them to permit of a sight being taken, and locks and ham-
mers so delicate that the first discharge, it almost seemed, would
break them. Also she had around her neck, in place of her cat's-eyes,
a string of carved green stones, and on her shoes two new buckles
set with brilliants. I knew nothing about the necklace and the
buckles: but I had trafficked a little in guns, and knew a fowling
piece such as my mother held was worth four times what I had paid
for the shawl.

The mellowness of the buttered rum, I saw, had done its work on
Sir Arthur; for when he addressed my mother, he was all loquacious-
ness and spoke as though his mouth were half filled with hot mush.

"You prob'ly don't know what you got in that gun," he told her.
"You never saw one like it, I'll venture to say. There ain't a gunsmith
in Belgium nor Spain nor Italy nor this whole America of yours that
can make a gun like that fowling piece. A Joseph Manton, that gun
is! Deadliest li'l' thing y'ever saw! Load her up with slugs and she'll
kill a stag at a hundred paces!"

"Foxes too?" my mother asked.

"Fockshes!" Sir Arthur exclaimed, his face a horrified mask. "Shoot
fockshes!" Then he laughed. "Thought you meant it! 'Pon my word,
one must watch you Americans every moment to find out whether
you mean a thing. You're very shavage here, but you wouldn't shoot
fockshes! You're wigging me, eh?"

I could see my mother had an answer on the tip of her tongue, and
I suspected she wished to say that fox hunting was not much sport:
that we only shot them when there were. no Englishmen to shoot.
She kept silent, however, so I felt Sir Arthur was so easy for her that
she took no further pleasure in baiting him.

"You're wigging me!" Sir Arthur repeated thickly. "Talking about
war and shooting fockshes! War, indeed! Fancy you making war on
England!"

"Well, there's this about it," my mother told him. "People who deal in ships belong to a brotherhood and have ways of knowing things. I'll say this much to you and no more: get your young wife down to Boston or New York as soon as you can, and take her home with no loss of time."

Sir Arthur stared hazily at my mother. "I think it's nothing but moonshine!" he said at length. "The thing's absurd on the face of it! Why, your country's helpless! Your army ain't worth mentioning; and where's your navy, hey? You ain't got one!"

"You're right," I said, though I disliked siding with anybody against my mother. "We have no ships to fight England, and no desire, either! I've no reason for fighting England, and I won't do it. Neither will any man in this town. Our living comes from the sea! Why should we let ourselves be driven off the ocean because a lot of fools in Washington who never smelled salt water say we must fight?"

Sir Arthur nodded. "You've more sense than I thought," he said. "We've a hundred ships, and more too, for every one of yours, and our soldiers are the finest in the world, able to whip the strongest nations of Europe. What could you do against our ships and our armies?" He laughed shrilly. "Did you ever hear of Dartmoor Prison, where we've shut up thousands and thousands of Frenchmen since they set out to fight us? It's the stoutest prison ever built; and within a month after you declared war on us, your cockleshells would be blown to pieces and your men behind the walls of Dartmoor."

My mother, slender and small and straight, rose suddenly to walk across the room and back. This, I had learned, she only did when boiling with words and fearful of exploding with the press of them inside her. She stood behind her chair, picked it up and thumped it down again.

"I believe it's the custom for a mother to be older than her son," she said. "In my time, too, I've done a fair amount of sailing, so maybe I can tell you things neither you nor my son would otherwise hear. You English are a great people, good sailors and brave fighters; but you've done things in certain ways for too many years. You're slow to realize other methods may be better than your own. I know the best ships on the seas, once, were English; but that's past. The best and fastest ships to-day are built by French and Americans, who've been driven by necessity to build better than you. I know there was a time when English mariners were the ablest of all the world's seamen, but that time has gone, too. To-day the greatest seamen in the world are Americans."

Sir Arthur threw back his head and crowed.

"I know how you feel," my mother told him. "The Englishmen who came over here during our revolution were scornful of our manner of fighting; and even when they found themselves disarmed and made prisoners, they thought it was all a terrible mistake. I'll say that for your countrymen: they're obstinate, especially about admitting defeats."

"Not at all! Not at all!" Sir Arthur protested.

"Well, I'm glad they've changed," my mother told him, "because soon they may have opportunity to admit another defeat. What you don't know, and what may mean nothing to you if you do know it, is that there's no house in this town—not one house—that hasn't a seaman living in it. There are more master mariners along our river road and the Saco road than there are Frenchmen in your English town of Quebec. In some houses you'll find five and six and seven sons, all captains. What's more, they're deep-water captains, born with salt in their noses and the feel of the sea in their bones; and you can believe it or not, but it's the truth: there's something about these New Englanders that makes it possible for them to sail their craft into places where the captains of other nations won't go. All up and down our coast it's the same—in Wiscasset and Damariscotta and Portland and York and Portsmouth and Newburyport and Salem and Boston and New Bedford, and in the little towns between; all the length of Cape Cod, and farther south, along the Connecticut and Rhode Island shore, and in New York and New Jersey and in every creek on Chesapeake Bay and in a hundred other places: everywhere you'll find master mariners who can handle craft as they've seldom been handled before, and seamen who are wild and rampageous."

Sir Arthur made as though to speak, but my mother thumped her chair on the floor again and wouldn't hear him. "I've seen our people go out like hornets against the French and Indians," she told him. "I've seen 'em drop their hoes and plows to pour out in rivers against your great Burgoyne, when he and his fine army proposed to batter the last of our resistance from us. You may think you can crush us with your hundreds of great ships; that we'll let ourselves be swallowed up without a struggle by this dark monster of a Dartmoor you talk about; but I tell you these New England mariners aren't easy to crush! They'll sting you and outrun you and sting you and outrun you until you're as fuddled as a horse with a foot through a beehive."

Even then she would listen to no reply from Sir Arthur, but suddenly declared Lady Ransome was half dead with sleepiness, and so hurried the two of them upstairs.

"Remember what I tell you," I heard her saying to Sir Arthur. "Get yourself over to New York and on your way to England."

Sir Arthur assured her, in his reediest voice, that he'd make every effort to do so, not because he feared a war but because he feared to hear further talk of it.

*   *   *

When my mother returned, she closed the door carefully and took a letter from the front of her dress. "I'd have told you sooner," she said, "but I wanted you all together and these English people out of the way. This letter is from Captain Callender in Boston. It came by express this afternoon. Here's what he says:

"'We have to-day received advices from Washington that Congress will immediately pass an act of embargo for ninety days. This will become a law on the 4th April, after which date no vessel will be allowed to clear from an American port. This is in anticipation of war

with England and is designed to prevent American ships and sea-
men from falling into the hands of the enemy, as well as to prevent
the carriage of necessary supplies to the British armies in Spain.

"'It is my duty to inform you that the shipowners of this section*
are nearly unanimous in refusing to submit to this embargo, the feel-
ing being that supplies furnished to the British armies in Spain will
not materially affect any military operations which may take place
in America. Kindly feel free to pass on this information to any in-
*terested parties.'"

My mother folded the letter and tapped it on the table. "Well,"
she said, looking from one to the other of us, "there it is! Pretty advice, I must say! The shipowners of Boston setting up to know more
than the government of their own country! Advising us to dodge out
ahead of the embargo so the embargo can't do what it's intended to
do!"

"It's intended to ruin us!" I reminded her.

"It's intended to keep food from the British!" my mother protested.

"Nonsense!" I said. "If they don't get it from us, they'll get it somewhere else! I'll set out for Portland to-night, and be off for Spain as
quick as you could skin an eel."

"I say No!" my mother cried, shaking the table to emphasize her
words. "If we're going to fight 'em, let's fight 'em: not trade with
'em!"

"Let those fight 'em who declare war," I said. "I won't fight Englishmen, who've done nothing to me, just because some damned old
landlubber from South Carolina votes to have me do it! Why should
I? Didn't my grandfather buy French rum from the French while
we were fighting the French?"

My mother turned to Nathan. "You'll stand by me, won't you?"

"It appears to me," Nathan said, moving his fingers clumsily, "it
would be a sin if we let every other shipowner beat the embargo and
just laid and rotted in harbor ourselves."

My sister Sarah squirmed in her chair. "Me too," she cried. "Bring me a shawl when you come back from Spain, will you, Richard?"

My mother stared at the table before her for a time. At length she looked up at me. "Is there anything you need, Richard?"

Since there wasn't, I left it to her to send my dunnage by Jeddy and Tommy Bickford on the morning stagecoach, after which I said good-bye to her and Sarah and aunt Cynthy and set out to walk the twenty-six miles to Portland, Nathan going with me for company, and Pinky sticking his nose in every stump along the road and fluttering his tail with delight at being off once more.

VI

THERE was never anything seen, on the Portland docks, to equal the happenings of the next four days; and word reached us that the self-same things went on in Philadelphia and Alexandria and Baltimore and New York and Boston and every other port in America.

When we came up Fore Street in the early morning, the docks lay quiet, smelling of tarred rope and lumber and sacking and fish, no different from any other morning. By mid-afternoon, when news of the embargo had spread through the city, every dock was alive with men, howling and sweating, and hauling at flour barrels, grain bags, salted beef, bread boxes and God knows what. Drays were backing up to all the docks, laden with provisions, and clattering empty to the warehouses for fresh supplies. Men came out from stores and counting houses, eager to have a hand in forestalling the embargo, and worked, adrip with perspiration, alongside stevedores and wharf rats and seamen and teamsters and farmers.

Never since ships were built did supplies tumble into holds with such speed. The work went on after darkness fell, by the light of smoking torches that gave the workmen, wrestling at their piles of provisions, the appearance of demons clambering over the lava heaps of hell. It continued until the pinkness of dawn came into the sky over Peak's Island, and on through the day and around through the night again. There was a sort of madness among the people against the embargo and against a war—such a frenzy to defy the government that a stranger might have thought us engaged in a revolution.

There was free rum for the workers, and free food; and whenever a vessel left her dock and set her sails, there was as much hullabalooing and cheering as though a victory had been won.

Only for one departure was there no cheering, that being in the case of the brig *Riddle,* said to be bound for Nova Scotia with food for the British in Canada. Because of this the captain, Eli Bagley, a Portsmouth man, had fought five fights in Fore Street taverns, there being a feeling that there was something wrong in dealing with the British on our own continent.

Eli Bagley was an opinionated man with a thin face and great prominent jaw bones. His whiskers grew like a hairy frill underneath his clean-shaved chin, and extended from ear to ear. This is a style of whisker I mislike, since all those on whom I have seen it have been sanctimonious men, tyrannical and churlish, always able to consider themselves right and everyone else wrong. Those who knew him said he was a vain man, fond of fighting but not good at it, since he couldn't keep his head when he fought, and so shipped only smallish, timid men on the *Riddle,* in order to indulge his fancy for fighting with no danger to himself.

Eli was opinionated enough, God knows, in this matter, declaring it was no worse to sell in Canada than in Spain, which seemed unreasonable on the face of it, and I, being bound for Spain, felt obliged to give him a black eye in return for his belief.

When the *Riddle* moved out into the harbor along toward dusk of the second day, a sort of snarling growl followed her from every dock; and showers of rocks and bolts flew toward her, bouncing harmlessly from her sides.

Thanks to a good agent and a good crew, all from Arundel, and thanks, also, to my early knowledge of the embargo, we were loaded and set off late on the third of April, a bright, cloudless day with the wind still in the northwest and blowing great guns, as it often does off our Maine coast in the spring of the year.

When I packed away my good blue coat in my chest that night I did a thing I had been in two minds about doing since Jeddy and

Tommy Bickford had brought my dunnage from Arundel. In this dunnage was my good blue coat, which I had last worn when I walked with Lady Ransome in the pines by the marsh; and when I took it out there was a thin disk, something like a silver dollar, caught in the lining. In the bottom of the pocket was a slit that looked to me to have been cut with scissors. I worked my fingers through the slit and fished out the disk. It was a plaque of ivory surrounded by a band of gold in which brilliants and colored stones were counter-sunk, and the plaque was painted clear and beautiful with a minia-ture of Lady Ransome—a portrait so delicate and fine that I could almost count each strand of her copper-colored hair and the black lashes that seemed to shade a little the smoky color of her eyes. The lips were so fresh and warmly red in appearance that I feared to touch them, lest the paint be as new and wet as it seemed.

It was true this lady had wearied me somewhat with her change-ableness, being first hoity-toity and then friendly: yet I had hunted for an excuse, on the night of my departure from Arundel, to bid her farewell. More than once after I had left, I had regretted my failure to have a final word with her; and now this miniature called her to my mind once more and left me puzzled as to how it had come in my coat. I thought of asking Jeddy whether he knew how it got there, since he had brought the coat from Arundel. I was reluctant to speak of the matter to him, but I was even more eager; so in the end I sent Tommy Bickford to bring Jeddy to my cabin.

When he came in, his knee-long pea-jacket unbuttoned, I un-locked the small oak chest my father bought in Ireland, the one with the large eight-sided bottle and the two six-sided bottles and the four four-sided bottles, and we hooked our feet around the table leg and had a thimbleful of red rum to a quick trip.

At length I asked Jeddy whether he had seen Lady Ransome be-fore he left Arundel. He said he had. She had come down to breakfast with her husband, he said, seeming to be in a fret, most likely over the embargo, and in a twitter to be gone from the house. For a time I held the picture of her in my hand under the table, and finally brought it up and showed it to him. He whistled when he saw it, and I could tell he had never seen it before.

"There's a tidy craft!" he said, taking it gingerly between his salt-hardened fingers. "Fine sweeping sheer to her and no foolish top-hamper. Sweet bows, and as nice a tumble home to her dead-works as you'll find anywhere!"

There were times when Jeddy became so nautical in his talk that a porpoise might have sickened to hear him run on, though he had often enough heard my mother declare that no man with a thought for the comfort of others would speak constantly in terms of his calling. "Just because you set out to be a mariner," she said, "don't forget the manner of speech of those who can't understand sea terms." But it may be that Jeddy, having been a school teacher for so many years, was impelled by the very dullness of his former occupation to express himself in the terms of his new one.

"You talk like a ship chandler," I said, taking the picture from him. "I'm not blind! What I want to know is what to do with it. I don't know how it got in my dunnage nor anything about it."

Jeddy squinted at me knowingly. "I'll tell you this much! That picture's worth something! It's not one of those things done by a swab-artist out of a bumboat for eight dollars. You'd pay fifty pounds for a picture like this in London, even without any copper bottom or binnacle lights around it! Stow it away, Richard! Findings keepings! If ever you're without money in a foreign port, a little bauble like that would keep you for a month."

This was good advice, so I put the picture on top of the striped silk shirts in my chest, and Jeddy and I played piquet and had another thimbleful of red rum to fair winds and a smooth passage before turning in. But after he left me I took the miniature from the chest and dropped it in a pocket of my shirt, determined always to have it near in case there was need, as Jeddy had said, to sell it.

I was happy to be back on the old *Neutrality* once more, for she was a good brig and comfortable, having been planned by my mother. I have heard it said in Arundel that many masters plan their own vessels, but they are built the way the shipbuilders think they ought to be built—except in my mother's case. Where my mother was concerned it was not so; and either the vessel was built the way she drew it, or the shipbuilder was tongue-lashed into going away and living in another town. The bulkheads creaked, in a heavy sea, like a whole flock of crow-blackbirds walking in an oatfield; but the chairs and the bunks were big and comfortable, and a man could move around without having his head caved in by the bottom of a whale-oil lamp, they being out of the way and so fixed that they reeked less than most; though to my mind there is a homey scent to burning whale oil, perhaps because I was born aboard the *Orestes* in Copenhagen harbor and so learned to know the smell before I had formed other tastes.

*   *   *

It was a little before sunrise the next morning when Cephas Cluff, the first mate, banged on the door to say there was a sail to leeward, maybe two miles away, and that she had just hauled her wind to cross our course. A ship, Cephas said she was, probably homeward bound and wishful of speaking us to get news or bearings.

The wind had dropped, and the water was tolerably smooth; so, mindful of the embargo, I told Cephas we must warn her. With that I hustled into my clothes and pea-jacket and went on deck.

She had come up fast, a sturdy black ship with a white streak; too sturdy, it seemed to me—and in a breath it dawned on me that here was no merchantman at all, but a sloop-of-war. In that very moment she triced up a port, fired a gun, hoisted the British flag, hauled up her courses, hauled down her jib, took in her topgallant sails, and backed her maintopsail, all with a speed impossible for a merchantman.

Here was a fine mess, I thought to myself, feeling as though someone had stuffed my mouth with cotton—a fine mess, and never so much as a rat hole through which we could dodge.

The men stood looking from me to the sloop and back again, knowing well that one or more of them, before nightfall, would be wearing a British seaman's uniform; and I could hear Jeddy cursing a set of curses he never learned out of the Fifth Reader or Bowditch's Navigator.

She was pierced for eight carronades to a side and had long guns forward and amidships, so I knew we would be torn to shreds with grape if we tried to run for it, or overhauled in this breeze, even though we got through the grape unscathed. There was nothing to do but come into the wind, and bring-to under the lee of this damned sloop.

The captain, a portly man, stood on one of the carronades, looking at us. "This is His Britannic Majesty's sloop *Gorgon!*" he bawled through a trumpet, "I'm sending a boat!" and send it he did, with twelve men besides the oarsmen, and a thin, red-faced lieutenant important in the stern sheets.

There was no formality about this officer when he came aboard, except for his uniform, which was a natty blue affair with tight net breeches, and with a gold swab as big as my mother's mop on one of his shoulders. It made me uncomfortable to look at him, what with my pea-jacket and my red-flannel shirt and the high leather boots I found most comfortable at sea. Ten men came over the side behind him, hard-looking broad-shouldered men, blue jackets to their knees and cutlasses and pistols at their waists.

"Who's master here?" he snapped, looking at Cephas Cluff, who was as tall as I, but broader in the beam, and important looking.

"I am," I said. "Step in the cabin and look at my papers."

He whirled and stood staring at me for a moment, his head lowered a little. Then he flashed a quick glance at Cephas and Jeddy and turned his attention to me again.

"Call all hands on deck!" he ordered, without so much as a "sir" or "if you please." I think if I had met this lieutenant under other circumstances I might have felt a liking for him; but there was something about the hard roundness of the blue eyes in his thin red face, and the fixed, contented smile on his down-curved mouth, that soured everything in me.

Every last one of our crew was in the waist, watching us. "The men are on deck," I said, "and you'll find no Britisher among 'em. They're all from the same town: the town of Arundel. There isn't one of 'em you can touch."

"Call 'em aft!" he said. "I've heard that story before! I know more than to let any Yankee skipper pick men for me."

The men came aft silently. The lieutenant turned to me with more politeness than he had yet shown. "Was there any talk of an embargo when you cleared?" he asked.

I pretended ignorance. "What embargo is that?"

His smile hardened on his face, and his eyes, fixed on mine, were cold as those of a halibut. "You say you're master of this brig, and you ask what embargo! You Yankees think you're pretty smart, but we know a thing or two ourselves! We know you're a lot of tricky rascals, quick as snakes to turn against your own country or against the country that provided spawning grounds for your people!"

I had heard all I could stand. "Do what you've come to do and get off this quarter-deck," I said, keeping as quiet as I could, because of the long guns slewed around on the sloop to bear on us.

He turned and looked at the men. They were staring at the mastheads, or at the deck seams, mild and harmless appearing as though no word of what had been said had penetrated their skulls.

The lieutenant went down among them. When he came to Tommy Bickford, he stopped. Now, Tommy was like his father, who carried my father to shore when he was hurt aboard the Congress galley, on the day General Arnold outthought and outfought the British at the Battle of Valcour Island, though outnumbered ten times over. He was flat backed and handsome, with wavy light hair and cheeks like a girl, and so soft-spoken and pleasant and willing that he was no more like the ordinary run of boy than a tapering spar is like an alder fish pole. There was no man on our brig or in all Arundel for that matter who wasn't perpetually pleased with Tommy and forever going out of the way to coddle him; and it was my guess he would be master of his own ship at eighteen.

The lieutenant laughed. "You can't breed 'em like this in your filthy country!" He motioned to his line of waiting seamen. "Take this one!"

"Hold on," I told him. "That's Tommy Bickford from Arundel. His father was a soldier in the Revolution!"

"Gammon!" the lieutenant said, watching me closely, so it came to me he had a reason for speaking roughly. "There never was an American that told the truth about that tuppenny ha'penny business you call a war!" He motioned to his seamen again. "Take him!"

The slatting of the running rigging, the yawping of the chickens in the coops that filled our boats, and the creaking of the rudder sounded as loud in my ears as though I had never heard them before. There was an aching in the muscles of my upper arms. The corvette, no doubt impatient at the lieutenant's slowness, fired another gun. We stood like figureheads.

Two of the Britishers closed in on Tommy, taking him by the shoulders and wrists. At that my little white dog Pinky whipped out from behind me like the end of a parted tow rope; and with his whiskers bristling so they hid his furious little black eyes he went to haggling at the ankle of the nearest sailor, all the time making a hellish sucking noise in his throat.

The man kicked at him, shouting, and strove to draw his cutlass without loosing Tommy's wrist. At that the lieutenant shouted as well, and stooped to slap Pinky with his open hand. Somehow the little dog released himself like a chronometer spring, whipping up and turning in mid-air; and in a second he had slashed the soft, muscular edge of the lieutenant's hand, cutting it to the bone. The lieutenant yelled and kicked at him, and all our Arundel men shouted together. Pinky, whirling, ran between them and stood partly behind the mainmast, peering out at the lieutenant with his stump of a tail bent up over his back as though on the verge of breaking, his whiskers bristling fiercely, and his legs planted as stubby and straight as a brace of whitened hitching posts.

The lieutenant stared at his hand, flipping it in the air so that drops of blood fell on the scoured deck; then in a flash he reached in the bosom of his coat and drew a pistol, which he leveled at Pinky.

Now, I well knew my business, which was to take our brig and its cargo safe to Cadiz, regardless of the acts of British lieutenants who exceeded their authority, or of the misfortunes of our crew, or even of my dog, who was a better friend to me than most of the humans I had met. Yet it is impossible, as I must often say, to lay out a course in this life and stick to it. Much as I hated the British lieutenant for his treatment of us, I would have laid no hand on him or any of his men, but would have steered clear of his determined spite. Our undoing came because I couldn't see my little Pinky shot down without protest. Neither, as luck would have it, could Jeddy Tucker. I have no doubt, in view of what I later learned, that if our downfall had not come through this, it would certainly have come somehow; for the officers of the war sloop knew what they were about.

However that may be, I struck at the leveled pistol with a belaying pin that had got into my hands God knows how; and a fraction of a second later Jeddy Tucker, on the lieutenant's other side, undertook to do the same. The force of my blow must have been greater than I thought, for when I hit the pistol the lieutenant pitched forward as though he had stumbled, and the pistol exploded. It was then that Jeddy's belaying pin came down. He was able to soften the blow, he told me, but he couldn't stop it, and so the pin rapped the lieutenant lightly on the back of the head. He dropped to one knee and was up again immediately.

"All right! Keep back there!" he shouted to his men, who had their cutlasses out and were spreading toward us. He felt the overhang of his head with his good hand and looked from Jeddy to me. "Whose dog is that?" he asked.

Half inarticulate from apprehension, I said it was mine, whereupon the down-curving smile deepened on his lips, as if there were something about the fact that gave him malicious pleasure.

A faint angry bellow came down wind to us. I could see the captain of the corvette standing on a carronade, clutching a shroud, and I knew he was bawling to his lieutenant to come back.

"Under the circumstances," the lieutenant said, "I shall have to ask you to return with me and explain to the captain about this boy."

"My God, man!" I said, "this is an American vessel! You can't do a thing like that!"

The lieutenant indicated Jeddy. "This man one of your mates?" he asked.

"Second mate."

"Bring him, too. You'll want someone to corroborate your statements." He motioned to his men. They signaled their boat, and two of them went over the side with Tommy Bickford.

The lieutenant laughed at my irresolution. "Hurry along, Captain," he said, his voice seeming to mock me, "or I'll bring over the gig and press your whole crew. God knows we need 'em, and anybody with half an eye can see they're all Englishmen!"

He had us, and there was no way out. "We'll come in our own boat," I said.

"Suit yourself," he replied, grinning sardonically.

"Lower away a boat!" I shouted, thinking to have a moment to say a word to Jeddy and Cephas.

"I'll send two men with you," the lieutenant added, "to guard against Yankee tricks."

I could feel my muscles move under my pea-jacket. For the first time in my life I felt an ugly, coppery hatred, a great powerful bitterness surging through me, from head to foot, like the wave of heat from a tumbler of bad brandy, against men who would use their strength to change the lives of defenseless people. I hated this sneering lieutenant; I hated his ship; above all I hated the country that had sent him out to rob us of our rights and our freedom.

We went into our boat, Jeddy and I, followed by two English sailors; and Gideon Lassel and Seth Tarbox pulled us over to the sloop. The lieutenant, waiting for us when we came over the side, led us aft at once.

The captain, a walrus-like man, leaned against the weather rail and looked at us from under heavy eyebrows, each as big as a field mouse.

"Sir," the lieutenant told him, "this man claimed to be the master, but the whole thing was too fishy. No master would have assaulted a king's officer, as this man did. There's no doubt the affair was hocus-pocused to screen the real captain, who must have been English. This man admitted ownership of a terrier that bit me, sir, and the dog's an English dog, no fear of that!"

He had hardly finished before the captain snapped at him, "Pass the word to get under way, and turn these men over to the bos'n."

"My God, sir!" I exclaimed, "you can't press the officers of a merchant vessel!" The captain looked up to see the fore-topsail braced aback. I could hear the orders being given in the waist of the ship and see the men, swarms of them compared with our little crew, hoisting and sheeting home the sails. I thought for a moment of going overboard and swimming for it, but two red-coated marines stood near at hand, their muskets slanted toward us. As the sloop fell off, Gideon and Seth set up a shouting from our boat below; but before I could answer them the captain turned sharply on us.

"Oh, indeed!" He clasped his hands behind his back and teetered on his toes. "I can't, eh? And what's to stop me, if I may ask?"

"The customs of civilized nations," I said.

"Tchah!" The captain worked his bushy eyebrows up and down. "Tchah! Save your exalted sentiment for the marines!" He brandished his finger in my face. "We spoke the ship *Clio* out of New York yesterday. She told us every port on the Atlantic coast had been warned of to-day's embargo against England. Yes, by God, and here you are dodging out with a full cargo! Customs of civilized nations, indeed! You say you're an American, and yet you're doing your best to embarrass your own country!"

He bellowed with laughter. "Doesn't that seem a bit contradictory, Mr. Doyle?"

"It puzzles me completely, sir," the lieutenant answered.

"There you are!" bawled this red-faced walrus. "You *can't* be Americans if you're turning against your country! All Americans are noble heroes, willing to die for their glorious nation—eh, Mr. Doyle?"

"Yes, sir: so we've always heard."

The captain turned to look back at the *Neutrality*. A stretch of tumbling blue water lay between us. She had gone off on her course, flirting her taffrail in the air as if glad to be rid of us.

"Certainly!" the captain said, and he spoke jovially, as though doing us a favor. "That's what makes us sure you're Englishmen; but whether you're Englishmen or runaway Americans, here's your chance! War'll follow the embargo, and this is the cruiser that'll put the Yankees in their places."

He looked at us hard and sharp. We stood silent before him. God knows there was no fitting answer to be made to what he had said; and besides that, the captain of a British man-of-war is a harder and more dangerous taskmaster than any king and therefore no man with whom to argue.

"I have a word for you before you enter on your duties in this king's cruiser," he growled. "Play the man and keep out of trouble, and there'll be prize money coming to you and shore leave aplenty. Go to playing the fool with your fists or your mouth, and you'll get the cat at the gratings. As for this talk about being Americans, belay it, or I'll lay you a course for a haven that'll rot the skin off your bones. That's the tidy stone prison up among the Dartmoor snows that we built for those who try to trip us in our little wars!" He glowered at us from under his beetling, mouse-like brows; then nodded to his lieutenant. "Take 'em forward, Mr. Doyle."

VII

Wʜᴇɴ I had heard from the captain of the corvette, Sir Mungo Bullard-Jones, that I was a tricky Yankee, and from Lieutenant Drake Doyle that I was full of Yankee tricks, and from the bos'n that he was sick of seeing bloody Yankees brought aboard a decent ship, knowing he would have to set a watch to keep the tricky rats from stealing the copper sheathing from the corvette's bottom; and when these fine Britishers had played us the foulest trick that had ever been done me, and lashed the both of us like black slaves or baulky horses into the bargain, and set us to carrying slops and tarring ropes and messing with rabbit-toothed, twist-brained beasts out of the filthy cellars of the world's filthiest cities—Dublin and Liverpool . . . When all these things had happened, I said to myself that while I had so far had no training in trickiness, it was never too late to begin; and since they expected trickiness, I'd give them as much of it as I could rake and scrape together, and see them all in hell if ever I could.

Yet I also determined that never, while I remained on the corvette, would I show anything but a smiling and contented face to any Englishman, whether officer or sailor; for I knew that if I could trick them into thinking me harmless and not worth watching, all subsequent trickeries would be easier of accomplishment.

I was at home on a brig, whether full-rigged or jackass: consequently I was equally easy on a schooner or a barkentine or a ship. As to a cruiser such as the one into which we had been pressed, I could have sailed her with no trouble, for she was ship-rigged; but when it came to fitting in with her crew of some sixscore men, I was in a state of befuddlement for days, what with gun stations and bevies of half-baked midshipmen to issue senseless orders, and a half-dozen numbers to answer to, and captains of a score of different parts of the craft, and droves of marines to keep an eye on the movements of the seamen, and food that nobody on the *Neutrality* would have fed to Pinky for fear of poisoning him, and all the rules and regulations and officials and divisions and subdivisions that are necessary to keep an unwieldy body of men, most of them worthless, from turning a vessel into a madhouse in time of stress.

I made out after a fashion, and so escaped further rope-endings, largely through the help of a Wiscasset seaman in the next mess to mine, John Cromwell, a cat-footed man not overly tall, but quick and powerful. He walked with his stomach pushed a little forward, so that he looked fattish; but he was not, and his upper arm, where it joined his shoulder, was near as wide as his thigh. He came to me on the pretense of showing me how to ticket a bag of food for dropping into the great mess kettles called the coppers. The first thing he said was "Where you from?" I told him Arundel and he nodded his head, eyeing me covertly.

"I watched you come aboard. Captain, wa'n't you?"

"I suppose you might say so, but they say not," I told him.

"There's talk in the tops," he said, speaking from the side of his mouth, "that a captain wouldn't never have been took if we wasn't close to a war with——" He left the sentence unfinished, canting his head quickly in a half circle that seemed to include the entire British navy.

He narrowed his mouth still more. "There's eleven Yankees on this ship, all of 'em pressed. Three of 'em's waisters and don't count. Two of 'em's boys. One works for the master at arms, and he'd tattle on himself in his sleep, so to hell with him. There's the three of you, and me, and 'Lisha Lord."

"Who's 'Lisha Lord?" I asked.

Cromwell snorted as though I had asked who Bonaparte might be. "'Lisha Lord's captain of the maintop," he said. "He comes from Bath. There ain't anywheres he ain't been. He can shoot the ear off a horsefly with a musket or a long twenty-four. He knows all there is to know about this corvette."

"Why don't you let *him* tell you about the war, if he knows so much?" I asked, though satisfied Cromwell would do me no harm.

"You York County folks always was suspicious of us Down-Easters," he said angrily. "'Lisha Lord wants to know what there is in this war talk, and I want to know too. How long you think we'd stay on this damned weevil box in case of—in case of——" He canted his head again and worked a shoulder under his shirt. I suspected he, like many another American, must have had his back made into hash by a British nine-tailed cat.

"You're right," I said. "There was a three months' embargo put on, starting the fourth of April."

"And on the fourth of July we fight?" he asked.

"Looks so," I said.

"Well I declare!" he drawled; and with that he hurried away, light as a fox to the roll of the ship.

As a result of this, Cromwell passed the word to me at noon the next day to go into the maintop. It was a fine big top with rope railings, and when I came over the edge I found two men in it, one a tall man with black whiskers whose sheen gave them the look of having been rubbed with an oily rag. At sight of me, the man with the glossy whiskers rounded suddenly on the other. "Look at that breast backstay!" he growled. "Look at the way she's chafed! Anybody'd think this was a Portygee fisherman instead of a king's cruiser! Spratt, you hop down to the first luff and tell him I say to get somebody up here to serve that backstay with leather." The other immediately lowered himself through the lubber hole.

The whiskered man, I saw, must be 'Lisha Lord. Turning his attention to me, he went on growling. "My good gravy! I don't know what the world's coming to when they put boys in command of merchantmen! Had either of your mates been weaned, by any chance?"

"Both of 'em," I said, "and on good New England rum, what's more! Maybe you can tell me whether there's any talk of discontinuing the use of old women in the maintops of British sloops-of-war?"

He sniffed and peered down through the lubber hole; then sat at the edge of the top, his legs doubled under him and his glossy beard pointing between his knees at the slender canted deck far below, on which seamen moved as slow and maggot-like as sheep in a meadow seen from a mountain side.

"If I'm any judge," he said, "you're madder'n I was when they pressed me, and I was pretty gol-blamed mad."

I saw no reason to answer. When he twisted his head over his shoulder and looked at my face, he seemed to need no reply. "Yes," he continued, "me and John cal'late to cut loose from this durned old scow."

"How did you figure on leaving her?" I asked.

"Well," he said, "we figured you'd figure out a way; and we figured on hauling our wind when you do."

He leaned backward to peer through the lubber hole once more.

"You figure we'd have trouble getting off?" I asked.

He laughed shortly. "Brother," he said, "you ain't had dealings with these dirty sea soldiers on a British ship! Some folks think they have 'em aboard to fight; but what they have 'em for is to put a bullet between our shoulders if we make a move to slip our moorings. You can lay to it Jonah wouldn't have got out of the whale so easy if he'd swallered a few lobster-backs."

"Seems to me you and Cromwell could have left the ship long before this if you'd wanted to," I told him, wishing to be sure of him.

He laughed again. "Listen," he said. "The British never pay off except in home ports for fear the crews of their whole damned navy'd desert; and I'll bet you they would, too. They always hold back six months' pay and prize money for the same reason. They got a way of turning men over from ship to ship so you stay away from England for about three years—ten, sometimes—and then get back with a sheaf of pay notes fit to choke a swordfish! Then they got a lot of lunatics running their pay section, and you couldn't get your notes cashed if you spent all your shore leave in the paymaster's office. If you want money, you sell your notes to the Jews. They allow you six shillings to the pound."

"That's less than thirty cents on the dollar," I protested.

"Yes, by gravy!" 'Lisha Lord returned, "and that's why some of us New Englanders kept hanging on. Well, we're ready to quit now. I've got more than seventeen hundred dollars in pay and prize money coming to me, but I'll quit any minute."

"Well, there's this about it," I said: "I know Tucker and I know Bickford, and they'll do as I tell 'em; but you might find me too young to take orders from."

"Don't worry about that," he assured me. "I take orders from some of these half-grown midshipmen, don't I?"

"All right," I said, "only I'm no midshipman."

'Lisha Lord nodded. "You're the old man."

"See if you can find out where we're bound," I told him, "and contrive for Tucker and Bickford to get to know something about long guns."

"Hell," he said, "I can show 'em all there is to a long gun in half an hour, and we're bound for the Banks to chase Frenchies away from our fishing fleet. After that we'll make Halifax." He gave me a quick push. "Down you go—lee side: here comes the bos'n."

*　　*　　*

Lord and Cromwell, being old hands and used to English ways, were one thing; but Jeddy, who found a new grievance wherever he turned, was another thing altogether. He couldn't keep his feelings from his face when he spoke with me, but looked so murderous that any officer would have been justified in clapping him in the Black Hole on general principles.

"Wipe that look off your face!" I told him when he caught me alone one day. "Keep smiling if you don't want to get us all shipped to England for the next ten years!"

He grinned a horrible, blood-curdling grin, worse than the malevolent stare it replaced. "Dried peas!" he whispered. "Nothing but dried peas and pork for mess twice in a week! You know what pea soup does to me, Richard! I'm blown up like a bladder!"

He seemed to ooze profanity.

"Forget these things," I told him. "They're nothing."

"Oh, are they!" he snarled. "How about having to hang over a yard and take in sail when you're blown up like a bladder? I'd rather teach the rule of three to all the idiot children in Arundel than fold myself over a yard when I'm like that!"

"Look pleasant!" I told him.

He contorted his face in a ghastly simper. "If that's nothing," he persisted, "how about having to sling my hammock between two jailbirds so filthy I'm afraid of being poisoned, just sleeping beside 'em. You know what they do? They call me a damned Yankee! And I can't answer 'em, because it's the simple truth."

"Look here," I said to him as fiercely as I could say it in a whisper, "shut up! Wait! This won't last forever!"

"It'll be forever for me if they give me any more pea soup!" he growled. There were times, indeed, when I feared that Jeddy, unable to express his bitter rancor against the British, would die of an apoplexy.

*   *   *

We cruised for a week off the Banks, handing out medicine and rum to English fishermen; and though we wallowed through a gurry of fog and rain for a great part of the time, there was not enough of a grog allowance, so that we were half sick, all of us, and as full of coughs and whoops as a ledge full of seals.

Our red-faced captain was given, according to the crew, to a heavy consumption of port wine, and I think his liver or his stomach was affected by his anger and by days of inaction; for he was touchy while we lay in the fog. He watched the men continually, and had them flogged whenever he saw one of them so much as looking cross-eyed. He caught Jeddy at some sort of facial contortion one sticky, shivery afternoon. At once he began to bellow that Jeddy had malingered at the polishing of the monkey tail on a carronade; and the next second he ordered him to the after gangway for a catting.

I wanted to go below when they peeled off Jeddy's shirt, lashed his wrists to the hammock nettings over his head and made his feet fast to a hatch grating; but I dared not move, not even to shut my eyes, not only because the English require a flogging to be witnessed by all hands, so to teach them a lesson, but because I knew the captain would see me, which might have proved unpleasant, since he was aching to serve everyone the same way if he could find an excuse.

While Jeddy stood there, waiting, his eyes flicked over us who were watching in the waist and caught at mine for a second. Then he faced to the front with a small pale smile. When the bos'n's mate swung the cat against him, his head snapped a little and his eyelids flickered: the skin on his back jerked up as though drawn by halyards and then slipped slowly down; but in spite of the red wales that grew and grew across his muscles and crawled into the deep groove over his backbone, his lips were still curved upward, as though he faintly contemplated a pleasure yet to come. To me that smile meant more than all his profanity and scowling, and I thought to myself there were squalls ahead for any Englishman Jeddy might later encounter.

When, after his flogging, I came across him in the rigging or at the coppers, he said nothing, but he smiled that same pale smile; and his eyes looked red, like those of a weasel making up his mind to go down after a rabbit.

It was late in May when we raised the high hill of Halifax in Nova Scotia and stood into long, narrow Chebucto Bay, as fine a harbor as there is in the world, but the dreariest looking place I know, with one exception.

I knew, as we went through the western channel into the harbor, that this was where we must escape from the *Gorgon* if ever we hoped to escape at all; and while I racked my brains for a means by which the five of us could leave the ship, I caught sight of a brig that seemed familiar. As we came abeam of her, I saw a nick in the edge of the smoke pipe that stuck from the galley; and there came into my mind, suddenly, how I had stood on the end of the dock in Portland and thrown the half of a brick at just such a brig with just such a nick in the edge of her smoke pipe.

She was the *Riddle,* captained by Eli Bagley; and I felt, somehow, she was manna sent from heaven, though I could not see at the moment how it would nourish us.

I knew, however, that Eli Bagley, famous in every Maine seaport for being meaner than all get-out, would be aching to pay me for the black eye I had given him in Portland and, even without that score to settle, was not a man to help a distressed fellow countryman at the price of any risk to himself.

Nevertheless, I looked hard at the little *Riddle* and began to think about her even harder.

VIII

THE officers of the *Gorgon* watched us like hawks in Halifax harbor; for it was plain to them that every American aboard would cut and run if he had the chance. Therefore no American was given shore leave. Wherever we moved, from bowsprit to taffrail, there was always a marine with his eyes fixed upon us; and I, eager to devise a method of escape that would harm no one but myself if it failed, was near desperate before my plans at last were made.

There was a constant passing of bumboats between the shore and the *Gorgon* at all hours of the day and night, and a great hurroaring and screaming on the part of drunken seamen and their equally drunken women; for women come aboard British men-of-war when they are in port, do what they please, and stay as long as a seaman has a shilling to spend on them.

Always there were traders somewhere about the decks, dealing in trinkets and food, and illicitly in rum; and through the night drunken sailors were perpetually returning, some of them carried, and some still able to sing unmelodiously and fight each other.

With all these things in mind I had 'Lisha Lord get me two bottles of brandy, a long knife, a curved marlinspike, and a ball of spun yarn. At sundown on our second day in Halifax harbor, I gave out instructions and stations to Lord, so that he could pass them on to Jeddy and Cromwell and Tommy Bickford.

The noisiest and busiest time on the *Gorgon's* decks during the preceding evening had been at nine o'clock; and immediately after that hour on the night of our attempt, Jeddy Tucker came reeling around the deck, seemingly as full as a tick. He had a bottle of brandy stuck in the waistband of his trousers; and almost at once he laid hold of a girl, whipped out the bottle, and went to hullooing about everybody being shipmates together. At this the seaman on whose knee the girl had been sitting began to roar and bellow, but Jeddy took her by the arm and ran forward with her, the outraged seaman pelting after him.

They stopped by the starboard sheet anchor. Here Jeddy, dodging behind the girl as if for protection, worried the cork from the bottle and offered it to the willing Nova Scotia damsel. The seaman seized it, and he and Jeddy wrestled together, the girl pinched between them. Some of the brandy spilled upon her from the bottle. She squealed, and the sentry in the bow walked over to look at the trouble. Having been waiting for this, I moved forward, slid over the bulwarks by the larboard sheet anchor, went down the cable until I could go no farther, kicked off my shoes and dropped feet first into the water.

The water was as cold as though pumped fresh from the bilge of the North Pole: so cold I near opened my mouth under water to suck in my breath against the shock. I swam a few strokes; then came up with the back of my head toward the corvette, so the white glimmer of my face might not be seen in the bright starlight.

I moved slowly away. Two boatloads of drunken sailors passed within twenty yards. A little later a boat, returning to shore, came toward me, its oars thumping cheerily in the rowlocks. I could see there was only one man in it. When I had taken three quick strokes toward him I stopped, groaning and thrashing. He backed his oars and swore, startled. I threw up an arm and went under: then rolled to the top and gurgled; and at that the boatman sculled over to me quickly and thrust an oar beneath my stomach.

I groaned again and caught at the oar. The boatman took me by the hair and upper arm, heaving at me; and with his heaving and my scrambling I rolled over the thwart and into the bottom of the boat, lying there with chattering teeth and quietly freeing the marlin-spike from its resting place along the seam of my trouser leg, where I had tied it with spun yarn.

"Man!" he said, "ye must be froze! What are ye, fey or only drunk?" He turned the boat toward the corvette.

I thanked God for a Scotch blue-nose; for though the Scotch have no use for Americans, neither are they inclined to waste love on the English, though they will fight for them against Americans. From what I have seen of the Scotch, they hate the English, but hate everyone else worse.

"Not there," I whispered hoarsely, to hide my accent from the boatman, "not to that dirty box of slave-drivers! They'll press you and cut your hide off!" I pulled up my shirt and showed him my back, where the welts from my colting still showed blue when I was cold.

"The bloody lobsters!" he said, pulling the boat around again. "What'll I do with ye? Ye'll freeze in the fields; and there's a raft of sentries on the docks."

"There's a brig lying there," I whispered, pointing to the eastward. "If I can get aboard quiet, they'll ship me."

"Losh!" he said, "there's *thirty* brigs off there! What'll ye do: try 'em all?"

"I know her," I told him. "Let me at the oars to keep from freezing, and I'll be there before you could down a gill of rum."

When he had made way for me to come up on the seat he fumbled in a stern-locker and brought out a bottle. After sucking at it with melodious gurglings, he passed it to me. I think I let a pint slip down my throat; then, when I had given the bottle back, I fished in my soggy breeches and handed the boatman a dollar.

"Na! I dinna want this!" he said. He took it quickly, nevertheless.

"It's worth something to find a friend," I whispered, "who'll help a poor sailor out of a pickle and keep his trap closed in the bargain."

"Dinna fear!" he said, pocketing the dollar. "I never saw ye."

When we had found the *Riddle* at last and nosed our way to her bow, I went up the anchor cable hand over hand and clung to the cat-head for a while, to let the thudding of my heart die down.

The brig, except for the lap-lap under her counter and the faint clacking of a piece of loose gear, seemed heavy and dull, like a house filled with sleeping people. I went over the bulwarks at last and crept to the capstan, holding my knife and marlinspike in my left hand. Peer down the deck as I would, I could see nobody; so at length, knowing it must be done, I stepped softly toward the stern. As I passed the mainmast, I made out a figure, a small figure, leaning against the larboard rail by the cabin. I went for him, making no sound in my stocking feet. I heard him say, "What the hell you want?" Then I got my hand on his jacket and the point of my knife against his throat.

"Easy now," I told him. "It's all right, only don't talk or move."

"Git away!" he squeaked.

"One more like that and I'll slit your hawse hole," I said, pricking him a little.

He stayed as he was, bent rigidly backward in the attitude of a girl seeking to escape a kiss.

"All right," I said. "Now we'll go see the old man. Walk down to the cabin, open the door and pull him out of his bunk."

"He'll kill me!"

"He won't kill anyone! I'll look after you as long as you do what I say." I prodded him. With an anxious grunt he stepped toward the captain's quarters.

She was a slovenly brig, with a foul smell about her, as if she had never been cleaned. The cabin, lighted by a dirty little pewter whale-oil lamp, was fouler still. We had no sooner opened the door than Bagley thrust his head from his berth, making chewing motions with his lips. He had on a red knitted nightcap; and what with his thin bluish face and his protuberant jaw bones, he looked like somebody thrown out of hell for meanness.

"Knock before you come in, dum ye!" he protested; but the mate's only answer was to lay hold of his arm and haul him over the side of the bunk. He bounced upright, a raging fury in a red flannel night-shirt.

"Here!" he yelped at me, "what you doing here? Who be you?"

"A fellow countryman," I said, "in trouble and needing help."

He peered at me, moving his chin whiskers. "Nason!" he snarled. "You set up to be pretty high and mighty down in Portland! Better'n me, you was! You wun't get no help here!"

I took the ball of spun yarn from my pocket and tossed it to the mate. "Tie his hands," I said, "then light the big lamp."

"By gorry!" Bagley said. "I'll have the law on you!"

When his hands were tied and the big lamp lit, I took the yarn and tied the mate's hands as well.

"You'll have a fine time doing it," I reminded Bagley. "You're carrying cargoes to the British!"

He eyed me venomously. "You're dretful pious, you are! I s'pose *you* ain't doing it, nor nothing like that!" He paused uncertainly. "I thought you cleared for Spain."

"I did, but something happened, and I've seen a light. Where's your Bible?"

I knew Bagley to be as superstitiously religious as he was mean, so that the Bible would bind him more securely than any spun yarn.

"Bible!" he exclaimed, watching me warily out of little pig eyes as hard as snail shells. "I wun't trust ye, Nason: not even with a Bible!"

I found it, at last, in a pocket beside his bunk. "All right," I said, pushing it against his tied hands. "I'm leaving this brig: leaving it in your boat. Swear on this to lower it away for me, help me off, and keep your mouth shut for two days, so help you God."

Bagley glared at me. "What you think I am!"

"A traitor!" I told him. "Hurry up and swear! I haven't got all night!"

"Gol dum ye!" he said. "I wun't!"

I pulled the whale-oil lamp from the wall, kicked the wood box from behind the stove, and smashed the lamp over it with a chunk of pine. "You've got one minute before I set her afire!"

"Gimme that Bible!" the mate said.

They took their oaths, the both of them; and half an hour later I was under the *Gorgon's* bow in the *Riddle's* boat.

* * *

I was pleased to hear from the deck above a prodigious drunken singing of hoarse voices. The chorus was so loud that Jeddy, peering down at me, could have spoken in his natural tones, I think, without fear of detection; and the disorder was so happily useful that four figures slid down the anchor cable and into my borrowed boat with what I might almost call comfort.

We sculled softly away from that well detested vessel, then, under cover of dark, pulled hard for safety. Almost in the harbor mouth we had a great fright and an astounding piece of luck, even while we wrangled among ourselves as to whether we should set out afoot for Annapolis or capture a pink by boarding. The American schooner *Nancy* of Kittery, Captain Rich, which had cleared at sundown for her home port, but lay a little inside, becalmed, had caught a breeze and was running out, and in so doing almost ran us down. Captain Rich took us on board, was astounded to find men from a town neighboring his in such a plight, showed himself a hearty patriot, swore by Job's Turkey he'd land us safe on our mutually native soil, and kept the potent Maine oath. On the second afternoon after he made it we stepped again on Arundel ground.

* * *

There was nobody in sight when we crossed the creek and came again to our comfortable gray farmhouse nestled above the dunes and the curving crescent of beach: nobody, that is to say, except Rowlandson Drown, that violent-tempered man, who sat beside the front door in the golden rays of the late afternoon sun, his mottled gray face and his bull neck hunched over a chair he was mending.

"Hey!" he said, working at the turnings of a rung with a draw shave, "you're back quick!"

"Yes," I said, feeling quarrelsome inside, and glad for the opportunity of letting out on one who was against a war because it would hurt the chair trade. "Yes, thanks to the English, who have more friends around here than they rightly ought to have."

Rowlandson Drown picked a sliver of hickory from his draw shave. "Do tell!" he said, looking quickly at 'Lisha Lord and Cromwell and then fastening his eyes on Jeddy.

"You're damned right," Jeddy said, watching Rowlandson with round, unblinking eyes. "They licked me twice, once with a cat. You'd be real friendly with the British, I suppose, if they took a cat to that fat back of yours!"

"You keep out of this," I warned Jeddy. Then I turned to Rowlandson. His face had grown darker, so I knew violence was rising in him.

"Jeddy was whipped," I told him, "and I was whipped too. That isn't much. We can pay 'em back for that. But you know what they did to me, Drown? They came aboard my brig and called me a lying, tricky Yankee. They tried to kill my little dog Pinky. Then they pressed me; me, her master! Took me right off my own vessel, by God! Said I was a Britisher! Said my dog Pinky was British! Said Tommy Bickford was British because we couldn't breed people like Tommy in our filthy country. Maybe you'd like to say a word or two for the English, Drown."

His face grew darker, and he grunted at me, a groaning sort of grunt that made his shoulders heave.

"Now," I said, wagging my finger in his face and marking the little lump on the side of his jaw where I proposed to hit him, "I'm going to take out a privateer against the British; and if God's good to me, I'll pay 'em back for what they did; and what's more, I'll take every opportunity to deal harshly with any man who tries to tell me the British are friends of ours. That's what Caleb Strong, the Governor of Massachusetts, has been telling us for years, Drown, and I've believed him. Now I know he's a liar, and as much my enemy as the English. All the ministers and merchants of Boston have been talking like Strong, Drown, and I was fool enough to trust 'em! I trusted the Timothy Pickerings and the John Lowells and the Francis Blakes and the Harrison Gray Otises, Drown; but now I've got the welts of a British colt on my back, and I know better! I know they're all liars; and if you hold with Caleb Strong and the Boston Federalists, Drown, you're a liar as well!"

Just as I was about to hit him he dropped his head. "Your little white dog? They tried to kill your little white dog?"

"Yes," I said, hoping he'd have to be carried home on a shutter.

He turned back to the chair and picked up his draw shave. "Well," he growled, "I'm a good cabinet worker, which is a more valuable trade than carpenter, and I'm as good a carpenter as any man, and a damned sight better than most I can name, so I'll ship as carpenter on your privateer."

"Carpenter?" I said, taken aback by the suddenness with which his sentiments seemed to have altered. "I don't want a carpenter!"

He turned on me, snarling. "You *got* to have a carpenter," he said violently. "You got to cooper and uncooper your water barrels and fish your busted masts, ain't you?"

"Yes," I admitted. "I guess I have."

"I guess you *have!*" Rowlandson Drown sneered. "I can carpenter and I can fight. If you got any good reason why I shouldn't ship as carpenter, I got some money saved, and I'll buy some shares in your privateer! I'll buy 'em anyway, by gosh!"

The five of us stared at Rowlandson, who growled and grumbled to himself, wobbling the chair on its front legs to make sure it was stout and rigid. Before I could say anything I heard a familiar clicking sound. I looked up to see my mother standing in the front yard, one hand on her hip and the other rattling the string of cat's-eyes at her throat. She smiled a pleasant, one-sided smile.

"Welcome home," she said.

IX

People knew nothing about vessels, my mother told me when we got to arguing about the proper sort of craft for privateering. "You can't expect a man who hasn't been to sea," she said, "to know or care that a sloop-of-war isn't a sloop at all, but a brig or a ship, and that she's a corvette at the same time because her guns are all on one deck, whereas those of a frigate are on two decks, and those of a line-of-battle ship on three. I tell you that for every man who knows a full-rigged brig has two masts with square sails on both, whereas a brigantine is square rigged on the foremast and fore-and-aft rigged on the mainmast, there are twenty thousand who can tell you nothing about a brig except that she's a ship, which she isn't. Who knows, do you think, that a corvette carries a crew of a hundred and fifty, and a frigate a crew of five hundred, and a line-of-battle ship a crew of a thousand, whereas a 700-ton armed merchant ship carries only twenty-five or thirty? Nobody, or next to nobody!"

"I thought we were speaking of a proper vessel to be a privateer," I ventured to remind her.

"So we were. Let me repeat you're aiming too high when you think to use a brig for a privateer. Also a Baltimore clipper schooner's no good, because she'll crush like an eggshell if you undertake to lay her alongside a heavy ship in any kind of sea. They're too delicate, these Baltimore clipper schooners. Furthermore——"

"But if we wait for the *Neutrality* to come home," I interrupted, "we can add to her speed. She's familiar to me, and it'll be a great saving of money."

My mother snorted. "It won't be a saving of money if a British sloop-of-war makes sail in chase of you and your topmast carries away. Listen to my arguments, now, and remember I know more about sailing and war than you do. No doubt you consider yourself almost better than Stephen Decatur; but you must bear in mind it was little longer ago than yesterday that I was paddling you with a hairbrush to keep you out of the cooky jar."

"Go ahead," I told her. "You'll be telling me I'm still a child when I'm sixty years old."

"It may be," she admitted, smiling her one-sided smile, "but let's stick to the matter in hand. You say you care less about taking prizes than about harrying the British and sinking their ships."

"Yes," I said, "but at the same time I wish to overlook no opportunities to enrich ourselves at their expense."

"Certainly not," my mother said. "You'd be a fool if you did! At any rate, you wish to capture and sink Britishers. Now I've marched with fine fighters in my day; and they've all persisted in saying that the true art of war is the art of ambushing and surprising your enemy, and of inflicting the greatest possible loss on him at the least cost to yourself.

"If you attempt to carry this theory into sea fighting, you'll find few ways to ambush and surprise an enemy. You can do it by night attacks, which are dangerous unless you're sure of the enemy's strength. You can do it by sending your boats into a harbor under cover of dark and cutting out an enemy craft; but that's even more dangerous. I've given the matter some thought, and it seems to me the surest method of surprising British ships would be to lead them to hold you in contempt—to underestimate your strength. I think it's the surest method, because the British have always underrated us as opponents and always will, so it'll take no great skill to lead them astray.

"Suppose, now, you privateer in our own brig. In the first place she must be rerigged, so to be speedier. Then you must raise a crew of a hundred men for her, or a hundred and twenty; for it's impossible to do with less if she's to be properly fought; and you must find supplies for these men, which is no child's play. Then, when you've got to sea, you'll be the prey of every British frigate and sloop-of-war that sights you; for any brig is a good prize, and they'll chase even a small one as long as they can keep her in sight.

"On the other hand, if you go out in a smaller craft—a sloop, say— you can get along with fewer men; you can come down all unsuspected on some lordly merchantman and blow him out of water just as he's preparing to be gracious and give you your latitude and longitude. You can tack three times, if you're caught in a box, to anybody else's once. You can sweep out of gunshot if you blunder into an enemy in a calm. You can depend on prizes for much of your supplies; and frigates and sloops-of-war won't waste time on you if they see you have any chance at all of getting away."

"Then you give the word I must use a sloop?" I asked.

"I think so," she said, working her fingers in and out of her cat's-eyes. "Go somewhere and get a strong, fast sloop of about sixty tons burden, and you'll have a craft that can be handled by a few men. Thirty or forty can fight her as well as a hundred and twenty could fight our brig, and she can be made to look as harmless and unimportant as a porgy fisherman. Yet she'll carry enough guns, and there'll be room for all of you as well as for a fair load of prisoners in case of need; and if she's the right sort of sloop there's no British-built vessel of any size whatever that can catch her."

So the end of our argument was that I was to get a sloop; and we had no sooner decided on it than I took Jeddy and 'Lisha Lord and Cromwell, and started off toward Salem and Boston to see what we could find.

I thought to leave Tommy Bickford in Arundel; but he spoke his mind to my mother to such good purpose that she told me to take him along, she having a weakness for the boy because of the manner in which his father had dragged my father ashore through a shower of bullets at Valcour Island, and also because he was a handsome, polite boy with a broad smile that won the women, and the men too, for that matter.

With me I carried fifty-five hundred dollars, forty-two hundred being my mother's money and my own, and two hundred belonging to my aunt Cynthy, she having made it in a venture of twenty dollars during my first year as captain of the *Neutrality*. Four hundred and sixty belonged to that violent man, Rowlandson Drown, seventy to Jeddy, and five hundred to Dominicus Lord, the shipowner. Fifty-seven dollars of it was the sole wealth of Tommy Bickford's widowed mother, and I wouldn't have taken it if my mother had not insisted, saying it was a good thing to have a responsibility like that on my mind.

In Portsmouth and Newburyport we found only the regular run of brigs and snows and sloops laid up by the embargo, none of them fit for our purpose. All through the taverns and along the waterfront the people were talking against the war, which was fairly on us, since the President on the first of June had sent a message to the Congress, telling of the wrongs we had suffered at England's hands.

Much of this hatred of the war was due to the knowledge that there would be fighting in Canada, Thomas Jefferson having said in one of his frequent moments of lunacy that the capture of Quebec was merely a matter of marching, and that we would therefore invade Canada to take it from the British. Having no dislike for Canada or the Canadians, and being with good reason suspicious of Thomas Jefferson, our New Englanders declared hotly that any war fought in Canada would be fought without them.

When we reached Salem, we found little outcry against the war and no argument in favor of a Canadian campaign; but everywhere there was talk of privateering and privateers: how the Crowninshields would take off the upper deck of the ship *America* and fill her sides solid between planking and ceiling, like a man-of-war, and fit her for a privateer; how Holton Breed would take out a privateer for the leading merchants of the place as soon as a fast enough brig could be found; how twenty-four Salem captains had formed a company to go out in their own vessel against the British.

At Crowninshield's wharf, by good fortune, I found Captain William Webb, who had helped me buy the shawl for my mother in Cadiz. He was superintending changes in a pink little larger than a ship's longboat. She had two six-pounder carronades, one mounted aft of her mainmast, and one between the main and foremast, so arranged that both could be pivoted and fired from either side. There were twelve or fifteen men crowded on her deck, working at this and that, and it took no more than a glance to see they were not common seamen.

"Hey!" Webb said, when I nudged his elbow, "what you doing here?"

"Looking," I told him.

Webb scanned the drifting white clouds overhead. "If you're looking to sign on with me," he said, "it can't be done. She's all divided: twenty-four owners. All masters. We're taking her out ourselves."

"I'm looking for one of my own," I said.

Webb studied the sky to the westward: then to the eastward. "What you think of this craft?" he asked.

"Good for her size," I said. "She'd make a nice cutter for my brig."

"Yes," Webb said. "She'd run all the way around your brig twice while you were shaking the reefs out of your topsails. Built in Chebacco in 1804. There's a pink that *is* a pink! Thirty tons burden, and I'd take her to Canton as quick as to Boston."

"What's her name?" I asked.

"*Fame,*" he told me, smiling affectionately at the little craft. "That's her name, and I hope it'll be her nature. Fame for her, fortune for us, and hell for the British."

Never was there a vessel, it seems to me, so aptly named; for there was no American privateer afloat who didn't learn, before the war was five months old, how the *Fame,* in spite of her diminutive size and her thirty tons and her two little sparrow guns, took eight British prizes in no time at all, one an armed British ship of 300 tons, and

another a 200-ton brig, and all of them together representing a loss
of two hundred thousand dollars to the English.

"Well," I said, "I've had something the same idea, only I want a
sloop."

"You're making a mistake," he said gravely. "Everybody in Salem
tells me I'm crazy, going to sea in a toy like this. What I ought to
have is a Baltimore clipper schooner."

"Yes," I said, "I've heard there's nothing like a Baltimore clipper
schooner. I want a sloop."

Webb laughed. "Good sloops are scarce. You'll find plenty of
sloops laid up here but none that I'd——"

A thought came to him. "By gum!" he exclaimed, "how big a sloop
can you do with?"

"Well," I said, "I don't rightly know till I've seen her. Fifty tons.
Sixty maybe. Maybe more. I figure on thirty men, and I guess I could
scare up thirty-five."

"Then I guess this won't interest you," he said. "A North River
sloop slid in here yesterday, loaded with grain, and clumsy-looking
as they come; but she had an old h'ister of a stick in her. Prob'ly she's
too big for you. Seventy tons—eighty, maybe: it's hard to tell about
those North River sloops."

"Where is she?"

"She's up toward Whipple's Wharf," he said.

In ten minutes the five of us were scattered along Whipple's
Wharf, scanning, with apparent indifference, the towering mast of
the *Lottie Green*. It was the tallest stick I ever saw on a craft of
her size, ninety feet high if an inch, with so few shrouds and stays
that it seemed likely to whip out of her at the first blow. She was
broad beamed; and a litter of hen coops, old sails, and lumber up
forward distracted the eye from her flush and level decks. A part of
her seeming clumsiness was due to her heavy bowsprit and her solid
bulwarks, as well as to the manner in which she was daubed with
paint, as though the owner's money had run out and he had bor-

rowed some light green here and some dark green there. As soon as I had looked hard at her I knew she was worth thinking about.

"But," I said to myself, as I stood staring at her, "she'll never be the *Lottie Green* if I should come to be part owner of her, and her master."

Straightway I fell to thinking how I should name her, and thereupon a curious little thing happened. The green of her sides made me think suddenly and with little relevancy of a green dress I had seen; and unconsciously I put my hand to my breast pocket and felt the round contour of the miniature I carried there as a provision against poverty.

In that very moment I renamed the sloop: the words came murmuring upon my lips without my knowing well just how they got there.

"The Lively Lady!" I whispered. "The Lively Lady!"

That was how the *Lively Lady* got her name.

* * *

I turned to 'Lisha Lord. "What about guns?"

"She'll carry anything," he said confidently.

I went down onto the sloop's deck, where a tall man with a large stomach was wearily supervising the unloading of grain from her hold. "You cap'n?" I asked him. This was flattery; for we merchant captains are masters in theory, and only the captain of a war vessel is supposed to be called a captain.

"Yes, I be," he said, shifting a straw in his mouth.

"War's going to catch you, isn't it?" I asked, thinking to pave the way for a trade by frightening him.

"No, it ain't. There ain't nothing going to catch me. You looking for a privateer?"

"Well," I admitted, "I might be and I mightn't be. If I got a fast craft cheap, I might."

"Listen, mister," said the large-stomached man, blowing the straw from his mouth, "this sloop come off the ways at Newburgh in 1809.

She's staunch and she's gentle and she's fast. You might not think it to look at her, but this sloop can do thirteen knots."

"Thirteen knots your grandmother!" I said, for thirteen knots is better than any of His Britannic Majesty's frigates can do, even if they throw over all their guns, their reefers, and their bos'n's mates.

"Thirteen knots and nobody's grandmother," he said impressively. "She can do better than ten knots for twenty-four hours on end, and she ain't never been pushed. This little old sloop, she's sweet as a nut and sound as a bell; and what she'd do if she was pushed I'd hate to say."

"If she was pushed," I said, "she'd carry away the top of that coach whip you've got in her." From the inward movement of his eyes I could tell I had touched him on a tender spot.

"Mister," he said, "you're all fouled up! She's sweet as a bell and sound as a nut from stem to stern, blow high, blow low. She's ninety-six tons, and you know the rule for masting North River sloops: a foot of length for every ton."

"She looks about seventy-five tons to me," I said, for the sake of saying something. "How many men you carry, and what you asking for her?"

The large-stomached man waved his hand toward the three men who were swaying up the grain. "There they be, and I got to get sixty dollars a ton for a craft like this."

"Good grief!" I said, "that's nearly six thousand dollars figuring at ninety-six tons. I see now why you claim she's ninety-six. I'll bet she's not an ounce over eighty; and no sloop afloat's worth more than forty dollars a ton."

"Mister," he assured me, "you New Englanders beat anything I ever see! Durned if you wouldn't turn your back on a dollar to hunt for a copper. This sloop'll make you a hundred thousand dollars—a million, if you know how to handle her—and yet you're shaking in your boots at spending fifty-seven hundred and sixty for her. Well, there ain't nothing mean about me! I'll knock off the sixty and make it an even fifty-seven hundred."

The upshot was that I gave him four thousand dollars for his sloop, which may have been a whisker less than she was worth; and as soon as her grain was out we took her in hand, slipped away from Salem and scudded up the coast with as little fuss as a loon moving out of gunshot.

Thanks to General Dearborn, with whom my mother had marched to Quebec in her youth, we had an order on the Portsmouth Navy Yard for guns, so we ran up the Piscataqua that afternoon and anchored off Kittery.

"Our order calls for six thirty-six-pound carronades," 'Lisha Lord told me. "I don't know how you feel about carronades, but I wouldn't give 'em house room. They ain't bad for clearing an enemy's decks at close range; but at long range their shot just bounces. If you want to take vessels without boarding, you want long guns that'll throw a shot clear through a ship."

"I'm afraid of long guns," I objected. "Their pivots are too high and they weigh too much. They'd make us top heavy and slow."

"Not if you mount 'em on carriages," 'Lisha said. "We'll fire 'em through ports; and if she blows too hard, we can sway 'em into the hold in five minutes."

'Lisha, being from Bath, would, I knew, have profited by all the mistakes as well as the wisdom of the British under whom he had learned about guns.

"If you want to know what I think," he said, "I'd ask for two long eighteens—traversing pieces. For carronades I'd take two eighteen pounders, so I could use my long-gun ammunition in 'em if there's need, and a twenty-four pounder betwixt my bow ports to throw langrage wherever it's handiest. Then I wouldn't be over-gunned, and there'd be few craft as dangerous."

By langrage Lord meant the old iron and scraps of lead and odd bullets that are loaded into guns at close range to chop up stays and shrouds and clear the decks of an enemy vessel.

We got our guns the next day, and in addition to them our barrels of powder, pistols, forty cutlasses, forty boarding axes, twenty board-

ing pikes; round shot, grapeshot, and double-head shot; musket and
pistol cartridges aplenty, cartridge boxes, rammers, and sponges;
worms and ladles; tubes, priming wires, lanthorns, blue lights, wads,
cartridge paper, gun tackles, gun aprons, bed and quoins, gun hand
spikes, tompions, gun breechings, kegs of manila rope, hooks for
breeching; and a mighty mess our sloop was when we had all this
aboard.

We had only a part of it stowed when a pleasant young lieutenant
came down to tell me war had been formally declared. "The British'll
be down from Halifax like hornets," he said, "and all our ships are
in New York; so if you see a frigate or a sloop-of-war, cut and run,
for she'll be British."

Fortunately we had not far to go, yet in the short distance after
we had scudded between Boon Island and Cape Neddick and stood
away across Wells Bay for home, we sighted eleven brigs, all of them
back from foreign parts—and all of them, as I knew from my own
caution and watchfulness, feeling as hurried and harried as a dog
that scuttles past a master wishful of kicking him.

From far off we could see the squat chimneys of our house behind
the Arundel dunes, rising against the green slope of the high land
across the river. Behind the house, as we skirted the half circle of
brown reefs that guard our river and beaches from the sea, we spied
a brig's topgallant sails moving slowly upstream with the tide. We
rounded Mile Ledge, slipped easily over the bar and followed the
topgallant sails around the bend.

They belonged to the *Neutrality;* and on her quarter-deck, his feet
on the taffrail and his stump of a tail cocked over his back as if
hoisted up and sheeted home, barking and barking in a sort of ec-
stasy, as if he knew he'd find me on our river, was my little white dog
Pinky.

X

No MAN, I have learned, is qualified to say what brings joy or sorrow to another. There was a man in our town of Arundel whose home and worldly goods were entirely destroyed by fire, and two of his children as well; yet the one lost thing for which he mourned loudest and longest was a snuffbox made from a cow's horn.

We should have been in a state of excitement because Cephas Cluff had brought the *Neutrality* safe home, laden with salt as instructed, so that we not only had our brig, together with her crew to join with us aboard our sloop, but a handsome profit on our cargo —a profit so large that my mother would be well fixed, no matter how long the war might last; for salt had shot up in price as the war came close. Yet the thing that stirred me was neither of these things, but the knowledge that I had my little white dog Pinky again; whereas my mother seemed to have no thoughts for the brig because of her interest in the sloop.

She had me row her from one side to the other and back again, and she climbed around the deck and in and out of the cabin until I was in a mind to order her home so we could set to work undisturbed. When I spoke of this she set her hands on her hips and stared up the mast as though looking for a twist in it, and said nothing could be done until she had gone out in her and got the feel of her.

"Look here," I said, "I won't have it; not with your back apt to be lamed again. Besides that, this country's at war. We've no time for pleasure cruises."

Her eyes seemed to scoff at me. "I suppose not," she said. "I suppose you only have time for a trip to Dartmoor Prison. You're saving all your time for that, no doubt."

"Stop fretting about how she feels," I told her. "She feels good. There's nothing to worry about, and I'd like to get out and pick up a couple of Britishers before they're all gone."

"Try to contain yourself," she said. "This war won't be over in a week or two. If it lasts till we get an army, I think it may even last two or three hundred years. What I want to find out is this: Is that stick of yours all right?"

"Well," I said, "to tell the truth, I think it's a trifle long."

"I see." Smiling a faint one-sided smile, she twisted her fingers rapidly in her string of cat's-eyes. "That was something you'd forgotten to mention! You thought it was too long, and you were willing to go to sea without making sure! Richard, Richard! Haven't I taught you better than that?"

"She logged over ten knots coming down here," I told her, which would have been enough of a defense to satisfy anyone except my mother. She only turned her shoulder to me and lifted it a little; then scanned the sky and sniffed the wind. "It'll come in from the southwest this afternoon," she said. "We'll take her out and see about this."

* * *

There were times, that afternoon, after my mother had all sail cracked on and was conning the sloop around the ledges off the southerly tip of the point we call Hell's Two Acres, when I wished we had left our gunners' stores on the river bank, being sure we must rip off our bends against the barnacle-covered rocks.

My mother was in high spirits, humming constantly with her lips tight closed, and seldom opening them except to call, "Luff!" or, "Nothing off!" to John Cromwell, who was steering. The wind holding constant, we logged her again and again. She showed always just short of eleven knots.

"Let's reef that mainsail," my mother said at length.

I saw what was in her mind, so we reefed it. "Now," she said to me, "work her!" I took the wheel from John and worked her. There was a lift to her, as though a whale were fast to us, drawing us forward; and she hissed in the water, so there was a noise beneath her counter like streams from a dozen pumps pouring overside.

We logged her again. This time she showed eleven knots and two fathoms.

"There you are, Richard," my mother said. "I suspected it, and now I know it! She's got too much mast and too tall a sail. It forces her head down. I say take off ten feet of mast and ten feet of canvas. If you do, she'll sail as well as most Baltimore clippers and keep you twice as dry."

We went to work on her the next day, Rowlandson Drown in charge of the carpenters, and 'Lisha Lord supervising the mounting of the guns.

On this little sloop of ours, only sixty-eight feet over all, we made living quarters for forty men, and a cabin and a gun room aft, if you want to call it a gun room, though I think Jeddy Tucker was nearer the truth when he called it the popgun room; for it was about as big, Jeddy said, as a pint of rum half poured out.

Also we had to allow for water casks and gunners' stores and a place for prisoners; because, though I wanted no prisoners, we well knew the day might come when willy-nilly we'd have them. And, finally, we needed plenty of space in the hold for whatever we might take from prizes, though I'm not ashamed to say now that none of us spoke of making prizes without knocking on wood or spitting over our left shoulders, these two precautions having long been known, in our province of Maine, as sure preventives of disaster.

It was not until late July that a commission was brought to me by post. It bore the signature of James Madison and authorized the private armed vessel *Lively Lady* to cruise against the enemies of the United States under the command of Captain Richard Nason. With that we made more haste, laying in supplies and rounding out our crew, which was not easy because nine tenths of the folk in Arundel and neighboring towns were bitter against the war and those who had forced them into it. It would put an end to their prosperity, they said, and they wanted nothing to do with it.

What I most needed were men handy with small arms; and by bribery and arguments of one sort and another I got eight of the best marksmen the town afforded, among them Moody Haley, who in a morning could shoot enough Eskimo plover to fill a hogshead; and Moses Burnham, whose rifle, though carrying a ball no larger than a pea, would kill rabbits and moose with equal thoroughness; and Pendleton Quint, who could drop a flying partridge without raising his fowling piece above his hip, he having learned to shoot in this fashion, he said, because of the weight of his weapon, which made it a nuisance to lift; also Bezaleel Bird, whose eyes were so keen he could distinguish goslings from ganders in a flock of geese and kill only goslings. I was fortunate in signing Jotham Carr, he having worked at rolling pills and holding forceps in Dr. Wiswall's office, so that we wouldn't be without a doctor. With him came Alley Mc-Alley, an Irish tailor who had appeared in our town from some place to the south and been cured of the itch by Jotham, so that he was Jotham's ardent follower, and glad for the opportunity to ship with him.

Also, in a cabin near Durrell's Bridge on the river road lived two black men named Pomp and Sip, which are names given to all black men in our part of New England, and these two I persuaded to sign on the *Lively Lady,* both of them being good-natured and handy at fishing, snaring, or shooting, as well as at cooking simple messes such as lobscouse and fish chowder.

By the end of August, thanks to the defeat of the *Guerrière* by our splendid frigate *Constitution,* and the news of the privateering successes of the little *Fame* out of Salem, our Arundel folk had become heartier for the war, so that we had more than enough men from whom to choose when our work was completed. Nevertheless, I held the crew to thirty men, over and above Jeddy and Cephas Cluff and

'Lisha Lord and Cromwell and myself, for I figured this number would answer my needs.

If we were lucky, the smaller the crew, the richer they'd be; for the owners were to receive one half of our taking, the other half going to the officers and crew. In this, there was matter to trouble the mind of any conscientious privateer captain, especially that of a young one; for the swelling of the shares by the taking of rich prizes was all too likely to become the main object with the crew, to the exclusion of what was more patriotic and important.

* * *

The crickets were loud the night before we sailed. I sat with my mother in the large room; and since then I have never heard a cricket's monotonous plaint without recalling the fragrant perfume of a Maine August—sweet grass and pines and wet sea sand and uncovered ledges—and without seeing quick pictures in my brain: the sharp current riffles in our river; a distant sail on the horizon; a handful of men standing silent and staring by the side of a long gun, their mouths hanging open against the explosion; and other pictures not so pleasant.

"There's a number of things I've had it in mind to tell you," she said, rounding off the toe of a white woolen stocking she was knitting. "War's a dirty business. They talk a lot about chivalrous enemies and land knows what-all; but chivalry doesn't help much if you have to be sewed up in a topsail and dropped overboard with an eighteen-pound shot at your feet. The chief idea in war is to kill and destroy. If you feel a bit of chivalry coming on, I'd recommend fighting it off till there's no chance of being killed and destroyed yourself."

"Don't worry about me," I told her.

"Privateering," she persisted, "has its bad points. Any Britisher that gets an opportunity will treat you like a pirate. You'll find, oftentimes, they'll keep on firing after one of our privateersmen strikes his colors. They did in the Revolution, in between some of their talk about chivalry. You needn't look for much mercy."

"I don't figure on giving 'em the chance to show me any."

"Weight of metal's a thing you can't do much against," she continued. "It may look cowardly, but don't lose time in running when you see a big one after you. Do what damage you can, and take as little as may be."

"That's why I shipped Moody Haley and Bezaleel Bird and the others."

"That's right," she said absently. "Pick 'em off at the top. That's how we won at Saratoga. The British don't like it, but that's because they aren't as good at it as we are." Her needles clicked rapidly. "Were you figuring on leaving her that dirty green color?"

"Yes," I said.

"I thought you might be planning to paint her a nice fresh green, like that green dress of Lady Ransome's." She eyed me sharply.

"I hadn't thought of it," I said. I had, but there seemed to be no reason to say so to my mother; and I had decided, finally, that the very dirtiness of the green was an advantage, since it might make us less easily visible to enemy craft. Once or twice, too, I had been tempted to speak to her of the miniature I had found in the pocket of my coat; but I knew nothing would be gained by idle chatter on the subject, so I remained silent about that as well.

She moved restlessly in her chair and sighed. "Get your charts," she said, not looking up from her knitting. "I've been thinking about the British trade routes. It's easiest to go to the Grand Banks and so intercept the merchantmen bound to Halifax from Britain and the Indies; but I'm beginning to suspicion it would be a mistake."

"I've been thinking," I said, unrolling a chart for her, "that all our privateers will run for the Grand Banks at the same time."

"That's been my thought," my mother said. "If I were captain of the *Lively Lady*, I'd head out across the Gulf Stream and bear south to the sugar trade route." She tapped her finger on the point that coffee and sugar traders from the West Indies must cross in sailing to England: the same point where there are always slow-moving merchantmen laden with English goods, heading for the West Indian markets. "It'll be hot down there," she said, "but you can't let a little heat stop you. What's more, I think you'll find next to no enemy war craft and few enough of our own privateers to compete with you."

"That's what I'll do, though I'd mislike to be caught by one of those tidy little hurricanes."

My mother lifted her shoulder. "They won't hurt you," she said. "You're lucky. They'll only stave up the merchantmen so you can take 'em easier."

Again we sat in silence. The crickets chirped on and on. I stared at a picture of Rome on the wall paper, a picture showing a sheep herder putting his arm around a handsome, dressy girl, though from what I had seen of sheep herders in Spain and Portugal they'd be given a wide berth by any girl not weak in the head.

My mother finished the stocking. "There," she said, "that's the fastest knitting ever done in this town! If you're going out on the flood tide you'd better get forty winks."

We stood in the door, listening to the soft, slow, irregular plunge and murmur of the surf on the hard beach, and to the chirping of the crickets. Then she patted me gently on the shoulder, and we went upstairs.

I've heard it said we New Englanders are cold folk, taking no pleasure in life or love. I don't know how such beliefs spring up, for there's as much marrying among us as among people said to be more passionate; and our families couldn't conveniently be larger. And I, at least, knew that although my mother failed to scream and burst into tears because of my departure, as more excitable and less sensible mothers might have done, she took no pleasure in my going and would be happy when I came back.

XI

It was early on the fifth day out that Pendleton Quint sighted the first sail, bearing north with the Gulf Stream. We made sail in pursuit; and since it was our first chase the men were excited and in high spirits, though they made an effort to remain calm, leaning over the bulwarks and spitting when asked a question, and looking always at the sky before answering, though there was no cloud in sight and no chance of a change in wind.

As we drew up on this first sail of ours we cleared for action. The muskets, except those for the sharpshooters, were ranged in a rack by the main hatchway; each man was at his post, a cutlass buckled around him, the two long guns were cleared of their screens, the hatchway coamings were set with eighteen-pound shot; and ready on the decks were boxes of grape and langrage, water buckets, tubs of wadding, rammers and sponges, among which Pinky sniffed as though they were there for the sole purpose of letting him locate the rat that had made free with them.

She was a slow brig of some three hundred tons. The closer we came, the more Jeddy Tucker licked his lips, pleased and eager at what was about to happen. Just then the brig hove-to and hoisted Russian colors, so I was certain she was a neutral and our first chase a vain one. All around the deck the men settled back on their heels, growling and swearing; while I, wishing to make no mistake, spoke her and found her to be the Russian brig *Moskva*, Captain John Blanton, eight days out from Havana bound to St. Petersburg with a full cargo of sugar, logwood, and coffee. Jeddy Tucker went on board to examine her papers, log book, letters, crew and passengers. All was in order, as I had felt sure would be the case; and from Blanton, a Louisianian, Jeddy picked up intelligence that did us little good—that he had been boarded five days before by His Majesty's brig *Scorpion* but had sighted no other sail; that there were many British vessels at Havana, several ready for sea, and that a convoy was expected to set out within the month.

We sent the *Moskva* on her way and made sail to the southwest. Finding only light airs and calms, such as are often found in this section of the Gulf Stream in the month of September, we got out our lines and trolled, which I do whenever I can in the Gulf Stream because of the innumerable fish that cruise on its surface—ferocious fighters and as good eating, or better, than halibut.

When the breeze picked up we moved along to the southwestward. Toward evening of the second day we sighted another sail, but darkness fell. Jeddy was exasperated by this disappointment. We were, he said, carrying a Jonah aboard, one that soured our luck; and from various of his phrases having to do with chair makers and gray-faced wild men, I gathered he had somehow got it in his head that Rowlandson Drown would be at the bottom of any ill success we might have.

We laid a course, that night, calculated to hold us in the neighborhood of the sail we pursued; and when dawn came, the lookout spied it four miles astern. She was a brigantine, a clumsy, slow thing; and when we ran down toward her and fired a gun, she hove-to and hoisted the American flag. She seemed to have a familiar look; so when we boarded her I went myself with Jeddy to see what it was that stirred my memory. As our boat came up to her side, I saw a nick in the galley stove pipe. A moment later the lean face of Eli Bagley stared over the rail, as inflamed and congested as when I had bound him in his cabin in Halifax harbor.

"Well, Captain," I said, as I came aboard, "this seems like old times."

He smiled a sick smile, and I suddenly remembered he was what we call a fish-chowder sailor: one who lacks the courage or the skill to navigate out of sight of the coast.

"Aren't you a little far from home?"

"Oh, a leetle; a leetle. I—I got me a sailing master."

"Well, well! You're coming up in the world! You'll be working a tea ship before you know it! Let's look at this sailing master of yours."

Bagley hesitated, his jaw bones moving like the gills of a fish. I could see he wanted to question my authority, but felt he might be treading on delicate ground. "I hold a commission from President Madison," I told him, "to capture, burn, sink, or destroy all enemy craft."

"Gosh," he said, "I ain't no enemy craft! You know me: I'm out of Portsmouth."

"Where's that sailing master?"

He hesitated: then pointed to a lean, red-nosed man who stood at the lee rail, looking fixedly at nothing and chewing busily.

"What's your name?" I asked him.

"His name's Thomas," Bagley said hurriedly.

"Tammas *McAndrew*," said the red-nosed man, a hint of sourness in his voice.

"A herring choker!" I said. "I don't like it. Let's see your papers."

"There ain't nothing wrong," Bagley said. "You know me, Nason. You won't find nothing out of the way."

"Let's see your papers."

We went into his smelly little cabin. The pewter whale-oil lamp, unmended, had been hung back on its hook beside the door.

"Well," I said, when I had finally wormed his papers from him, "you're bound from a British port to a British port with lumber for the British. You're as good as a Britisher yourself."

Bagley's lumpy jaw bones moved convulsively. "Why, that ain't so! I'm just a poor man with a living to make! Why, Halifax harbor's full of New Englanders running flour to the Canadians! Gosh almighty,

Nason, them poor Canadians couldn't live a week if we didn't run flour to 'em!"

"Nor the British army in Canada," I said.

"No," he agreed uncertainly.

He seemed to have no idea he was doing anything out of the way. "Will you tell me how in hell we're going to whip the British if we keep feeding 'em before we fight 'em?"

"We got to live, ain't we?"

"I don't see what's gained by it. I'll keep these papers, and you can make for the nearest port in the United States."

"No," he protested, "I'm going to Jamaica! I got to have those papers."

"You'll never hit Jamaica in a thousand years. I'm taking your sailing master with me, so you'd better head for more familiar waters."

"You *can't!*" he shouted, his face a mottled green and crimson, like a half-ripe apple. "I can't find my way without McAndrew."

"Yes, you can," I said. "All you need to do is steer west. You've got to hit land if you do that. Columbus did it, and so can you, if you know where west is."

"Gosh!" he said, his eyes round and staring, "what'll I do if a British frigate chases me?"

"It ought to be worth watching," I said. "Maybe you can outmaneuver her."

We threw overboard his deckload of lumber. As an afterthought I sent Jeddy to the cabin to hunt for rum. He found a keg; but after tasting it I left it with Bagley, fearful it might poison my crew if I took it with me.

McAndrew made no protest when I ordered him into the boat. "Accept my apologies," I said, "for taking you off that tidy little craft; but this is a war, even though some haven't sensed it."

He spat over the side. I saw he was chewing slippery elm. "Tidy!" he ejaculated.

"Didn't he set a good table?" I asked.

"Ghastly!" McAndrew said.

I shook my head at Jeddy. "Life can be very disappointing. Under the circumstances we'll have to let Mr. McAndrew mess in the gun room—at least until we take other prisoners to keep him company."

*　　*　　*

We were not long in doing that. On the third of November we came up with a brig flying the Spanish flag. We brought her to, for I hoped to buy a few pipes of Spanish wine from her, so our crew might not brood over our failure to take prizes. She was the *Dos Hermanos* from Pernambuco to Portsmouth—a fine craft, coppered to the bends and clean as the inside of a mussel shell, which isn't usual with Spanish vessels, all those I have seen being thickly crusted with dirt and smelling villainously of rancid oil, garlic and mold. To add to these suspicious circumstances, she had two Englishmen aboard as passengers, one of whom was standing with the captain at the rail as we came up; and her cargo was composed entirely of India goods: silks, guavas, opium, indigo, tea, ivory, carpets, and spices, chief among these being ginger and turmeric. Now it seemed unreasonable to me that this brig out of Pernambuco should be laden with India goods, rather than with sugar or coffee or aguardiente or cigarros, which are Pernambuco products.

The captain was a Spaniard and held the backs of his thumbs against his breast when I sought to question him, flapping his fingers limply in the air and looking stupid as a goat.

"All right," I told Jeddy, "bring down those two Englishmen."

They came down, polite and affable, and we had a glass of Spanish wine together.

"You gentlemen took passage from Pernambuco?" I asked them. They said that was the case.

Jeddy walked around them and around the captain, looking at them front and rear. I could see he made the Englishmen uneasy.

"You gentlemen have lived in Pernambuco for some time?" I asked.

One of them, a squatty red-faced man, looked helplessly at the other, a small man with the protruding upper front teeth that seem

almost a fashion with so many of the inhabitants of mighty Albion.
He said quickly they had been traveling.

"For business or for pleasure?"

"Pleasure," he answered readily enough. The squatty man, I
thought, relaxed gently in his chair.

"And where have you traveled?"

"Oh," said the man with the teeth, waving his hand loosely
as if to indicate far-off lands, "China, India, Ceylon, Madagascar,
Brazil——"

Jeddy laughed, his eyes as wide and blue as those of a china doll.
The glance of the buck-toothed man shifted and wavered.

I poured him another glass of wine, and we drank, all of us.

"A pleasant trip, indeed," I said. "You make it often?"

"No, we've worked hard for a number of years, and now we feel
it's time we enjoyed ourselves."

"Of course," I said. "And what may your business have been?"

The squatty red-faced man, I could see, had grown tense once
more.

"Really," said his buck-toothed friend, thoroughly English in his
manner but smiling sweetly none the less, "such interest in our affairs
is complimentary, I assure you."

"A natural interest," I told him, "for I recently spent some little
time among English people and became almost excited about them.
Now for a few more questions—after I learn your business?"

"Land," said the buck-toothed man sourly. "We dealt in land."

"Where?"

"London, of course. Land and houses."

"Your families didn't accompany you?"

"No; my wife is dead—ah—my children are too young to travel."

"So you left them with relatives?"

"Here!" he protested, "you've no right to ask these things!" His lips
were tight across his teeth; but when I looked at him without speaking and Jeddy laughed under his breath, he smiled again, albeit a
trifle weakly.

"Of course," he said, "I left them with my sister: two sweet little girls and a little boy."

"And you learned to speak Spanish while selling land in London?"

"Why, yes; that is, no. I don't speak Spanish."

"Probably you were talking to the captain in Russian when we came up, then, or was it Malay?"

He glowered at me, and Jeddy laughed again.

"Oh, well," I said, "that doesn't matter. Suppose you show me the trinkets you picked up in China and Ceylon and Madagascar for your two sweet little girls. And for the little boy. And for the kind sister who has been caring for this lonely little family."

Both Englishmen stared at me.

"Well," I said at length, "I'm waiting. Let me see some of the things you bought somewhere except India."

"This is a damned outrage," the red-faced man said huskily.

"No doubt," I returned, "but if we start exchanging outrages, we'll be here all night, and we must be on our way. This is an English brig carrying English goods to an English port, and it's as plain as the nose on my face that the captain's no captain at all, but a cat's-paw put aboard for you to hide behind. Get your dunnage together. We'll shift you to the sloop."

"I protest," said the man with the buck-teeth, though it was plain he knew he was caught. "What's to become of the brig?"

"Well, it's a shame to harm this fine new English vessel, even though she does masquerade under the Spanish flag; but I'm going to shift her cargo to the sloop and burn her." With that I told him to tell the Spanish captain that if all of them would help shift cargo, we would put them aboard a smaller prize some day, so they could sell it and have the money: otherwise they would be ordinary prisoners of war with the chance of being carried to America.

We laid the sloop alongside and worked at shifting cargo all that afternoon and through the hot, calm night. An hour after sunup the next day we had what Cephas Cluff and Jeddy and I figured was close to eighty thousand dollars' worth of the best India goods under hatches, to say nothing of a lot of new spars and sails, kegs of Spanish wine, and barrels of powder to replace that shot away in practice; and the crew were sluicing themselves with buckets of clear cool water from the blue Gulf Stream.

At eight o'clock we hoisted her sails, lashed her helm, and set her afire. Ten minutes later we ran up to windward and used her as a target. There was an oval keg of Spanish wine at the foot of the musket rack by the main hatch; and when the crew had given her a few rounds out of long guns double shotted with grape and ball, there were so many white splinters showing around her bends and bulwarks, and so much gear at loose ends, that Jeddy went down and told the crews to have a small tot all around. With that we wore ship under her stern and let her have both long guns through the cabin windows. The grape and solid shot went in with a crash that could be heard above the roar of the guns—such a crash as might be made by a horse falling through a roof. Her mainmast was cut four feet above the deck and her foremast halfway up; so that in less than five minutes she had become a torn and shattered hulk, belching a column of smoke amidships, and trailing masts, sails and shrouds over her sides.

'Lisha Lord turned from this sad wreck to shake his fist threateningly at the crews. "By Ory!" he shouted, "I told you to keep that fire low, and here you've gone halfway up the foremast with your shot! What the hell you think you're shooting at? Angels?"

XII

We had worked well down toward the trade route when Pomp, seated at the masthead like a black cloud, shiny and happy from the heat of the noonday sun, caught the flash of a distant sail on our starboard quarter. We put about, and when we drew up on it in the late afternoon, we made her out to be a ship: a good one; partly laden so that she rode high out of water, and pierced for twelve guns, five on a side and two in the stern. We stared hard at her, but could find no trace of a long gun.

"I tell you," 'Lisha said, "she carries carronades and nothing else, like most running vessels."

The men in the waist of the ship were shouting "Take her! Take her!" so we piped to quarters and loaded and double-shotted the long guns. Tommy Bickford brought me the double-barreled fowling piece my mother had traded out of Sir Arthur Ransome, placing it on the deck where it would be handy; and my little dog Pinky came and lay beside it, helpful and obliging, his whiskers resting on its stock.

We ran up the British flag and bore off to windward of her. Her ports were open, and we could see men at the guns, but not many, and I was sure there would not be enough of a crew to damage us with musketry fire when we closed with her.

She hoisted no answering flag, so we hauled down the British flag, ran up the American flag, and fired a gun. She ran on as silently as before, a beautiful, high-sided ship, her mass of sails ruddy in the late afternoon sun. A cloud of pink smoke puffed from her stern; and a spout of water shot into the air two hundred yards ahead of us well off line.

"Hell," 'Lisha told me, "that's a twenty-four pound carronade! We can outrange her and take her from here."

"Go ahead," I said, having determined long ago never to risk losing a man if I could avoid it.

'Lisha sighted his long eighteen. The deck jerked; the gun roared; the white smoke came down around us. There was a distant crackle, like a dog crunching a stick between his jaws. The boat at the after davits seemed to fall apart reluctantly.

'Lisha cursed bitterly while the gun crew sponged and rammed, moving with seeming laziness, as they had been taught, but having the gun ready almost before the smoke from Pendleton Quint's gun had blown into our throats.

"There, by gravy!" said 'Lisha, squinting after Pendleton's shot. "Caught her that time!" A star-shaped patch of white splinters appeared at the stranger's water line.

'Lisha pulled his lanyard, and the ship's mizzenmast swayed drunkenly, just as she turned slowly into the wind. She ran up the British flag, only to haul it down instantly.

She was the ship *Auchterlonie,* Gilbert Lubbock, master, from St. Thomas for Bermuda, 518 tons and twenty-four men, armed with two twenty-four pound carronades and ten nine-pound carronades, and half laden with sugar and rum. I went aboard with Jeddy and found Lubbock feeling unhappy, as well he might.

"Here," I told him, "it's not your fault. If I didn't take you, somebody else would."

"Aye," he said, gazing bitterly at the *Lively Lady,* which seemed too small and battered, lying off to windward, to be anything but a tender for his splendid vessel, "but I could have stayed with the convoy another day or so."

Here was news indeed—news that might, if our luck held, result happily for us and sadly for the British. "That's true," I said, hoping to lead him into giving me further information, "but doubtless we'd have caught you in the end; for it's probably a small convoy, and weakly guarded, like most we find in these waters."

Lubbock nodded angrily. "Weakly!" he growled. "The word's as weak as the guard! If the Governors of the Bank of England followed the methods of the fools in the Admiralty, they'd toss their money in the street and set a sleepy midget to guard it! Thirty-two sail there were in our convoy when I hauled away, and no protection save the *Turnstone* sloop-of-war."

Delighted at what he told me, I assured him we would do all we could for him.

"Aye," he groaned, "in America."

"No," I said, "we'll try to get you another vessel somewhere. Anyway, America isn't so bad. All our prisoners are paroled."

"I dinna like the place," he growled. "It's either too hot or too cold, always, and not too bonnie, neither." As an afterthought he added, "But bonnier than the stone box the British have for prisoners. *They'll* give ye no parole!"

"I know," I said hastily, having heard enough of Dartmoor. "Where's your specie, Captain?"

He shrugged his shoulders and pressed his lips together stubbornly; then, evidently figuring on making the best of a bad bargain, he showed me the panel behind which he kept his specie kegs, they being made and marked to look like nail kegs. We rolled out twelve, containing thirty-five hundred English pounds, or in the neighborhood of eighteen thousand dollars. We took out some rum and small articles from the *Auchterlonie*, and bales of pink flamingo skins—birds that must look like patches of Maine sunsets, so beautifully rosy are their feathers. Then, though I disliked the thought of so many prisoners, we sent the captain and the crew to the *Lively Lady*, wheeled a carronade to the *Auchterlonie's* main hatch, and blew a hole in her bottom—though I couldn't help but hear the men growling while they did it.

We had brought Rowlandson Drown with us, in anticipation of

needing a carpenter's help in scuttling her; and I think his grumbling was loudest. "We'd get forty thousand dollars for this ship if she was manned out for home," he told Seth Tarbox, his face dark with sourness; and unfortunately he was right.

*   *   *

It was dark when we set her afire and tumbled into our boat; and we wasted no time on rum or Spanish wine, for every last one of us panted to see the convoy of which Lubbock had spoken.

We paroled Captain Lubbock, the two Englishmen from the *Dos Hermanos,* the Spanish captain and McAndrew from Eli Bagley's brig; but we had to be watchful of the seamen lest they rise against us and seize the *Lively Lady* for themselves, which was why I disliked taking prisoners if I could avoid it; yet I couldn't turn them loose in a good ship when it was my purpose to distress the enemy in the greatest possible degree.

We bore off to the eastward, hunting for the convoy, and cruised for three days, with the weather what it so often is in those parts—bright blue overhead, fleecy beds of cloud near the horizon, and occasionally a sharp squall banging past with a thunderstorm in its arms. Toward mid-afternoon on the third day there was a bellowing of "Sail ho!" from the bow and the masthead at the same time, a distant squall having uncovered a white speck like the tip of a hen feather.

Hoping we had found the convoy, we held on our course, and soon discovered the stranger had hauled her wind and was bearing straight for us. Since there was no other sail in sight, we concluded she was in chase of us. We ran off on the other tack, figuring on getting to windward of her, whereupon she went off on the other tack herself, and we saw she was a schooner with a raking stern and bow and almost no freeboard, so that she seemed plastered to the water. She had tremendously tall raking masts and next to no top-hamper, there being only two shrouds to the foremast and one to the mainmast; and the masts, bending like fishing rods, seemed to spring the schooner ahead as though she were alive and being whipped along. She had a beautiful clean run, and she slipped over the waves, rather than through them, seeming to have no keel at all to hold her back.

"Well," I said, "there's only one place where they build schooners like that, and that's Baltimore." The others agreed, but we manned the long guns for the sake of safety and watched her whisk through the water. We saw she could weather us with no difficulty. Indeed, she was the fastest schooner I had ever seen. If we were logging twelve knots, which I think we were, she must have been logging thirteen and a half. I even think she was doing a knot or so better than that, but I am reluctant to say it for fear there will be folk to snort and declare no craft afloat can travel with such speed. I knew no Britisher could have overhauled her in a chase, so it seemed to me that she must be an American privateer. If I had not felt sure, I would have run from her long before; and I think I could have kept ahead of her until dark and then given her the slip.

We ran up the American flag, and I maneuvered to get under her lee; but a hen might as well have maneuvered to get under the lee of a kingfisher.

She came about and ran down on us. We could see she carried fourteen guns—two of them long guns—and had a sizable crew on deck. She hoisted the American flag and slipped alongside, not a half pistol shot away; and since there were no muskets leveled at us we knew her captain was certain of our nationality. None the less, her gun crews were at their stations, and a dark, slender man with a small black mustache, flashing white teeth, and elegant-seeming clothes clung to the ratlines, one hand on his hip, and shouted down wind, "What sloop is that?"

I rapped Pinky on the snout to stop his barking, he being beside me with his forepaws on the rail, considerably affronted by this stranger's question. "Private armed sloop *Lively Lady*, Nason, out of Arundel," I called back.

The dark man took off his gray beaver hat and made me a polite bow. "Schooner *Comet*," he shouted, "out of Baltimore; Boyle commanding. Would you do me the honor?"

We hove to, and I was rowed over to the *Comet*, where Boyle met me, hat in hand, as mannerly as though Commodore Truxton himself were coming over the side.

This Captain Thomas Boyle of Baltimore was the most affable man I have ever known, and the gentlest-seeming. Indeed, if I had not seen more of him at a later date, I might have thought his deference assumed; for it seemed to me, at times, that no man could be as gracious as he and still be serious about it. Yet he was always courteous, even to his men and prisoners; though there are captains of a score of British war craft and masters of almost a thousand British merchantmen who have declared he was the most tantalizing and troublesome man that ever lived.

He was, as I have said, gentle—so gentle, almost, as to seem harmless—and appreciative of things said by others. I noticed early in our acquaintance that if I was speaking with him and he was forced, for some reason, to interrupt the conversation, he would apologize profoundly at the earliest opportunity and ask me to be kind enough to proceed from the point where he had, as he put it, so rudely broken in on me.

He was quiet, too: the most deceptive man, it seems to me, that ever lived. His seamanship was a thing for seamen to marvel at, and I have never seen his equal for boldness. It was this boldness that so addled and fuddled the British; and it was common talk in French ports at one time that the captain of a British frigate had been so infuriated at Captain Boyle's behavior in the Channel that he had wept openly on his own quarter-deck from rage.

He took me below to a neat small cabin as pleasant to look at as his beautifully fitting broadcloth coat and pale-colored trousers buckled under his boots, and had out a mahogany chest inlaid with a satinwood lion and unicorn.

"I *do* hope you'll like this, Captain," he said, drawing out a five-sided bottle made from purple glass—the prettiest bottle I had ever seen. "It seems to me not half bad. I took it from a ship with a delightful captain: thirteen pipes of old Madeira wine, he had. This is from the oldest, and I find it passable, but I'm eager to have your opinion."

He took a goblet from the slots in the cover—a purple goblet, like the bottle—filled it for me, and watched me anxiously while I sipped. If the wine had been sea water and sour milk I would have praised it, because of his eager hospitality, but it seemed to be a blend of delicious fruits and faint perfumes and the essences of tropical nuts.

"Well," he said, when I spoke enthusiastically of it, "that is very kind of you. *Very* kind. Let us have another glass. Then you must tell me about your cruise. I hope and trust, Captain, that your cruise has been successful. Your idea of a small boat is excellent—excellent! Next year you may find a larger craft advisable; but what we need now is speed. I think you're exactly right."

"She's a tub beside yours," I said.

"No, your sloop is very fast, Captain Nason. You're too modest by far. You could have lost me in the dark if you'd tried."

"Yes, and if I'd tried, I might have been raked with a long twenty-four around midnight."

Captain Boyle laughed, a musical Southern laugh, quite in keeping with his voice, which, being soft and flat, was easy on the ear. "No, sir; I always talk things over with an enemy before I shoot, if it's possible."

"Well," I said, "I saw she was a Baltimore schooner, so I suspicioned you were American, but I never saw a Baltimore schooner behave like this. Sometimes she gets right up out of the water and flies."

"It's a pleasure to hear such appreciation from a seaman like yourself, Captain Nason," Captain Boyle assured me. He held up his purple goblet and stared through it at the scuttle overhead. "Now that you mention it, I feel free to tell you that so far as I know the *Comet* is the fastest Baltimore clipper ever built. She's faster than the little Baltimore-built government sloop *Enterprise*. Doubtless you remember her, Captain Nason. Before the navy cut down her masts and made her into an unbreakable brig she was said to be the fastest craft afloat. I'm *very* averse to saying it, sir; for I might be misunderstood; but you've seen the *Comet*, sir, from the deck of a fast sloop; so I'll tell you she's logged over fifteen knots."

I could make no reply to this except to whistle, which I did; and we had a drink on it.

"Well," I said, "I've had fair luck, but I hope to have better. There's a convoy of thirty-two sail bound for England under the sloop-of-war *Turnstone*."

"A convoy!" Boyle exclaimed, and his eyes, velvety brown eyes, seemed to glow with yellow lights. "A convoy! And only one sloop-of-war to guard it!"

We sipped our Madeira silently. I knew he was thinking longingly, as was I, of that diversity of vessels with the sloop-of-war fussing around them like a hen with a family of addle-pated chicks.

Finally Boyle shook his head. "I should be off about my business. I've taken nine prizes on this cruise and manned out six for American ports. My crew's reduced to forty-two men instead of the hundred and twenty with which I started; and I've a swarm of prisoners aboard, eating me out of house and home."

I asked him whether many privateers were putting to sea.

"Lord!" he said, chuckling a rich Southern chuckle, "the sea's full of 'em!" He threw himself back in his chair, hung a fawn-colored leg over its arm, looked up at the scuttle, and checked them off on his fingers. "Out of Baltimore alone there's Barney in the *Rossie* with a hundred and twenty men and fourteen guns, Grant in the *High Flyer*, Richardson in the *America*, Miller in the *Revenge* with sixteen guns and a hundred and forty men, Dooley in the *Rolla*, Wilson in the *Tom*. That's six. There's the *Dolphin*, the *Nonsuch*, the *Globe*, the *Wasp*, the *Hornet*, the *Liberty*: twelve. There's the *Sparrow*, thirteen, and the *Sarah Ann*, fourteen, all out of Baltimore. There must be three thousand Baltimore men at sea in privateers and letters-of-marque: all fast vessels, sir; fast and well armed; commanded by able men. Speaking of able men, Dominique Diron's out of Charleston in the *Decatur*. He's a Frenchman and a pirate, but he's able! There's some out of New York that you'll hear from, too: fast and dangerous—the *Governor Tompkins,* and the *General Armstrong*—by jolly, Captain Nason, there's a brig, the *General Armstrong,* with nineteen guns and a hundred and forty men, that would make trouble for any British sloop-of-war! There's the *Yorktown* and the *Holkar* and the *Anaconda,* each with a hundred and sixty men: there's the *Saratoga* and the *Orders in Council* and the *Benjamin Franklin*—and over a dozen more I'll call to mind in a minute. Why, they're coming out of the Chesapeake like a swarm of bees and pouring out of New York; and I've heard, Captain Nason, that New England's not being backward in the matter."

"They must be coming out of Salem and Boston almost as fast," I told him, "and they'll be out of Portsmouth and Newburyport in fair numbers, if they haven't started already."

He nodded. "If I knew how to do it, I'd bet a thousand dollars to a pipe of old Madeira that American privateers will capture or destroy five hundred British merchantmen in a year's time, and do more than a hundred million dollars' worth of damage."

"Don't you ever bet?" I asked him.

"Whenever I get the chance," Captain Boyle replied politely, "but I can't find anyone to take me up on that one."

"This convoy, now," I reminded him: "It would be an education to watch you in chase of it."

"That's very kind of you, sir: very kind," Captain Boyle said. "Not only kind, but gracefully expressed." He meditatively touched his small black mustache with his finger tips. "I should be getting home with my prisoners and refitting for another cruise." He stared at me thoughtfully. "But it would be mighty pleasant," he added, "to keep company with you against that flight of doves."

"I must get rid of my prisoners, too," I reminded him, "and I'll refit from one of the convoy if my luck holds." At this both of us rapped the table top with our knuckles.

He sighed gently. "I don't like to sail short-handed. It's an uncomfortable feeling if you have a sudden need to fight. Still, we may find a few Britishers who'll prefer our service to their own. It *has* been known to happen—" he smiled at me gaily—"so I'll go along with you a little way, though we can't expect to do much unless we get a bit of dirty weather."

I knew that here was a rare piece of good fortune, running into a seaman like Boyle and finding him willing to keep company with me against a convoy; for while it's not overdifficult to harry a convoy alone, provided you have luck, it's easier and surer when two together make the attack. None the less, I didn't begin to know how fortunate I was; for all I knew of Boyle was that he was a good seaman.

We arranged that the first to sight the convoy should run down to the other so that plans might be made, and that if the convoy should be sighted by one while we were separated, the discoverer should hang astern of it for three days before attacking, in the hope that the other would come up.

So we cruised off to the northwest, being already on the trade route; and I was almost discouraged at the manner in which the *Comet* outsailed us, even though we cracked on all we had. Yet we hung together by dint of Boyle making long reaches to windward and to leeward, and so worked up in the general direction of the Azores.

The bright blue sky that had favored us so long was filmed with a loose gray veil on the second or third day, and the wind had started to pick the tops from the waves, shake them to pieces and toss them against our mainsail, when Pomp, riding high and darksome at the masthead, shouted that the *Comet* had put about. We made her out shortly, bearing down on us like a distant gull; and ten minutes later, when she had taken on size, Pomp went to shouting, "Sail ho! Sail ho! Sail ho!" until I thought he had lost his mind.

But the men in the bow moved excitedly and looked back at us, so I knew we had sighted the convoy. With that I put the sloop into the wind, hoping we had escaped their notice; and in the southwest I saw, faint and far off, a small gray dot that came and went, and then another, and then two more close together. I didn't bother to hunt for others, for they couldn't be far away, I knew, and it was a pleasant thought that within our reach were more than thirty West Indiamen laden with millions of dollars' worth of rum and sugar and India goods, and God knows how many kegs of specie.

The *Comet* came slipping up under our lee as easy and graceful as a seal, and Boyle waved his gray beaver to me, affable and polite and anxious to please.

The men crowded up to look at him when he came aboard; and I could tell from this how they felt toward him; for our Maine men won't stir two feet to see a person like the Dey of Algiers, who has nothing but wealth and position to his credit.

He glanced around at them and smiled a bashful smile, very friendly. "Well, Captain," he said, bowing a quick little bow to me, but speaking, I was sure, for the benefit of the crew, "it looks as though England might find herself somewhat poorer by dawn to-morrow."

XIII

W<small>HEN</small> we had made our plans, we payed off to the southward till dusk; then turned to the northeast in the track of the convoy. It was a night of pale darkness with a smart wind from the east; yet it was not bad, for the stars shone, and the sea was nothing to cause us inconvenience, though the decks were wet with scud, and there was a moaning in our top-hamper that foretold heavier weather.

The *Comet* stood along within half pistol shot of us under a reefed mainsail and jib, so we might hang together. We could make her out clearly, skimming along as easily as the deep-sea birds that follow craft for days in mid-ocean, remaining always a foot above the waves. She was as silent as though she sailed without a crew, with no figure showing on her decks except that of the helmsman. Not a sound could I hear from her above the complaining of our mast, the screaking of the boom and the gun carriages, and the gushing rush of the waves along our sides. Yet I knew her people were on deck, as were our own, armed with cutlasses and boarding axes, the sharpshooters ready with their muskets, and all of them lying under the bulwarks or sprawled around the long guns.

When we had held our course for two hours, there was a hoarse half shout of "Sail ho!" from the bow. In the same instant I heard the same half-stifled call from the deck of the *Comet,* and as if she had been nothing more substantial than a fog she sheered away and was gone in the gloom.

I saw the bulk of a smallish vessel on our lee bow. We came up on her fast. I caught sight of the light from her binnacle and made her out to be a small brig. We hauled a little away; then ranged alongside. There was a shout from the man at the helm of the brig. With that Jeddy clapped his hands, and our boarders came out from under the bulwarks and went over the brig's side and into her waist, fast and silently.

There were four men on the brig's deck, unarmed and with no thought of attack, so when Jeddy led a boarding party of ten toward the stern and Rowlandson led another ten toward the bow, all with cutlasses swinging, there was no opposition and no noise save another shout or two and a little thudding of feet on the deck.

In five minutes Rowlandson's ten boarders were back again. The brig came about, according to plan, and the two of us bore off to the southwest, all without a shot being fired or a flare kindled to give the alarm.

For fifteen minutes we drove back on this course, keeping the brig close under our lee; then, having put five miles between ourselves and the convoy, we hove to once more and settled the business.

The brig proved to be the *Star of the Indies*, Fagin, master, two six-pounders and a crew of nine, from Jamaica for Liverpool, laden with rum, sugar, and fresh fruits. Also she had two thousand dollars in specie, which we promptly seized. Having no time to waste, I proposed to the captain that if he would put his men to work transferring a part of his fresh fruit to the *Lively Lady*, receive on board our prisoners, and engage to sail northwest for two days, so that he would be in no likelihood of picking up the convoy again, I would transfer one third of the brig to him and one third to Captain Lubbock, who had told me of the convoy, and one third to the remainder of the prisoners and his crew and set them all free. Otherwise, I told him, I would take him and his men prisoners and scuttle his brig to boot.

I thought, when I was done speaking, that the captain would jump down my throat in his eagerness to accept; and two hours later we were once more on our way to the northeast, free of prisoners and keeping a sharp lookout for the *Comet*.

A little after half-past ten we made out a sail on our weather beam and were sure we had again come up with the convoy. When we found this craft to be another small brig, we fell away from her, wishing bigger game. We were soon rewarded by sighting a large ship, and without more ado ran under her lee and ordered her to wear immediately and head southeast, or we'd sink her. This was the plan made between Captain Boyle and myself—that I should run my second prize off to the southeast while he ran off to the northwest. Thus if one of us should be pursued by the convoying sloop, the other would have time to strip his prize.

Instead of obeying our order, the ship held on her way, firing a gun. We heard no wail from the shot; so she may have fired it to warn the others. At this 'Lisha Lord rapped out a quick order to the musket men, as we had agreed. A crackling of small arms sent pale flashes against her sails and the smoke wisps that still clung to them. There was a crying-out on her deck, indicating that Moody Haley and Moses Burnham had poured their fire into the helmsman.

"Wear ship!" I shouted again, "or I'll blow you to pieces."

She came about slowly. Ahead of her a blue flare blazed in a ship's bows, revealing faintly luminous mainsails, topsails, and topgallant sails against a wavering background of blue light. Two miles to leeward another blue flare shone out; and then a third, almost a mile away. There was no way of telling whether they had been set off out of fright at hearing the gun, or whether Boyle had swooped down on another of the convoy and so put all of them into the tremors.

Now a strange thing happened when we had run this ship five miles to the southeastward and hove her to; for when I boarded her I found a person I had known before; and though I had no thought of meeting an acquaintance, I felt no surprise at the encounter any more than as though I had expected it.

The ship was the *Lord Startham*, James Houie, master, from

Kingston to Falmouth, 407 tons, 10 guns and eighteen men—or what had been eighteen men; for our musketry fire had killed the helmsman and wounded the first mate. She was laden with sugar, rum and indigo, and carried 8,250 English pounds in specie. Not liking the groans of the first mate, poor man, who had been shot through the lungs, I sent back the boat to bring aboard our doctor, Jotham Carr, ordered the indigo to be swayed up from the hold for transfer to the *Lively Lady*, and rapidly proceeded to an examination of the ship's papers, knowing the sloop-of-war might come down on us at any moment.

I discovered there were three passengers aboard, one of them a Mr. Sanderson, manager of a sugar plantation in Jamaica, and the others his wife and her maid. I had no liking for this; for there was no place on our sloop for women, nor had I any desire to encumber myself with prisoners.

"Have these people brought here," I said to the captain, for whom I had little sympathy because he had kept on his course when I hailed him. "I think they should have something to say concerning their disposition."

Sanderson proved to be a young man with a pleasant dignity about him and a look that struck me as vaguely familiar. With him came his wife, a pretty blonde girl of a washed-out appearance, as though she had stood too long in tropical rainstorms, and behind her a maid whom I could see but dimly in the light of the whale-oil lamp, which swung in figure eights with the uneasy rolling of the ship.

"I'm sorry for all this," I said to them, wondering where I had seen Sanderson before, "but I hold a commission to take, burn, sink, or destroy all enemy craft, and this ship must be sunk. Now, I can do either of two things, and because of Mrs. Sanderson I'll let you say which it shall be. Either I can take all of you as prisoners to my sloop, which is small and uncomfortable, and destroy this ship; or I can stand by you till morning, run you within sight of the convoy, and set you afire. Then the sloop-of-war will take you off, or you can go in your boats to one of the other vessels. There's some danger in the first course, for nobody can tell when we'll be fired on ourselves. As for the second course, if you go aboard a merchantman, she may quickly be captured herself, so you'll have it all to do over again."

When I said this my eye caught a movement of the maid behind Mrs. Sanderson. I stared hard at her and saw she had a gray, reminiscent look. Her face seemed to soften a little from its grimness, as though she wished to smile but couldn't quite decide on it. I knew then I had seen this grim gray woman in a field near Saco. Her name, I remembered, was Annie; she had given Jeddy and me a glass of wine at the behest of Lady Emily Ransome. It seemed a queer thing, the thought that flashed through my head when I recognized her; for it was the thought that this was quite right and proper: that the whole affair had happened this way before, which of course it hadn't.

Having glanced at me, she looked quickly down at the cabin floor again. It occurred to me it might be well to wait before seeming to recognize her, lest the Sandersons annoy us with questions and make it more difficult for me to do what I had to do. Also she put other thoughts in my head: thoughts of Lady Ransome's hoity-toityness: of how she had looked with my knife clasped tight in her hands, cutting her initials on the old beech tree: of my miniature of her, which, as it happened, I had in my breast pocket even now. It happened, too, that I had a thought to speak to Annie alone.

Before the Sandersons could answer my question, young Jotham Carr came in at the cabin door. "Captain," he said, "the mate's dead."

"Well," I said, looking at Houie, "I'm sorry to hear it. It would never have happened if you hadn't been so injudicious as to run from an armed vessel at night."

"Captain," said Sanderson, "we'd be obliged to you if you'd let us remain on board this ship to-night. I'd prefer not to trust my wife to a small boat in a choppy sea."

"Very good," I told him; "and how'll you feel if it comes on to blow a gale and you have to get off in it to-morrow?"

He stared at me without speaking. I strove hard to fix my mind on the colting I had received aboard the *Gorgon,* for I had no more love for the business than Sanderson had.

"My wife has been ill," Sanderson said. "I'm taking her home in the hope she'll recover."

There it was: what I had dreaded. If I have learned anything about war in the little I have seen of it, it's that you mustn't think of the enemy as human beings, like yourself, but as some sort of devouring monsters capable of doing any wicked deed: that you must think of everyone as nothing more than worthless playing cards or chessmen, to be tossed away or crushed or destroyed so long as advantages are gained and battles won; otherwise there seems to be nothing worth fighting about. Yet in spite of knowing all this I had let Sanderson mention his wife's illness; and on top of everything I had been such a fool as to listen to him.

"Well," I said, thinking hard of how I could learn more about Annie without seeming to ask, "your wife will probably be all right, with the sea voyage and all. She's fortunate to have a woman to look out for her. I should think it would be hard to get such a woman in the Indies."

"Oh, we'd never have got her in the Indies," he said. "I wrote to my sister in England, and she sent her out to me."

"Oh, did she!" I said weakly, for his mention of his sister in England, coupled with Annie's presence, had made it plain to me at last why I had found a familiar look about him. It was because his sister had married Sir Arthur Ransome.

I strove to decide what should be done, and the more I strove, the more I regretted my misfortune in encountering such people as Sanderson and his blue-eyed ailing wife. For a moment I considered sending for Jeddy, knowing he held himself merciless where Britishers were concerned; but I could see it was a matter I must settle myself.

"Well," I said at length, watching Sanderson carefully to see whether he might not give me reason to be harsh with him, "I've heard that turn about is fair play, and if this is so, I must remind myself that a few weeks before this war broke out I was taken from my brig by a press gang from the crew of the *Gorgon* sloop-of-war and whipped for nothing except to gratify the spleen of her captain, and be damned to him."

Sanderson twisted up the corner of his mouth and looked at me out of eyes the color of smoke, so that I stared at him in a sort of confusion because of the memories of Lady Ransome that crowded my brain. "All Englishmen aren't like that," he said.

"Probably not," I admitted, "but since England filled her ships for this war out of jails and poorhouses, the Englishmen that Americans see are worse than anything we've ever been able to imagine."

"I've heard so," he said. "It's a great pity."

"Oh," I said, "there's no use going over and over all this! If you and the captain will give me your word to keep away from the convoy and make no further effort to join it, I'll turn you loose with your cargo. But I wish a paper signed—a paper saying it's done because of Mrs. Sanderson, and for no other reason, and stipulating that half the sale price of the cargo belongs to her."

"Sir——" said Sanderson in a choked voice; but I had no time to listen to further talk.

"Is that agreed, yes or no?" I asked.

Since there was nothing else for the captain to do, he agreed.

"Very well," I said gruffly to him in response. "You'll step into Mr. and Mrs. Sanderson's cabin and draw up the paper instantly." As he seemed to demur and cavil, "Instantly!" I repeated sharply. "I mean the three of you!"

They obeyed me, and I turned to Annie, who seemed about to follow. I frowned, to cover an unreasonable embarrassment. "You'll remain here," I said, and I fear I looked foolish. "You're not needed in the drawing up of such a paper, I take it."

"No, sir," she returned meekly, leaning against the table and swaying with the slow rocking of the ship. "You have something you wish to say to me, sir?"

I stared at her sternly. "No, I haven't."

"You didn't wish to ask——"

"Well," I said negligently, "I seem to recall having seen you. I seem to have seen you in attendance on Sir Arthur Ransome at——"

"No, Captain," she said quietly, "upon Lady Ransome."

"It may be; it may be," I returned. "I suppose they were both quite well when you last saw them? They reached home safely?"

"Quite safely," she said. "They went straight to Ransome Hall, near Exeter."

"Exeter?" I asked. "Oh, yes: they went to Exeter. But this ship is outward bound from Jamaica. She—they left home again, possibly."

"It was I," she said, looking down at her feet. "I was not to stay there long myself. We were home in May, and in June Lady Ransome sent me to her brother's wife in Jamaica."

"Oh," I said, "to her brother's wife! Indeed!"

She glanced toward the door of the Sandersons' cabin, which was just off that of the master, in which we stood. "Yes, Captain."

I stroked my chin. "You've been long in Lady Ransome's service?"

"Since she was twelve years old, Captain." Suddenly she gave a hiccup and went to sniveling and catching her breath, most distressing.

"I can't see how she could let you go so far away, if she thought so highly of you," I said.

"It was over something that was lost."

"You mean something belonging to Lady Ransome?" I asked. "Something she thought you'd stolen?"

"Oh, no, sir! It was S'Roth! This thing was lost, and I was the last one to see it; and S'Roth was angry and kept saying I should take better care of m'lady's things."

It seemed as though I might burst in this small cabin, what with the heat and all. "Did he nag at her?" I asked. "Did he nag at his— at Lady Ransome?"

"Oh, sir," she cried, "he's a devil! He's forever peering and prying! He kept at m'lady and kept at her about it, and kept at her to get rid of me and get somebody who could be trusted not to lose valuable things, and at last he said I'd have to go."

I could see Sir Arthur's thin, pale face before me and hear his whining voice chewing at his words and pushing them up against his teeth.

I stood and simmered for a while, rolling Annie's revelations through my head. Talk, I knew, would remedy nothing; my best procedure was to let well enough alone and hold my tongue. Yet I could not bring myself to drop the subject, not until I had asked Annie one more question; so I coughed and cleared my throat, and finally said to her: "What was it she lost? Was it—was it a piece of— was it a piece of jewelry?"

At this Annie nodded violently and burst into a storm of tears, so that it would have been difficult for me to question her further, even though I had wished to.

Somewhat uncertainly, I fear, I watched her and thought of many things to say but didn't say them. Instead, I finally broke out with, "Well, it's too late to mend matters now," and I added, not quite knowing what I meant myself: "A present's a present and couldn't be returned without insult, so stop your sniveling!"

Upon this, much befuddled in my mind, I strode out to the main deck and gave a great many orders in an angry voice. Among them was one to Jeddy, which he heartily misliked—to take fifty gold sovereigns from the specie kegs and carry them to Annie.

Seeing he was averse to the task, and being a little clearer in my mind, I took the sovereigns myself and went below. Truth to tell, I could not leave the ship until I had seen Annie once more. She was sitting in the cabin where I had left her, staring down at her folded hands.

"Now, here," I said, dropping the sovereigns in her lap, "I don't understand this. I can't wait around here all night listening to hints. Do you understand?"

"Yes, sir," Annie replied.

"Well, then," I said, "well, then—ah—you say there was—that is to say, you could see that this man—this gentleman we were speaking of—you could see he wasn't always—ah—pleasant?"

"Yes, sir."

"Well," I said, impatient at her slowness, "speak up! Don't beat about the bush!"

"Oh, sir!" Annie said, "it was a great mistake, and such a pretty little thing, always gay and happy; and now sour looks if she so much as laughs at anything! She'll be old and bitter while she's still a baby."

"Old and bitter!" I repeated, recalling how Lady Ransome had bound up my head in Arundel, and how I had felt her soft arm against my cheek. "I won't—a man can't—there must have been some help for it!" I looked up at the whale-oil lamp, jerking at its chains with the wallowing of the ship. I thought it burned dimly. The reek of it seemed to irritate my eyes and throat. "You can always get—I mean, couldn't anybody help—couldn't you help her? Couldn't you do anything?" I may have shaken the cabin table overstrongly, for I heard the mahogany crack.

She looked away from me thoughtfully. "I?" she asked. "I? What could I do? Now, you——"

"I?" I asked. "What could *I* do?"

"I think," she said, moving uncomfortably, "I think she'd like to see you again."

"See me?" I demanded. "Why should she want to see me? How could she see me when my country's at war with England?"

"And will you be fighting forever?" she asked.

I thought the matter over and over, but I could make next to nothing out of it except that it would be well if I did what I could to see that this war of ours was as short as I could help to make it.

* * *

It must have been one o'clock in the morning when we finished loading the indigo and specie aboard the sloop and hauled away from the *Lord Starham.* Toward morning the east wind that had threatened us the night before died completely, and we lay and wallowed on a turbulent gray-blue sea. On the following day the breeze came up again from the west, and we moved along in search of the convoy, without finding it. During the night, however, we heard the sound of guns and guessed that the *Comet* was at them again. Early the next morning we found them, twenty-seven sail, huddled together so close that from where we watched them they looked as though a skysail could have been thrown over the lot, barring one, which hung in their rear, so that I knew it was the *Comet*.

While we watched, one of the convoy put about and started back toward the single sail, all very small and distant to the eye; and we heard guns, though we were too far off to see the smoke, even.

It seemed plain to me that the *Comet* was harrying the convoy for the deviltry of it, and that the *Turnstone* was seeking to chase her away or get within striking distance of her. If Boyle wished to play that game, I thought, I could do nothing but help him; and with that I crowded on all sail and moved off to the westward; then bore north; and in two hours' time we had run well ahead of the convoy and were bearing down on its weather bow.

The *Turnstone* was still playing at long balls with Boyle, and I hoped to reach one of the convoy before she could return; but it was impossible; for when the convoy sighted us they ran together like frightened quail and fired guns, whereupon the cruiser put about instantly and returned to them.

We lay off, a little out of gunshot in case the *Turnstone* took it into her head to let drive at us with her long guns; and while we lay there, studying the convoy and picking out the craft that looked most likely as prizes, Boyle did a thing I was glad to have seen, so that if ever I could have a fast enough craft, I might some day find myself in a position to profit by the lesson.

He bore off to windward of the convoy, which was closely bunched, with the sloop-of-war herding them along in the rear, and then came running along toward us, as pretty a sight as ever was. The masts of his graceful craft seemed to bend and give like willow branches and to thrust her along by their bending, as a strip of whalebone, pressed against a slender board, might spring it through the water. The *Comet* came close up under our lee; and Boyle, affable and dapper, clung to a stay and waved his hat.

"You'll dine with me, Captain?" he shouted.

I nodded.

"Pray put about," he called. "I'll be back in half an hour."

We payed off and watched him. He stood past the convoy; then tacked suddenly and shot across its bow. With that the *Turnstone* moved out from behind the merchantmen and set off after Boyle. But Boyle, having rounded the head of the convoy, hauled his wind in a flash and slipped down the opposite side, having put the entire fleet between himself and the sloop-of-war; and to us it seemed, and was indeed the fact, that the *Turnstone's* movements, by comparison with those of the *Comet*, were like those of a clumsy, flustered crow attempting to escape the agile dartings of a kingbird.

While our crew, and our officers as well, for that matter, stamped their feet at the bulwarks, shouting with laughter and waving their caps at this display of speed and agility, the *Comet* rounded to and shot alongside a fine large ship. What happened then we could not see, except that the *Turnstone* labored slowly around the head of her clumsy charges. Before she had rounded them we saw well what it was that had occurred; for the *Comet's* head payed off again, and she flew on her way down the convoy's lee side, while from the deck of the ship at which she had stopped there rose a pale wavering haze of smoke—a haze that grew thicker as we watched; then suddenly billowed out and puffed upward, enveloping the mainsail, topsail, and topgallant sail in a pillar of smoke and flame. We could see the *Turnstone* come up with the burning vessel and heave to, so the crew might be picked up, and all the while the *Comet* foamed along behind us, as swift and innocent-looking as a teal duck skimming the surface of a marsh.

She drew abreast, so close we could see the rings in the gun tompions and the gold key dangling at the end of Captain Boyle's watch fob as he stood by the wheel, beaming at us and feeling tenderly of his small mustaches.

He lifted his hat debonairly as our crew manned the rail to cheer him.

When I stepped aboard the *Comet* a few moments later he said apologetically, "I hope I haven't made you hungry, Captain! I'm some minutes late; but dinner's waiting in my cabin."

XIV

I T WAS on the fifteenth of December that the *Lively Lady* came through the teeth of a blow into the Bay of Biscay, got under the lee of the land, and made the mouth of the Loire; and I know of nothing that had ever looked more welcome to me—barring our own oblong patch of farmland in Arundel—than the calm surface of the river, the bright green islands in it, and the small stone houses on the low-lying banks.

We had clung to the lee of the convoy until a gale of wind blew up from the northwest, whereupon that had happened which always happens with a convoy: it had been scattered by the blow, some heaving to, some scudding under bare poles, and some setting a few rags of sail and holding their course as best they could. While they were thus scattered we captured, in two days' time, a ship and two brigs without the firing of a gun; and it was with the last of them that our trouble started.

The brig *Loyal Nancy* was laden with 146 puncheons of Jamaica rum and some mahogany; and we took out her crew and burnt her. The brig *Hesperides* was laden with rum, sugar and coffee, and 2,300 English pounds in specie; and we took out her crew, used her as a target, and sank her. The ship *Rose of the West* was laden with 320 hogsheads of sugar and 90 seroons of indigo, the latter having a value of $18,000.

This *Rose of the West* was a handsome ship of 400 tons; and after we had taken the indigo from her with great difficulty because of the roughness of the sea, I gave orders to burn her, though I regretted the destruction of so staunch a craft. Before my orders were carried out, Rowlandson Drown, with three of the men, came to me. Rowlandson, his dark gray face pushed forward by his thick bull neck, looked mulish and lowering.

"Captain," Rowlandson said, "there's been some talk among the men about the destruction of these vessels. It seems to us as how it might be possible to make a dollar out of this ship if she was handled different."

"How would you propose to handle her, Rowlandson?" I asked, fearful that I had overlooked something, and desirous of getting as much prize money as could be got.

Jeddy thrust in a contemptuous oar. "He wants to make chairs out of her and raft 'em ashore."

"Go ahead, Rowlandson," I told him. "Let's hear what's on your mind."

"Well," he said, "it appears to us we must be close to some port or other after all this sailing. We could put a prize crew aboard that ship and run her in."

"No," I told him, "I won't do it, Rowlandson. We came out intending to man out no prizes, and we're not equipped for it."

"Couldn't you spare four men?" he asked.

"No," I told him, "I'd have to send a navigator with them. I can't spare them, anyway. We've got barely enough men as it is."

"We could sell that ship for forty thousand dollars!"

"You could if a sloop-of-war didn't take you prisoner, which it probably would, and if you got to port, which you probably wouldn't. I won't do it."

"A dollar's a dollar!" Rowlandson grumbled. He stood looking at me, gray-faced and glum, but I shook my head.

"It isn't safe," I told him. "What I'm doing is best for all of us."

In spite of his dissatisfaction and that of a good part of the crew, when we slipped into the yellow waters of the Loire we had a cargo aboard that weighed little but was almost as valuable, we later learned, as those brought in on the first cruises of the *True Blooded Yankee* or the *Comet* or the *Grand Turk* or the *Governor Tompkins*, or the *General Armstrong* or the sloop *Polly* out of Salem, or the *Harpy* of Baltimore, privateers that made enormous sums from the beginning, and harried the British until the very mention of their names was enough to cause a flutter in the insurance rates.

*   *   *

We found Nantes a good town, as Captain Boyle had told us, though there was an air of depression and sorrow to the place, and unusual numbers of womenfolk. For every man that met the eye there were three women—all on account of the millions of men that Bonaparte had slaughtered in the making of his vainglorious wars.

There was infinite detail to the sale of our cargo, which had to be done slowly by French agents; and after that there would be the figuring of shares and the refitting for another cruise, so I left the crew aboard the sloop and went to take lodgings at the Golden Eagle Inn—L'Aigle d'Or: a tall, narrow building facing the Place du Commerce, near where the small river Erdre flows through the city and into the Loire.

Captain Boyle had told me that all American captains patronized L'Aigle d'Or when they were in Nantes, because the proprietor, M. Marcel Solbert, had spent several months in America and learned what he believed to be English. M. Solbert met me at the door and immediately proved that he thought he spoke our tongue.

"Ah!" he said, clasping his hands in front of him like a woman. "Ah! Gentiman, you are *capitaine*, eh? Ah, *oui!* Gentiman, you live Philadelphia, no? I have work wiss *livres* in *maison de livres de mon ami*, M'sieu le Comte Moreau Saint-Méry in Philadelphia, eh?"

He took me to my room, a narrow room with windows opening on a courtyard smelling peculiarly of stables, soapsuds and cheese rind; and when I came down I met three other American captains, all waiting impatiently in Nantes until their cargoes should be sold —Captain Dawson of the letter-of-marque schooner *Ned* of Baltimore; Captain Troutman of the privateer schooner *Lion* out of Marblehead, and Captain Hewes of the privateer *Leo* out of Boston.

Through them I found agents—the Latour brothers: polite men with bushy whiskers large enough for squirrel nests—and thought to settle down to wait for our rich booty to be turned into money; but there was such an air of discomfort about the country, what with Bonaparte's terrible battles and the ghastly news of the death of four hundred thousand Frenchmen on the steppes of Russia, and the conscriptions that were forever taking place to provide more men to be slaughtered, that none of us could rest easy.

We set out again in February to chasten the British, believing that when we were back from our cruise the Latours would have settled our affairs. Yet I think I would have done better to stay on shore: for we were twice chased away from prizes by British frigates; and when the cruise was over the men, headed by Rowlandson Drown, were grumbling louder than ever, demanding a larger vessel and crew so we could man out our prizes.

When we were back in Nantes, furthermore, I found the Latours had disposed of our cargo to such good advantage that I dared not tell the crew for fear their newly acquired wealth would make them unwilling to risk their skins in fighting; since every ordinary seaman's share now amounted to something better than twenty-four hundred dollars. Consequently I kept my own counsel, banked the money with the Latours, refitted the sloop; and early in May, when the hawthorns were pink-and-white clouds against the rich green of the swelling fields, we slipped down the Loire again and stood off to the northwestward on a cruise that, for general cussedness, would have been difficult to beat.

We ran straight into one of the hellish westerly gales that blow into the Bay of Biscay with hurricane force, kicking up such seas that a sloop the size of ours is stuck against the face of one of them like a fly against the page of a book; and we, clinging to our canted deck, must look upward to the crest of the wave and downward to the trough of it, with no horizon at all save that furnished by our own wave and the next one to it.

The gale seemed bent on wringing the *Lively Lady* as a woman wrings a towel, twisting the stern in one direction and the bow in another. We were obliged to heave-to under a double-reefed mainsail, nor did one of us dare move without a leg or an arm hooked around something, lest we be snapped through the air like a whip lash.

Fearing for Pinky, I tied him tight in a blanket and corded him to the roof of the cabin, where he hung with head protruding and whiskers a-bristle, barking passionately when lamps were broken from their fastenings and every loose object sent flying from one side of the cabin to the other. After four hours of this a tremendous sea came down with a roar in the wake of our starboard shrouds. It seemed to me we were gone; but the sloop struggled gradually upright, and I found the force of the blow had broken one of the top timbers and split open the plank-sheer, so that I could look directly down into the hold.

Knowing one more like this would leave us clinging to splintered spars in the cold green surges that towered around us, I sent Jeddy and 'Lisha Lord and Cromwell and Rowlandson Drown to cut loose a spare boom. This we spanned with a piece of new four-inch rope; and to the bight of the span I had them fasten our small bower cable. The other end of the cable we fastened to our mast. Thereupon we threw over the boom, paying out sixty fathoms of cable, and at once the sloop came head to the wind, riding as easily as a mallard; for the boom not only acted as a floating anchor, holding us in place, but it broke the ragged crests from the seas and forced them to march at us in a more orderly manner, instead of rushing from every direction like becrazed things. Thus it gave us a chance to nail tarred canvas over our broken plank-sheer; and we rode out the gale without further injury.

Following this we gave chase to a ship, lost her in the darkness, cruised two days in search of her, picked her up again, and lost her

for good during the night. We sighted a brig and hove her to, only
to find she was an ancient craft, in ballast and not worth sinking, so
we let her go. Then we lay and creaked in a calm for two days, a
hot, steamy, uneasy calm, smelling of newly caught fish, after which
we suffered from light and variable airs that left us wallowing here
and there like a drunken seaman.

We were well over toward the coast of Cornwall one dismal morning when the lookout sighted two craft in the southwest. We made
all sail in chase of them, and when we discovered that one was a
ship and the other a small xebec—a xebec being a three-masted craft
with square sails on the foremast and lateen sails on the main and
mizzenmasts—it seemed to us our luck had taken a turn for the better.

When we came up with the ship, she hoisted English colors. It
seemed strange to me that she should be so slow a sailer, for she
had the appearance of smartness; so we hoisted American colors,
bore up and gave her both long guns, hulling her near the water
line. I thought for a moment she had struck, for she lowered her
ensign. The men set up a roar; but there was something about her
I misliked. She kept a small yellow flag at her main, which seemed
contrary to good sense; then, in merchantman fashion, hauled up her
mainsail slowly and clumsily backed her maintopsail.

I shouted to 'Lisha Lord that something was wrong and immediately wore ship, passing into her wake. When we were in a raking
position, 'Lisha and Pendleton Quint gave her both long guns, and
we could see the distant cabin windows go out as the grape and the
round shot went in.

The gun crews stood with open mouths, waiting for her to come
into the wind in token of surrender. Instead of that, she wore; and
as she wore she ran up her ensign again. Ports flew open along her
gun deck, and we saw she was a heavy sloop-of-war, disguised by
closed ports and by having a tier of ports painted on a strip of canvas stretched over the channels, so to look like a merchantman.

"My God!" 'Lisha shouted. "It's the *Gorgon!*"

Her side disappeared in a white cloud, above which we could see her sails spreading, fast, as no merchantman ever set them.

The round shot from her broadside went over us, wailing like giant sea gulls, and there was the clattering hiss of passing grapeshot, a most unsettling noise.

I heard a grinding thump from the waist. When I looked along the deck I saw a round shot had caught poor black Sip, the brother of Pomp, and taken his hip away. He lay there looking first at the great raw hole in himself; then up at Pendleton Quint; then back at himself again, with a terrible look of anxious surprise on his face.

Pendleton jumped over him and sighted his gun, careful and delicate, as if sighting at a distant goose. He pulled the lanyard, and the smoke blew down across us, setting us to coughing and filling our eyes with moisture. When it blew away, Jotham Carr had got Sip out from under the feet of the men, so they could load with no interference.

We made sail upon the wind and left her very fast; but fast as we left the *Gorgon*—if indeed it was the *Gorgon*, as 'Lisha Lord said and swore—it was nothing to the quickness with which Sip left us. He lay in the scuppers for a time; for Jotham Carr refused to let us move him, saying it would be no use and would only hurt Sip. He smiled a gray smile up at me. "Gosh," he whispered in his flat Maine speech, that seemed to me so strange to come from a black man's lips, "smoky wind, Cap'n Dick—good troutin'—Kimball's Brook—le's go fishin'—to-morrah——"

So Sip went home to Arundel; and I, remembering it was I who had persuaded him and Pomp to leave their little cabin on the high land above the marshy banks of our river, wished myself back where I could hear the red-winged blackbirds chucking and whistling in the bayberries at the edge of our creek—where I would never have to smell gunpowder again.

*　　*　　*

It was the devil's own work to hold the men in hand and get the *Lively Lady* out of the Loire again that autumn. The amount of our prize money had leaked out and been magnified in the leaking; and so sure were the men that they were close to having the wealth of merchant princes that I was hard put to it to make them remember our country was still at war. They let slip no chance to remind me they were set on sailing in a larger vessel than the *Lively Lady;* and I knew it to be true that the increasing wariness of the British made it advisable for privateersmen to use larger craft, heavily armed and manned. None the less I knew the *Lively Lady* was a lucky boat, whereas God alone could tell what our fortune might be if we changed.

Finally I got her to sea again, and the cussedness of this cruise was greater, even, than that of the preceding one.

Again and again we were robbed of prizes by the alertness of British cruisers; and once a fast British merchantman struck her colors to us toward dusk, let us slip alongside her, then ran up her colors, opened fire once more, cut up our rigging so that our mainsail came down on the run, and finally escaped us in the dark. To cap it all, while we were cruising off the Spanish coast, we found ourselves one dawn in the midst of the whole British fleet supporting Wellington's armies. We tacked like a fly dodging a broom, got some holes in our sails and one through our hull, and to escape had to throw over our carronades, so that the only guns left to us were our two long eighteens.

When, therefore, we saw the islands of the Loire again, the men were glum and dark and truculent, and I was no less gloomy than they.

*   *   *

There were new faces in the narrow front room of L'Aigle d'Or when I came into it on a dark night in early December, though Captain Hewes was still there, a bottle of Vouvray before him and a stranger sitting across from him—a stranger whose hat perched precariously on the side of his head.

Hewes pushed a glass of Vouvray into my hand before I could unbutton my jacket. "We needed you," he said. "Dawson sailed for

home, and Troutman was captured; and France has too many
Frenchmen in it for our taste. Captain Hailey and me, we're getting
lonesome."

"Hailey?" I asked, looking quickly at the stranger.

"You hit it!" Captain Hewes laughed. "He's the one: captain of
the *True Blooded Yankee*, out of Brest."

Now there was no American seaman who hadn't heard wild yarns
of the brig *True Blooded Yankee*, though she had been privateering
only since late in February or early in March; but, accustomed as I
had become to hearing fantastic tales of our privateersmen, I didn't
believe the tenth of what I heard about the *True Blooded Yankee*,
any more than a grown man believes fo'c'sle rumors of the *Flying
Dutchman*.

"Well, sir," I said to Captain Hailey, "I'm glad to meet you and
find you're flesh and blood and not some sort of corposant that's been
fevering the brains of the British."

Hailey laughed and lifted his hat, replacing it on the opposite side
of his head, tilted at the same dangerous angle.

"Why," he asked. "What have I done now?"

"We heard you'd captured an island in the Channel and held it
two days," I said.

Hailey scratched contemplatively at the corner of his mouth.
"That wa'n't quite so," he said.

"Well, it didn't sound reasonable to me," I told him.

"What happened," Hailey said, "was that we rammed a wreck off
the Irish coast and had to careen ourselves somewheres and fit two
new planks; so we picked ourselves a nice island and took it and
put the natives to work. There was an armed schooner that thought
different, but we mounted our long guns on shore and sank her."

"How long did you hold it?" I asked, goggling at him.

"Heh, heh, heh!" Hailey said. "Six days!"

Hewes raised his eyebrows at me. "He took nine towns in Scotland and Ireland and held 'em for ransom; and he went into one
harbor and burned seven vessels. He came home with two hundred

and seventy prisoners and a four-million-dollar cargo, in addition to
the prizes he manned out."

"Oh, here, here!" Hailey protested. "It wa'n't four million dollars!"

"How much was it?" I asked.

"Gosh, I don't rightly know," Hailey said. He checked on his fingers. "There was twelve thousand pounds of raw silk, eighteen bales
of Turkey carpets, twenty boxes of gums, a hundred and sixty dozen
swan skins, twenty-four packs of beaver skins—oh, gosh! Say three
million and a quarter, or three and a half, or so. I'm going up to
Paris now to see Mr. Preble. He's owner."

"Well," I said, "you made a great haul!"

Hailey hitched forward in his chair. "I tell you, I've got a fast brig.
She's *fast!* And I got a crew that won't be took. They'll outshoot and
outfight anyone."

"Why will they?" I asked. "They won't outshoot and outfight my
crew, man for man!"

"Yes, they will," Hailey said. He tilted back in his chair with an
air of confidence. "Yes, they *will!* We couldn't pick up enough Americans; so Preble, he had some hokus with the French, and we searched
the prisons for seamen: American—English—anybody that wanted to
chance it."

We stared at him in silence, and he smiled at us.

"Was you ever in a French prison?"

We shook our heads.

"No," he said, "and you don't want to be. These men of mine,
they wanted to get out, and they don't want to go back. And the
English among 'em, they don't want to be took. If they're took they're
swung from the yardarm quick. Quick! *Real* quick! Why wouldn't
they fight? I've got a big crew, two hundred of 'em; and you never
saw anybody shoot faster and straighter than they shoot, when they
have to. I've got a fast brig, and there ain't anything going to get
away from me when I start out after her; not *anything!*"

I began to see why the *True Blooded Yankee* had become such
a terror to the British, and I wondered how I would like a crew

taken out of French prisons; but before I could make up my mind, I heard someone running along the flagstones that edged the river.

There is little running in French towns on dank December evenings, when all good Frenchmen are snugly sealed in steamy kitchens; so we fell silent and looked toward the door, where M. Solbert, his hands cupped around his eyes, had pressed his forehead against the glass to see who it was that pelted so unceremoniously beneath the silent elms of Nantes.

The rapid footsteps came closer. M. Solbert fell back suddenly from the door, and in that moment it opened. Tommy Bickford stood before us, blinking and peering about the room. There was a smudge of soot on his cheek and a charred hole in the front of his pea-jacket.

He came to me. "Cap'n Dick—the sloop! She burned!"

He made a quick little bow to Captain Hailey and Captain Hewes, and smiled at me uncertainly.

"Did she burn to the water?" I asked.

"Yes, Captain."

"How'd she catch?"

Tommy looked at Captain Hailey and then at Captain Hewes. "Speak up!" I said. "I think I know. They set her, I'll bet! They saved my papers and the long guns, didn't they?"

"Yes, Captain: they saved pretty near everything."

"Then they set her," I said. I turned to Hewes and Hailey. "They wanted something bigger, so to carry more men and man out prizes."

Hailey laughed dryly. "I can tell you where to find the extra men," he said. "I can show you all the nicest jails in France."

So there was I, who wished to shorten the war, left without a vessel. I thought of the miniature in my pocket and stared at Hailey, while it seemed to me clear that I'd have most earnestly preferred his jailbird crew to my own simple downright fellows from home.

XV

THE brig I got to take the place of the old lucky *Lively Lady* I bought from a fox-faced Frenchman, Robert Surcouf: she lay in the basin at La Rochelle, and we were three months reconditioning her. Privateering was no new venture for her: the fox-faced Robert Surcouf had sailed her and fought her years before against the English —sailed her and fought her in such a manner as to bring him undying fame. Her figurehead had been a white shrouded woman of wood; and Surcouf had called her the *Revenant,* which means the *Ghost;* and always, in Surcouf's hands, she had disappeared like a wraith from the fastest British frigates that hunted her. But six years before, rich from the taking of prizes, Surcouf had married and given his wife his word that he would fight no more; and being determined that the British should never touch her, yet wishing to have her somewhere within reach, he had dismantled her and laid her up, a dismasted hulk, in La Rochelle.

It took a power of persuading and 4,000 English pounds to get her from him; and on top of everything I was obliged to sign a paper that I would never allow her to fall into the hands of the British. Having gone that far with him, I brought my crew from Nantes to work upon her, and they did it with a good will too; for not a man of them but could see, under the lumber and the pigsties and the steep-roofed penthouse with which she had been disguised and disfigured, her beautiful run and great breadth of beam.

"Fifteen knots!" Surcouf had bragged. Yet when I saw her made fit for the sea again, I doubted that he had bragged at all. We rigged her as she had been rigged when Surcouf had sailed her—as a taunt-rigged brigantine: square-sails, that is, on her foremast only, and high-masted. Her mainmast was a handsome tapering stick; her upper spars drew out into topgallant, royal and skysail masts that seemed as slender and fragile as the new wands that spring from a willow stump in June. Her shrouds and stays, beautifully fitted and served with hide wherever they lay in another's chafe, were so few in number that a landsman would have deemed her as sparsely rigged as two fishing poles, and therefore useless.

Our two faithful long guns stared grimly from their ports amidships; and sixteen carronades, which had come with the brig when I bought her, were lashed snugly on their slides.

Her decks were scrubbed; the bolts and rings in her high and solid bulwarks shone clear and bright. Except for her riband she was painted a dull green, against which her copper shone like newly minted gold. We gave her a black streak, set off from the green by stripes of gilding; and I went down over the bows myself with Rowlandson Drown, bent on making her figurehead into something that would keep me from forgetting I must do whatever lay in my power to help make this war a short one.

We cut away the shroud from the head and body of the corpse Surcouf had built, leaving a tight braid of hair around the brows, and making the shoulders smooth and sweetly rounded: then fashioned a snug little dress that flowed back into the cutwater. The lips and the eyes I carved myself with my jackknife; and when she was done we painted her carefully, the face a creamy ivory with a faint flush to the cheeks, the lips a brilliant red, and the hair a copper color, like that of a copper bolt chafed by the rubbing of a rope. The dress was a beautiful shimmery green with shadows and high lights, so that a breeze seemed to be whipping it around her.

When she was finished, one evening early in March, I walked down to see how she would look in the moonlight, and Jeddy went with me, and Davy Maffett, captain of the privateer brig *Rattlesnake*

out of Philadelphia—the same Davy Maffett who had sent prizes val-
ued at one million dollars into Norway during the winter just past,
and as daring a captain as ever sailed.

We stood on the quay of the basin, the odor of drying fish nets
in our noses and St. Nicolas Tower bulking against a moon of bur-
nished silver. Davy Maffett looked and looked at the figurehead and
whistled a little. Then he crossed the quay to a near-by tavern and
returned with three bottles of sparkling white wine. We popped out
the corks, and Davy held up his bottle toward the green-clad figure
under the bowsprit. It gave me a strange tightness in my throat to
see her there, smiling a faint, tremulous smile, as though she well
knew what we were doing but was too much of a lady to look around
at us.

"Here's to the *Lively Lady*," Davy said. "May all of 'em want her
but none of 'em catch her!"

"The *Lively Lady!*" we shouted, and drank; and that was how we
rechristened her.

*   *   *

One hundred and twenty men she carried, but I had not taken
all of Captain Hailey's advice, though I had taken some. All of the
hundred and twenty were Americans, and I think the last ten of
them to arrive in La Rochelle were the roughest and wildest of the
ten dozen.

They came in charge of Alley McAlley of the old crew, that little
Irish tailor from Arundel who had signed with us because of his admiration for Jotham Carr, who had cured him of the itch. He had
picked up an intelligible jargon of French and had been combing
the coast towns for stranded fellow countrymen of the right, rough
sort. With them he also brought, sewed into the waistband of his
trousers, a letter given him in Nantes by Captain Jacobs of the Baltimore letter-of-marque schooner *Kemp*.

It was from Captain Boyle; and when I saw his name written at
the end, he flashed into my mind, dark and handsome and polite,

standing on a carronade, his *Comet* slipping over the waves like a
flying fish and he waving his hat at me.

"ESTEEMED SIR AND FRIEND," the letter said, "*by good chance I have
fallen across my brave friend Captain Jacobs, of the letter-of-marque
schooner* Kemp, *Baltimore, and by him I send you my wishes for good
health and success. Until the fifteenth March I shall hold station
about one hundred miles west of the Scilly Isles, to intercept vessels bound into the English Channel or the Irish Sea. If it suits your
wish and convenience we can keep company there or thereabouts.
If not, I will run for Nantes on the fifteenth March, hoping to have
a snail or two with you before refitting for another cruise. I am in
a new brig,* Chasseur, *sixteen long 12's, and she is able to sail a little.
If you come out, be so kind as to hoist a pair of blue pantaloons to
your main peak, so there may be no mistake, and I will run up a
green silk petticoat with ruffles. I am in great hopes of encountering you, and trust that if you come out, you will bring a few bottles
of sparkling wine and a cheese or two. I have a partiality for the
white Roquefort cheese, though any cheese will do. The more powerful the better. Accept, dear sir, the assurances of my distinguished
regard.*

"THOS. BOYLE."

I read it again to make sure of the date and the cheese. "Get your
men aboard," I said to McAlley. "We were only waiting for you."

I touched my breast, feeling that little oval of mine under the outer
cloth; and I bethought me of how Captain Boyle rounded the convoy, burned a British ship, and came blithely to have me for dinner
with him. I thought, too, that in Captain Boyle's company I might
at least help a little to shorten this war.

"Get your men aboard," I said again, "I'm going to buy some
cheese and wine to take to Captain Boyle on his *Chasseur* a hundred miles west of the Scillies."

*   *   *

It was late in the day, with a cold westerly wind seeming to hold up the sun in a smutty sky the color of a newly blacked eye, when we rounded the point on the northerly side of the harbor and dropped our pilot.

We knew the brig was very fast, for there was a lift to her, almost like that which I felt as a child, when I swung in the long rope swing hanging from the high oak on the far side of the creek in Arundel—a lift that caught my breath and filled me with the exultant sensation of being about to soar on and on, into another world.

The harbor of La Rochelle is a pleasant harbor in ordinary times, and as safe as any harbor anywhere; but in 1814 it was bad because of the manner in which blockading frigates and sloops hid themselves behind the shoulders of Ile de Ré, and pounced on Americans coming out of shelter.

We were a quiet lot as we bore to the north, past La Pallice and toward Breton Pass, the seventeen-mile sound separating the Ile de Ré from the mainland. There were lookouts at the mastheads; and I had put 'Lisha Lord in the larboard fore chains and Cromwell in the starboard fore chains to con the brig. Jeddy and Cephas were driving the men, clearing the decks of the litter that covers them when a craft first puts to sea, and so keeping them occupied; but they were as quiet as the rest of us, for until we were clear of the narrow channel, and the greenish half light had thickened into a comfortable blackness, there could be no feeling of security in the mind of anyone.

This presentiment of danger was justified as we slipped past the eastern end of the Ile de Ré; for the two men aloft shouted, "Sail!" sharply and simultaneously. A second later 'Lisha bellowed, "Cruiser in the lee of the island!" and in the same moment I saw her topsails dimly—topsails with such a tremendous high hoist that they could belong to nothing but a frigate.

I remember saying to myself, "To hell with this!" for due to the narrowness of the channel, we couldn't possibly escape a broadside if we held our course. We went about, then: almost we spun around, as if some vast hand had taken the brig by the bowsprit and turned her on her heel. I heard laughter from the men in the waist, and a whoop or two, and knew they were laughing with delight at her swiftness.

We slipped back along the eastern tip of the island in the gathering gloom. I find it hard to make clear the feel of swiftness in a vessel. It is a little like that which comes into the body of a runner at times—a quick consciousness of lightness and suppleness, as though running were no exertion, and could be continued indefinitely. Our sloop had been a fast craft; but there was no such feel to her as to this brig, which seemed to pour herself over the waves without effort, adjusting herself to irregularities in the water like an otter gamboling in the rapids of a fast stream.

She moved, it seemed to me, with a soft rush, a tireless swoop, a smooth unchecked flight, devoid of bumpings and squatterings such as mark the progress of slower craft. I have watched kestrels come into the wind and hang there motionless, except for a little shivering of the wings: then turn without effort and soar away on a straight, effortless flight, very rapid; and it was like a soaring kestrel that the *Lively Lady* seemed to move.

There was still light in the west when we hauled our wind to pass out along the southern side of Ile de Ré; but the light was dim and faintly greenish, which was fortunate for us. Against this dying paleness, as we opened the island, the lookouts made out two more sail, two miles off our starboard bow, running down with the wind on such a slant that they were bound to intercept us. I could feel in my bones they were British frigates or sloops-of-war, and I knew they must have learned there were American privateers in La Rochelle and so been sent to blockade the port.

I had no love for this situation. Our canvas was new and bright; and since they had surely seen us I knew they would separate, one edging in toward the Ile de Ré and the other off toward the Ile d'Oleron. I also knew that if either of them passed within gunshot of us, which was likely, we would get a broadside that might wing us and leave us swinging in circles on the water like a wounded duck.

How long it was before darkness hid those two sail from us I cannot now recall. It may have been two minutes; it may have been four; but to me, watching this beautiful brig slash over the waves like a frightened swan, it seemed like an hour out of a sleepless night.

I shouted for lanterns and called 'Lisha Lord aft to step a mast in the longboat; and while he worked at it with his men I sent a seaman part way up the foremast ratlines with a lighted lantern.

When it was dark at last, a thick gray dark, we came into the wind and hung there. 'Lisha lowered away the boat, lashed its tiller, made fast a lighted lantern to the masthead, scrambled back on board, and cast her off. He shouted, whereupon the man in the ratlines doused the lantern he was carrying. The empty longboat bobbed away from us toward the Ile d'Oleron, the lantern bright at its masthead. We watched it a moment, then wore ship and stood back toward the Ile de Ré.

We may have been a quarter mile off shore when Jeddy spoke and the men jumped for the topgallant clew lines and the fore clew garnets. They worked as though bawled at by the Bull of Bashan; yet I had to strain my ears to catch Jeddy's muted whispers. "Peak and throat halyards! Jib downhaul! Rise tacks and sheets! Let go! Clew up!" I heard him whistle a shrill little whistle between his teeth and add, "Settle away the main gaff, you!"

In another two minutes' time we were slipping along with every inch of canvas furled, as dark and silent as a deserted brig, so that an enemy vessel would be obliged to run us down, almost, in order to see us, and would, in such case, shoot by us too fast to bring guns to bear.

There was a creaking as the head yards were squared: then we bore up before the wind and lay there, listening. There was a small moaning of the breeze in the rigging, and a slatting somewhere above us, and the lap, lap, lap of the waves against our bends. Far off to larboard we could see a pinpoint of light, blinking and blinking; then disappearing for a second; then blinking and blinking once more. We watched it and watched it, until it seemed nearly gone: only a spark now and again. We peered for it until moisture ran from our eyes and lay cold on our cheeks; and as we peered there was a flash like sheet lightning seen through a rift in a cloud: then a thud, as though someone had dropped a weight far down in our hold. We saw two lights, one close under another, rising, and knew one of the cruisers was hoisting her signal lanterns. Immediately, farther away, two more lights went up. With that I snapped at Jeddy to make sail. Jeddy shouted, and the crew sprang up from under the bulwarks, cheering and whooping; for like the rest of us they knew the cruisers had gone too far afield after our longboat to locate us again—that there was nothing now between us and the open sea, and that, once free of the land, no British cruiser ever built could overtake us.

In four minutes' time our sails were set and drawing and we were running to the northwest, all clear.

XVI

It was early March still, a blustery bright day, and we were casting around in a circle west of the Scillies when we made out a sail on our weather quarter, coming down on us fast. When she proved to be a brig, we bent on the pantaloons—a pair belonging to Cephas Cluff, who was large in the bends and with next to no tumble-home about him—and ran them up. Instantly a billowing green ensign of some description went to the brig's masthead; and Cephas, watching her through the telescope, said, "There's ruffles on it!"

"The Irish navy!" Jeddy shouted; and since we were delighted to encounter Boyle again, we combined business with pleasure while waiting for him to come up, hove over a cask, circled it, and banged away at it fifteen times with our lee battery, thus giving him a salute of fifteen guns.

This brig of Boyle's, the *Chasseur,* was as beautiful a vessel as it had ever been my fortune to see. She was brigantine rigged, like the *Lively Lady,* but with a lighter bowsprit and foremast and more of a rake to her sticks, so that she seemed to me to have a quicker and more elusive look than the *Lively Lady*—the look, almost, of a slender girl running hard, her head back and her stomach thrust out before her.

When we had fired the fifteen guns, we tacked twice and came back onto the *Chasseur's* course, slipping along beside her not fifty yards away, so close we could see the patches in the mainsail where the passage of a bushel of grapeshot had been repaired, and the wind-blown hair of the grinning crew that lolled, close-packed, over the hammock nettings to watch us come up, and the fluttering ruffles on the bosom of Boyle's shirt. He stood on one of his long twelves, clutching the main shrouds and waving his bell-topped gray beaver at us.

"Very kind!" we heard him shout. "Too many guns! Hope I can live up to the compliment!"

He looked around at his helmsman, making a little circular movement with his hand. The *Chasseur* hauled her wind and ranged closer. We could hear the crackling and whipping of the green silk petticoat at her main peak, the patter of the foam clouts skittering from beneath her raking bows, and the babble of her crew as they talked and laughed.

"Delighted you came out," Boyle called over. "Did you bring the cheese?"

I nodded.

"I'll come aboard for dinner when it's dark," he said.

He did not, however, for the day turned gray and dirty, and the wind shifted into the northeast. In the afternoon it stiffened to a gale, so that both of us lay-to under double-reefed mainsails. That night it eased up, and by morning the wind had come around into the south, and there was a light fog that began to burn off around ten o'clock. When it lifted we saw a sail to the southwestward; and since Boyle was the nearer to it, he hauled his wind in chase, while we bore on toward the northeast.

Toward noon we made out a column of smoke in the southwest and concluded Boyle had found his chase to be a small craft of little value and so set her afire. A little later the shreds of mist in the northeast cleared away still more, and we made out a large ship off our lee bow, heading in a southeasterly direction—a magnificent, freshly painted, high-sided vessel, bearing all the earmarks of a merchantman. When she ran from us, as she soon did, we knew we were right and so piped all hands to quarters.

We came up on her fast, and I could see she was armed with

stern chasers. Therefore I kept off and sailed past her, sending extra muskets and loaders to Moody Haley and Moses Burnham and the rest of the sharpshooters in our tops. Then I came down on her bows, wore across them in a raking position, fired a gun, and shouted to her to heave-to. Instead of this she attempted to wear in order to give me a broadside. This she could not do, because of our speed; for, seeing what she was about, I came up into the wind very sharp and crossed her bows again, wearing immediately afterward. Even then she would not strike, thinking perhaps that because I was moving straight away from her I was running. Therefore I turned once more and ran back to windward of her. As we came up, 'Lisha Lord shouted to the men in the tops, and they opened on her with muskets. We saw man after man go down at her guns, so that when her broadside let off it was ragged and useless, and the shot passed around us and over us. Also two men in succession were shot down at her wheel, and an officer on the quarter-deck slipped to his knees, clutching at his shoulder. Immediately after, a man ran out from the cabin hatch and hauled down her colors, and she slowly hove-to, at which we came about and ran up to leeward of her, with our crew shouting so triumphantly and stamping so delightedly at their good fortune as to drown the slatting of the reef points against the mainsail. Nor was my own pleasure any less than theirs, for we had suffered no damage whatever in the encounter, and the *Lively Lady* had outsailed her bulky antagonist as readily as my little dog Pinky runs in circles around a cow.

I boarded her myself, to see what disposition to make of her people as well as what manner of prize crew to put into her; and I had no sooner stuck my head above her bulwarks than I hankered for her myself, because of her cleanliness and her broad, scoured decks, splotched here and there with the red stains that had resulted from our musketry fire.

Even before I made a move to take possession I began to plan how I could have her for my own some day.

Five men were laid out in the shelter of the main hatch, and the remainder of her people, gathered around them, glowered at us as we came over the side. The officer who met us, a young man, seemed to expect harsh treatment; for his lips were pressed tight together and his face was pale.

"Captain?" I asked him.

He cleared his throat. "Second officer. The first was shot through the shoulder. The captain went to his cabin when—when we struck."

"Lower away your longboat," I ordered, "and send your men aboard my brig. What is this ship?"

"The *Pembroke*, West Indiaman," he said, getting a little color back in his face, "London for Port-au-Prince."

"Well, get your boat away. I'm putting a prize crew aboard."

I left Jeddy in charge of the deck and went to the cabin. I had heard about the richness of big West Indiamen, but I had never been aboard a wealthy Londoner before; and here was one indeed. She was 540 tons: a roomy, comfortable ship; and when I stepped into the cabin, I was staggered by what I saw. Two silver lamps were hung on long silver chains; and beneath the lamps was a dining table, covered with gold brocade weighted at the corners with silver tassels. Behind the table rose the rudder case, carved and colored to represent a close-packed stand of bamboos; and these, at the top, branched out in feathery green fronds, all carved out of wood, which spread interlaced across the ceiling. Behind that, in turn, were the stern windows, hung with blue brocade. The cabin walls were paneled with gray wood, some of the panels filled with mirrors edged in gold, so that the bamboo of the rudder case was reflected back and forth. Doors let into side berths, three doors to a side; and in a recess stood a piano colored gray to match the cabin panels. There was a scarf, a green scarf, across the piano bench; and it seemed to me I caught from it a singular delicate fragrance.

A sallow-faced man sat at the table, his chin sunk on his chest, staring at a handful of papers that lay before him. When I came in he rose and bowed, a quick, angry bow, as though he would rather be whipped than do what he was doing.

"Captain," I said, "I must ask you to take whatever personal belongings you require and go at once aboard my brig. Do you have passengers?"

"You have the authority for this, no doubt?"

"A commission from President Madison, sir, to Captain Richard Nason of the private armed brig *Lively Lady*."

What answer he made I cannot say, for at that moment one of the cabin doors swung open.

I stared and stared at what I saw; for beyond the open door, swaying to the uneasy motion of the ship, stood a slender girl, a girl in a green silk dress, her pretty arms bare to the elbow, and her hair, tight braided around her head, the color of a copper bolt chafed bright by rubbing. As for her face, it was the same as that on the miniature I had carried in the pocket of my shirt, for fear of losing it, ever since the distant day when I sailed from Portland in the *Neutrality* to carry foodstuffs to the English in Spain.

Just then it did not seem to me so necessary to shorten this war.

XVII

IF EVER I saw a man in a rage so powerful that he was on the verge of being poisoned by it, it was Sir Arthur Ransome when he learned he must leave his comfortable West Indiaman and go aboard a crowded brig not half the size of the vessel he was leaving. I was in a hurry to man out the *Pembroke* and send her on her way to Nantes, for I had learned she had been driven from a convoy by the gale of the day before; and there was no knowing when a fast frigate might come prowling down in search of this fine fat chicken that had straggled from the flock.

But say what I would to Sir Arthur, I could not hurry him in his preparations. He stood by his berth, quite helpless, asking his wife in his whiny voice where he had put this and where he had put that. He would pick up a thing and stare at it helplessly: then hand it to her to hold, looking like a baulky horse; and with each passing moment he seemed more and more impatient with her, though she had only tried to help him.

At length I asked her if she was ready to go. She said at once, without looking at me—and indeed, she had not looked at me at all except when she opened the door of her small cabin—that she was. At that, unwilling to endanger our crew or our prize by further delay, I called to Jeddy to send down Gideon Lassel and Seth Tarbox. When they came, I told them to enter Sir Arthur's cabin, take every movable thing except Sir Arthur, and dump the whole in a blanket. This they did, regardless of Sir Arthur's angry protests. Then Gideon threw the loaded blanket over his shoulder, and Seth took Sir Arthur by the back of the coat and pushed him on deck. I sent Lady Ransome after them and followed her out myself; and as we went we could hear Sir Arthur expostulating with Seth, telling him to take his hands away.

They tumbled him into the boat and jumped in after him; whereupon Jeddy and I handed down Lady Ransome, and I gave Cephas Cluff his final orders: to head for Nantes and sell the *Pembroke* to the Latours for one hundred francs, so she might lie safe at her French quay, and be readily repurchased when all danger of seizure was past. Also I wrote the Latours, giving Cephas authority to draw on them for funds and live aboard the *Pembroke*, keeping her neat and ready for sea, until I should come for her.

No sooner had I gone over the side than the *Pembroke* slipped off to the eastward, toward Nantes.

Raging as Sir Arthur was, he was silent in the boat—not, I felt, from good sense, but because it was a part of his scheme of life to show no feeling publicly before menials; and it was as a menial, I knew, that he regarded me. At all events, he sat stiffly on the thwart beside Lady Ransome, staring over my head at nothing. I was glad of this for two reasons, one being that if he had opened his mouth, the boat crew, being in high spirits over the taking of the *Pembroke*, would have mocked him in some dreadful way, since nothing seemed to strike them as being as laughable as the speech of an Englishman; and the other being that it kept his eyes from encountering the figurehead of the *Lively Lady* as we came down on her lee bow, although he was a dull man about some things and might not have seen it even though he looked directly at it.

I could have wished, even, that Lady Ransome had been less curious about her destination; but as luck would have it she cast a glance over her shoulder at the brig when we were less than ten paces from her dolphin striker; and as a result she looked squarely at the figure Rowlandson Drown and I had fashioned and painted with such care in the harbor of La Rochelle—at the copper-colored hair, the brilliant

red lips, the bare pink arms and the shimmering green dress with
the look of being whipped back by the wind into the duller green
of the cutwater.

With lips a little parted, she stared and stared; and I, watching
her, had the singular impression that only a few days had passed
since I first saw her sitting in a field near Saco, with my little dog
Pinky on his haunches before her; but I had no heart to dwell overlong on this strange feeling, for when she turned from the figurehead, her eyes met mine in a glance so level that it appeared almost
to have something of enmity in it.

I think Sir Arthur would have resumed his arguing as soon as we
set foot on deck, had I not sent him, with his wife and Captain
Parker, to my cabin until the brig was squared away toward the
south on the lookout for the *Chasseur,* and until the wounded first
mate was comfortably stowed in one of the side berths off the gun
room. I had the feeling that I had done something wrong, nor was
this feeling lessened when I went into my cabin and met the accusing
gaze of Sir Arthur and Captain Parker and saw how Lady Ransome
refused to look at me and stared at nothing from the stern windows.

"Well," I said. "I regret this had to happen to persons I know, but
war's hard on friendships."

Sir Arthur whinnied, a short, angry whinny. "Friendship!" he
exclaimed.

"Oh, well," I said, feeling sorry for them, "it's hard on everything,
and since we must live on this craft for some time, I'd like you to
know I don't relish making prisoners of people who have been in
our house and eaten our food."

With that I went to logging them, and so discovered from Captain
Parker that Sir Arthur was on his way to Jamaica, where he had been
threatened with the loss of vast sugar lands through litigation. It
came into my head, when I learned this, to ask Lady Ransome
whether Annie had come safely to England in the brig in which I
had placed her and the Sandersons; but when I looked up at her
I thought I saw apprehension in her eye and so said nothing.

"Just what do you mean, may I ask," Sir Arthur said, when I had put away the log book, "by saying we must live on this craft for some time?"

"Why," I said, "I mean just that! I can't set you adrift in an open boat, and I think you'll agree that the water's a trifle cold for swimming."

Sir Arthur stared at me along his nose, an unpleasant look such as he might have given to a servant. "I warn you," he said, "that you'll be held to blame for any harm that comes to my wife or myself or any of our property, and that you'll be treated like any other pirate when you're taken, as you must be."

"Well," I said, "no harm's going to come to any of you if I can help it, so make your mind easy on that point. And since you bring up the matter of blame, I'd like to ask your captain what was in his head when he allowed this lady to remain in the cabin and refused to strike his colors to me."

Captain Parker moved uncomfortably in his chair but made no answer.

"Captain Parker is an experienced navigator, in whom we have the utmost confidence," Sir Arthur said. To me his voice sounded finicky and unpleasant.

"In that case," I told him, "I can only remind you that if my brig hadn't been faster than anything Captain Parker had ever seen, I'd have been justified in raking you through your cabin windows, which is something I don't like to think of."

They stared at me without speaking.

"There's another thing," I said, as calmly as I could. "It seems to me it's a little singular to choose this time to travel, even in a convoy and with a captain in whom you repose confidence."

"Oh, indeed," Sir Arthur said. "Indeed! Words fail me to express my gratitude for your interest in my personal affairs! It would doubtless mean nothing to you to know that a fair part—a very fair part—of the island of Jamaica is at stake in our lawsuit."

My answer was both gruff and awkward. "I don't see," I said, "why you should bring a lady along."

"Don't you?" Sir Arthur asked quickly, his face the color of fresh putty. "That's truly unfortunate!"

Lady Ransome bent her head over her clasped hands and spoke for the first time, her voice so low and husky I could scarce hear it. "A lady that has to be watched," she whispered, "would need to be brought along."

Sir Arthur turned on her. "Hold your tongue!" he said quietly. "Is this any place to discuss our private affairs?"

Into Lady Ransome's eyes came a foggy, wavery look that set me off on another tack, talking more loudly than I might otherwise have spoken. "Now, here!" I said, "if you'll give me your paroles to do nothing that can damage or hinder this brig or its people, I'll try to land you in a safe port."

There was venom in Sir Arthur's glance. "And what if I don't choose to give my parole?"

"Well, sir," I said, "if you won't give it, I'll have to demand it. The lady must be put ashore."

At that Captain Parker gave his parole, as did Sir Arthur, and I sent for Tommy Bickford to help make them as comfortable as was possible in our cramped quarters.

Late in the afternoon we fell in with the *Chasseur* again; and when Boyle, standing in his main chains, shouted gaily at me to tell him what I had been doing, I thought it best to lower a boat and go aboard the *Chasseur*, so my passengers might not hear me spreading their affairs to the world.

I told Boyle about Sir Arthur and asked him to join me for supper so I wouldn't feel like a voiceless fool when Sir Arthur became talkative over his wine and favored me with his rudeness. Boyle laughed. "Since when have you been voiceless under such conditions?" he asked.

Not wishing to tell him it was because I didn't want to hurt Lady Ransome's feelings, I contented myself with saying I became voiceless because Ransome persisted in addressing me as though I were a groom or a scullery boy. Boyle nodded thoughtfully. This, he said, should amuse rather than anger me. "His wife," he said, "has thick ankles, no doubt, and a raw, carroty look, like so many English-women."

My reply, perhaps, was overwarm. "Not at all! She's rather good-looking."

"Indeed!" he said, "and what's the color of her eyes?"

"They seem to be green, but in reality they're a sort of smoke color," I told him; whereupon he turned from me to open his chest of old Madeira. I saw he was smiling, and wondered whether I had made a mistake to admit knowing the color of her eyes.

I thought many times that evening that if I had sat alone at supper with Sir Arthur and Lady Ransome and Captain Parker we would have been a glum and silent gathering; but men from Baltimore are prattlers, seeming to talk for the pleasure of hearing the sound of their voices, which are soft and slurry, doubtless from living in close proximity to Negroes.

Boyle had no sooner come into the cabin, with his white teeth, his clear, sallow skin, his gentle politeness and his soft, warm voice, than Captain Parker brightened up, and Sir Arthur took a reef in his chin, so that his nose came down out of the air and left him looking like any normal human being, while Lady Ransome smiled for the first time since I had seen her open the door in the cabin of the *Pembroke*. Indeed, no woman could have helped smiling if Boyle had bowed over her hand as he bowed over Lady Ransome's, saying as he did so, "This repays me, ma'am, for being a sailor! We get to thinking there can be nothing in life but lobscouse and dirty weather, and then Heaven sends us—" he straightened suddenly and looked earnestly at her—"and then Heaven sends us a pair of eyes the color of smoke in the swamps of Maryland."

He looked around at me, as if to make sure I heard what he said, whereat I flushed as red as the turkey cover on the table.

"Lud 'a' mercy!" Lady Ransome cried with an air of unbelief, "you're never from America, sir, speaking such poetic nonsense to me."

"Now your ladyship is paying compliments," Boyle said, "whereas I was telling the simple truth! Tell me, now, what part of England you think I come from, if I'm never from America, as you say?"

"Oh, not England!" Lady Ransome exclaimed hastily. "I meant I didn't know American men spoke—I didn't know they were in the habit of——"

Boyle chuckled, and there seemed to me to be little pinpoints of mockery in his eyes. "It's a large country, Lady Ransome," he said. "Our products vary widely. Now in the North we have the Province of Maine, where the people never speak for fear of committing themselves to something; but farther to the south we have Maryland, where we're trained from childhood to fall in love at first sight continuously throughout our lives."

"You're speaking now of the training of maidens and ladies?" she asked, "or do you mean your gentlemen would never fall in love unless trained to? If you mean the latter, your ladies must all be perishing of broken hearts, I take it!"

Captain Boyle laughed lightly. "No, ma'am; it's only our own hearts that break, and that without any training."

Sir Arthur cleared his throat with what I considered unnecessary loudness. "Are you the captain of a privateer, Captain Boyle?"

"I have that honor, sir," Boyle said. "The *Chasseur* of Baltimore; sixteen long 12's."

"Do you ever find men of standing serving as captains of privateers?" Sir Arthur asked almost genially—due, probably, to the rapidity with which he had tossed off his wine.

"Never, sir!" Boyle assured him quickly, "only a lot of scamps like Captain Nason and myself. Some of our privateer captains have been downright notorious." He rolled up his eyes at the ceiling and went to checking off names on his fingers. "Truxtun, Porter, Biddle, Decatur, Barney, Perry, Murray, Rogers, Cassin, Little, Robinson, Smith, Hopkins . . . terrible low fellows all of them; but they reformed and entered the navy, as I have the greatest fear you already have the displeasure of knowing, sir."

He sipped his wine smilingly, and then went on: "Now, let me see: Captain Nason wants to send you to England, and he said something about taking a small brig and turning her into a cartel for you." He raised his glass toward Lady Ransome and drank the remainder. "It seems to me I wouldn't advise a cartel. She might be taken by another American before reaching port. As you doubtless know, our government pays a bounty for each prisoner, and you might possibly be taken to America."

"But we're nearly in the English Channel!" Captain Parker protested. "There can't be Americans in the Channel, my dear sir!"

Boyle raised his eyebrows at me. "Had you understood the Channel had been cleared of our privateers?" he asked.

"No," I said. "We're in it already, and Captain Hailey of the *True Blooded Yankee* is fond of cruising in the Channel when he isn't holding towns for ransom in Scotland and Ireland. The *Scourge,* the *Rattlesnake* and the *Grand Turk* are Channel cruisers, and there are seven or eight others standing off and on the coasts of Great Britain, though they may not be in the Channel at the moment."

Captain Boyle shook his head sadly at Captain Parker. "I fear, sir, your mind has been less on the war than on other matters—or, possibly you've listened to unreliable information."

It was Lady Ransome who finally said she was quite sure Captain Boyle's advice would be worth following, at which Captain Boyle bowed and flashed his white teeth at her. "That's kind of you, ma'am," he said, "and I appreciate it. I must tell you, too, that you can have complete confidence in Captain Nason's judgment, for though he's young and a great believer in Maine taciturnity and not committing himself to anything, he's as good a seaman as ever I kept company with."

The fiery heat of my face was not cooled by the somewhat discouraging silence that followed these words of Captain Boyle's; and at length, in desperation, I quickly swallowed a glass of wine and said it seemed to me the best thing to do would be to run to the Channel Islands, which were a little out of the beaten track, and set our prisoners ashore on one of them. From here, eventually, I said, they would get passage to England in a government sloop or schooner, and would be safe with English folk meanwhile.

"There!" Boyle cried. "What did I tell you! A perfect arrangement!"

The others, however, had nothing to say, but sat and pecked at their supper.

At length Sir Arthur observed dryly that after Captain Boyle had boasted of the manner in which Americans were making themselves at home in the Channel, it seemed not unnatural to hope his party might be landed in Plymouth harbor.

Captain Boyle smiled at him as sweetly as a newly wakened babe smiling up into his mother's face. "Where our privateers go," he told him softly, "depends a little upon the reward in prospect. When they risk themselves out of kindliness, they must take some account of numbers. You are three, and Captain Nason and I have a hundred men apiece to consider. Those two hundred, Sir Arthur, might be willing to venture their skins for a prize worth the good part of a farm to each of them. But I think they'd mislike Plymouth harbor as the scene of a Christian deed performed without even the prospect of being thanked for it."

Lady Ransome raised her eyes to mine for a moment; then dropped them immediately.

"Ow," Sir Arthur said at length. "Remarkable, your speaking of thanks, Mr. Boyle! Attacking us without a word of warning when we were harming nobody—that might be defined as somewhat cowardly, mightn't it? You put it all as a wholly commercial matter, you and your men, as I understood you to say, thinking only of how much money's to be made out of it. If you're to do a brave act, there would first have to be a calculation of the pennies to decide how many of them your bravery may be worth."

For my part, I could have wrung his neck, so deep was my resentment of his words; but Captain Boyle seemed undisturbed.

"Yes," he said, "I've heard that before; but as it just chances, I've always heard it second hand. Not before has it been said to me directly. I feel a little unfortunate that it's thus spoken at last by a captive; but since we're so happy as to have a lady with us, I'll explain these matters more fully than I would ordinarily do. Thus you may be able, hereafter, to state the case properly."

Captain Boyle rose, walked to the stern windows, drew aside the curtains and peered out. "A fine starry night," he said. With that he returned to his chair, and, as he came, fixed the back of Sir Arthur's head with a hard, level gaze.

"Well, now," he said, "this is the way of it. Most people in this world seem to be in the position of doing things for money. Your kings and our presidents; your doctors, lawyers, generals, admirals and ship-builders; your poets and your writers of books: all these men earn a living by what they do; and by stretching a point you might say it's a commercial matter with them. Why, I've even heard it said your great families in England marry oftener to gain a few acres of land or a sure addition to their incomes than for love."

He paused and looked shyly at his fingers, the most harmless-looking gentleman I had ever seen, and I was astonished to discover that Lady Ransome was as white as the linen at Captain Boyle's wrists, and that Sir Arthur's leathery, dust-colored face had gone a muddy red.

"Yes," Captain Boyle went on gently, "we're most of us money chasers in this world, though some of us chase it more grimly than others, and others chase it because they're whirled along with the chasers.

"Now, you gentlemen may or may not be aware that in the American navy there are only seven frigates and fifteen sloops-of-war to cope with your tremendous fleet of eight hundred men-of-war; but this is a fact. It's also a fact that many hundreds of Americans—

many thousands of them—are eager to do battle with a nation that has so flouted and insulted their country as has England."

Captain Boyle leaned forward and looked wistfully into Sir Arthur's face. "What's to be done in such a case?" he asked. "These men are seamen: all their lives they've known nothing but the sea. They're lost on land; and the ways of landsmen are beyond them. They'd be worthless in an army; and besides, they've no quarrel with England on the land. It's on the sea that England treads on our toes and denies us the right to be our own masters; and it's on the sea that Americans wish to fight for free trade and seamen's rights and no impressment."

Captain Boyle, it seemed, could not sit still. He rose again from his chair to stand with his back against the oak rudder casing, swaying as the brig, rising to the lift of a wave, swooped with it and lowered herself gently to the bosom of the following wave.

"What can these people do who want to fight you?" he repeated, looking from Captain Parker to Sir Arthur. "There's no room for 'em in our navy, on our few small government vessels. What am I to do when I want to fight you? I'm a navigator. I can work a brig or a ship, and work her well. I can fight her. Shall I go as a common seaman on one of our twenty-two government craft, where my knowledge of seamanship will be lost? What are the rest of us to do?"

Captain Boyle's voice fell almost to a whisper, so that I leaned forward for fear of losing his words in the slight screaking of the rudder and the lapping of the water against our sides. "You have a vulnerable spot, you English," he said. "It's your merchant fleet. We're striking home, Sir Arthur Ransome, when we send the price of flour in England to fifty dollars a barrel—to sixty dollars a barrel."

"Ah, yes," Sir Arthur said. "And getting the sixty dollars yourself, Mr. Boyle!"

Taking a handkerchief of gray silk from his breast pocket, Boyle smoothed it between the palms of his hands; and as he did so he lowered his head and looked into Sir Arthur's face as intently as though there were nothing else worth seeing in all the world. "I think I've made myself quite clear," he said. "I beg, therefore, you'll indicate in some way to me that you've labored under a misapprehension."

Sir Arthur met this intent look now bent upon him for a moment or two only; then lowered his eyelids and glanced aside.

"Oh, I've no doubt it's a fair enough sort of fighting, according to American ideas," he admitted.

Captain Boyle bowed gravely, resumed his seat, and lifted his glass to Captain Parker, then lowered it. "On second thought, Captain," he said, "I can't ask you to drink with me to the fortunes of war just at present."

"No," Parker returned gruffly. "And they wouldn't be what they are for us just now except for the damned laziness, saving Lady Ransome's presence, of our damned blockading fleet that's supposed to hold your privateers inside your own ports. How you get by them I'm damned if I can see, saving Lady Ransome's presence again."

"Oh, but it's the simplest thing in the world!" Boyle said. "We back out."

"Back out?" Parker repeated, with a kind of hoarseness. "Back out?"

"Let me explain it," Boyle said winningly, and turned to Lady Ransome. "You see, ma'am, your people have a heavy blockading fleet cruising up and down before the entrance of every harbor in America, so we come out stern foremost: that is to say, backwards; and your people look at us carefully and think we're going the other way. So they don't bother us. Sometimes we have to back halfway to the Scilly Islands; but, after all, what could be simpler?"

Captain Parker sputtered, grunted, and seemed to be swearing internally. Lady Ransome said, "La!" and looked purely scornful, whereupon Boyle lifted a protesting hand toward her.

"You'll not betray me, ma'am," he said, "for giving this information to the enemy—I'm afraid I must regard your husband and Captain Parker as enemies; but I'm sure they'll be honorable and not betray the secret. Doubtless you know yourself, ma'am, that Sir John Bor-

laise Warren had it published in England how well he holds the
Chesapeake blockaded; but as a hundred and fifty American privateers are constantly passing in and out of those lively waters, Sir
John could only be excused on the ground that he sees nothing but
their sterns and therefore thinks they're all inside."

When he had said this he sat staring at Parker. His face had suddenly become as blank as a clam shell. His eyes seemed turned inward, and his lower lip sagged, so that he looked to be gone entirely
from us. Then, as abruptly, a little glow appeared upon his cheek.
He came to life, smiling, and turned to me.

"Blockade!" he said. "Why, what fools we've been, Captain! Warren's in America, blockading us; and we're here, so why shouldn't we
blockade them?"

"Blockade who?" Sir Arthur asked.

"The British!" Boyle cried, striking his fist on the table. "Captain
Nason, we'll blockade England."

"Good!" I said.

Captain Boyle clapped his hands softly and rubbed them together. He slid from his chair to walk up and down the end of the
cabin, beaming delightedly at me, as though I had done something
mighty pleasing. "Pencil and paper, Captain!" he said. "Pencil and
paper! This blockade must be effected at once!"

I went to my dispatch box for writing materials; and thinking
all eyes were on Captain Boyle, I stole a glance at Emily Ransome,
only to find she had looked suddenly over her shoulder at me. It
was the same level glance she had given me once before; but now I
saw no enmity in it; for when she turned quickly away, her face and
throat flushed hotly red. I fumbled in my dispatch box as though my
fingers were turned to thumbs.

I forgot, almost, what I had come to get; I heard but dimly the
voice of Captain Parker, plainly outraged by Boyle's remarks. "It
seems to me, Captain Boyle," he said, "that what you say is in ex-
tremely poor taste!"

Boyle stopped abruptly in his pacing. "Poor taste, Captain?" he asked, as if he doubted his ears. "Surely you didn't say poor taste!"

Captain Parker made a sound like an outraged goose. "Such a thing's impossible of accomplishment," he said, "and you'd never say it to our naval officers; so it must be said for the purpose of irritating us, who are helpless here in this cabin."

"Why, sir," Captain Boyle said, and I thought he spoke regretfully, "I'll ask you to pardon me if I've irritated you. That wasn't my intention." He raised his eyebrows at Lady Ransome. "Have you found my words irritating?"

"I find them pleasantly fantastic," she said, smiling at him.

Boyle shook his head sadly. "Not fantastic," he said. "They're meant more soberly. Why, here—" he turned to Captain Parker— "it's not half as impossible for me to blockade England as for Sir John Borlaise Warren to blockade America. And I question your judgment, my dear sir, when you tell me I'd never say such a thing to naval officers. I'm quite willing to say it to anyone." He seemed struck with a new idea. "I shall *insist* on saying it to everyone! You shall carry my proclamation to London, Captain Parker, and post it in Lloyd's Coffee House!

"Take it down for me, Captain," he said, seeing I had brought pencil and paper. "Take it down! We'll make three copies, so all Great Britain may be warned."

Thereupon, with a mocking spark in his velvety brown eyes and the gentlest of smiles playing about his lips, he wandered around the table, dictating to me, seemingly oblivious of the rigidity with which Sir Arthur and Captain Parker sat in their chairs.

"At the top," he announced, "the word 'Proclamation,' printed large, and flanked by American eagles with ruffled feathers, if you're any hand at drawing eagles: if not, we'll get along with American ensigns. After that, in red ink, the word 'whereas,' large and italicized, and with that we can start." His voice rose a little and became flat and monotonous. "*Whereas,* It has become customary with the admirals of Great Britain, commanding small forces on the coast of the United States, particularly with Sir John Borlaise Warren and

Sir Alexander Cochrane, to declare all the coast of the said United States in a state of strict and rigorous blockade without stationing an adequate force to maintain said blockade;

"I do therefore, by virtue of the power and authority in me vested, possessing sufficient force, declare all the ports, harbors, bays, creeks, rivers, inlets, outlets, islands and seacoast of the United Kingdom of Great Britain and Ireland in a state of strict and rigorous blockade."

"Ow!" Sir Arthur protested.

Captain Boyle held up a warning hand and continued his dictation: "And I do further declare that I consider the force under my command adequate to maintain strictly, rigorously, and effectually the said blockade."

"Adequate!" Captain Parker protested. "Two small vessels *adequate!*"

"Why not?" Boyle asked. "Look at Warren!" He nodded at me and resumed his flat, monotonous dictating voice: "And I do hereby caution and forbid the ships and vessels of all and every nation in amity and peace with the United States from entering or attempting to enter, or from coming or attempting to come out of, any of the said ports, harbors, bays, creeks, rivers, inlets, outlets, islands, or seacoast under any pretext whatsoever. And that no person may plead ignorance of this, my proclamation, I have ordered the same to be made public in England.

"Given under my hand on board the Private Armed Brig *Chasseur*, THOMAS BOYLE, Commander."

Captain Boyle came and looked over my shoulder. "I date it as from my own ship, as more fitting and proper, if you'll pardon me, Captain Nason. Have you it all?"

"I think so," I told him, pleased to see Sir Arthur looking at me sourly. "In reference to the supposed British blockade of America, it might be nearer to the truth if you inserted, before the words about stationing an adequate force, the words 'without possessing the power to justify such a declaration.'"

"My dear Captain," Boyle said, starting back wide eyed, "the proclamation would have verged on the inaccurate without such a phrase. I thank you a thousand times for the suggestion! Pray make it so!"

With that, smiling graciously upon us, he caught up his hat and swept a quick bow to Lady Ransome. "Charming evening," he told us. "I shall hope for others before the blockade ends."

XVIII

IT WAS thick as pea soup in the Channel on the following morning: thick and choppy; and it seemed to me there was trouble in the air; for Pinky lay in my bunk, his head hanging across my legs and his beady black eyes wide open, now elevating one bushy yellow eyebrow at the stern windows, then twisting the other toward the door of the cabin, and between times growling faintly deep in his throat; so in the end he drove me to dressing and going on deck at an early hour.

I could make out nothing in the fog. Pomp, standing his trick at the wheel, his face like polished ebony from the wetness of the air, jerked his head to larboard and said he had caught a glimpse of the *Chasseur's* topgallant sail half an hour earlier. There was no breeze to speak of; only light airs from the west that left us wallowing and creaking in the oily cross-seas, with steerageway but little more; so from our reef-points and top-hamper there was a slatting and whacking reminiscent of a hailstorm on a barn roof. The suggestion of a barn, indeed, was one that came to me readily, because of the barnyard flavor of our waist, where there were sheep pens and crates of fowl.

One of the men brought me a cup of coffee, stout enough to hold up a nail, and I mooned idly over it, with that early-morning numbness of eye and brain which often accompanies changeable weather.

Pinky stirred himself between my ankles, where he was resting, and peered out around my leg. Feeling his stub of a tail begin to thump, I looked around myself and saw Lady Ransome had come on deck, a dark green kerchief bound around her head like a Spanish fisherwoman's, and her fur cloak wrapped tight about her. I gawked at her, my cup half raised.

"Well," I said, staring. "Well—what are you—where——"

"Is it hot?" she asked, looking at the cup.

"Yes," I said, holding it before me as if waiting for someone to throw a marlinspike at it.

"Let me have a little," she said, and took it.

"Wait; I've been drinking from it. I'll send for more."

Even while I said it, she drank what was left, watching me over the rim as she did so. I couldn't, for the life of me, think of another thing to say, and only stood looking at her until she put the cup back in my hand, which was still half open in mid-air.

"What would your aunt Cynthy say if you gave her coffee like that?" she asked. "What do they put in your coffee? Rusty iron?"

"It seems to me," I said, "it seems to me you look thinner than when I saw you in Arundel."

She seemed almost to study over her answer. "How is your mother, Captain Nason?"

"She's very well. She helped me with this sloop. No: this is a brig: she helped me with the sloop I had before this."

"When did you see her last?"

"Why, only a short time ago. Last fall. No: it was longer ago. A year ago. No: it was over a year ago: it was a year and a half ago."

Speech deserted us, and we stared at the tide streaks always to be found in the dirty gray water of the Channel, which has as many cross-currents as one of our marsh rivers within a few minutes of flood.

Only the night before, it seemed to me, there had been scores of things I wanted to say, if I could catch her alone for a moment. Yet now that I was alone with her, and she surprising me by seeming to be in a friendly mood to boot, my brain was as muddled as a plate of lobscouse. Nothing would rise to the surface.

"There are sticklebacks in England," she said at last. "They live in the ditches. In London I found a print of a woodcock flying with one of its babies held between its knees, as you said. Has your head hurt since that day?"

I told her it hadn't, and wondered why I had to be so dull and stupid.

"I suppose you've helped other girls cut their initials in the beech tree," she went on. "Better carvers than I. La, how crooked my letters were!" She laughed a gay little laugh, though it seemed to me she laughed overlong. "I fear you're always following after the women."

"No, I'm not," I said, hoping my voice sounded stern and truthful.

"Why," she said, "there's one under your bowsprit at this moment. Aren't you afraid she's leading you on, Captain Nason?"

"Leading—leading me on?" I stammered. "She was a ghost when we got the brig. She was pale—she looked entirely different."

"And you had her changed afterward, Captain Nason?"

"I changed her myself," I said. I intended my words to have no double meaning, but I thought she eyed me strangely.

We stared at each other. She stooped suddenly and picked up Pinky, pressing her cheek against the top of his head.

"I saw your brother," I told her awkwardly. "A pleasant young man. I saw Annie too. Did you see Annie?"

She nodded. "You said nothing to my brother about knowing me?" she said.

"No, I didn't. Did you?"

I knew she hadn't because of her sudden interest in adding to the roughness of Pinky's eyebrows. "Why was it you said nothing to him?" she asked.

"I don't know. Maybe because we're at war. No: I don't know why. Perhaps for the same reason I didn't tell my mother about your picture."

"What picture?" she asked, wide eyed.

"Why," I said, wishing I had held my tongue, "the one you—the one Annie——"

"Where is it?"

I fumbled under my coat and had to rip the button from the pocket, so clumsy were my fingers. I got out the picture at last and unwrapped the silk handkerchief from it. I glanced at it before I gave it to her. Certainly, I thought, she had grown thinner, and there was a look in her eyes that had never been in them when I first knew her, and that was not in the eyes of the miniature—a look I have seen only in the eyes of prisoners.

She gazed steadily at it, turning it between her fingers: then, before I realized what she was doing, she dropped it inside the collar of her dress.

"Here," I said, "here!" and I found myself with my hands stretched out toward her, as if to snatch it back again.

"There's been a deal of trouble over this, Captain Nason."

"But," I said, "it's—I've carried it—you can't——"

"Where did you find it?"

"It was in my coat when I sailed. It had slipped through a hole in the pocket. I've never let it out of my hands. It brings me luck!"

"Luck! Lud! It brought me more talk than was ever caused by the Great Plague! Now there'll be no more of it." She hummed a tune under her breath.

"You mean you'll tell your husband you've found it, and he'll stop talking?"

She nodded, without interrupting her humming.

"Stop a minute," I said. "Shall you tell him how I happened to have it? And where I was carrying it?"

"Of course," she said, looking abstractedly at the masthead.

"Well," I told her, "if you've been talked at till you're sick of talk, as I suspect you are, I'd give the matter more thought. I think it would be safer with me. It's brought me luck, and I'll try to see no harm comes to it."

The man at the masthead shouted, "Sail on the larboard beam!"

The fog, I saw, was lighter; much lighter; but still there was no breeze to speak of.

Peer into the fog as I would, I could make out nothing.

There was confused shouting near the forecastle. 'Lisha Lord came aft to say the lookout had caught sight of a craft with two royals when the fog lightened for a moment. How far away, 'Lisha said, he was not sure. A mile; maybe less: maybe more.

"Was he sure of the two royals?" I asked him. If there were two it couldn't be the *Chasseur*. She was a brig-schooner like ourselves and carried only one.

"He says two," 'Lisha insisted.

We peered to larboard, but the fog hid what lay beyond us. We could see it drifting like smoke above the water, with little rents and alleys in it, as though it were being pushed aside, here and there, by objects invisible to us.

While we stared and stared into that blank gray wall, our mouths open and our muscles tight from our anxiety to sharpen our senses a muffled, cottony thud struck our eardrums like a ghostly finger pressed against them. We seemed to float in a thick, motionless world—a world without breath or life; and as we waited so, a burst of cavernous thuds tumbled on each other's heels irregularly, like the distant barking of two monstrous dogs.

I knew on the moment what had happened, as surely as though I had looked through the curtain of fog and seen it. The *Chasseur* had blundered into an enemy craft of some sort; and what would happen to her, with no breeze for maneuvering, God alone could tell. In no other way could the matter be explained, and our duty, as I saw it, was to find out whether it was indeed so. There were two ways, I knew, of finding out. I could send away our boats loaded with boarders; or I could run out the sweeps and move the brig herself in range. Since the *Lively Lady* moved easily, I figured she might be swept up almost as quickly as the boats could be manned and got away and rowed to an attack: also I felt that our guns would be needed, and if I depended on boats, the guns would be useless.

"Get out the sweeps, clear the waist of lumber and pipe to quarters," I told 'Lisha Lord.

He ran down the deck. Irrelevant thoughts popped into my head, such as that 'Lisha was from Bath and as smart-looking an officer as could be found on any British man-of-war, and that we were lucky to have him to point our guns. The brig was a turmoil of running and shouting, with the shrilling of the bos'n's whistle threading through it, as is always the case in a sudden call to quarters; and over everything continued the hot, sepulchral roaring of the guns, pressing thick, moist air against our faces.

Jotham Carr ran past, to turn my cabin into a hospital, Tommy Bickford at his heels to stow my dunnage and bring me my fowling piece. The thought of the fowling piece put Sir Arthur into my head, so I caught Tommy by the arm and turned to Lady Ransome, who had been wiped from my mind by the thudding of the guns. From the waist came a disquieting baa-ing and cackling, as the men hove the livestock over the bulwarks; but there was a faint fixed smile on Lady Ransome's lips, a smile that would stay there, once she had put it on, it seemed to me, even though the whole world fell to pieces around her.

"Go with Tommy," I told her. "Get your husband and Captain Parker. Tommy'll take you below, where there'll be no danger. Don't be afraid."

"I'm not afraid," she said.

I knew there was something I wanted to ask her, but there were too many things on my mind, such as how these other vessels might be lying, and whether 'Lisha had kept shot hot in the galley, as he had spoken of doing. She stared at me over Pinky's head, and while I was trying to remember what I wanted to say, I saw Captain Parker step on deck. Behind him was Sir Arthur, weak looking and the color of the little sponges that grow in the rock pools of Arundel, near low-water mark; so I knew he had been made ill by our wallowing in the calm. As they appeared a burst of gunfire stopped them in their tracks.

Parker.shot a quick look at the fog that hemmed us in; then peered at the men casting loose carronade slides, tricing up ports, manning the sweeps, and running like ants with shot, powder, water pails, rammers, and muskets.

"Look here," he said, stepping up to me, "what's happening here?"

"Nothing you need worry about. Go below with Lady Ransome."

Sir Arthur's face was green. "Ow!" he said. "I can't permit this."

I remembered, then, that I had wanted to speak to Lady Ransome about the miniature; but now it was too late.

"Take your husband below," I told her, "and be quick about it. Keep the dog. He'll be company. Don't let him loose. He likes the guns."

She nodded, a bright nod, and went away with Tommy, the two Englishmen following her, and Pinky peering back at me from around her arm.

Moved by the sweeps, the brig was swinging to larboard, toward the hoarse bellowing of the guns. I told myself we must see the vessels soon, since they could see each other; that it was the Ransomes' own fault, getting into this trouble; that if they hadn't wanted trouble, they should have stayed in England, where they belonged; that I hadn't lost a man so far, only poor Sip; that my mother would say that what I was doing was all right, if she were here. That's the way of it with me, I'm sorry to say: When close to trouble, I can only think small thoughts that have next to no bearing on the matter in hand.

A spout of water shot thirty feet in the air off our starboard quarter, giving me a picture of how they lay, broadside to us and two cable lengths ahead. The gun crews, silent at their stations, pointed and whispered when they saw the spout. We swept off to larboard again, so we could come up under their bows or sterns, in a position to rake. I felt movement in our topsails, the beginning of a light breeze. In the same moment the lookout shouted again, and as he shouted we saw them dimly, their top-hamper showing through the dissolving fog, their hulls hidden, except for patches here and there, in layers of smoke.

We came around more, until we lay broadside to them, our bow to the westward. They were pointed northeast, a pistol shot apart. The nearer one was a ship-rigged sloop-of-war, a corvette, with British colors at her peak. Her foretopmast was cut through at the head, its spars and gear lolloping from the cap in a tangle. The mizzenmast trailed over the counter, with the jagged stump of the mast rising from the wreckage. Through the smoke we saw her people hacking away with axes to clear the decks.

Yet there was life in her, and plenty of it. The *Chasseur*, dimly seen through the smoke, seemed a ragged wreck of the swift brig that had skimmed the waves beside us on the day before, though I well knew that a vessel, though apparently cut to pieces, could be nobly patched by a skillful crew in an hour's time. Her main-boom was shot through, her foretopgallant yard was broken in the slings, and her bowsprit dangled in splinters and festoons from her stem. Her sails were riddled and shredded from the passage of grape and round shot, so I knew the Britisher's gun crews were shooting too high. In the moment when the two craft became clear to us through the thinning fog, a man pitched over the side of the *Chasseur's* maintop, hung by a knee; then sprawled downward to the deck, turning slowly in the air and vanishing in the smoke.

"Get at them with muskets," I told Jeddy, "whenever our people can shoot without hurting the *Chasseur*. I want no gun fired till we can rake."

The breeze died again, and the guns roared thunderously, almost in our ears. A little futile spattering of musketry set in from our tops. The men were under the bulwarks, stripped to the waist; for even in cold weather there is a feeling of greater security if no coats or shirts hamper the arms or shoulders, and if belts are pulled tight at the waist to ease the shrinking in the stomach that comes with fighting.

Our eyes burned and watered with the fierceness of our peering, for there's no time to meditate when creeping into position within easy range of an enemy, waiting for the gunfire you know must come. And creep we did; for though the men drove the sweeps through the water until it whirled and sucked, we seemed to lie motionless in the oily chop, except for the lifts and lurches of the brig as the waves had their will of her. Yet we moved; for there was a sheep pen clinging against our side, with three half-dead sheep in it; draggled, wretched, staring-eyed beasts that blatted and blatted as the cold Channel chop slapped unendingly at them; and this pen moved slowly backward from our waist.

We had swept a little beyond the Britisher before she opened fire. It may be that between the men needed to work her guns and muskets against the *Chasseur* and those who chopped at her tangles of spars and cordage, she had no men to waste on us, or she may have hoped to force the *Chasseur* to strike and then engage us. Whatever the reason, we were nearly ready to turn again and sweep under her stern when she let go her starboard battery.

There was a whirring and rattling of grapeshot above us as the smoke jetted irregularly from her side, a small downrush of severed tackle, and the rasping shudder that comes from being hulled with solid shot. I moved forward to reassure the men, but they stayed where they were, those at the sweeps pushing hard; the men under the bulwarks lying tight, some with their arms over their heads to guard against splinters, and some with their faces screwed around toward the quarter-deck, grinning.

I could see the Britishers ramming home charges at the starboard ports. We would have two minutes, I knew, before the next broadside: maybe three, and maybe even four. I could make out officers on the quarter-deck as the smoke drifted away; and I wished, as I had never wished for anything in my life, for a breeze to drive us around under her stern so we could rake them off.

'Lisha Lord moved from gun to gun in the waist, tinkering with them, almost like a woman prodding at her hair, striving to get it just so. Suddenly he straightened, whirled, and jumped for the quarter-deck.

"By God!" he shouted, "it's the *Gorgon!* It's the damned old *Gorgon!*"

She let off at us again, as though in protest at 'Lisha's words. We felt the push of air against us, and a hellish clattering and whirring all about us, so I knew she had pointed her guns better. To this day I cannot kick a gray-winged grasshopper from the dune grass of Arundel in late summer without feeling my heart turn over in my breast; for their whirring is like that of flying wood splinters ripped from masts and yards and bulwarks by round shot. I could see splinters pass in a shimmery yellow mist, and felt a quick ache in my left shoulder, where a small splinter had driven into me, point first.

The men at a starboard sweep were sprawled on the deck, knocked there when the sweep was shattered by a round shot. Our foretopmast swayed, then buckled with a sound of rending timber, and hung loose and draggled. A man toppled over the edge of the foretop, twisted in mid-air and clung by his hands. I saw Moody Haley reach down, clutch him by the back of his shirt, and heave him back into the top. One of the men crawled out from beside a carronade. Blood gushed in spurts from his neck. He reached the musket stand by the main hatch, pulled himself to his feet, then fell again and lay still, a black stream moving slowly from under him.

Jeddy hustled a new sweep to the starboard sweepers, and Rowlandson Drown bawled at his men to cut away the foretopmast. I pulled the splinter from my shoulder, thankful when it came out easily from the bone, and told Pomp to put over the helm.

"All ships look like the *Gorgon* to you," I reminded 'Lisha. Automatically I figured that if nothing happened to us we would be in a position to rake in three minutes.

"Like hell they do!" 'Lisha said, his voice shaking as if with cold. "That's the *Gorgon!* I thought it was the *Gorgon* when I got a look at her through the fog! Now I know it! Look at her maintop netting, made in diamonds! That's mine, by God! I made it!"

It was in diamonds, as he said; and as I peered at her, wrapped in smoke and littered with her tangled top-hamper, it seemed to me I could recognize, on the quarter-deck, the burly figure of Captain Bullard-Jones.

Smoke gushed from her starboard battery once more. "One—two —three!" 'Lisha counted, above the howling and rattling that followed the discharge. "Three! They can't bring the others to bear!"

"Give 'em a gun," I said. "Keep it away from the *Chasseur*." I thanked God, as 'Lisha jumped for the long gun, that the *Gorgon* had been able to bring only three to bear; for these three had left a ragged, furry hole in our mainmast, shattered the bottom of our long-boat, and stretched Rowlandson Drown on the deck; while something, though there was no way of knowing what at the moment, had happened to our steering gear. The wheel had whirled suddenly in Pomp's hands, throwing him to the deck with wrists half broken.

I saw Jeddy run to Rowlandson and pull at his arm, looking at his face; and from the way he let his arm drop and turned away I knew Rowlandson was dead.

'Lisha worked at his gun, squinting and squinting. The deck jerked as he fired, and in the same moment the sternmost gun of the *Gorgon's* starboard battery, struck fair on the muzzle by 'Lisha's shot, kicked backward and exploded.

The crew of the long gun leaped like jumping jacks, sponging and loading. "Load with one shot!" I heard 'Lisha tell them. "There's a hot one goes on top."

He ran down the deck toward the galley, slapping at the gun crews. "Steady as a rock!" he shouted. "We'll never have no such gun platform again! Right into her guts, boys!"

We crept in and crept in, closer to the *Gorgon's* stern, but slowly: as slowly, almost, as the moon comes up beyond the brown rocks of Cape Arundel. Her masts, wrapped in a tangle of sails, spars, shrouds and running rigging, drew closer together as we brought them in line, and up through them rose white wreaths of smoke from her guns; for still she hammered at the *Chasseur*, and still the *Chas-*

seur hammered back, though the roars of both had a labored, weary slowness.

'Lisha ran from the galley, behind him two men with pails.

I saw a long gun emerge from one of the *Gorgon's* stern ports and slowly come to bear on us. My muscles were tight as barrel hoops, and I wanted to crouch behind the bulwark for a second—for half a second even—to do anything except stand and wait.

'Lisha Lord shouted to the gun crews of the long guns. They dumped the shot from the pails into their guns, and 'Lisha ran for the forward carronades.

The *Gorgon's* stern gun bellowed at us. It was langrage—old iron and bolts and pieces of kettles and nails—and it screamed around and over us as though the sky were filled with angry cats.

'Lisha's first shot went through the cabin windows of the *Gorgon*. His second smashed her rudder. Our men came up cheering from behind the bulwarks, all a-drip from waiting. They cheered and swabbed and cheered, and last of all 'Lisha ran to the long guns loaded with hot shot.

Perspiration dropped from Jeddy's chin as he shook his fist at the *Gorgon* and screamed at her, in a shrill, cracked voice, to strike her colors.

The long guns roared out of a welter of white smoke. Aboard the *Gorgon* we heard a muffled, anguished cough, as though some great hulk of an animal had coughed in deathly sickness. The smoke lifted; the cough died; then rose immediately into a roar. The wreckage of her mainmast and mizzenmast reeled; and up from her midship section sprouted a bell of planks and cordage and men and gear, a bell that blossomed into a mushroom of smoke and suddenly climbed up and up into a flame-shot column, in which moved black, broken objects, turning slowly as they mounted.

A strange silence came down upon us and on all the sea as well. It was silence, and yet not silence; for in the distance there was a rushing noise from within the column of smoke that still mounted upward from the *Gorgon*, until it seemed to hang over us like an enormous maple tree in full leaf. We heard a rasping and creaking from our damaged top-hamper, and a sickening moaning from a wounded man in the foretop.

"Lower away the boats," I told Jeddy. There was a walloping splash hard by our counter, and thumps here and there on our deck, followed by a rush of falling fragments, hurtling down at us from the sides of that cone-shaped cloud.

The hull of the *Gorgon* had opened out like a melon suddenly dropped on the ground, but now her bow and stern came upright again. The opening seemed about to close; then slowly and wearily widened once more; and the bow and stern, wavering and groping as though feeling their way beneath the surface, settled deeper and deeper into the gray water of the Channel until it came to us suddenly that they were entirely gone: that there was nothing left of the *Gorgon* but a welter of planks and broken spars and splintered fragments, with heads here and there among them, and over them a vast, ever spreading umbrella of smoke. From those heads among the wreckage there rose a faint, thin piping, like the distant calling of young frogs such as we hear in Arundel on warm nights in the spring of the year.

XIX

THE men were knotting and splicing the rigging, plugging the shot holes in our hull and nailing lead over them, and making ready to fish our wounded masts and spars as soon, almost, as the boats had been lowered away; for they knew, as well as I, that the English Channel was no place in which to waste time celebrating a victory, especially when we were helpless as a shark with his tail cut off. We would be fit to maneuver, I knew, in a half hour's time if there was nothing to worry us but our masts and spars and rigging; for no seamen in the world are so quick and handy at repairing ship as are American seamen. But in addition to our top-hamper we had our rudder to consider; and when we came to look at it we found we had no rudder at all, the rudder post having been cut by a shot, and the whole machine having wrenched away. Thus we couldn't move until we made a false sternpost, or preventer sternpost, reeved a rudder of plank to it, fixed it in place, and fastened the false rudder in turn to the main chains by guys and tackles. This is the devil's own job, and we laid out the necessary gear on the quarter-deck, to save time and trouble; and into this turmoil came Sir Arthur Ransome and his wife and Captain Parker.

I think there is some good in most men, at least in those brought up among decent people, although some Englishmen seem to take pains to discourage Americans in that belief. To me Sir Arthur Ransome seemed to be such an Englishman; and I wondered where I could stow that green-faced nuisance before he offended my crew with one of his ill-considered remarks, and so got himself thrown overboard. Even as I did so he came to me, radiating offensiveness. "Look here, Nason," he said, in that whiny voice of his that set my teeth on edge.

"*Captain* Nason to you," I told him, feeling savage from anxiety as well as from the discomfort in my shoulder. "For God's sake, hold your tongue till we've put ourselves in order!"

"Ow!" he said, stiff and contemptuous, "Lady Ransome asked——"

"She's not hurt?" I snapped, conscious that the very thought made the deck seem to lurch beneath me.

"She wishes to be of assistance to your surgeon in the cabin," he said, staring at the clotted splotch on the shoulder of my shirt, so that I was reminded to put on my coat again. "I couldn't myself: very squeamish stomach on the water."

I thanked him as well as I was able. The cabin, I told him, was no place for a woman; and we could somehow make out by ourselves. I never had any doubt that Sir Arthur Ransome thought me a boor; and just then he was no doubt entirely right, though I tried to console myself by thinking he had never had to supervise the making of a preventer sternpost and rudder.

The fog was growing steadily lighter. Directly overhead was a patch of blue sky. The cat's-paws were steadying, so I knew we would soon have a breeze from the west. The boats were coming back from the wreckage of the *Gorgon;* and men were swarming in the rigging of the *Chasseur* like snails on eel grass. Her bowsprit was in place once more, though the bobstays and shrouds were not set up; a new foretopgallant yard had been swayed onto the cap, and the main-boom had been fished. I tried to make out Boyle through the glass but couldn't find him.

Jeddy came over the side while we were reeving guys through the preventer sternpost. "It was the *Gorgon*," he said. "Those people from the *Chasseur*, they say they'll make you King of Maine when we get home."

"Well," I told him, "I'd rather have their rudder, so we'd be sure of getting home. How many did you pick up?"

"Seventeen. The *Chasseur's* boat got about thirty."

"Any officers?"

"No; only seamen and petty officers."

"Any wounded men?"

"No; they sank."

"Is Boyle all right?" I asked him.

Jeddy looked at me thoughtfully. "They got hit pretty bad, I guess; but Boyle, he only got a bullet through that gray beaver of his."

I think the thought of Rowlandson Drown lying on the deck came to both of us at the same time, because Jeddy coughed and cleared his throat and said we couldn't all be lucky; then turned away quickly to attend to the *Gorgon's* men.

A patch of sunlight showed on the water near us. Ripples lapped against our side, and it occurred to me that if my luck were what it should be, the fog would have held on and the breeze held off for another hour.

"How long, boys?" I asked the men rigging the tackles on the rudder.

One said twenty minutes; another an hour. A man screamed in the cabin, so I knew Jotham Carr must be taking off an arm or a leg. It came to me that he lacked practice in such matters: that it would be better for me to help him than to stand on deck with nothing but my thoughts to keep me company. I had no more than started for the cabin when I saw the *Chasseur* wear to the north before a light westerly breeze. I thought Boyle was coming down to see what he could do for us, and I was wishful of seeing him; but it seemed strange he should wear to the north when we lay southwest of him.

I saw him crowd on his studding sails, holding steadily to his northerly course; and so rapidly did he leave us under this press of canvas that even while I gazed blankly after him, the figures on the *Chasseur's* quarter-deck faded to specks and then to pinpoints.

Jeddy came and stood beside me, looking after her. "Well——" he said. "Well——" And with that he launched into a string of curses that he never got out of any book, not even one of Tobias Smollett's. It was in the midst of his cursing, when he had become so involved and fanciful that the men at work on the rudder sat back on their haunches to stare up at him, that the man at the masthead shouted "Sail!"

Jeddy stopped abruptly. The men flew at their work again. We made out the sail, far to the northward, beyond the *Chasseur*. I realized instantly that the *Chasseur* had seen it first and set off at once to intercept it; and I thought to myself that this is the way of it, often, when a friend seems to go off unfaithfully on other affairs, so that we curse him and soon thereafter lose him as a friend.

What the sail might be we couldn't tell. It looked to me like a ponderous craft. I had my suspicions, and they were such as to give me an empty feeling in my stomach and a coppery taste in my mouth; for I had no desire that our cruise should end here in the gray waters of the Channel, with us caught like a rabbit lurching and squeaking in a trap.

I could see Boyle holding straight for the sail, and knew he would do what he could; but I also knew we must make a try at helping ourselves. If she should indeed be an enemy, as I suspected, she might turn off in pursuit of Boyle if only she could see us under way. It was this, I was sure, for which Boyle was hoping.

The hole in our mainmast had been fished, and a new topmast swayed up, fidded, and stayed; so that nothing stood between us and safety except our rudder. Due east, if my reckoning was good, lay the Island of Jersey, largest of the Channel Islands. With a light westerly breeze, provided we were able to maneuver, we could turn the Ransomes adrift close to the island and be safe on the Norman coast in the little harbor of Carteret or St. Germain-sur-Ay before sundown.

I thought about it; then called Jeddy and 'Lisha Lord to the quarter-deck. The *Chasseur* was hull down, but the strange sail, which she had not yet reached, showed the tops of her bulwarks above the water. We needed no word from the man at the masthead to tell us that a ship of this size must be a seventy-four—a ship-of-the-line; and since America had no war craft larger than a forty-four-gun frigate we knew she had to be a Britisher.

"Well," I said, "we'll try steering with the sweeps, unless somebody knows a better way. If we can keep before the wind for five minutes she may run off after Boyle." They said nothing, but stood staring into the north. As we watched, the *Chasseur* hauled her wind and went off to the northwest, to windward of the seventy-four. We peered and peered, hoping to see the seventy-four go off on the same tack after her, though we knew no seventy-four ever built could sail half as fast as the *Chasseur*.

"Some of these seventy-four captains," 'Lisha said, "they ain't so bad. Either they're moss-backed old pigs, not fit for eating or killing or anything else, or they know their business."

There was a dull, distant thud, more of a throb in the air than a thud; then another; but the seventy-four came straight on. 'Lisha grunted. "Threw a couple thirty-six pounders at random! He knows his business."

"Get out the sweeps," I told them. "Run 'em through the stern ports."

We made sail and wore around. As we came before the wind the sweeps seemed almost to hold her steady. She got fresh way rapidly, held on her course for half a minute, then yawed suddenly to larboard.

"Starboard!" Jeddy bawled. The men at the sweeps pushed hard at them. The *Lively Lady* shivered a little, wallowed back toward her course, hung for a moment, then yawed again and broached to.

The seventy-four may have been three miles off; but so accurately was she pointed that if she kept on as she was, her stem would slice us neatly in two, unless we could take ourselves out of her path. The *Chasseur* had come about and shot past her to windward, and now wore across her bows once more. Boyle, we knew, was armed only with long twelves, whereas the seventy-four must carry thirty-six pounders or forty-two pounders: consequently it was clear to us that there was nothing more for him to do. Yet he would not give up. He hove a shot at her as he passed her bows: then tacked twice in quick succession, letting off a gun each time, though he could no more hurt the lumbering hulk that surged contemptuously on her way than a woodpecker could hurt the side of a house.

Rowlandson Drown's assistant had been a gangling young man from Quincy in Massachusetts, one James Combs. At Rowlandson's death he had become ship's carpenter; and it was he who straightened up from the rudder, shouting, "Get her over." With 'Lisha Lord and Jeddy climbing around and among them like two inquisitive cats, the men put this rough machine overboard, then lashed the upper part of the preventer post to the brig's sternpost, and bolted the two together to keep the false sternpost from rising up or falling down. There were men under the stern, working half submerged, with one or two entirely under water at times.

Seeing that his attempts were useless, evidently, Boyle had left the seventy-four and was coming down on us under a cloud of sail. Behind him the seventy-four, less than two miles distant, towered upward like an iceberg, glistening white and no less pitiless and dangerous.

The men worked at the tackles like figures in a nightmare, slower than anything I had ever seen; and I was so desirous of getting free of this enormous black-stemmed vessel and the triple line of guns along its side that I was hard put to it to get enough air into my lungs. I stood silent, my hands clenched tight in my pockets and the nails biting into my palms. The machine was done at last, so that Jeddy set up a shout from larboard and 'Lisha from starboard.

With two men handling the larboard tackles and two the starboard tackles of our makeshift rudder, the *Lively Lady* wore slowly around. She made as though to yaw; then held steady and slipped more and more rapidly through the water, to the south, straight away from the seventy-four. She was a mile off by now, a tremendous big ship, making the *Chasseur*, close astern of us, look like a pilot boat. As we picked up speed she fired a gun. Jeddy laughed and waggled his fingers at his nose. "Growl, you black bitch!" he said; and indeed there was a look about her of a big black dog showing white teeth at us, in a rage at having a dinner snatched from her jaws.

The *Chasseur* came up under our lee, her crew swarming along her bulwarks and high on her ratlines, bawling and hurrooing at the top of their lungs, and waving their hats and hands until the whole brig seemed aflutter. Boyle was perched on his aftermost long gun, but his bell-topped beaver was not on his head, so that he did not make us one of his fine sweeping bows. Instead of that, he reached up his hands, tightly clasped together, and shook them at us without a word. It occurred to me he might be feeling the same tightness in his chest and throat that I felt—a tightness that came from knowing him to be safe and grateful for our help—and so be averse to attempting any speech.

He dragged out his gray silk handkerchief, blew his nose violently; then smiled and nodded at me. I thought he was about to say something; but even as I cupped my ear with my hand I saw him cast a quick glance at our foretopmast and stand staring at it, his mouth half open. At the same moment I saw the heads of all his crew swing upward as if drawn by one string, so that every eye on the *Chasseur* was fixed on our foretopmast.

I needed nothing more to know that we were done: not even the ripping, splintering crackle that followed immediately as our new foretopmast gave way two thirds below its head and toppled to leeward; nor yet the second crash following close on the heels of the first when the foremast, weakened no doubt by the break during the engagement and by this additional strain, broke off close to the deck.

A hissing groan went up from the decks of the *Chasseur* as she shot ahead of us, and as we veered around, dragged by the wreckage. There was a queer, absent-minded look on the faces of our crew and of Jeddy and 'Lisha as they stared at the wreck of the foremast, al-

most as though they watched a cat sleeping on the deck or some
similarly harmless and familiar spectacle.

Boyle, I saw, intended to speak us once more. He came into the
wind, then wore around, starting to circle us. The seventy-four, still
a mile astern, lumbered relentlessly on her way. I turned my eyes
from her, knowing I would see enough of her before the day was
done.

"Work fast," I told Jeddy. "Get out boarding axes and cut all rigging. Lower away the boats. Get the prisoners on deck and into the
boats, and the wounded too."

Boyle ran under our stern, his crew as silent and watchful as
though we were strangers.

"Do anything!" I heard him shout. "Anything! Prisoners? Can I
take prisoners? Any belongings? Can I take anybody? Anything?"

There was the least possible chance that one boatload of people
had time to pass from us to the *Chasseur*.

I turned to look at the Ransomes and Captain Parker. There was
a smug look about Parker and Sir Arthur, for which I could not blame
them; but Lady Ransome's face I could not see, because she was
sitting on the deck, with Pinky still in her arms, and was too busy
with him to notice me.

"No, indeed, thank you," Sir Arthur said, in answer to my un-
spoken question, and I remember how mislikable I found his pro-
nunciation of "thank you," which was "think yaw." "No, indeed!
We'll stay where we are!"

I waved to Boyle to go on. "Stand by," I called to him, "until the
Lively Lady's gone. I don't want her taken!"

Boyle nodded vigorously; the *Chasseur* slipped away into the
south; and to me her departure seemed like that of an old, dear
friend, so that my heart was like lead.

The seventy-four was close on us: no more than a half mile away.
Our prisoners were on deck and our boats in the water, and Jotham
Carr was seeing to bringing the wounded from the cabin. There was
only one thing left to be done. Since I wished to be sure it *was* done,

I warned Jeddy not to strike our colors till I returned; and with that I ran forward and down into the carpenter's quarters.

There was an old roundabout jacket belonging to Rowlandson Drown lying on the bench, where he had dropped it less than ten minutes before he was killed. I picked it up and hung it on a nail and tried not to think about it as I poured varnish over the shavings and worked with my phosphorus bottle and a match to get a light.

The drenched shavings burst into flames with a roar, and I fled back on deck pursued by a blast of heat that singed my shirt. The seventy-four, hove-to at pistol-shot distance, was like a black cliff, bristling with guns. Her bulwarks, rigging and ports were a-swarm with men—as many as can be found in Arundel and Cape Porpus put together.

At the sight of me, Jeddy pulled down our colors with such eager-ness that I knew the seventy-four had been threatening to throw a shot at us if it was not done speedily.

I looked around, but could see nothing else that needed doing. Lady Ransome sat in the stern of the longboat, still with Pinky in her arms. Beside her sat her husband, his blanket full of belongings at his feet. I sent them away; then shouted up to the gold epaulettes shining above the gaily painted taffrail that we were on fire and needed boats. After that, as well as I could for the growing heaviness in my head, I took my last look at the *Lively Lady*.

They wasted no time getting us aboard, for a burning privateer is no welcome neighbor to any ship. Knowing the customs of our cap-tors, I thought they would put us in that stinking, three-foot-high den in the bows known as the cable tier, and leave us to rot in the dark on the slime-covered coils of the cable. I have no doubt that if this seventy-four had been one of the ships used for transporting Ameri-can prisoners, we would have received the same inhuman treatment suffered by thousands of captured Americans during the war; but it had fallen to our lot to be taken by the *Granicus*, Captain Wise commanding, and this Captain Wise was as pleasant and as easy to be with as any of our own great captains. Why Decatur and Perry and Lawrence and Hull and MacDonough should be quiet, companionable, polite, pleasant, thoughtful men, and the greatest of our fighters to boot, and why our incompetents should have been selfish blusterers, I do not know; but that was the truth of it. The captains I have named would not, I have heard men say, permit their crews to be whipped for offenses, and this was also true of Wise; but throughout the entire British navy of more than eight hundred ships there was hardly an officer who would not tie up any member of his crew for the smallest infraction of discipline and see his back chopped into bleeding mincemeat. I say here, in no spirit of rancor, that British naval officers, taking them by and large, were more cruel and brutal than can possibly be realized by persons who are sheltered in peaceful homes, and sleep securely on soft beds under warm blankets; so to find myself in the hands of a man like Wise was as great a surprise as to drop a hook among a school of sculpins and catch a fat beefsteak.

We were paraded before him as soon as we were aboard. He stood at the quarter-deck rail, staring down at us, a thin, tall man, possibly fifty years of age. His hair was crinkly brown, heavily shot with gray; and he had a habit of half closing his eyes before he spoke, so that he seemed about to deliver himself of an angry remark.

"I'm told," he said to us gruffly, "that the prisoners aboard your brig were well treated, and I'm a believer in turn about. I'll therefore put you to lodge on the orlop deck, and you'll be in charge of your own officers until you pass out of my control and into the hands of the Transport Office. I expect orderly conduct from you, even though I've heard that such a thing is seldom found where American seamen are concerned. Until I'm disabused you'll receive the same rations issued to the people of this man-of-war."

He turned on his heel; then swung back to us again. "I'd like to see your captain in my cabin."

When I stepped forward he nodded curtly, spoke briefly to a young officer near him, and walked off without another word.

Tommy Bickford would have followed me with my duffel bag; but a red-coated marine took it from him.

I cast a final look around as I mounted to the quarter-deck of this towering vessel. Back under our lee, a smudge of black smoke pouring from her forward hatch, lay the *Lively Lady*, forlorn and untidy, her foremast dragging in the Channel chop; her mainsail lying half over the side, slack and useless, like a broken wing. A mile to the south I saw the *Chasseur* slipping toward the southeast. Even as I looked she hauled her wind and stood back toward us again, so I knew there would be no better days in store for the poor hulk we had just left. Boyle would sink her if she didn't sink herself. I tried to remember, watching her, when it was I had brought the cheese to Boyle; but I could only remember it was long, long ago.

The young officer spoke to me, sharp and haughty, ordering me to follow; and I stumbled after him with a slack and gone feeling, as though my legs and brain were stuffed with straw.

The captain's cabin in one of these British seventy-fours is a palace by itself, rising from the rear of the quarter-deck like a rich house set down at the end of a village green; and I, entering it, felt myself shabby, with something of mendicancy and disgraceful misfortune about me.

The young officer rapped at a paneled door and stood aside for me to pass in, looking as though he wished me the worst luck in the world. I entered a low-ceiled room that seemed enormous, larger than our living room in Arundel, and stood before this tall, thin, crinkly-haired captain. He had laid aside his great cocked hat and was sitting at a polished table with a hand on either knee and his lips pursed as though he intended to clap me in chains for life.

"I've been told, sir," he said, without preamble, "that you purposely set fire to a prize."

"No, sir; I did not."

"I have the word of an Englishman for it!" He eyed me coldly. "I have his word you shouted to the commanding officer of the privateer brig that annoyed me so determinedly before I came up with you. You told him to stand by until your vessel had been destroyed."

"I didn't strike my colors until after the fire had broken out," I said.

"Then you set the fire?"

"Yes, sir."

"Then in effect you set fire to British property; for you had no means of escaping and were as good as captured."

"It wasn't a prize till I struck my colors," I repeated, feeling dull and numb. "You might have blown up."

Despite my hair-splitting, he gave me a courteous reply.

"So I might! So I might! I never thought of that!" He compressed his lips again and made a flirting motion with his hand. "That's no reason, however. If you destroyed a prize with no greater justification, I shall be forced to take steps. I'll be forced to make representations to the Transport Office."

There was a dull roar far astern, like the muffled rumble of a nearing thunderstorm, and I knew I would never set eyes on the *Lively Lady* again. Something seemed to go from me, so that I could hardly stand on my feet before this captain, who suddenly appeared to me more powerful than any man I had ever met. I saw he was waiting for me to speak.

"Well," I said, "there was no way out of it. I passed my word."

He frowned. "Come, come, Captain! You'd better tell me the full tale. And let me have your name, while you're about it."

"Nason; the *Lively Lady*, eighteen guns and——"

"Yes," he said, flirting his hand again, "yes, yes! Wise is my name: *Granicus*, seventy-four. Now, Captain Nason."

"Well," I said, "there it is." For the life of me I couldn't remember what he'd asked me.

Captain Wise eyed me closely. "So you passed your word, did you?"

"Yes. I couldn't get the brig till I passed my word she shouldn't fall into the hands of the British. I passed my word, and so I got her."

"Indeed! And to whom did you pass your word?"

"Robert Surcouf," I said. "Fox-faced man. Damned French pirate. Asked double what she was worth and made me give my word to boot."

"Was that Surcouf of St. Malo?"

"Yes. Surcouf. Look out for him. Had to have her, and he traded close, damn him. There's worse people than Yankees, and you can tie to it."

"And where did Surcouf get her?" he wanted to know. It seemed to me his face had come loose from its fastenings, for it appeared to slip sideways: then waver back into place.

"Get her?" I asked. "He built her! The *Revenant*. Meant *Revenge*, Jeddy said. He's a crazy little fool. She never meant *Revenge*. She's a ghost. I mean she *was* the *Ghost*. I took her out of the grave, Captain, and made her the *Lively Lady*, but now she's a ghost that's laid for good, green dress, red hair and all."

With that, feeling somewhat upset because of the throbbing in my shoulder, I laughed at the thought of the ghost that had been laid— laughed till the tears ran down my cheeks and till I had to hang to the table. Then I found myself in a chair, drinking a glass of brandy, and heard Captain Wise at the cabin door, passing the word for the surgeon.

"Well, well," he said, "well, well, well, well! So that was the *Revenant!* Well, well, well! I should have you shot for that, my boy! Well, well, well, well! The *Revenant*."

I might have fallen asleep from the persistence with which he repeated himself and the regularity with which he nodded his head as he sat staring at me, if the surgeon had not come in, a man both pompous and obsequious, followed by a pimply-faced assistant smelling of medicines.

"Now," Wise said, "anything wrong with you? Get hurt this morning?"

"No," I said, not liking the looks of the surgeon. "Nothing. Nothing at all."

The surgeon's assistant had my coat off and whipped the shirt over my head before I could down the last of my brandy.

"Pretty!" the surgeon said, looking at my shoulder. "Sweet as a daisy. Very finely cushioned by the deltoid muscle." He prodded me with a forefinger like a red banana. "Hm! Hard! Surprised the splinter didn't bounce off! Take out half a pint of blood and he'll be better than ever!"

He bled me, as I knew he would; for these navy surgeons bleed a man for everything under God's heaven—for headache, toothache and footache; for burns, frostbites, loss of memory and even loss of blood. Whenever they don't know what to do, they bleed their patients; and since they seldom know what to do they're forever bleeding someone. Yet I must admit that when he had taken a cupful of blood from my arm I felt relieved.

"How'll he do for dinner?" Captain Wise asked the surgeon, while the assistant helped me on with my shirt.

"Admirably," the surgeon said. "Ten minutes' rest and he'll be fit to eat a sheep!" He went away with his assistant, wheezing mirthfully like a porpoise clearing his nose of a vast accumulation of air and water.

"Yes," Captain Wise said, "a bite of dinner'll do you no harm. It'll occupy your mind and improve my own. I've heard monstrous strange tales about Americans, but I've had few opportunities to speak with them."

The wheezy surgeon was right; for after I had stretched myself for a time on the berth in the small gun-deck cabin in which I was stowed by the captain's orders, and had freed myself of blood and powder stains and struggled into the clean clothes Tommy Bickford had stuffed in my duffel bag, there was a stiffness in my shoulder; but the blackness that filled my brain after the blowing up of the *Lively Lady* had fallen away, as the tide falls on our Arundel beaches, though now and again a black wave came out of the receding tide and lapped at my brain once more, as I suppose must always be the case whenever a tide goes out.

Sir Arthur and Lady Ransome were in the captain's cabin when I went to it, and Captain Parker as well; and I cannot deny feeling bitter when I saw how they had become gay and light-hearted and inclined to toss scraps of gaiety to me, whether I wanted them or not.

"Ow, Captain," Sir Arthur said, as I came toward them, "we owe you an apology, I fear, for making you a trifle late for your appointment at the Island of Jersey."

I smiled as pleasantly as I could.

"Jersey!" Captain Wise exclaimed. "Weren't you getting a little deep in enemy waters?"

Sir Arthur laughed spitefully. "You'd not have thought so, Captain, if you'd heard Mr. Nason making free with our Channel, no longer ago than last night! You'd have thought the place was full of his friends! He was talking, even, of blockading Great Britain!" He stared at me. I looked from him to Lady Ransome and felt a sudden tightness in my breast to see her bend down her head as if to hide the wave of color that mounted suddenly into her face.

"I think that was Captain Boyle," I said. "It's Captain Boyle who intends to blockade you."

Captain Wise made a mildly explosive sound in his throat. "I've heard of him!" he said. "In the Indies. The whole British navy has heard of him. It wasn't Boyle—why, by God, sir, of *course* it was Boyle who squittered around me like a petrel! So that was Boyle! I nearly ran off after him when you got under way this morning. Why, I'd as soon expect to mash a flea with my best bower anchor as catch that gentleman!"

He led the way to the table and, when we were seated, looked at me sharply. "Your brig, now," he said. "How did she sail with Boyle's brig?"

"About the same," I told him. "Under favorable circumstances we did fifteen knots."

He shook his head wonderingly. "I can't account for it. Boyle's vessel was American built, I take it."

"Yes. Baltimore built."

"We can't build such vessels," Captain Wise said, "and if we could, we couldn't sail 'em."

Sir Arthur widened his eyes slightly. "Don't you think it possible, Captain, that Americans brag a little faster than they sail?"

Captain Wise studied Sir Arthur carefully. "No," he said at length, "no, I regret to say that doesn't explain it. We've taken a few of these fast American vessels, but had the devil's time trying to use 'em. We're afraid of their long masts, so we shorten 'em. We strengthen the hulls and find we have tubs."

"And may I ask, Captain Wise," Sir Arthur asked, "whether or not you've ever been in America? You appear to display a peculiar tolerance for its people. Ah—they shoot birds sitting!"

Captain Wise coughed. "Then I wish to God, sir, they'd be as thoughtful of us and wait till we sit!" He turned to me. "You people are different from us on sea, and I've heard you're more so on land. Yet most of you are only two or three generations out of England. How do you explain the difference, Captain Nason?"

I think I got red, and I know I spoke foolishly; for what came upon my tongue were only the stock phrases of our politician orators. "I think it's the air of liberty we breathe that makes us different. Our fathers won our freedom from British bondage; we cast off the shackles——"

Suddenly I stopped, remembering in what plight I stood myself at that lamentable moment, and seeing that the others thought it strange I should speak just then of freedom and the casting off of shackles.

Captain Wise coughed again; not even Sir Arthur looked at me, and the air seemed heavy with discomfort. It was Lady Ransome who spoke; her voice was low, and her eyes hidden by her lashes.

"Freedom," she murmured. "Yes, Americans seem to love freedom; and what will so many of them do when they're in our prisons?" She spoke the last word in so faint a voice that it was scarcely audible.

I stared at the table, unwilling to trust myself to look at her. Her husband laughed comfortably. "It's to be feared, my dear," he said, "that you've asked a question Mr. Nason will unfortunately soon be able to answer. Fortunes of war, fortunes of war!"

Lady Ransome didn't look up, and Captain Wise cleared his throat. "I was thinking about your little dog, Captain Nason. Lady Ransome tells me the dog she brought aboard is yours, but is nevertheless English. My thought was this: for a time American prisoners in English prisons were allowed to keep dogs, but there got to be too many of them, and someone gave an order they should all be killed. I'm afraid there was great lamentation: rather hard on the poor men, because seven hundred of those little comrades of theirs were destroyed on one day. Too bad, too bad!"

He assumed an air of gruffness that deceived no one. "Too bad, of course! Ah—since your little dog's already in Lady Ransome's custody and seems happy with her, it might be—you know your own business best, of course—Sir Arthur being a sportsman—ah, I thought it might be well if Sir Arthur could persuade you to—ah——"

"I'd consider it a great honor," I said, "if Lady Ransome would accept my dog: a great honor and a great relief, for to have him killed would be worse than——"

"No," Sir Arthur interrupted promptly. "The dog has points; I've noticed him, but I shouldn't want to be indebted. I don't mind purchasing the dog for my wife; but no gifts! No gifts!"

Lady Ransome looked up; her hand was at her throat, flat against it, so I could see the little indentations in the smooth skin over her knuckles. Yet the fingers seemed almost to flutter, as if she were about to make a gesture toward me; and I wondered, if her impulse carried, what that impulse would be.

"Of course," I said to Sir Arthur. "However it's done, it's a favor to me. Make the price whatever you like."

"Ow!" Sir Arthur said, "I never make an offer. *You* make the price, you know: if it's reasonable, I accept: if not, I won't, eh?"

I have no doubt, as I have said, that the man tried always to be just and fair; yet to my way of thinking he could do and say nothing gracefully.

"Would two pounds be too much?" I asked.

"Ow, not in the least," Sir Arthur said. He drew a wallet from his breast pocket, took out three bits of paper, and tossed them across the table. "I think he's worth all of three pounds, you know!"

I picked them up and put them in my pocket, unmindful of his manner in my relief at Pinky's safety.

"That's right," Captain Wise said, "that's right. You'll find use for that before you know it."

There was a knock on the door, and the captain's polite young secretary entered and bowed. "Land, sir," he said. "Wembury Point."

"Plymouth!" Sir Arthur said. "We're nearly home, eh, Nason?"

At the word "home" I turned to Lady Ransome sharply, as though she had spoken. She was staring full at me, almost haggardly; and for that moment it seemed to me, strangely, that we were actually speaking to each other, though I could not have said what the words were or even what they meant.

Suddenly she sprang up. "Plymouth?" she cried to Captain Wise, "Plymouth? But that means—Dartmoor!"

"Yes," he said, and he seemed ill at ease. "I—that is—well, really, there's nothing to be done about it: you'll go to the depot at Dartmoor, Captain Nason."

XX

T<small>HE</small> harbor of Plymouth is cup shaped, with deep green hills rising abruptly from it; and because of the persistent rain that fell as long as I stayed there, it gave me the feel of a large green funnel that was gathering all the misery in the world and pouring it down my neck.

We moved up, in the early morning, past a partly finished breakwater between the sound and the inner harbor; and I, thinking to myself that I must, if possible, have a final word with Lady Ransome before I was taken ashore, set out to go on deck, only to find myself stopped by a red-coated marine on guard at the cabin door.

"Captain's orders," he said, barring my way with his cutlass. "Prisoners to be took to the berth deck for disembarking."

I backed up and sat on the edge of my bunk, half desperate with disappointment. I had watched and watched, the night before, and vainly tried for a word alone with her, for I couldn't forget the little movement of her hand at her throat. It had seemed to me, the more I thought of it, that there was something she wanted to say to me but couldn't. Later, half asleep in my berth, I could have sworn I heard her voice in my ear: not a dream voice, but a living voice, saying nothing of importance, but saying it so distinctly that I started up on my mattress, dry throated and my heart pounding fit to push my ribs apart.

The marine shuffled his feet outside the door and coughed. "Cap-

tain's orders," he repeated. "Prisoners to be took to the berth deck
for disembarking."

"Now?" I asked him.

"Yerss," he said.

There was nothing for it but to go, so I picked up my duffel bag
and followed him into the bowels of the ship.

Our men were peering from ports at the slanting drifts of rain that
tinged the green hills of Plymouth with a bluish haze. They were
guarded by so many marines that I thought there must have been a
mutiny, though I soon found this to be the custom of the British
where American prisoners were concerned.

Tommy Bickford took my bag. "Where we going, Cap'n Dick?"
he asked.

Jeddy and 'Lisha Lord pushed up close to hear the answer. When
I told them Dartmoor, they blinked, as a dog blinks at a threatened
blow.

We came to anchor in that portion of the harbor known as
Hamoaze, and no time was wasted getting boats into the water and
us into them, so that the *Granicus* might be relieved of the burden
of feeding us. As we lay in the boats and cutters, sopping up rain
like sponges, I stared and stared at the quarter-deck of the *Granicus*
and at the cabin windows, unwilling to admit I had looked for the
last time on the face of Lady Ransome, and her hair like rubbed
copper, and her smoke-colored eyes that had silently asked me for
God knew what. But in return for all my staring I saw only rivulets
of rain water trickling from the galleries, and an occasional scowling
face peering from the after ports.

They put us ashore in the drizzle; and even at this hour in the
morning we found ourselves surrounded by drunken sailors out of
grogshops, trulls with voices like knives, old women carrying jugs of
ale and baskets full of cakes, fried eels and boiled sheep's heads;
by Devon farmers in corduroy breeches, red vests that dropped half
down their fat thighs, and little tight brimless yellow caps like the
scooped-out half of a pumpkin.

Some pitied us and others didn't. "Look at 'em!" a trull screamed, pointing at Jeddy and me, "look at 'em, sayin' they're Amairicans, when there ain't nobody as don't know Amairicans has red skins."

The English sailor with her looked at her gravely, raised her chin with his forefinger, and hit her fair on the jaw. She went down in a heap in the mud. He swayed on his feet, wagging his head at us drunkenly. "Sportsmen!" he said. "Tha's what we are! Treat prisoners like sportsmen even if they *be* a lot o' blasted rebels!"

Our escort of a hundred moon-faced Devonshire militiamen started us off at last, up the steep streets of Plymouth and away from the sour smell and the mud. As we went, Plymouth seemed more than ever like a funnel; for a piercing wind roared down the abrupt roadways, rain beat into our soggy garments, and brown driblets of water wriggled from foothole to foothole in the claylike mud.

I expected, when we reached the top of the hill, to march off on a level to wherever we were going. Yet when we had toiled up we found the top was only the beginning of another range of hills, somewhat less green than those near the ocean; and when we had labored up the second range we found a third before us, brownish and sad looking, drenched with rain, and wreathed in ragged veils of fog. Beyond the third was a fourth, and beyond the fourth, a fifth; and through all the length of that sullen, interminable day the hills mounted before us, so that the road was like a never-ending river of mud pouring down from some monstrous reservoir high up among the dirty scud of cloud and mist and rain.

The color of those hills changed gradually from brown to gray, and then to a dark gray; so that the country was as somber as it was chill and watery. There were no trees or shrubs on that vast expanse of rolling countryside, and no houses—only here and there, at wide intervals, a hut that seemed to shrink into itself at the threatening hills that frowned upon it. As we went higher there were patches of snow, and a biting dampness to the air such as I have never felt on any ocean.

We plodded upward all that cold wet morning, and in the afternoon we came to the longest of those long hills, its top lost in a driving gurry of snow and rain. There were stupendous granite pinnacles and knobs jutting from its dingy surface as though an angry God had pelted it with the leavings from the rest of the world.

There was a confused babbling before and behind us, and I caught the word "Dartmoor." Jeddy pulled at the sleeve of the moon-faced Devonshire militiaman beside us. "Is this Dartmoor?"

The soldier looked at us stolidly. "Dartymoor be oop," he said thickly.

It seemed to us the hill would never end; but we topped it at last and found ourselves looking off at a country faintly like that through which we had already mounted, and yet unlike it. It was more gigantic, as though we were seeing what we had already passed through, but seeing it magnified and distorted by weariness and hunger, or by a sick man's dream. The ground before us swept off into a broad valley, and then up to tremendous remote heights, treeless and houseless, and dotted here and there by fingers and spikes of granite, small-seeming things in that enormous expanse. The road, empty of all life and unsheltered by any tree or house from the drive of the rain and snow-laden wind, stretched off ahead of us like a dirty string.

The valley and the distant hills were almost black, except where snow lay on them; and what was more, the drab soil around us, when I poked at it with my fingers, was not good clean dirt, but a slimy black peat, unhealthy and decayed.

"Dartymoor," the soldier beside us said, and I thought there was complacency in his voice. Certainly there was pride in the gesture he made with his musket toward the dreadful land that faced us, though how any person could look at it except with horror was beyond me; for if ever a place looked like an abode for devils and lost souls, it was that swarthy, sinister moor.

We were like blind insects, it seemed to me, crawling and crawling up the roof of a great black barn: insects that might be blotted from the face of nature with little exertion and no regret.

They gave us no rest, these pie-faced Devonshire soldiery, but drove us on, across the somber hills, past up-thrust granite arms that seemed to threaten us; up and up, and down and down, and up and up again; and late in the afternoon we came to a wretched square stone house, rising from pools of water in which sad ducks paddled. Beyond it we saw another, and beyond that a bend in the road and a downward path to a shallow, desolate valley where there were more houses.

Beyond the houses, sprawled against a dingy hill slope, lay a circular mass of granite; a sort of giant millstone.

We stared at it and stared at it, lurching drunkenly down the slope like mud-caked scarecrows; but if any man of us had a thought in his head, either fearful or otherwise, about that dark and hulking prison, he kept it to himself.

XXI

THE shape of that miserable place, as I have said, was vaguely the
shape of a monstrous millstone or cartwheel. The outer rim of the
wheel was a stone wall a mile in length and twelve feet in height;
and thirty feet from it was the inner rim of the wheel: a similar wall,
twelve feet in height as well. Around the top of each wall was
stretched a wire to which bells were hung, and if any part of the
wire was touched, no matter how lightly, the bells set up a clangor;
and every guard in hearing came running with his loaded musket.

Projecting from the inner rim at intervals were loopholed bastions;
so when the guards ran into the bastions and up the steps with which
they were supplied they could sweep the entire prison yard with
their muskets and cut down any person who might be striving to
mount the wall.

This enormous tilted cartwheel was divided into equal parts by a
high stone wall running through its center. On one side of the wall
were offices, guardhouses and storehouses. On the other side were
the prison buildings, seven of them, each one shaped like a huge
New England barn, but their walls built entirely of stone, and all of
them pointing inward to a common center, like clumsy spokes in this
vast wheel. The seven buildings were again divided, three being in
a yard by themselves on one side of the semicircle, and three in a
yard on the other side; and in between, standing alone and walled
off from the three to the right and the three to the left, was the odd
prison, Prison Number Four, which was the deepest and darkest in

the place, barring the Cachot or Black Hole itself; for it was in Number Four that those Frenchmen who were known as Romans lived, and King Dick and his court, and all the Americans who had been captured up to this time.

The high wall that separated the prison half of the cartwheel from the other half was pierced in the center by a high barred gate, and the gate led from the prison half into a market place, a hundred feet square, which might be regarded as the hub of the wheel.

We were driven like sheep beneath a stone archway in the outer wall, taken in hand by a detachment of bare-kneed Scotch soldiery, and herded down through the inner gate and into a small stone house that stood on our left, near the hospital. Our clothes were soaked and covered with mud. There was mud in our hair, even; and some of us could not stand upright because of the blisters on our feet.

They wrote our names in a book, giving us numbers: putting down our rank, when we were received, where we were born; our ages and statures and appearance; the shape of our faces, the color of our hair and eyes, the marks on our bodies—all the things that would help them catch us again in case we escaped.

While we stood waiting for this wearisome duty to be completed there was a shouting of sentries outside, and a stir and bustle among the clerks who were taking our names, and with that in came a florid-faced, hook-nosed man with a high chest and thick upper arms and curly brown hair, dressed in the uniform of a naval officer. This man was Thomas Shortland, captain in the royal navy: agent for prisoners of war at Dartmoor; and we were not long in discovering what thousands of Americans already knew—that if ever a man deserved to burn in hell, it was Thomas Shortland.

I was sure, as soon as I looked at him, that he would have a touchy temper; for this is something, I have found, which often accompanies curly brown hair.

"My God!" Shortland exclaimed angrily to one of the clerks, "what's Pellew thinking of to send me this number of men! A hundred of them, and there's already nine thousand in the prison!" He stamped up and down; and I knew, from the look of him and the rage he was in, that to attempt to speak with him about getting a parole would be doing all of us a disservice.

"Give these men hammocks, blankets, and mattresses," he snapped. "Yes, and mess equipment. You, Hawkens: see they get mess equipment, and spun yarn for slinging their hammocks."

They brought us our bedding: a hammock of fair quality, a mattress about an inch in thickness, stuffed with something that felt like wet wadded newspaper, and a blanket that might have held out wind if it could have been tarred.

When the clerks were done with us we shouldered our bedding and limped into the rain, to find our bags waiting. We picked them up, whereupon the Scotch soldiers marched us through still another gate and down across the empty square market place, which would have been the hub of the hulking wheel to which I have likened the prison. We could see the square front of Number Four Prison ahead of us, with dim lights shining from its six end windows: windows that gave it the look of glaring at us out of ancient, rheumy, hating eyes.

The soldiers pushed us through iron gates at the far end of the market place, and a warden led us between two strong walls, up to the face of the building and around a corner to an entranceway. He fumbled at the door, rattling a key in the lock. There was a stale, sour smell around us, in spite of the bitter wind that whipped the raindrops through our sodden garments.

When the door creaked open, a volcanic blast of noise and fetid air surged out. "Git along in!" the warden shouted. "'Urry up! Don't tike the 'ole bloody night!"

I don't know how I had come to think of Dartmoor as a place of small stone cells in which manacled men lay eternally on the floor, groaning. This was how I had thought of it; but now that the iron-studded door had closed behind us I saw there were neither cells nor manacles. If there were groanings, they were completely lost in a deafening hubbub of gabbling, laughing and hurrooing, shot through with scraps of song, shrill whistlings, and a clatter of iron against iron.

An enormous room lay before us, with colonnades of slender posts extending from floor to ceiling along the length of it, as though hundreds of small schooners, stripped of standing and running rigging, were moored close together, not only along the walls, but down the center of the room as well. Thus it had the look of the most tremendous stable in the world, with stalls for hundreds of horses; but instead of horses between the masts or posts or stanchions or whatever you wish to call them, there were men squatting around kettles in groups of six, eating, drinking, laughing and shouting; men sewing at garments, or searching themselves for vermin, or reading in books and newspapers, or playing games, or busy at pursuits that were mysteries to us. Among them were flickering candles whose yellow beams seemed to make their garments and their faces yellow, but to cast no illumination whatever on the remainder of their prison. Thus the masts or stanchions vanished into the upper murk, and the yellow company was outlined against a wall whose swartness glittered strangely, though it was not till later that I saw the glitter was caused by the reflection of the candles on moisture that trickled unendingly down the face of the dark stones.

The pressure of the men pushed me into an alleyway between the stanchions, an alleyway that ran the length of the building. The men in the stalls, most of them clad in sleazy roundabout jackets, saffron yellow in color and stamped back and front with the black TO TO of the Transport Office, never so much as raised their eyes. We dragged ourselves wearily a little farther down the alley, and then a little farther, helpless and friendless, but ever hopeful of finding a spot where we might squeeze in and rest.

It seemed to me that every inch of floor space in this great prison house was occupied, and we doomed to wander through laughing, yelling prisoners until too exhausted to move farther.

Yet we were strangely succored, and by one who aimed to persecute us, as is sometimes the case in this life. Jeddy Tucker, suddenly dropping his bag and hammock at my feet, reached silently for a gangling, saffron-colored figure hunkered on the floor, searching his body for vermin like a yellow monkey.

When Jeddy pulled him to his feet, I saw it was Eli Bagley, whom we had last seen heading to the westward in his crazy brig, hopeful, like Columbus, of reaching the American continent.

He stared at us open-mouthed for a moment; then burst into malevolent laughter. "Gol durn ye!" he said to Jeddy, and his wandering gaze included me as well, "they got ye!"

He was a miserable object, dirty and with no shirt beneath his yellow roundabout jacket; and when I looked into the stall in which he had been squatting I saw men no more savory-looking than Bagley.

He laughed again, excitedly. "I thought you wouldn't never get took! By gorry, I wished you was here last winter, when we didn't have no clothes nor fires nor nothing."

"Where can we hang these hammocks?" I asked him.

"You go to Tophet!" he squealed, his lantern-jawed face a fiery red, and his chin whisker trembling with rage. Then he grew calmer, as though realizing we were all Americans together. "Well," he said, scratching himself uncertainly, "well——"

"Go on, Bagley," Jeddy urged him. "We never did anything to you that you didn't deserve."

"You belong up on the next floor," he said, peering at us sharply. "All your people are up there. Go on up them steps—" he pointed to a long flight of stone stairs opposite the doorway through which we had entered, stairs that ascended into the darkness in which the ceiling was shrouded—"and when you've clumb 'em, ask for King Dick."

He pressed his nutcracker lips tight together, then doubled over, slapping his knees and cackling.

We shouted to the drabbled, mud-smeared men who stood crowded in the alleyway behind us, staring at the tumult and movement of this vast cavern of a prison with the yellow pinpoints of countless candles reflected in their eyes. They turned and made their way up the stone stairway, looking, as they mounted that steep slope, bent beneath the burdens of their bags and hammocks, like the picture in the Bible that my mother brought from England in her sailing days—the picture showing the building of the Tower of Babel.

Jeddy and I climbed the stairs last of all to find our crew huddled close together at the top. I saw there was trouble brewing; for the huddled men had lowered their bags and hammocks to the floor and were hitching at their trousers and sleeves, as men do when on the verge of using their fists.

When we pushed through them and came into the front rank, we saw we were in another vast stable-like room, no different from the one on the lower floor. Similar rows of stanchions extended as far as we could see in the gloom, and candles made innumerable golden points through its dim cavernous length. Yet there was a difference; for it had a ranker smell to it, a smell something like that in the den of a fox; and above all else the prisoners were different. On the floor below they had paid no attention to us, so that we felt alone and forgotten, and therefore helpless. Here, on the other hand, there were faces turned toward us wherever we looked: thin, mean, pockmarked faces that made quick movements, like animals watching in the deep forest, raising and lowering their heads as though to catch our scent.

They were ugly faces, gray-looking even in the yellow light of the candles, and gaunt. Some of these unsavory folk were clothed, and badly clothed, in yellow rags or grayish rags; whereas others wore nothing except pieces of cloth twisted around their loins.

It was easy to tell from the look in these men's eyes that we weren't welcome, and I knew we would do well to get away quickly, since we were in no condition to fight—not even to fight naked scarecrows.

"I want King Dick," I said. "Which is King Dick?"

A voice among these watching faces said something in French. They were all Frenchmen, I saw, and bad ones, too, if it's possible to tell anything from a man's face. A squatting, half-naked figure

close to us rose on hands and knees. A knife was tucked in his right
hand so that the blade extended halfway up his bare gray arm. He
snarled at us, using a word I had never heard before.

"Shut your mouth!" Jeddy cried. He threw his clothes bag at the
half-naked man, knocking him in a heap. He followed the bag like
a cat, dragged the man to his feet and drove a fist into his wind-
pipe, so that he sprawled to the floor and lay there. Jeddy snatched
up the knife which the half-naked man had dropped, and recovered
the clothes bag at the same time.

The rest of the ragged men scrambled upright and glared silently
at us. Most of them, I saw, had knives; and I quickly decided that
if blows were to be struck, we had best strike first. The thought had
no sooner passed through my head than I heard a shrill, high voice,
far away and beyond the circle of snarling French faces, shouting
querulously, "Frawg! Frawg! Frawg!" With that the angry Frenchmen sank back as if they had been puppets, deserted by their guid-
ing hand. The anger vanished miraculously from their faces, and they
cast only occasional glances at us from the corners of their eyes.

The distant shout of "Frawg!" was picked up by other voices, all
strangely high. It occurred to me suddenly that these were the voices
of Negroes.

We became conscious of a bustle not far from us: a scurrying and
hustling. Figures approached between the stanchions, one a towering, giant figure. As it came close enough to be lighted by the feeble
yellow candlelight, we saw it to be that of a gigantic Negro. He wore
a bearskin hat, so that he seemed eight feet tall; and in his right hand
he carried a long club, like the handle of a boarding pike, but thicker
and gnarled. His face was a soft, sooty black, like the black on the
bottom of a kettle, and his head seemed too small for his enormous
body, rather like a melon balanced on an up-ended long gun. Yet
his mouth and eyes made up in size for the smallness of his head;
for his mouth stretched all the way across his face, as though slashed
with a knife; while his eyes, possibly because of their whiteness

against the sooty black of his skin, had the appearance of china door-knobs set on swivels.

On each side of this tremendous man, as he bore down on us with eyes rolling from side to side, were two smaller Negroes: one a scowl-ing, bowlegged, ape-like man in a bright green coat reaching nearly to his heels—a personage whom we came to know later as the Bishop; and the other a worried-looking darky with a peculiar habit of con-stantly looking behind him. The worried-looking one, we afterward found, was known as the Duke because he claimed to have been one of the secretaries of the Duke of Kent.

The towering black man and his two attendants came to a halt over the Frenchman who had been hit. He still lay where he had fallen, clutching at his throat.

"Heah!" the huge Negro said in a plaintive, light voice, poking the Frenchman with his stick and rolling his eyes over us, "Wha's goin' on heah? Who stirred up all 'is whuppus?"

I took the knife from Jeddy and tossed it beside the Frenchman. "I was told to come up here and ask for King Dick," I said. "These Frenchmen figured on stopping us."

He stared at me solemnly. "Who?" he demanded. "Who tole you? 'At's me! Ah'm King Dick. Ah'm King up here. Who was it tole you?"

"Bagley," I said.

"Bagley? Ole Goat-whisker Bagley? Ole Bone-face Bagley?"

I nodded.

"You an' him friends?" he persisted.

Jeddy pushed up to him like an impertinent sparrow. "Friends!" he exclaimed. "How could we be friends? We know him too well! Hell, if he knew how to sail, he'd captain a slave ship!"

King Dick peered at him carefully, then dropped his head sud-denly on one side, half closed his eyes, and giggled as though a finger had tickled him. Jeddy laughed, reaching up to slap this black hulk on the shoulder. King Dick gave way to immoderate mirth, opening his mouth until it seemed like a yawning cavern in his face; while his two henchmen viewed us somberly. His laugh eventually died, and he scanned us again with glittering roaming eyes.

"'Ese Frawgs," he said, "'ey doan' want no moh white folks messin' up 'is prison! 'Ey was fus' heah, an' 'ey get snippety when 'ey's crowded."

He turned and shook his stick at the Frenchmen, silently hunkered over mysterious pursuits. "You Frawgs!" he shouted at them, "you keep 'em stickers away fum mah sight, or you'll get youahsefs into a buckus 'at no Frawg ain't never seen nothin' like!"

He turned and waved his club over us benevolently. "Come on, you white folks," he said. "'Scuse mah delay, but we been havin' trouble wif ouah society in 'is place, so we gettin' picky an' choosy!"

XXII

I HAVE the vaguest of recollections of my first night in Dartmoor
Prison; because when I was sure my men would have food and a
place to sleep, I seemed to move in an ever thickening haze of drow-
siness, a haze that pressed against me as heavily, almost, as water;
and when my head dipped beneath its surface, as it often seemed
to do, I knew nothing, though it appeared I was able to walk and
talk and even eat a little while so submerged. I recall passing hordes
of half-clad Frenchmen, and coming among more black men than I
had ever seen together except in the West Indies. Above all else I
remember the tumult; for none of these prisoners were sitting quietly,
but were engaged in trades and traffickings, tending small shops,
crying their wares, peddling their products, crowding around gaming tables, or operating miniature restaurants and coffee stalls. All of
them, black or white, perpetually watched the movements of King
Dick, so there was no doubt about the high position he held.

He led us to the rear of the building, where one of the stalls between the stanchions had been set off from the others with strips of
canvas. In this stall was a large armchair, its frame brightly gilded
and its back and seat upholstered in red plush. Before it was a table
at which sat two white boys dressed neatly in blue roundabout
jackets, duck trousers, and varnished black hats.

King Dick took Jeddy and me into the stall with him, the Bishop
and the Duke entering close behind, as a matter of course; and indeed, unless he sent them on errands they were always trailing him

like a double shadow cast by two strong lamps. As soon as he entered, the boys leaped to attention. They, he carelessly explained, were his seckataries.

He threw himself on his red plush throne. "Heah you, Namiah!" he said to one of the seckataries, "you go git Jesus Fenton an' Pigtail an' Goose Huck an' Ayun-Haid. I want 'ose boys come a-flyin'!"

Namiah darted away.

"You, Albert," he said to the other, "you go tell Chickenfoot he doan' sell no more beer, seppen to mah frien's, 'nen git 'at plum gudgeon man an' 'at lobscouse man an' 'at freco man, an' tell 'em I say come a-runnin' wif ev'y las' scrap in 'eir kids."

He nodded and winked at us as Albert hurried off on his errand. "Ain't nobody sells no beer in 'is yah Number Foh, on'y me!" He had the proud, aloof look of the man who has reached a position of affluence and power and is telling how he did it. "You lemme 'lone in 'is prison long enough," he said confidently, "'an I'll buy it right off 'ose English white folks."

Negroes, singly and in pairs, pushed up to the opening in the front of King Dick's stall to stare at us with glistening eyes. King Dick rapped the cement floor sharply with his gnarled stick. "You, Jesus," he said to a pale Negro with thin lips and a Spanish look about him, "you git on up in 'at cock loft an' tell 'ose Frawgs in mah boxin' 'cademy Ah needs 'at space to-night. You tell 'em not to make no muckus 'bout it, lessen 'ey lookin' to git sent to Plymuff wif 'ose odder Romans."

He explained the matter to us quickly. "'Ose Romans," he said, "'ey never wore no clo'es a-tall, jus' gamble, gamble, gamble, wussen any white folks in 'is world. Ain't nobody can't stan' 'em, so we sen' 'em down into Plymuff, so's 'ey kin live in a hulk, all by 'emse'fs. But, mah lan'! We's gitten mo' of 'em ev'y day. Looks lak 'ey's allus somebody gotta be Romans!"

"You, Ayun-Haid," he continued, turning back to his henchmen and addressing a Negro whose close-cropped skull had a hard, metallic look to it, "you cut out sixty of 'ese new white folks an' take 'em up into mah 'cademy in 'at cock loft an' show 'em where 'ey hang 'ose hammicks. You an' Jesus stay wif 'em. You heah me? You stay wif 'em, an' doan' go 'way till 'em hammicks is all hung, lessen you want mah fis' bounced off yo' pan!" He flirted his stick at Iron-Head, who at once scurried among our men, gathering his flock together.

King Dick rose from his throne and addressed them tersely and to the point. Even in my half-conscious state I could feel, in this enormous, smiling Negro, an air of assurance and authority that would have done credit to the quarter-deck of a 74-gun ship.

"'Ey's close to 'leven hund'ed men in 'is Number Foh Prison," he said, "an' room foh 'bout th'ee hund'ed; so you do like Ah tell you, else you won't fin' no place to hang yo' hammicks, not a-tall. Ah's King in 'is Number Foh, an' Ah likes good white folks; but bad white folks, Ah takes an' bends 'eir jaws roun' into 'eir eahs! You go 'long up, an' Ah'll sen' up somepin foh you to chew on.'"

Seating himself, he went on with his orders: orders to Goose Huck to take one Frenchman from each of the center stalls on the second floor and bid him sling his hammock under the beams at the side of the building; then to empty six stalls entirely and scatter the occupants among the places made vacant by the single removals; orders also to Pigtail to follow Goose Huck and instantly report any insubordination on the part of the Frenchmen.

"'Em's mah odors!" he reminded Goose and Pigtail. "You tell 'em Frawgs Ah wouldn't do it, seppen it's gotta be done, an' if 'ey make huckuss 'bout it——" He pushed out his tremendous black fist, then flicked it forward, twisting it as he did so, and somehow it had the look of a projectile that would pierce six inches of oak plank.

It was about then that my senses began to slip from me for a minute at a time. In no way could I keep my ears or eyes open. I heard King Dick's voice saying, "Heah, white boy, bite yo' teef on 'is plum gudgeon," but what became of the plum gudgeon I would never have known if Jeddy had not told me, when he roused me on the following morning, that I had swallowed it in my sleep. King Dick himself, Jeddy said, had peeled off my coat, found my shoulder swollen, and so had slung my hammock in his own stall, lifting me in his arms and placing me in it as easily as though I had been five feet tall and no bigger than Emily Ransome.

Jeddy shook his head as he stood peering into my hammock. "What beats me," he said, "is the stuff this black elephant knows. I was going to call Jotham Carr to doctor your shoulder; but the King said no. He got out a chicken bone and a feather and a piece of horsehair. Then he tied the feather onto the bone with the hair and stuck it under your shoulder and said it would be all right in the morning. How does it feel? You can't cure anything with chicken bones, not that I ever heard of."

I looked at my shoulder. The soreness was gone from it, and there was a ragged shred of cloth protruding from the puncture where the splinter had entered. After I had drawn it out, the wound looked no worse than a flea bite.

"Well," I said, "he took a shine to both of us, and a good thing he did!"

King Dick came hastily into the stall while I was donning my still-damp clothes. "Slip yo' cable!" he said in his plaintive, high-pitched voice, slapping his black paws together with a smack like a longboat coming down with a run on still water. "Git yo'se'f six white folks togevver foh yo' mess, 'nen go 'long down an' git raidy to count out in messes. New men come in, prisoners allus count out."

Our mess of six included Tommy Bickford, 'Lisha Lord, Jotham Carr, and John Cromwell. We joined the throng in the rear of the prison's first floor. After we had stood there a while, jammed in with a thousand filthy Frenchmen, Negroes, and ragged, starved-looking Americans, the doors were opened, and we filed into the rain-swept prison yard. Every sixth man got the number of his mess on a ticket, and the ticket holder, in turn, received a day's rations for his mess from the prison cooks—two loaves of brown bread, a chunk of beef weighing three pounds, including bone and gristle, and a handful of vegetables.

Number Four Prison had looked evil enough the night before, with its pale eyes glaring through the rain; but in the gray light of early morning its appearance put a weight like an eighteen-pound shot in the pit of my stomach. Some of the feeling may have been caused by the sour stench of the half-naked Frenchmen who slunk through the crowded yard in twos and threes. Some, certainly, was due to the perpetual drizzle of cold rain, and the barren hills we dimly saw beyond the outer walls—hills blackened as though by fire. Most of all I think I was oppressed by the granite barriers that hemmed us in; for I now perceived that the reality of escaping over those towering walls would take more study than I had ever given any problem in navigation.

We had been in the yard less than five minutes when Jeddy spied a man with whom he had drunk a pitcher of ale at the Ship Inn in Salem when we went there to buy the North River sloop that became the *Lively Lady;* and in three seconds he had his arm across this man's shoulder, the man's name being Josiah Pettengell, a master's mate; and the two of them were as thick together as though they had married sisters.

Because of this we were soon surrounded by a dozen Salem men, a few in decent coats and breeches such as we ourselves wore, but most of them in strange saffron-colored roundabout jackets and trousers, marked with the broad arrow and the letters T. O. The jackets and trousers were undersized, as if made for children, so that their wearers looked half starved and forlorn.

They shook their heads dubiously when told how King Dick had found us places to sleep.

"You want to watch them blacks," Pettengell said; "they'll steal the nails out of your shoes if you ain't careful. They was scattered all over the building when we first come here; but they got to stealing so much, they was put all together up on the second floor."

"I notice the stealin' ain't stopped," one of the Salem men said. "Them niggers was awful handy to blame anything onto."

"They treated us all right," I told Pettengell.

"Maybe they think you got money," he said, "and aim to gamble it out of you. You better move down with us as soon as some of our Frenchmen die off. They die off pretty fast."

"Well," I said, "for a while we'll stay where we are. What's the matter with those Frenchmen up on the second floor?"

With one accord the Salem men looked over their shoulders, as men do when asked for information on odious topics.

"They're the fellers that took the place of the Romans," Pettengell said. "Give 'em time and they'll *be* Romans." He spat on the ground. The others followed his example.

"What's a Roman?" I asked, having wondered about it since hearing King Dick mention them.

"Bad Frenchmen," Pettengell said. "Bad! By God, we don't know nothing about being bad, alongside those fellers. I've shipped with tough ones, but I never see nothing like those Romans. They never wore no clothes."

"At night, you mean?" I asked.

"Hell!" said one of the Salem men, "not *never!*"

"They'd freeze," I protested.

They laughed. "Look," Pettengell said, "they was as hard all over as the sole of my foot from sleeping on stone floors without no bedding nor nothing. They slept nested against each other to keep warm. They rolled over on orders, all together, and never got took sick. They never had nothing the matter with 'em."

"No smallpox even," one of the others said.

"Hell," someone said, "that was because they'd all had it before they was weaned."

"No, it wa'n't," Pettengell said. "They never got typhus, nor colds, either. They was the healthiest folks ever I see, and the worst."

"Murder, you mean?" Jeddy asked.

"Murder!" Pettengell said. "Murder wa'n't nothing! By God!" he made a hissing sound, expressive of disgust, and the others growled assent. "You wouldn't believe it," Pettengell said. "There ain't nothing in the world as bad and dirty as a bad Frenchman, and the percentage of bad ones is awful high."

The others told what they had seen these Frenchmen doing, publicly and unashamed, and the telling made my stomach quake like a shivered topsail.

"What's the chance of escaping?" I asked, "or don't you ever think about it?"

"Escaping!" Pettengell said. "We don't think about nothing else! Listen!" He tapped me on the chest. "Until last month we ain't had anything in here. We ain't had *anything!* Nobody had no money. Most of us didn't have no clothes, only the rags we wore when we was took. The British wouldn't give us clothes. Our own government wouldn't send us clothes. Our own government wouldn't send money. You heard about Beasley yet?"

I said I hadn't.

"Reuben G. Beasley?" Pettengell persisted. "Ain't you never heard the name Reuben G. Beasley?"

We shook our heads.

Pettengell's lip drew up like an angry dog's. "Reuben G. Beasley," he said, "is American agent for prisoners of war in England." He broke into bitter profanity. "When we was dying off like flies with smallpox, he came up here and wouldn't see but one of us for fear of catching it himself. Stood and talked to one man out of all our hundreds, holding a perfumed handkerchief to his nose, and saying, 'Oh, mercy! What a confounded stench!'" Pettengell made his voice high and lisping, like a silly woman's. "That's the only time he ever come to Dartmoor; and him the American agent! When we wrote that we were starving and freezing and herded in with Frenchmen out of cesspools, he never answered our letters. When we had to lay on the stone floors of this prison with typhus and pneumonia, Beasley let us lay and die."

He eyed us furiously, and we stared back at him, wondering if it could be true.

"Well," he went on, "that's why we ain't made any escapes. It wa'n't till last month we got clothes out of Beasley—these damned yellow rags—and a prisoner's allowance: five half pennies a day.

We're rich now. Two and a half pennies a day, we get: nigh onto seven shillings every four weeks. We can buy tools. We can keep shops and make money. We can have a quid of tobacco every day or two. Give us time and we'll show you some escapes!"

There was a movement among the prisoners in our section of the yard, and I noticed there were fewer than when we had come out. Pettengell looked around. "Market's open!" he said; and with that he and his yellow-clad companions hastened away.

Jeddy laughed defiantly. "Well," he said, "that sounds pleasant, don't it!"

I left him to prowl among the French, well aware that in a short time he would know near everybody and everything worth knowing, and went back myself into Prison Number Four to see King Dick, as I had been told to do.

I could see from the activity among the Americans in our prison house that work was no hardship to them, but a Godsend. The hammocks had been triced up against the stanchions, setting off each stall or bay from the one beside it; and in nearly every bay was a group of men at work: three or four, and sometimes even the full population of the bay, which was six.

From the seriousness and diligence with which they labored, they might have been making jewelry or tapestries that would bring them thousands of dollars in wages: yet the majority were cutting soup bones into small pieces that would serve as planks in the fashioning of ship models—models that might take six months in the making. Some were plaiting straw into baskets and boxes; others were manufacturing lobscouse and plum gudgeons in kettles over small stoves.

The first and second floors, however, were quiet by comparison with the third; for the gambling tables on the third floor were already open, and the vendors of coffee and tea were shouting their wares. At the far end a Negro band practiced wild and tuneless music, rich in ragged drum-beats and wailing discords; and in another quarter Negroes rehearsed a play that had a sound of Shakespeare, but a Shakespeare grandly mangled.

I found King Dick holding court in the space which, I learned, he had reserved as a boxing academy; for he taught boxing when free of his royal duties. He was seated on a green-topped table that I was to know later as the Bishop's altar on Sunday, the royal judgment seat on weekday mornings, and a Wheel-of-Fortune table during afternoons and evenings. On one side of him was the Duke and on the other the Bishop, both glowering darkly at an abashed Negro who stood before King Dick. There was something of a crowd in attendance, mostly black men; while stretched on the floor at the outer edge of the crowd was a Frenchman in a soiled yellow Transport Office suit. As I came up, the Frenchman struggled to a sitting position and felt his jaw in a gingerly manner, moving it from side to side as though doubtful of its security.

King Dick poked the abashed Negro in the chest with his stick.

"Ah give you warnin' two weeks back, Ashmodeus Jones," he said, in a high, almost breathless voice. "Ah tol' you not come pussuckin' aroun' nat' t'eater wif so much beer in yo' stummick. Din' Ah tell you, Ashmodeus?"

The eyes of Ashmodeus rolled spasmodically in search of succor. He was manifestly unable to answer.

"Tha's what Ah done," the King went on, prodding the culprit with his staff, "an' how you foller mah odors? Ah had a complaint las' night fum Clerphus Lapp 'at when he was a-mekkin' a speech to Ot'ello, playin' he was Des'emona, an' all painted nice an' white, you was a-sittin' in nat t'eater wif anodder stummick-full of beer, jes' awful drunk, an' bus' right out a-laffin' an' a-laffin' so's he's 'bliged quit bein' Des'emona an' holler 'at you be th'owed out. 'At's what you done!"

"Ah wa'n't drunk," said the culprit feebly.

"Ah s'pose," the King said, in a faint, reedy, skeptical voice, "Ah s'pose you din' have no beer a-tall? Ah s'pose not!" He flapped one huge flat foot against the door, in time with the ragged drum-beats of the Negro band.

"Nuh-nuh-nuh, Ah had two li'l' mugs," Ashmodeus said fearfully. "Ain't nobody goin' git drunk on two mugs beer."

King Dick rapped his gnarled stick on the floor. "'At's what you say, Ashmodeus! 'At's what ev'y drunk man say. Nex' time you see someone git drunk for th'ee-foh days, you ast him how much he put into hisse'f, an' he say he had a glass or two—jes' two li'l' glasses! 'At's what he'll say! Hyuh, hyuh, hyuh!" He laughed darkly. "What Ah say is 'at you was drunk, else you wouldn't go lussuckin' aroun' nat t'eater, yellerin' an' bellerin' when Des'emona right in a purty speech. 'At's what Ah say! 'At's judgment nis co't!"

"Amen!" said the Bishop in his deep, booming voice.

"Judgment nis co't," the King went on, rising to his feet and adjusting his enormous bearskin hat upon his small head, "is 'at you git yo' jaw wiped. Nen you keep away fum 'at beer an' outen nat t'eater lessen you want git wiped th'ee-foh times, all togedder."

The eyes of the waiting audience widened expectantly. Ashmodeus looked over his shoulder like a hunted animal, saw no way of escape, and sought to hide his face behind his arms. King Dick made a quick movement with his huge left fist, a movement that caused Ashmodeus to jerk his hands convulsively toward his stomach, as if to protect it. With that King Dick's vast torso rolled to the left, and his right arm came up a short distance. Ashmodeus's head snapped back. His body became rigid and elongated. He seemed to float upward from the floor, as though drawn by a wire, and in the next instant he fell with a lummocky thud on the cement-covered floor, jerked his right knee weakly, and lay still.

"Co't's adjourned!" King Dick said. He turned indifferently from his admirers, leaving them to dispose of the insensible Ashmodeus in any way that suited them, and came to me.

"Wheah's 'at li'l' Feevolus?" he asked.

"Jeddy?" I asked. "He went around looking for someone he knew. What's a feevolus?"

"Li'l' bird," King Dick said faintly, yet shrilly, making what he may have considered a bird-like motion with his tremendous big hand.

"Li'l' pickety bird, li'l' quickety pickety bird." He flirted his hand vaguely and led me down the center of this long attic, bright by comparison with the ground floor, which was a dank and gloomy cave; brighter even than the second floor; but there were pools of water on the cement underfoot, showing that the roof leaked. There were stanchions in sections of it, as on the other floors, except at the two ends, which were airy open halls. At one end I could see a rough stage—doubtless the theater where Clerphus Lapp, painted white to represent Desdemona, had been enraged by the drunken laughter of Ashmodeus Jones. At the other end, toward which King Dick was leading me, were tables encircled by prisoners both black and white. As we came closer, my ears told me that the white patrons of the tables were French as well as Americans.

The tables were arranged in a rough circle, in the center of which were two barrels of beer on wooden trestles, and two smiling black men waiting for customers. From the players rose a shrill and perpetual gabble, an occasional bellow of "Keno!" and a peculiar ear-piercing shriek, that sounded to me like "Rit! Rit! Rit!" All this uproar, somehow, seemed a fitting accompaniment to the wailing discords of the black musicians.

King Dick signaled imperiously to one of the beer guardians, who ran out from behind his trestle.

"Gim us 'ose stools, Shellac," he said. He beamed on me engagingly. "Had yo' breakfas'?" he asked. When I shook my head he added to Shellac: "Gim us 'ose stools, 'nen tell 'at Gawge Washington Dinwiddie bring 'ose fritters ovah heah, 'nen bring us two mugs 'at beer an' wipe 'at foam off 'em. Ah doan' wan' no foam 'is mawnin' or any odder mawnin', you heah me, Shellac?"

"Yarsuh!" Shellac said. He shuffled rapidly away, to return immediately with two rough stools and two brimming mugs of beer. We were approached by a small, bowlegged Negro, shrieking at the top of his lungs and peering at us over the pile of puffy fritters that filled his tray. His monkey face was distorted by strange twitchings resulting from the trilling half scream, half whistle with which he cried his wares, "Frrrrrit! Frrrrrit! Git yo' frrrrrits!"

King Dick rapped the feet of the fritter vendor with his gnarled stick and eyed him severely. "Heah, Dinwiddie! Doan' mek all 'at noise when you see me talkin' business wif a frien'! Ah kain't think about nuffin' wif all 'at whussickin' goin' on!" He reached forward, engulfing a dozen fritters in his gigantic hand. "He'p yo'se'f," he said to me. "Ah got credit wif Dinwiddie." Dinwiddie smiled a weak, monkey-like smile; and when I had taken four of the fritters he tip-toed away, a withdrawn look about his rump, as though fearing to be called back.

King Dick stared at me out of doorknob eyes, popped two fritters into his cavern of a mouth, and washed them down with a draft of beer.

"Ah doan' mek frien's easy," he said at length. "Less you meks, less you loses." He studied his beer mug thoughtfully. "Ah heahs what you done to 'at ole Bagley; an' Ah heahs 'at li'l' boy Tommy call you Cap'n Dick. Ah doan' like Bagley; an' Dick's *mah* name, too; so Ah guess Ah's oblessickated to be frien's wif you."

"Well," I said, "we need a friend, God knows."

He nodded solemnly.

"'At li'l' Feevolus, he tol' me you figgerin' on gittin' out 'is ole prison."

"I've got to get out!"

He closed his eyes wearily. "Whuffoh you want to be like all 'ose white Americans? Allus pussuckin' roun' bout gittin' out! Whyn't you hol' yo' tongue an' be good white boy?" He washed down two more fritters.

"Don't you want to escape?"

He laughed. "Mah lan'! Ah guess Ah doan'! Ah's mekkin' money, an' Ah's keeping odor in 'is ole prison."

"Keeping what?"

"Odor," he said, chewing his fritters. "Wif mah club an' mah fis'. You seen me keepin' odor jes' now. 'Ese prison folks, Cap'n Shoatland an' 'em, 'ey's obleeged to me foh keepin' odor, an' if Ah wants to git out, Ah gits out. Ah gits out any time an' stays out th'ee houahs, foh houahs, sem houahs! Come sunny days, Ah puts on mah blue clo'es an' goes into Princetown; 'at's whah Ah goes! Whuffoh Ah want to escape, wif plenty money, an' bein' King of 'is ole Number Foh, an' goin' ovah to Princetown when Ah feels lak dussuckin' aroun' a li'l'?"

He leaned forward suddenly and closed his huge fingers around my biceps. "Mm, mm!" he said. "Kin you hit?"

I said I could hit as much as was necessary to keep a brig in order.

"Stan' up," he said, "an' take a whup at mah chin." He rose to his feet, a towering, smiling figure, and held out his chin invitingly.

"What for?" I asked.

"Ah want to see kin you hit," he said, and I saw he meant it. "Hit hahd as you kin. Ah ain't goin' to feel it."

I took him at his word and drove my fist at his velvety black jaw. To my surprise it slipped out from under the blow, so that I missed and nearly lost my balance, though I felt my knuckles graze his cheek.

He caught me with an arm like a jib boom when I staggered forward. "Mm, mm!" he said in a hushed, faded voice. "You kin almos' hit, on'y if you go lashin' out wif yo' right fis', you ain't never goin' get nowheres." He stared at me thoughtfully, caressing his cheek with fingers the size of marlinspikes. "Heah!" he said at last, "Cap'n Shoatland say 'is French war goin' be ovah one of 'ese days, 'nen all 'ese Frawgs, 'ey goin' back to France; an' all 'ose Americans in Plymuff an' Chatham an' Stapleton, 'ey comin' up heah. How you lak Ah learn you how to hit, 'nen you be king in anodder prison when 'ey all filled up wif Americans?"

"I wouldn't do it if I could," I told him. "I don't want anything except to get out."

"Ah show you plenty ways mek money," he said hopefully.

"I've got some."

He nodded, tapping his stick on the floor. "Yarse," he said. "Ah wouldn' say nuffin' about it. Ah doan' know nuffin' about you escapin', but effen Ah heahs somepin', Ah tells you or 'at li'l' Feevolus."

He popped the last of his fritters into his mouth and upended his beer mug against his broad, flat nose. "You talk French?" he asked me then, and I suspicioned from the restlessness of his doorknob eyes that he had a reason for asking.

"A little."

"'At ain't enuff," he said, and I was sure, then, he knew something he was unwilling or unable to tell me.

He studied the narrow skylight that stretched the entire length of the slant-roofed cock loft in which we sat. "Ain't no use not wukkin' in 'is ole prison," he said at length. "Folks 'at does nuffin', 'ey goes bad. Frawgs, 'ey git to be Romans. Americans, 'ey git to be Rough Alleys."

"Rough Alleys?" I asked.

"Yarse," he said. "Rough Alleys. Fellers 'at won't wuk an' won't keep 'eyse'fs clean, on'y gamble an' steal an' go mussuckin' aroun' mekkin trouble."

"Why do they call 'em Rough Alleys?" I asked.

"'Cause 'at's what 'ey are," he said. "Rough, an' belong in alleys."

Not until later, when I knew more French, did I discover that the Rough Alleys, who caused such grief among us before we were finished with Dartmoor, got their name from the French word *raffalés,* a term applied by French prisoners on English prison ships to those among them unfit in dress, person, and manners to associate with folk who made any pretense to decency. "Whyn't you start wukkin' on French?" King Dick continued. "'At ole Gin'ral Le Feeber, ovah in Prison Number Sem, he give lessons in French, an' talk clear an' nice, not all yockety, yockety, yockety, lak mos' Frawgs."

"Number Seven?" I asked, to make sure.

"Yarse; Sem," he said.

He warned particularly against gambling, declaring it was a curse, not only to his old Number Foh, but to all the other prisons as well, inasmuch as prisoners who became addicted to gambling would sell their clothes and even their daily food ration in order to gamble.

I asked him how they lived if they sold their food rations.

"'Ey picks up 'at ole swill behine 'ose cookhouses," he explained. "Doan' you gamble, an' doan' you let none of yo' white boys git started, not lessen you want to see 'em runnin' aroun' wifout no shirt nor nuffin'."

Keno, he said, was not particularly bad, but Faro and the Wheel of Fortune, which he said the Frawgs called Roulette, were sure poison.

"If they're so bad," I asked him, "why have 'em? You could drive them out if you wanted to, being King."

He let his head sink on his shoulder and giggled weakly. "Whuffoh I wan' do 'at?" he asked. "You ain't seen 'em Frawgs ovah in 'em odder six prisons! 'Ey'd tek money offen a li'l' baby what hadn' had nuffin' to eat foh a week! Whuffoh Ah let 'ese folks in ole Number Foh go ovah an' frow 'eir money at 'ose Frawgs? You t'ink 'ey stop gamblin' effen Ah frow out Faro an' Wheel o' Fortune! Nawsuh! Not no moh nan 'ey stop drinkin' effen Ah say ain't goin' be no moh beer in Number Foh! Ah keep 'ose gamblin' tables right heah whah nobody starts no russickin wivout Ah knows it!"

A shrill outcry rose from a near-by table. "Lookit 'at!" King Dick said. "Go on down git yo' dinner!" He strode swiftly to the table, his bearskin hat towering above the excited players.

"'At ain't nobody's fault on'y yourn!" I heard him shout. "Effen you goin' gamble in heah, do yo' gamblin' wifout no hussuckin'!" He drew two yellow-clad figures from the milling throng and made what looked to me like gentle jabs at them, jabs that traveled about six inches. Yet both gamblers bounced from his keg-like fists: bounced, fell violently to the floor and lay still.

There was, I could see, much to be learned about Dartmoor Prison; and as I hobbled down to our bay on the second floor I thought to myself I would have plenty of time in which to learn it.

XXIII

W<small>HAT</small> it was about our life in Dartmoor that weighed heaviest on us, I find it hard to say. At one time I think it was the stench of the place—the bitter-sweet, flat, choking odor of unwashed bodies and fragments of food and hidden filth; for though some of our bays were scoured daily, others were given only a hasty sweeping—what Arundel housewives call a lick and a promise.

Again I think it was the cold; for the windows had no shutters, only iron bars, so that the bitter winds, the daily rains and snows, and the penetrating fogs that curse Dartmoor for nine months in every year poured in on us day and night. At other times I think it was our despairing rage at the wrongs inflicted on us by our jailers —inflicted not because we had committed crimes, but because we had fought to protect our country and our homes from conquest.

It may have been the lack of certainty as to our fate: we might, for all we knew, be kept in this dripping stone tomb for the remainder of our lives, unless we could escape; nor was this a groundless fear; for on every side of us were Frenchmen who had rotted either in the hulks or in Dartmoor for eleven long years, forgotten and forsaken by their country, their families, and their friends.

It may have been the myriads of fleas that lurked in cracks of the floor or folds of our hammocks, creeping out in the night to raise rows of welts on our bodies, welts that kept us awake and in torment with their burning and itching. Lice I don't mind. They are clumsy slow creatures, and any man who takes the time and trouble to be clean can keep them from his clothes and often escape them entirely. Fleas are different. They are too quick to be easily caught, and cleanliness is no guard against them.

It may have been the threat of disease—of smallpox, pneumonia and typhus—that hung over us constantly; or the clamminess that soaked up into us from the reeking floors; or the manner in which our wardens and guards taunted and jeered us. God knows they got back more taunts and jeers from the Americans in five minutes than their thick British wits could think up in five days, but none the less we brooded over their lying tales of American defeats when we had gone back at night into our prison house, and wondered and wondered whether, when we returned to our homes, we would be doomed to spend the rest of our lives paying taxes to keep a half-witted prince regent in women, liquor, and gambling funds.

In our own prison and the other six, prisoners had set up schools for the teaching of every subject under the sun. There were classes in navigation, knitting, tailoring, barbering, fencing, dancing, French, German, Spanish; in cooking, mathematics, boxing, painting, wood carving, Latin, Greek, chess playing, and the use of the globes; in gambling, even, and theology and violin playing.

I cannot remember all the things taught in Dartmoor; but for the expenditure of a penny an hour I truly believe a man could have instruction in any known subject, so that the prison was as good as a university, provided a man was hearty in his desire for knowledge. And to a man who lacks that desire, no university is better than a prison.

*   *   *

The Frenchman whom King Dick called Gin'ral Le Feeber proved to be General Le Febvre, an officer who had served with General Rochambeau in the French expedition to Santo Domingo. Like many other French officers, he was no longer admitted to parole, because of the frequency with which his paroles had already been broken.

He was a tall, thin man, and under his eyes were dark pouches that seemed to match in shape the enormous drooping mustaches that curved down like sickles on each side of his mouth. He had strange ideas, telling in one breath how he had broken his parole, and in the next speaking of his honor, eagle eyed and fierce; then caressing his mustache and boasting how he had got three girls with child during his stay in the parole town of Wincanton. Yet I liked him. He seemed not only kind, but even honorable, as that term is understood by most. I am sure I could have left money with him and had no penny of it touched, unless he was starving; and I know he would have seen France in hell before he lifted his sword in behalf of any Bourbon king, though he would have marched alone with Bonaparte against all the cannon in the world.

He made us welcome when we told him why we had come, and stood proudly before us, a huge cocked hat on his head, and holding under his arm, pressed against his coat of fine black broadcloth, a cane made of bone rings fastened together and polished.

"Yes," he said, speaking English well enough, "this king of yours, this king of Number Four, he is not appreciate'. There is nothing like him. He is a leader; and like all leaders, he finds out the affairs, both great and small, and places them together, do you understand, to discover the cause—the drift—the pattern. Perhaps he has told you something new, this king?"

We watched him silently, because we knew nothing, except that King Dick must have had a reason for sending us to Le Febvre.

He shrugged his shoulders. "Nobody knows nothing," he said, "but I feel here—" he struck his breast with his clenched hand—"that things in France are bad—bad! Yet if things are bad in France there may be a wind to blow good to us, eh?" He pulled at his sickle-shaped mustaches and peered at us sharply. He rolled an eye toward the next bay, where two Frenchmen were playing chess with a set of bone chessmen; then glanced up at the barred window overhead, through which the Dartmoor fog drifted in wisps that vanished at once in the gloom of the prison.

"You desire to speak French, eh?" he said finally. "Whence does it spring, this desire?"

"King Dick put it in my head," I told him. "He told me to learn French so to keep myself busy."

His eyes seemed to search the air above and beside me; and as they moved from point to point, they swept repeatedly across my face, never lingering but always returning. At length he smiled. "Yes," he said, "I teach you all the French you need. You find my French very useful; useful, but expensive. Maybe you find it cost too expensive."

"How much does it cost?"

"Five pounds each man."

There was something here I could not understand; but I sensed that this general, like King Dick, knew something we didn't. He had something to sell, and we couldn't afford to go without it.

"Five pounds!" Jeddy exclaimed. "I got some French already! I couldn't use more than a shilling's worth."

"Five pounds is all right," I told the general. "Five pounds apiece. When do we start?"

The general smiled grimly at Jeddy. "Truly!" he said. "Say me some French, so I see about your accent."

"Well," Jeddy said, "I speak the pure Nantes French. Maybe you don't know that brand, but it takes me in and takes me out." He cleared his throat, stared round-eyed at the general, and spoke up boldly: "*Mon Dieu, mon général, commez vous portez vous? Il est très méchant aujourdui, n'est pas; il fait plouit tout le temps.*"

The general seized his head in both hands and rocked it. The face of one of the chess players appeared suddenly around the canvas screen that separated the bay where we stood from the next, stared blankly at Jeddy, and withdrew as suddenly as it had appeared.

"Dear sweet mother of God!" the general said. "*Il fait plouit! Il est très méchant aujourdui!* What horror! If this is the true Nantes French, then I know at last why the citizens of Nantes were treated so badly in the Revolution. *Il fait plouit!* Ah, my God! My God!"

"What's wrong with it?" Jeddy asked.

"As well ask what is wrong with England!" the general groaned. "It is all wrong! The gouvernment, the people, the prisons, the houses, the women, the dress, the speech—all, all is wrong. So it is with your French."

He turned to me. "You speak the pure Nantes French also? Speak something to me, so I know the worst."

"Mine's canal French," I told him; and with that, speaking stiffly, since I have never felt free in foreign languages, I said: *"Je vois depart de cette prison ici."*

The general glared at me, breathing heavily through his nose. He drew a folded silk handkerchief from his breast pocket, flung it open, enveloping us in a wave of violent perfume, and dabbed at his brow.

"Look now," he said, when he had folded most of the odor back into the handkerchief and placed it in his bosom again, "you are strange people, you Americans, laughing and mocking at all things, but doing it stiffly, without unbending. Being mockers, you fear others will mock you. Therefore you do not speak easily."

"General," Jeddy said, touching him lightly on the chest with the backs of his fingers, "with a quart of brandy in me I can say anything in French."

"But certainly!" the general cried, flicking Jeddy's chest with his finger tips in turn; "the stiffness is relaxed by the brandy. For a moment you forget yourself! That is the truth. Therefore we find a way to make you forget yourself so that you speak easily, even without the use of brandy, eh?"

There were chairs in the general's bay: chairs and a chest; and attached to stanchions were two paintings, one of a naked woman and one of a woman not quite naked, but almost, so that the place had quite an air. The general drew our chairs close together.

"You know how we do this?" he went on. "We make you become other persons. No longer are you Americans when you come here to study with me. You become French persons—new persons. Thus you forget yourselves and your fear of being mocked, and talk like Frenchmen, waving the hands, raising the eyebrow, lifting the shoulder, curling the lip. You see? Ha, ha!" He bunched his fingers, kissed their tips, and tossed the kiss toward the picture of the almost naked woman.

The thing seemed reasonable. At least there could be no harm in trying it; so I nodded.

"Good!" the general said. "We start this minute." He tapped me on the chest. "You are Jean Marie Claude Decourbes." He repeated the name slowly, raising his shoulders and opening his eyes wide, so that he had a look of almost childish innocence. "Jean Marie Claude Decourbes. *Mais oui!*" He leaned forward and stared searchingly at me. "Who are you?"

"Jean Marie Claude Decourbes!"

He shook his head. "Shoulder!" he criticized. "Lift the shoulder! You are surprised I ask you! Everybody know you are Jean Marie Claude Decourbes—" his voice rolled sonorously—"enseigne de vaisseau de la Marine Impériale de France! Raise the shoulder! Use the face! That is what a face is for—to show what passes behind it. You droop the eyelid and raise the chin one sixteenth inch: you are insult because the name is not known. You raise one eyebrow: you are patient with an ignorant man. You raise two eyebrows: you are surprised an intelligent man should not know. You see? Use the face! Why did God give you the face? Not to be blank toward all the world, like the sheep or the goat, *hein?* But to speak silently to women of things that cannot at the moment be said in words! To mislead the enemy! Very good! Who are you?"

I drew down my mouth and raised my eyebrows. "Jean Marie Claude Decourbes," I protested.

"Damned if it ain't!" Jeddy said.

From his breast pocket the general drew out a small mirror. He breathed on it, wiped it on his sleeve, examined his face in it first on one side and then on the other; then handed it to me. "Look in this and say to yourself one hundred times who you are. Jean Marie

Claude Decourbes, a seaman of Provence. Never forget. You are Jean Marie Claude Decourbes!"

He turned to Jeddy. "Give attention, small one! You are Felix Berthot, Capitaine du navire *Ma Mie* de Nantes. Who are you?"

Jeddy lifted his shoulders until his head seemed almost to sink beneath their level, drew up his eyebrows and splayed out his hands. "Felix Berthot!" he plaintively declared, and anybody with half an eye could see from his gesture that he considered the general both rude and ignorant for asking.

The general rubbed his hands together. "Good!" he said. "It marches!"

Before we left the shelter of the dripping stone walls of Number Seven I had learned not only that my name was Jean Marie Claude Decourbes, but that I was born in St. Rémy de Provence, that my parents were Agathe and Antoine Decourbes, that I had one brother and five sisters, that I had been captured by the British frigate *Garonne* in the year 1809. Jeddy, being more flexible with his face and hands and shoulders, had delved deeper into his private life, and was taking pride in having wed a woman of Morlaix during the year 1804 and in being the father of two daughters.

Having arranged to return on the following day, we crossed the stone-flagged yards, slimy from dirt and the unending moisture of the Dartmoor mists. Swarms of yellow-clad prisoners were walking, gabbling, yelling, playing childish games and working at various pursuits while waiting for their noontime soup to come from the copper boilers of each prison's cookhouse. Something about the tumult dulled my sense of individuality, and suddenly it seemed to me that I was no longer Richard Nason, but was indeed Jean Marie Claude Decourbes, and that I had truly been shut up in this dank and sour-smelling prison since the year 1809. Yet this day was the fourth of April, and we had been where we were for less than a week. I was moved to wonder how we would feel about it if we had been there for years, instead of for a day or two. There came a time when dates meant little; but this date of April 4th was one that will never slip me, any more than will some of the dates that closely followed.

*   *   *

We had no sooner reached our bay and set out our plates and cups in preparation for the coming of Tommy Bickford with the bucket of soup than King Dick passed, attended by the Bishop and the Duke.

He grinned at me languidly, but went on without speaking. Yet he had no sooner vanished into his own bay, with the Bishop and the Duke popping in after him like two dogs popping into a cave after a bear, than he reappeared again alone and came lightly down the alley to me.

"Heah," he said faintly, wrinkling his forehead until the lines on it looked like the depth lines on a chart, "you an' Feevolus been ovah to Number Sem to see 'at old Gin'ral Le Feeber?"

I said we had.

He made a slight movement of his melon-like head: a movement that seemed to indicate he wished to see me alone.

Even as I got to my feet my heart began to pound against my ribs like the strokes of a gunner's sponge. I knew as well as though he had written it out that somehow he was bringing me the news I had known I must have ever since I sat in the longboat in Plymouth harbor, peering vainly through the slanting curtain of rain at the dripping stern windows of the *Granicus*, 74.

I walked with him away from our bay. "'At old Gin'ral Le Feeber," he said, turning a lackadaisical eye on me, "he'll learn you moh French 'an anyone."

I could hardly speak until I had gasped a lungful of sour prison air. "You've got something for me," I said, when I could talk without choking.

"Yarse!" His black paw half opened before my face, and I saw a square of soiled paper resting against his pink palm. I took it from him. "White man come into 'at market 'is mohnin', sellin' aigs. He

ast Agnes foh somebody 'at knowed 'em Americans; an' Agnes, she
sent Clerphus Lapp foh me." Agnes, I knew, was the pretty vege-
table seller from the near-by village of Tavistock, who came each
day to the market. "Ah wouldn' tell nothin' to nobody, 'f Ah was
you," he added darkly. "Don't do nobody no good, seppen to give
'em somep'n to talk about."

The note was printed roughly in pencil:

*"Please be selling something in the market one week from to-day
that will be 11 April."*

It was unsigned, but I needed no signature to tell me who had
sent it.

"Wipe 'at look off yo' pan," King Dick said severely. "Doan' go
lookin' 'at way lessen you want somebody follerin' you roun' to see
effen he kain't git to know about somep'n wuff sellin'."

I showed him the message.

"Whah 'is lady comin' fum?" he wanted to know.

"What makes you think it's a lady?"

He chuckled a fluty, hysterical chuckle. "'At ain' no way answer
King Dick! Whuffoh you got 'at li'l' sizzicky look in yo' eye effen
'tain't a lady? Mebbe you git 'at look foh an ole man wif whiskers,
huh? Nossuh! Naw SUH!"

"Well," I said, "I don't know for sure, but I think you're right, and
I want to sell something in the market a week from to-day."

"'At ain't no trouble," he assured me in his weakest, weariest voice.
"What you want to sell?"

"Anything," I told him. "I want you to buy something for me;
something that'll let me into the market: something a lady'd like to
buy."

He nodded. "'Ey's some nice li'l' ships finishin' up ovah in Number
One," he said. "Hund'ed gun ship, foh feet long: make a nice li'l'
present foh a lady."

"No," I told him, "that's too large for a lady."

"Nice li'l' frigate ovah in Number Five," he said. "No bigger'n mah han'." He opened his gigantic fist and stared admiringly at the vast spread of bone and sinew. "Got a lady foh a figgah-haid."

"That's what I want," I said. "Get it for me, and tell the man to paint the figurehead with a green dress."

* * *

I think I might have sickened from impatience if my waiting had not been leavened by the news that came into the prison on the ninth day of April and sent the eight thousand Frenchmen into a shrieking frenzy.

Because most of these Frenchmen had been in Dartmoor since 1806, which was the year the prison was built, they had found means to circumvent their jailers in the matter of newspapers. The British tried to deprive the prisoners of all news, but French newspapers and English too were delivered to the Frenchmen neatly baked in loaves of bread.

When these loaves came into Prison Number Seven on the morning of April 9th there arose such an uproar from the prisoners that the soldiery came out of the barracks on the run.

Frenchmen poured from Number Seven like a swarm of hornets, and the din brought other swarms from Number Six and Number Five. The uproar swelled and swelled until gamblers, Negroes and half-naked French came tumbling down from the second floor and the cock loft of Number Four. It spread to the yard beyond us, where the gray bulks of Number Three, Number Two and Number One crouched with noses pointed at a common center, like three enormous mangy cats glaring at their prey.

We ran to the covered walk along the wall between the prison yards and the market place; for it was only along the walk that we could pass from the yard of Number Four into the others. When we entered the yard of Numbers Seven, Six and Five, there were four thousand yellow-clad figures in it, weeping, embracing and kissing, as Frenchmen so often do. Somewhere among them started the song that goes, *"Allons, enfants de la Patrie, Le jour de gloire est arrivé"*

—a song that sends quivers along my spine. Others ran about in a frenzy, shouting *"Vive l'Empereur!" "Vive la France!"* in strange, cracking, trembling voices, or stood helplessly in their grotesque, pinched-looking yellow suits marked with the broad arrow of the criminal and the staring letters T. O.—stood with tears trickling and trickling from their eyes as if there would never be an end to their weeping.

We watched them in silence, wondering what ailed them, while the soldiers on the walls lowered their muskets to stare round eyed. At length General Le Febvre and another man came pacing toward us, watching their excited countrymen out of eyes that seemed too hard and old for tears.

General Le Febvre nodded curtly. "You know about this?" he asked, gesturing toward the yellow-clad thousands.

We shook our heads.

His features were rigid, in spite of what he had said to me about expressing the feelings through the face. "It is done," he said. "The wolves have pulled down the lion. Bonaparte is finished, and the Allies have taken Paris. Now the wolves have nothing more to fear, and we shall go back to our own country."

He stalked off with his friend, his eyes as tragic as those of a man who has lost all he loves; and it was plain to be seen that the butcher Bonaparte, who cared no more for him than for a fly crawling on the wall, had held as much of his heart as had France itself.

"To our own country!" Jeddy repeated, echoing the general.

It dawned on me, then, why the general had insisted and insisted until we had almost come to believe it ourselves, that Jeddy was Felix Berthot and I Jean Marie Claude Decourbes, enseigne de vaisseau de la Marine Impériale de France.

XXIV

THE market square of Dartmoor Prison was a busy place, even under the worst of conditions, for all the petty shopkeepers among the
prisoners were in constant need of replenishing their stores of tobacco, pipes, needles, thread, awls, boots; pots, pans, and pails; butter, eggs, cloth, coffee, tea, beer, rum, meat, fish, soap, and God
knows what-all. But on this eleventh day of April it was busier than
I had seen it in my short stay—busier, I think, than it had ever been.
Not only were patches of blue sky showing now and again through
the low-lying fog bank that hung perpetually over the prison when
rain was not falling, so that the market folk were out in full force;
but the news of Bonaparte's defeat had brought French *émigrés* by
the score to congratulate their countrymen on the end of their imprisonment, and to seek supporters among the old soldiers—supporters for the king who was now to be hoisted back on the throne
of France by the English.

Against the side walls of the square were rails to which were tied
the donkeys of the market folk who had ridden in from Tavistock
and Widecombe-in-the-Moor and Moreton-Hampstead—donkeys that
added to the turmoil by bursting into brays so mournful that they
might have been an embodiment of the hopelessness of all the nine
thousand prisoners.

The market folk were ranged behind long trestle tables set in a
double row down the center of the square, while the Jews occupied

the choicest positions, close against the barrier between the market place and the prison yards, where they could easily carry on their traffic in obscene toys with the French prisoners, giving smuggled brandy and dirty books in exchange for the toys. To get these places they scrambled for them at the opening of the market, while the prisoners pressed against the railings and cursed them for the manner in which they crowded the women out of the way, sometimes even oversetting them and trampling on them in their anxiety to snatch the most desirable places.

On that morning, truth to tell, I saw none of them; I had eyes for nothing save the main entrance to the market from the moment when the double sentries at the gate, seeing the small frigate made of bone that I carried, admitted me to the mud and deafening racket of the great square.

I can hear now, as though I still stood waiting among them, the howling of the Jews, the bellowing of the Devonshire wood and charcoal and poultry sellers, and the wild, coarse voices of the fishwomen, in particular of a terrible old woman with stringy gray whiskers, who wore a fisherman's boots and jacket and a dragoon's forage cap, brimless, and boasted of a wide knowledge gained in unsavory ways. She seemed to be at my elbow with her screaming. Move as I would, her voice sliced perpetually into my brain, making an agony out of the waiting that was a torment in itself; waiting that seemed to hover on the edge of eternity.

It came to an end when, above the heads of the yellow-clad French prisoners at the entrance, I caught sight of a small three-cornered hat, like the one my father wore as a captain in the last war. I could not see her face, what with the guards at the gate, and the elbowing countrymen and French *émigrés;* but something about the hat told me it was hers, so I was prepared to see her and armed against the making of any sign of surprise. I had it in mind, as soon as I caught sight of her, to go closer to the gate, so she might have less distance to walk through the black mud that covered the entire market square; but when she had come far enough through the gate to let me make out her face, I saw she had seen me at once, and I forgot about the mud.

The yellow-garbed scarecrow Frenchmen swirled around her, offering their small wares, and I feared it would be necessary for her to stop and speak with them; but they fell away before her and she came straight to me, a half smile on her lips.

I looked at the frigate I had brought her. My hands were shaking, and I knew I must be careful not to break it. When I lifted my eyes again I saw that her green riding habit was spotted with mud. There was a dab of mud, a small dab, on her cheek, which seemed to me almost as white as the face of the figurehead on the *Lively Lady*.

"It has a green dress," she said, then. "Is it for me?" She drew a deep breath and added uncertainly, as if she had half forgotten it, "Richard?"

I nodded, being in two minds what to say in reply, and so saying nothing.

"May I see it?" she asked. So faint was her voice that I barely heard her, what with the screaming of the fishwomen, the braying of the donkeys and the yammering of the crowd. She took it from me.

With the little frigate gone, I felt freer to think about saying something; so while she studied it, I coughed and said, "I knew you'd come."

She seemed lost in contemplation of the toy. I was conscious of a movement beyond her. When I looked more carefully I saw a small, thin, bowlegged man, and behind his shoulder the head of a dog that stared at me and moved his nose as a dog will when uncertain. It was my dog Pinky; and in the moment I saw him he leaped outward and was snubbed by a cord fastened to his collar, so that he swung in mid-air, scratching and scrambling. I ran to him and found he had leaped from a small wooden seat, like an inverted bracket, strapped against the bowlegged man's back, near his waist.

As soon as I got him in my arms he spread himself against my chest to root at my neck with his cold nose.

"Well," I said, when I had my hand around his muzzle, so he

could only lie against me, snorting and jerking his head in an effort to free himself, "what's all this?" I was speaking to Lady Ransome, but she had turned away and gone to look at the donkeys tied against the high granite wall.

The bowlegged man grinned and touched his hat. "'E wuddn't 'a' fell off, sir," he said, "for anything 'ceptin' 'is marster. 'E's rid there for near a fortnit nah, sir, like a bloomin' lamb. 'E's a grand little dog with the 'ounds: tikes to it like a cat to a 'erring. Reg'lar little lion, 'e is!"

Lady Ransome came back to us. "He's safe with Captain Nason, Mark," she said. "Unleash him and leave him." She drew another deep breath. "Look after the horses, Mark, and I'll come out soon."

He touched his hat and slipped the leash from Pinky's collar. "Please to remember, m'leddy," he said, "them horses got to walk back, and this moor ain't no place after dark."

She made no answer, so he touched his hat again and went spraddling toward the entrance, the little bracket sticking out from his back as though he were off for a load of bricks.

She looked up, as if waiting for me to say something.

"What's the sense of having him ride on that shelf?" I asked, though I didn't care why he rode on it.

"Because that's how we carry them," she said, moving her shoulder impatiently. "When a terrier's what he should be, he'll never give in, but runs with the hounds till he wears his pads to the bone; so we carry him on what you call a shelf till the fox goes to ground."

"Then what?"

"Then," she said, "he's tossed off, so he can go down after the fox and fight him out." She looked at me quickly from the corners of her eyes. "Lud 'a' mercy!" she added, "I think you must be studying to be an Englishman, so you can spend your life talking about dogs and horses." She raised the little frigate above her head, studying its delicate bone planking, and again there came into my mind the thought of her pressed against the old beech beside our mill creek in Arundel, laboring to carve her initials on it. It seemed strange to me that with all this turmoil surging around us I should be conscious of nothing but peace.

"I knew you'd come," I said, forgetting I had told her this already; but it seemed she had forgotten it as well, since she said, "Did you?" without ceasing her study of the frigate.

"Yes," I said, and could recall not one of the things that at some far day in the past I had planned to say to her.

She looked at me quickly, then slipped off her gauntlet, undid a button in the front of her long-skirted riding coat, and brought out a small package. "This is yours, Richard," she said. She placed it on the deck of the little cruiser so I could take it without being seen. "I didn't—I don't know—I've wished I'd never taken it from you."

I knew what it was; and I stared at it, lying there. It seemed to me I had wanted this miniature back more than I had ever wanted anything.

"Don't you wish it?" she asked, in her soft, husky voice.

There was almost a breathlessness to her laugh when I snatched it up and buttoned it into the pocket of my shirt, where it seemed to lie against my breast like greatly needed armor.

"I've hated it," she said, "ever since I took it from you. You said it brought you luck; and when you lost it, you lost your luck as well."

"No," I said, "we sank the *Gorgon*."

"Oh, yes," she said, "but after that! Dartmoor!"

"Well," I reminded her, "you're here, and I've got it back. That's luck."

"I'd have given it back before you—before you fought," she said, "or on the *Granicus*, but I couldn't. There was never a chance." She stamped her riding boot in the mud. "That awful Captain Parker! That awful Captain Wise! They never left me alone!"

"Was that what you meant when Sir Arthur bought Pinky and you made a motion with your hand?"

"What motion?"

"Why," I said, "you had your hand at your throat; don't you remember?"

She put her hand to her throat, staring at me.

"Yes," I told her. "Like that. You moved your fingers a little. There was a look in your eyes—I thought you wanted to say something to me."

"La! How could you remember a thing like that?" She put her hand on Pinky's head; and Pinky, twisting suddenly, brought our hands somehow together. The unexpectedness of it gave me a start, and I couldn't blame her for hurriedly making adjustments to her hair with the hand that had touched mine.

Embarrassed, we stood and looked at Pinky.

"Well," I said, when we had been silent overlong, "that night on the *Granicus,* in my berth, I'd have sworn I heard your voice close by my ear. When I tried to go to you in the morning I couldn't. The sentry wouldn't let me. I wanted to see you. I wanted—I wanted——"

"Yes," she interrupted me. The huskiness was in her throat again. "I—I wanted you to have the miniature. I wanted you to know I felt badly, Richard. It was our fault. It was my fault. You'd be free now if—how could I know you'd—I'd never——"

"Look here," I said. "Put these ideas out of your head! It was the fog. It was the fortunes of war. Nobody can tell what'll happen in war times. If Rowlandson Drown had stopped to hang up his jacket before he came on deck, he mightn't have been killed. Our mast might have been more stoutly fished, and we'd have got clean away. But Rowlandson wasn't to blame for not hanging up his jacket."

She raised her eyes to mine. They seemed to swirl like the swift water of the Arundel River on an August day.

"Don't cry here," I said. "Look at the green dress of this figurehead. It seems years ago that I first saw your green dress. It's a beautiful color—green. Do you remember telling me I couldn't pronounce the name of my own home?"

She smiled tremulously. "Of a Rundle!" she whispered. "I've learned a lot since then."

"What have you learned?"

"Oh, la! I've learned Baltimore gentlemen are taught to fall in love at first sight, and why beech trees are planted in America."

My thoughts skipped about, evading me. "Did you ride from Exeter this morning?"

"We were away before sun-up," she said. I had a sudden picture of her, small and gallant in her saddle, outlined against a golden sunrise.

"For God's sake," I begged her, "tell me things I want to hear. The day'll be gone before you know it."

"What shall I tell you?"

"There's something wrong with you. I see it in your eyes. You're thinner. Your eyes are hurt all the time. If there's—if there's something in your life you can't bear——"

At that she stood straighter and seemed haughty. "I think you misunderstand," she said. "I came to-day to let you see your dog again and to ask if there's anything I could do for you, because I had your acquaintance in America."

"Well," I said sadly, "there's one thing you didn't learn. Somebody should have told you an American can't be made to feel like a whipped dog by calling him 'my good man.'"

"What do you mean?" she asked. "How could I call you 'my good man?' I'd never say it."

"It was in your voice," I told her. "You were kicking me out of your way for saying something you thought presuming and too intimate."

She stamped her foot. "Don't you dare! Don't you dare! I kicked you out of my way! I!" She stopped and looked at Pinky. "No," she added, softly, so softly that I held my breath for fear a word might escape me, "no, Richard."

"Well—" I said—"well——"

"It's only that you don't understand the English, Richard. I've had the thought that you think hardly of Sir Arthur, but he's a fine honest man and a just man. He's kind to animals, and religious, and it's a great honor to be his wife." I thought she flushed a little. "He's

a believer in Joanna Southcott. The newspapers are full of her proph-
ecies, and he's gone up to London to see her."

"Has he?" I said feebly. Then, in spite of me, I laughed, and perhaps the laugh was unpleasant.

"Please be kind to me," she said. "I've ridden a long way to see
you, and now there's so little time!"

I fear I laughed again, and more unpleasantly, but I was ashamed
of it. "I'll be kind in the way you mean," I said. "I'll make no words
to trouble you."

At that her under lip trembled; she was all compassion. "Strange,
isn't it?" she whispered. "Strange I should be asking you for kindness,
poor prisoner!" Then she went on, speaking low and rapidly, "I can't
be very kind to you; I can only do what I can: that's to bring your
dog to see you and tell you a friend thinks of you, Richard. Your
friend would help you get away if she could."

I looked down at her little boots that were sinking in the mud. "I'm
afraid you mustn't stay much longer in this cold."

She laughed ruefully. "The cold's nothing, but there are pixies on
this moor, and everybody says you mustn't be caught on it after
nightfall."

"What in God's name is a pixie?" I asked her, and regretted the
words as soon as they were spoken. "Don't tell me! I don't want to
know what a pixie is! Tell me something I can think of in this damned
prison! How do you live? What do you do all day? Who do you talk
to and what do you talk about?"

"No," she said, "there are things I must ask. Do you know it was
two years and three weeks ago to-day that I came to your house in
Arundel?" She pronounced it "a Rundle," like one of our Arundel
people. "I've often wondered what the winters are like there? Is
there a sweet smell to the air always?"

"Wait," I said. "How can I——"

"There's something I must say to you, Richard," she said. "This
little boat——"

"It's a frigate."

"I know," she said, "I know, Richard. Some other time. You can teach me these things some other time. I want to know them. But this little boat: I must speak about this little boat. You bought it, didn't you?"

"Well," I told her, "that's one thing to be thankful for. My mother made me promise to carry money in a belt whenever we chased a sail, and by the grace of God it hasn't been taken from me. The little frigate is nothing. It'll remind you of American sailors."

She nodded and looked at me strangely, and in some way I knew she had next to no money with her: that the horse-faced Sir Arthur allowed her to have none.

"Now," I said, "here's something. No letters go out of this prison without being opened. Can you write my mother for me?"

"I've written already," she said. "I'll write her again."

"Tell her I'm well. Tell her I'll be home again some day—perhaps sooner than she looks for me."

"Ah, I hope so!" She leaned close to me, bending her head over Pinky's. Then, tousling him with her fingers, "Listen," she whispered, "I've wrapped a map in your package. It's forty miles to Exeter. There are press gangs at Plymouth and Teignmouth, and a watch is kept at Tor Bay; but Mark Tate, that man who carried Pinky, is a good man. He'll do anything for me. He takes his beer at the Goose with Three Heads, near Ransome Hall, almost in Exeter. It was Mark who brought the letter here. If you can reach him——"

"No," I said quickly, and in as low a voice as hers, "I'm planning with a Frenchman. I think it'll come about that way, through France: through France; but you know how I thank you, and I'll keep the dear map, as I keep the little picture."

At that I think she was disappointed, and yet glad I had better plans than hers. She sighed. "I fear your friend is useless to you, Richard."

I made bold just to touch her hand. "You haven't told me what you do all day and what you——"

But at that I saw the man Mark Tate close by us.

"Beggin' pardon, m'leddy," he said, shooting an apologetic glance at me, "but it's gettin' on in time. This moor ain't no place after dark, m'leddy, an' we'm near to forty mile to make. Hard going too, m'leddy, the first of it."

"Yes, Mark," she said. "Take Pinky. I'll follow in just a moment; in just a moment, Mark."

He took the dog from me, touched his hat, and spraddled away. Pinky, squirming in his arms, got his forepaws on Mark's shoulder and stared back at me, his brow wrinkled and his ears held high. He whined sharply.

She fumbled with her gauntlet. "I suppose I may never see you again."

"That might be," I said.

She gave me her hand. It was as cold, almost, as a bit of ice. I wanted to say more to her. It seemed to me we were standing there together in the mud, waiting for me to find words to say to her; but I could not even speak a farewell, and only formed "Good-bye" with my lips.

I swallowed hard and tried again. "Emily!" I said. "Emily——" But I could get no further.

She turned a little from me, and my eyes clung hungrily to the picture of her that was within them—her little figure straight as a lance in her three-cornered hat and her wide-skirted coat and her riding habit looped up on her hip, out of the way of her small muddy boots.

"Ah, thank you," I whispered. "Thank you!"

She drew her hand from mine, smiled as though we had met for a moment on the street; then turned and left me.

XXV

THERE were prisoners packed against the railing between the prisons and the market place on the morning of the twenty-first of May: prisoners peering from the end windows of every prison house, and crowded on the prison roofs; for on that day the first draft of Frenchmen, five hundred of them, passed through the iron-studded gates and down the road toward Plymouth; and if there's a sight to make a man sick and desperate, it's to see others march away to freedom while he stays behind.

We had pressed ourselves against the market barrier, Jeddy and I, to watch them hand in their hammocks and blankets and become their own masters after years of living death; and there was one I shall never forget. He was a thin, stooped Frenchman with gaping holes in the knees and elbows of his yellow Transport Office suit, huge flapping bare feet, and a crust of dirt down the front of his jacket. He came up to the guards, breathless, like a fluttering, frightened bird, to tell them his hammock had been stolen—though I think, from his looks, he had sold it for money with which to gamble.

The guards pushed him away, for the rule had been made that no prisoner could go free until his hammock was turned in. He came scuttling out past us and dashed for the prison to hunt for it, or to beg one from another man; but soon he came hurrying back again, so wild looking that I almost thought I could hear his heart thudding with terror beneath his ragged yellow jacket. We saw him run to the guards; and by this time the last of the five hundred were crowding through the gate; but the guards struck at him and drove him off, for he had no hammock.

Panting like a frightened dog, this tattered Frenchman went down on his knees. I saw he had an open knife in his hand; and even while I wondered what he wanted of a knife, he stabbed the blade into his throat and fell over on his side, pushing the blade away from himself, so that his throat opened out in a spurt of blood. He sat up and looked at us, dazed like, holding his throat together with his fingers. Before the guards could come out and pick him up, he had fallen back on the ground with no blood in him.

So only four hundred and ninety-nine Frenchmen crowded out into the wet Dartmoor fog, some of them weeping and some kissing the handful of soldiers that escorted them down the long hill. My heart was both glad and touched with envy by the secret knowledge I had that among them were more than twenty Americans who, being able to speak French, had answered to the names of dead Frenchmen.

The prison records had been badly kept at the time of the small-pox epidemics; and many prisoners who had died were not marked down as dead. For years, General Le Febvre told us, the Frenchmen had drawn the rations issued to these dead men and sold them, and drawn clothes and shoes in their names and sold those; and now, having no further use for the names, they sold the names as well.

The names of Felix Berthot and Jean Marie Claude Decourbes, we learned, would be called at the same time as Le Febvre's name, probably in the third draft.

The second draft of a thousand men was released on the twenty-fifth of May, and fifteen Americans escaped with them. The third draft of a thousand went out on the last day of the month; and something had alarmed the British, so that they were watching. General Le Febvre was in this draft, and Felix Berthot, and Jean Marie Claude Decourbes.

We had let our beards grow for three days, on orders from General Le Febvre; and when the draft was called we took our hammocks and bags and went out past the sentries and into the market place, wearing the patched yellow rags we had bought from Frenchmen.

The general, waiting for us, herded us along.

"Remember," he whispered, "you care no longer for these guards. There must be no apprehension! They are nothing to you—dogs under the feet! You are free men! You understand? You are Frenchmen, freed by the Peace! No man can stop you."

We watched the Frenchmen ahead of us pushing up to the gates at the far end of the market place, eager to be gone from the mud and fog and dripping walls of Dartmoor. Clerks at the gates took the names of those who passed out, checking them off in a ledger.

It is waiting, as every man knows—waiting and thinking of what is to come—that causes more trouble than almost anything in the world; and it was to shorten this waiting that I turned to look for the last time on the angry stone faces of the seven prison houses. For a moment I had the illusion that they were faces indeed, grotesques that gnashed their teeth at us. Upon the roofs stood lines and clusters of prisoners, following us hungrily with their eyes when we trooped through the gates; and other prisoners were pressed against the iron barrier at the far end of the market place, as we had been pressed to watch the first draft go out.

The front row was hunkered down like monkeys, so those behind could see over their heads; and as my eye ran along this crouching, ape-like line, it was caught and held by a weazened, malevolent face that had been gone from my mind for weeks; a face I had seldom glimpsed since the night of our arrival, when its owner welcomed us to Dartmoor with a snarl and sent us up the stone stairs to what he doubtless thought would be a pummeling from King Dick.

It was Eli Bagley who crouched there, glaring furiously at us as he had glared at me when I called him from his berth in Halifax harbor, and later when I had taken his sailing master from him and sent him wallowing off on a trackless sea with his brig full of British supplies. I turned away with a cold feeling behind my ears; for we had forgotten Bagley in making our plans to escape. If I had remembered him, I would have contrived to have him held inside Number Four until we were well out of the way; for I would have known he would make trouble for us if he could.

The general prodded me, and I turned to see Jeddy, just ahead, attempting to embrace and kiss the clerk, though hampered by his hammock and bedding.

"Hey!" the clerk exclaimed, disgusted. "*Allez vous en!* Save them kisses for somebody as wants 'em! Wot's yer name, yer little grasshopper! *Nom! Nom!*"

"Felix Berthot," Jeddy said, bursting into the set speech so carefully taught him by the general. "Ah, my friend, how I have a heart swollen with joy because of my wife Marie and my two beautiful daughters and that beautiful Morlaix——"

"Ah, the hell with *cette belle* Morlaix," the clerk said roughly, pushing him ahead and fixing me with a hard eye. "*Nom!* What's your *nom?*"

"Jean Marie Claude Decourbes, *m'sieu*," I said, drawing down my mouth and lifting my two bundles an inch.

"Gord!" the clerk said to a brother clerk who stood beside him, "wouldn't you think they'd name one of 'em Jack or Jim for a change!"

He flapped over the pages of his ledger and ran his finger down one of them; then looked at me impatiently. "Where from? "he asked.

I smiled and nodded, saying, as the general had told me, "*M'sieu désire?*"

"Oh, Gord!" he said. "*De quoi? De quoi?*"

"St. Rémy de Provence," I said, pushing the sounds up into my nose and letting them die there, as taught by the general.

"All right! Go ahead and good luck to you, Frenchy. *Bon chance!*"

I hurried away, and heard the general break into an instantaneous flux of French that must have fairly engulfed the clerk who had questioned me.

Before we knew it, almost, we were through the arched gate and out on the slippery road. The long line of Frenchmen stretched so far down the hill ahead of us—the hill at the bottom of which lay Princetown—that the head of the column was lost in the mist that had come to seem as much a part of Dartmoor as her fleas and the bells on the wires around the walls.

I had long looked forward to the day when I should find myself on the outer side of those iron-studded doors; but now that the dream had become a reality I felt only a profound depression at the thought of Eli Bagley glaring hatefully from behind the bars of the market place.

I told General Le Febvre about Bagley: how we had first taken his boat in Halifax harbor; then punished him on the edge of the Gulf Stream.

The general turned and looked back, up the hill toward the prison walls. There were four guards at the end of our long column. Strung out behind the guards were baggage wagons, loaded with our duffel bags. The road itself was a trench cut in the slippery black peat of the moor; and we could see at a glance there was no way for the two of us to scramble from it unseen.

"Holy name!" the general said, tugging at his mustaches. "Sweet Jesu! here is an affair out of hell!"

We looked desperately for drains into which to crawl, but there were none: only the barren river bed of a road, slimy with mud. We looked for thickets in which to hide, but the land was treeless and grassless: a desolate rolling expanse, with fingers and humps of granite thrust up through it here and there, but all of them far removed from our line of march. There were no houses: nothing—only the vast stretch of black moor, to which spring had brought a faint swarthy green, such as comes over the face of a Negro afflicted with seasickness.

"Well, now," the general said, "I think of nothing!" He struck his forehead with his hand. "Holy God! There must be a way! If we could get to Plymouth——"

Jeddy laughed a fierce short laugh. "Plymouth!" he cried. "We'll never reach the halfway mark!"

We looked behind us again, fearing to see a messenger posting after us; but there was nothing in that slot of a road, only the four guards and the baggage wagons.

"Here," Jeddy said desperately, "have these friends of yours start a fight, General. Everyone'll climb on the bank to watch it, and we'll climb up with 'em and hide somewhere till they've gone on."

"It's no good," I told him, and my mouth was dry, as though stuffed with cotton. "Look at these yellow suits! We'd get nowhere in 'em! We couldn't hide for five minutes, not even on Dartmoor."

"Truly," the general said, "you must do better than that!"

"Oh, for God's sake!" Jeddy said, "let's fight our way through 'em!"

"It would do more harm than good!" the general protested, staring helplessly around like an owl revolving his head in search of food. "Instead of ten days in the Cachot they give you one month—two month."

I looked back once more and saw a dim figure approaching through the mist. My stomach pitched down and came slowly up again, as it always does when hope departs. We walked on in silence. To me the gabbling of the Frenchmen in front and behind us seemed like sounds that were no part of our life, as the lapping of water under my cabin windows has often sounded between waking and sleeping.

We heard a voice, then, shouting blandly in our rear, "Ah gits mah beer 'is mawnin'! Mebbe Ah bus' open one li'l' bahl, 'count of all 'ese Frawgs gittin' out f'um under foot!" It was King Dick. When we looked around, we saw him towering above the four guards in his bearskin hat and smiling down at them as though they were his benefactors.

They cursed him affectionately. He flapped his ham-like hand at them and came on, singing happily and grinning from ear to ear at the marching Frenchmen:

"When Ah sees mah Lawd on Jedgment Day,
Ah's go'nter say, 'Lawd, Ah's heah to stay:
Ah kin fry yo' fish; Ah kin scrub yo' floh:
Ah's pow'ful handy wif a twenty-foh!

"'Ah needs you, Lawd, an' you needs me!
Ah's a bestest gunner 'at ever you see!
Ah kin pivot 'at gun; Ah kin shoot him right:
Ah kin blow ole debbil clean outa sight!'"

I made ready to hail him as he came abreast of us; but when his eyes met mine, I was warned to silence by a fleeting expression of almost Satanic ferocity that momentarily contorted his face and was instantly gone. He paid no more attention to us than as if we were strangers; but he lowered his voice and sang a third verse of his song in a half whisper:

"'Ere's somebody lookin' foh folks Ah knows:
Devonshuh Ahms is safe, Good Lawd!
Git inside quick: git into 'at attic!
An' doan' git out till Ah gits to 'at attic!"

He quickened his pace when he had finished, and broke into a fourth verse; and before he had reached the end of it he was forging rapidly toward the head of the column—like a frog through a goose, Jeddy said.

*   *   *

Princetown, named for Britain's dissolute prince regent by the pig-headed Englishman who built it, Sir Thomas Tyrwhitt, lies half a mile from the gate of the prison. More than once I have longed to change places with the prince regent for five minutes for the sole purpose of hanging Sir Thomas Tyrwhitt for naming such a town after me—and God knows he deserved to be hanged for persuading the British government to build Dartmoor Prison on his property.

We reached the Devonshire Arms in a sweat of apprehension for fear we would be overtaken before anything could be done to help us. The line of prisoners had halted; and the officers of our guards were standing expectantly near the door. As we came up, King Dick emerged with a barrel of beer clasped in his arms, making no more of it than of a bolster stuffed with feathers, and grinned a grin that threatened to split his head in two parts.

"Heah!" he shouted, "doan' ev'ybody stan' jus' nussickin' roun'! Git a-hol' 'is ole bahl while Ah gits a hawse!" The prisoners surged forward, forcing us toward the inn. They seized the keg and drew it toward the middle of the street, while King Dick went back indoors. We flattened ourselves against the front of the inn, near the door, and clung there, which was not difficult, since all the others sought to be near the barrel.

A carter in a rusty top hat and a long smock emerged from the inn carrying a stout wooden horse; and two boys, very important, followed him with a bung starter and a basket of earthenware mugs. We could hear King Dick, inside, laughing his oily, chuckling laugh.

"Ev'ybody gits mah beer!" he insisted heartily. "Ev'ybody's gotta taste mah beer!" He herded out an old man and a small girl; then stood like a colossus before the door, his arms benevolently spread. We edged ourselves along until we were behind him.

"Whoo!" he shouted. We heard the thumps of the bung starter, followed by the gush of beer and the slushy chuck as the spigot was driven home. Jeddy dodged through the door, and I after him. We stood in the stuffy, beery dimness of the inn's taproom, holding our breaths and listening for a cry of warning; but we heard nothing save the happy, thirsty babbling of the Frenchmen.

We looked at each other; then, at a slight sound, stared hastily around. In the doorway facing us a girl stood—a buxom, red-cheeked girl in frilled cap and short-sleeved dress. She nodded and turned away silently, evidently expecting us to follow. We tiptoed after her, and she led us up three flights of stairs; then stepped aside to let us enter a smelly attic with two pallets in the corner.

There was the sound of a slap and a scuffle behind me as I crossed to the dusty small window.

"Doan't 'ee be a zany!" the girl said.

"Bot you are so beauty-fool, *ma chérie*," Jeddy murmured.

"You Frenchies!" she exclaimed, and tittered. "They's cloaze under the beds, carters' cloaze. Boots be under pillows. Lay youmselves on they beds, and doan't forget ye're droonk. They's rum oonder they washstand, and if any o' they guards coom oop, zee as how 'ee's droonk raight!"

She scuffled with Jeddy; then left us. We tore off our saffron-colored Transport Office rags and scrambled into the carters' garb that lay neatly folded beneath the mattresses: leather breeches, red vests to the thighs, long dust-colored smocks, and worsted stockings that pulled over the knees. Under the pillows were enormous boots and rusty battered top hats, such as every Devonshire wagoner wears, so we knew we weren't the first escaped prisoners to make use of this attic.

"For God's sake, be careful!" I told Jeddy, as I laced the heavy shoes. "Don't make that girl angry! We're not a half mile from the prison!"

"Angry!" Jeddy whispered, raising his pale eyebrows. "She let me kiss her! If you can kiss a woman she'll never blab!"

The tumult in the street subsided. When we peered from the small dusty window we saw the barrel of beer had been lifted to the back of one of the baggage wagons and had started off toward Plymouth, with prisoners and guards trailing alongside. We became aware of distant noises below us, and stretched ourselves on the two beds with the rum bottle between us. Our retreat was invaded by the perfume of frying bacon and of coffee—genuine coffee, such as we hadn't tasted in months.

"Probably the bacon's rancid," I told Jeddy.

He removed his top hat, lay back on his bed, and stared dreamily at the rough timbers of the roof. "Do you know how much of that rancid bacon I could eat?"

I couldn't answer for the moisture in my mouth.

"Well," he said, "I'd start off with two fry-pans full: big fry-pans.

I'd eat it out of the pans. I'd shove the bacon on one side and push slices of bread into the bacon fat, and first I'd take a bite of the bacon, and then I'd take a bite of the bread. Then I'd have 'em cook me another fry-pan full, and drop six eggs into the middle of the slices; and when the eggs were half done, I'd stir 'em all up together and eat 'em with a spoon: a big spoon."

We heard a rasping sound, like that of sandpaper passing over wood with quick, regular strokes. We looked up to see King Dick in the doorway. He had mounted the stairs in his stocking feet as softly as an enormous black cat, and the rasping noise was his stifled laughter.

"Mah lan'!" he said in his faint, high, plaintive voice, "heah Ah gits mahse'f all whuffussed up 'bout you white folks, an' heah you is lyin' in bed lak 'at ole prince region an' not whuffussed over nuffin' seppen bacon!"

"How did they find out?" I asked him. "It was Bagley, wasn't it?"

"Ain't no way tellin'," he said. "'Ese infohmers, 'ey's foxy, so's 'ey won't be tattooed wif T. R. on 'eir forruds foh bein' traitors."

"Can we get away?" I asked him.

"Yarse!" he said. "Yarse SUH! Ain't nobody goin' look in 'is ole inn, account it bein' so close 'at ole prison." He stared at us innocently, then drooped his right eyelid slightly. "Ah gits all mah beer heah," he added irrelevantly. "Two bahls weekdays; foh bahls on Sadday; six-sem bahls on pay days."

He took a bundle from under his woolly black jacket and handed it to Jeddy. It held a loaf of bread and a wedge of cheese.

"Nawsuh," he said, "ain't nuffin' goin' happen to you long's you doan' try go buckussin' aroun' Plymuff or Teignmuff or Tor Bay. 'Is li'l' gull downstays, she goin' lem you know when ev'ythin' raidy tonight, 'nen you git up ovah 'at ole moor—up ovah 'at *high* moor. 'At road, she doan' run nowheres seppen Exeter, soon's you git stahted up. Effen you's still agoin' in daytime, ack lak you's drunk an' doan' know nuffin'; 'at's how 'ese Devonshuh folks acks when 'ey's natural."

My heart turned over in me at his mention of Exeter.

King Dick rolled his eyes at us. "Ain't nobody goes out on 'is moor night-times! Not nobody! Ah wouldn't, lessen Ah had to, an' Ah ain't never goin' to have to. 'Ey's ha'nts on it."

"Haunts hell," Jeddy said somewhat thickly, because of the bread and cheese in his mouth. "How do they know there's haunts if they don't ever get out where the haunts is?"

King Dick chuckled. "'At's all right foh li'l' Feevolus lak you," he said, "sayin' Haunts Hell; but me, Ah stick in 'at ole prison! Ah ain't goin' puckussin' roun' wif no pickies. 'At's what 'ey call 'em: pickies. 'Ose pickies, 'ey holler 'nuff to whuffle yo' haiuh raight offen yo' haid; so effen you sees anyone on 'at ole moor, jes start a-pickeyin' yo'se'fs."

Jeddy contorted his face at King Dick in a horrible grimace. The King stared at him, fascinated, then drooped his head on his shoulder and giggled weakly: the giggle of a brainless, foolish young girl.

He straightened his bearskin cap, looking, in that dim attic, like a tremendous, overwhelming black djinn out of the Arabian Nights.

"Effen you needs money——" he said, then hesitated.

"I've got some," I told him. "What about this?" I pointed at our clothes.

"'At ain't no 'count," he said.

Jeddy shook his fist at him. "You old rascal!" he said gruffly. "If I wasn't busy I'd get up and knock your old head off!"

This black mountain of a man stared soberly at us, while I fumbled for words to tell him how I felt. In the midst of my fumbling he stepped backward and left us without a sound; and to this day I have never found the words for which I sought.

XXVI

We came down from the cold, black hills into the warm, green, neatly hedged valleys of the Teign and the Exe, gawping and gawking at everything we saw as though we had never before set foot outside our native Dartmoor. When hailed or questioned, as we sometimes were, we stared as in a daze, scratching our heads and hanging our mouths so wide open that bats might have flown into them. This acting served us well, for it occasioned no surprise; and folk never persisted in their questioning after seeing the witless countenances we turned upon them.

The town of Exeter lies against a ridge above the river Exe; and the Goose with Three Heads Tavern crowds close to the road which joins the town to the pleasant fertile moorland behind it—the moorland that is the beginning of the steep ascent to the wretched heights of Dartmoor.

By dint of pretending to get ourselves drunk on Exeter spring beer, dark and fruity and smooth, and by lying in the field opposite the inn with one eye glued always on the front door, we caught bowlegged Mark Tate spraddling down the road for his evening's quart or two. Wishing to show myself no more than was necessary, I shouted at him from the field where we lay, "'Ey, Ma-ark Ta-a-ate."

He stopped, peering in our direction. "'Oo the 'ell's that?"

"Zhut 'ee va-a-ace an' coom 'ere!" Jeddy growled.

He took a step toward us, uncertain in the late English twilight, so I stood up and faced him.

"Well," he said, offended at such familiarity from a mud-stained wagoner, "of hall the blooming gall! I ain't tradin', an' ain't buyin' an' ain't got no time to waste to-night, neither."

He turned toward the tavern, but I got him by the arm and shook some sense into him. "Stow your clack!" I told him. "Look at me and remember where you saw me last." I took off my carter's hat and ran my fingers through my rumpled hair.

He thrust his small face close to mine, then fell back and swept me with a horseman's eye.

"Hods!" he exclaimed. "How the 'ell—get back in the field, ye wild man, before somebody suspicions something!" He pushed me back, and we jumped the ditch to where Jeddy sat.

"This is Jeddy," I told him, "my second mate."

"Aye, I heard about him! He's the little feller that got into a fight in Ameriky and got carried home, all bloody, on your shoulder." He scanned us, scratching his chin.

"So ye done it!" he said at length. "I dunno how ye got away, but ye certainly done something! What ye goin' to do now?"

Jeddy gave him a confidential answer. "We're going to send you for a five gallon can of beer and six feet of sausages," he said; and when we had done this and were seated in the soft, sweet-smelling grass, washing down sausages with long draughts of mellow spring beer, it seemed to me that we must be near the end of all our troubles and that there could be little more that was cold and cruel in a warm and pleasant world.

"This Exeter ship canal," Mark told us, "she takes boats up to nine-foot draft, and we can get you aboard one of 'em, if ye give us time— only we'll near have to buy the bloody boat, prob'ly!"

"How far is Ransome Hall from here?" I asked.

He studied me for a time. "All right," he said. "Blummy if I don't do it, though it'll mean a lashin' o' trouble if I'm cotched!"

"What do you think it'll mean for me?"

He laughed sourly. "Hods!" he said. "Ye don't know Sir Arthur!

He does what's right, even if he has to cut the ears off everybody in the world but himself!"

"I know him as well as I want to," I said. "Why work for him if you feel that way about him?"

"Work for him!" he said violently. "I wouldn't work three seconds for the damned old sharkskin! Me, I work for Leddy Ransome, same's I used to work for her old man. The money comes out of his pocket, but by rights it's hers. By rights he ought to pay her everything he's got, just for living with him! If she got what she deserved for doing that, blam it, she'd be richer'n the Duchess of Portsmouth!"

"You used to work for her father?"

He sucked at the can of beer and nodded. "There was the nicest old feller in the whole damned county of Devon. The nicest old feller and the worst Faro player! He'd go into the Regimental Club or Sadler's or the Boot and Bit, pour down four bottles o' port and get himself into a game of cards with some red-faced old buck as never took nothin' but toast and water before playin'. When he got through there wouldn't be a gorrammed horse in the stable or a gor-rammed dog in the kennels!"

I had heard tales of the gambling among the English, and of London gaming clubs such as the Cocoa Tree Club, White's, Boodle's, and the Thatched House, where it was no uncommon thing for an English macaroni who imagined he was playing the gentleman to lose five thousand pounds, or even his home, in a single evening's play. I had heard of these things, but had thought of them, always, as impossible tales out of a book. Yet here was Mark Tate sitting in a field in Devonshire, wagging a sausage at me, and telling me how Emily Ransome's father had been saved from the Jews and the debtors' prison: saved because Sir Arthur Ransome had taken over his broad acres and his daughter at a higher valuation than could be got from the Jews, since the Jews would make no offer on the daughter.

"There's gambling clubs in Exeter, is there?" Jeddy asked.

"*Is* there!" Mark exclaimed pityingly. "There's gambling clubs wherever there's gentlemen."

"*Is* there now!" Jeddy said thoughtfully. "And do they play the Wheel of Fortune at any of 'em?"

Mark laughed shortly. "*Do* they! *Do* they, when there ain't no man can play it without leaving his money behind? I'll love a duck if they don't!"

"And where's Lady Ransome's father now?" I asked, while Jeddy chewed contemplatively at his sausage.

"Dead," Mark said. "Shot himself. Lost some more and blew off the back of his head with a load of duck-shot. Nicest old feller that ever lived, too: always pleasant. Pity he hadn't learned earlier that he couldn't play cards, so he could 'a' hopped the twig before Miss Emily had the snaffle hooked on her!"

*   *   *

Late at night, when there was no more passing on the road, Mark led us back in the direction from which we had come; then bore off to the right, through a stone gate and into a grove of trees as black as the inside of a powder barrel. We caught the scent of newly turned earth; then the smell of stables; then the perfume of newly sickled lawn grass; and while the odor of lawn grass still hung around us Mark steered us off to the right again, and we felt ourselves close to a building. When Mark had pushed us through the doorway and lighted a candle, we found ourselves in a cottage little bigger than the cuddy of a Quoddy boat. There was a bunk in the wall, like the bunk in a cabin, and a fireplace in one corner with a kettle hanging before it. To the right was another room, smaller by a foot or two, which might also be called a kitchen or a bedroom, depending on however one's fancy happened to run; for it had another fireplace; but also it had a bunk in the wall and an outer door facing in the opposite direction from the one by which we had entered.

It was good to sleep on real beds again, after the hammock mattresses of Dartmoor, which might have been stuffed with clam shells for all the comfort we took on them. Our ears, it seemed to me, had scarcely touched the pillows before morning had come and Mark Tate, bowlegged and alert, was tugging at us to get us up again.

"You keep to the back room," he said, pitching my clothes at me, dragging me from the room in which I had slept and pushing me in with Jeddy. "Front room stays open: back room stays locked. Lock both doors an' don't let a yip out of you! Don't open nothing, only for me or Leddy Ransome! They's water in the pail in the corner, an' a razor under the window, an' bread in the cupboard over the fireplace."

He spraddled from the cottage. Jeddy stared resentfully after him; then fell back on his bed and took on the aspect of a dead man—as I might have done if it had not been for Mark's hint about Lady Ransome. With this in mind I could neither stay still nor get a decent breath into me. I set to work brushing off each piece of my wagoner's dress, though there was no way of making it look like anything but what it was; and I was slow indeed at my dressing, what with taking my miniature from my pocket to stare at it, and listening at the door, and peering from the small back window at the wide expanse of meadow stretching off among clumps of towering oaks, elms and beeches, to lose itself eventually in a warm, golden haze.

It was too regular for my fancy, this spread of English park; for I have a liking for our rough New England meadows, swelling and rolling among solid masses of pines, birches and maples, or for flat marshes threaded with twisting silver ribbons of salt creeks, or even for ragged dunes, green and gold against the blue of the sea. Yet knowing what I knew and expecting what I expected, I said to myself that this little part of England, soft in its golden haze, was more beautiful than any piece of land I had ever seen.

I waited and waited in this low-ceiled room, sitting down and jumping up a hundred times, and wishful of going out into the warm June sunlight where I would feel less stifled from the thumping of my heart. She might, it crossed my mind, have gone to London. She might be ill, even; and at this thought I was in despair for fear I might have to go away without seeing her.

I recalled, at last, what Mark had said about bread; and when I found it I remembered how I would go along the Arundel beaches, between voyages, to shoot plovers or yellowlegs for aunt Cynthy's pies, and how I could never sit down among the dunes to take a mouthful of food without having a flock of yellowlegs come flying along just out of gunshot; and I, my mouth clogged with food, unable to whistle them down within range. Thinking this, I cut off a slice of the bread and found it white and sweet, and so cut off another, and then another; and while I was biting at the third, I heard a clattering of claws in the next room: the clattering my little dog Pinky makes when he hastens eagerly around a room in search of something, alert and stepping on his toes.

I stopped and listened, my mouth half full of bread, and my heart pounding fit to choke me. I heard Pinky blowing at the cracks beneath the door—blowing, and then sucking the smells of the cottage into his black nose. He scratched at the door and whined; then barked three times, sharp barks, impatient and peremptory. A moment later I heard Emily Ransome's voice, soft and husky: "Sh! Stop it!"

I jumped to the door, opened it, strode across the threshold, and closed the door behind me. I think I would have had my arms around her in spite of the bread in my hand and the mouthful I could not swallow if Pinky had not leaped against my chest and set up such a squealing of delight that I knelt down and took him up for fear his outcries would bring someone in on us.

When I had his head under my elbow, he lay and blew against my ribs, fluttering his tail with pleasure. I stared up at Emily. She stood looking down at me, a queer half smile on her red lips, as a person smiles at the memory of some pleasant far-off happening that comes dimly into the mind. She seemed to me as beautiful as she was kind.

"You should never have come here," she said, looking intently into my eyes. "You should never——" She broke off and glanced around the room; then looked back at me again. "No, that's not true! I'd have felt—I'm glad you came! There's nothing I can do, but I'm glad! I've thought of you often. I thought—I thought——"

"Well," I said, "there was no end to my thinking of you." I reached for her hands, but she lifted them quickly to her throat and clasped them there, as I had often seen her do before.

"Why do you say that, Richard?" she asked. "It's useless to say it!"

"I say it because I want to say it—because I have to. Why, if you didn't wish to hear it, did you bring back your miniature?"

"Yes, I know. It was wrong; but you said it had brought you luck. I thought—I thought you might have need of it."

"Need!" I said. "Need of it! I'm afraid of wearing it out, taking it from my pocket and looking at it a thousand times a day."

She moved to a small woven rug near the fireplace and sank to her knees, facing me.

"I suppose," I went on, "it's useless to say that, too."

She nodded.

"You don't mind hearing it, though?"

"La!" she said with that queer half smile on her face, "I don't hear such things often enough to know whether I mind or not!"

"Well," I said, "that's easily remedied if you've no objection to hearing the truth about yourself—how your eyes are smoke-colored; how I see them in every mist and cloud, and in the sunlight and the dark, for that matter: how your lips are——"

She rapped her clasped hands against her knee. "Richard, it's no good, none of this! The more you say the more you'll want to say, and I won't listen. I've heard you boast how Americans keep their word; yet you want me to go back on mine!"

"Oh, for God's sake," I said, "that's entirely different!"

"Oh, of course!" she said, smiling ruefully, "it's entirely different since it's you who want it. If anybody else wanted me to forget my vows, it would be terrible, wouldn't it?"

"No, it wouldn't," I said; but when I saw the look in her eyes, I admitted she was right. "Yes," I agreed, "and the reason it would be terrible is——"

"No," she said. "No! You're my friend, and I'm yours, so——"

"Friend! I'm no friend of yours!"

"Yes, you are, and that's all you are, and I must do what I can to get you safely away. I've talked to Mark, and he says——"

A shadow fell across the window. Pinky jerked his head from under my arm, his whiskers and eyebrows sadly rumpled, and growled a ferocious, rumbling growl that set his body to vibrating like a halyard in a gale. I moved back against the closed door, and my hand behind me fumbled at the latch; but I had been too rash in the coming out. Emily rose to her feet as the front door opened quickly. There stood Sir Arthur, a fowling piece held easily in the crook of his elbow, and on his gray, horse-like face a look that seemed to me to have more of satisfaction in it than anything else. The fowling piece, I saw, was cocked.

"Ow!" he said, peering at me along his nose, "I was right! Here you are, where you're not wanted! You've a genius for it, on my wahd!"

He cast a glance over his shoulder. "Stay there!" he called to somebody beyond our sight. "I'll whistle when I want you!" He stepped in, shut the door behind him, and leaned easily against it, cradling the fowling piece in his arms. He looked from me to Lady Ransome, breathing heavily; while Pinky growled deep in his throat and blinked his eyes, knowing I would slap him, which I did, though gently.

"Countryside has word of your evasion from Dartmoor, Nason. Great bargain, really, that cur of yours! Saw him rooting about Tate this morning, and it came to me like that—" he snapped his fingers —"that he must have caught a rather rank scent, eh?" I watched him with some curiosity, wondering that he showed so little anger. "Had a feeling it was you he was snuffing for."

He lowered the right hammer of his fowling piece: then cocked it again, so it clicked sharply, twice, in the silence of that small room.

"Fancy you finding your way here, of all places! One would think you'd been directed!"

"No," I said, "it was an accident."

"Indeed!" he said. "More of a misfortune than an accident, I dessay!" He cast a calculating glance at Lady Ransome. "They never come singly, eh, my dear? Here's Tate, I mean, running to you about this fellow! It's my money he takes, and one would think it might enter his mind that I have the fahst right to know what's going on. I'm afraid we must let Tate go, eh? Not the thing for him to have done at all!"

"Please, Arthur," she said, "please don't blame Tate! It was only that he—well, I think he wanted to do what he could for a poor man in trouble."

Sir Arthur threw up his head, like a horse freeing himself from an undesired hand. "Curious!" he said, "so much sudden sympathy! I fear Tate must be given in charge for aiding and abetting, my dear!"

"You'll give Tate in charge?" Emily asked. There was no huskiness now to her voice, but a peculiar soft clearness that made it seem louder than it was. "Might that not involve your wife if Tate should tell the truth and say he did it for her?"

Sir Arthur looked at her; there was a spark in his eye, not a hot one—it was the gleam of the icicle. "You should have thought of that yourself, I fear, Lady Ransome. There might indeed be some such embarrassment for you."

"I see," she said, "and Captain Nason goes back to Dartmoor?"

He shook his head with an amused ruefulness. "Captain! Captain! Captain! Don't you think we've had a little too much of captaining for a species of hybrid, half inn-yard hostler, half petty pirate? It seems to me high time we had done with all your captaining, Lady Ransome!"

She stared at her hands, front and back, as though she found something strange about them. "So you'll send him back to Dartmoor!" she said. "What did he do for us when he had us at his mercy, as you have him now?"

"Oh, dear me!" Ransome said. "Do you expect me to argue? I confess I'm surprised, for I pay you the compliment of saying you've seldom lacked intelligence. I think, my lady, you understand very well that your present position doesn't entitle you to the grace of argument from me."

At that she seemed to become quickly a little paler. "My present position? My present position? What do you call it, Sir Arthur?"

"Precarious," he replied lightly. "At least precarious. I put it to you: what's the position of an imprudent lady with whom an enemy of her country finds a patently agreeable refuge? And doesn't the question present itself: by what means and by whose encouragement does this enemy of her country reach the lady's presence? I take it she must have connived. Ah, yes, indeed! 'Precarious' appears to be the accurate word."

She raised her hand to her throat. "That is, you put your wife in the precarious position!"

"I! *I* put her? Tut, tut, my child! How can I put a lady where she has most deliberately and carefully put herself?"

Emily had begun to breathe fast and audibly. "So you'll do it!" she said. "This is what we've come to! You'll do it because I've been merciful and grateful!"

He uttered a sound like the sour echo of an indulgent laugh. "I do it because you've been 'grateful'? It would be too much to suggest that our language contains such words as 'duty' or 'honor' or 'law'? But I fear it's discourteous to remind you of what you yourself have so long forgotten!"

At this I took a step toward him in spite of the fowling piece which he shifted to a readier position as I moved. "You might remind yourself of the word 'honor,'" I said. "You can't speak to her like that!"

Emily turned to me, and suddenly she was weeping. "I don't care!" she cried. "I'm thinking of your going back to that horrible place, the mud, the cold, those terrible men in yellow clothes——"

Sir Arthur interrupted shrilly. "How well you describe it, Lady Ransome! Now we have it indeed! So you've been there!"

She turned to him. "Yes, I went!" she sobbed. "I did go, Arthur! I wanted to help him. I want to help him now. There's no harm in that! There's no harm in that and none to you. There's never been any harm to you in anything I did; and there never will be in anything I do. Couldn't you just let him go now? I'll never see him again. Couldn't you——"

"Disgusting!" He threw the word in her face with the most fierceness I ever saw from him. For the moment it seemed that something like a real passion mastered the man. "Disgusting! You make this show of yourself before me! Do you think I've been blind? Do you think I was blind in America? You little fool—you shameless little fool! Falling in love with an inn-yard lout; throwing yourself at him! And then, when he turns pirate, letting him make calf's eyes at you before my face! Sneaking off to coddle him when he's in jail for his thieveries! And now, when he's skulked out of his cell to you, begging for him! Begging for a damned dirty Yankee runaway thief! My God! What a paramour for Lady Ransome of Ransome Hall!"

I had heard as much from him as I could endure. "Open that door!" I said to him. "Open that door!"

Then, as I moved toward him, he poked the muzzle of the fowling piece at me, but I was quick, slapped it aside and took it away from him.

I opened the door myself. There were three workmen grouped around it, listening, all of them with guns. I smashed the muzzle of the weapon against the floor, so that the barrels were bent, and threw it into a corner.

"This man is an escaped prisoner from Dartmoor," Sir Arthur said. "If he makes a move, kill him!"

Then he spoke quietly over his shoulder to Emily. "Go to the house and remove everything that is yours," he said. "Pray be careful to take only what belongs to you!"

XXVII

THEY put me in Exeter jail; and I had been there three days before I got a word out of the man who brought me my hard bread, thin soup, and water—tepid water that must have been standing in the June sun. When he did speak in answer to my questions, I found his lingo difficult to understand.

"Noa, noa," he said. "Us bant agoin' vur tew zend ee backalong tew Dartymoor dreckly minit: not till us cotches tha body as wuz wi' ee. Zir Arthur hiszel, 'e yerd at tha Hall fra Dartymoor az they wuz tew or ee. Tuther must be a urnin' tha moor. When us cotches tha body an' ast tha tew or ee lockit up yere, than'll be time tew zend vur sojers as tew such bad bodies can be trustit wi'."

I had a gleam of hope for Jeddy, since he was still at large, having had the good sense to lie hid in the back room of the cottage until they had taken me away.

"Well," I said to the warder, "you may not catch the other bad body; he's not so bad, by the way, and neither am I."

"'Ess shur that ee is!" the man said, and shook his head mournfully at me. "A bad, bad, bad body thee'rt! Zim they do zay in Exeter town az how they'm a purty bobbery an' stirridge at tha Hall, an' her leddyship put oot, an' banned fra' a' the gert vokes, an' gude vokes tew, an' a' on account ov a bad, bad body fra Dartymoor. 'Ess fay, thee'rt a bad, bad body, man!"

That was all I got from him; he called me a bad, bad body a

thousand times, I think; for I lay in Exeter jail two months, until mid-August, before they took me back to Dartmoor.

Dun-colored clouds were caught against the barren face of North Hessary as we made the final ascent from Princetown to the depot gates; and the wisps of fog that drifted across the top of the seven crouching, staring prison buildings seemed less like fog than like the prison smells rising perpetually from the yawning, never-shuttered windows.

In his office Captain Shortland, with his crinkly brown hair and his ruddy, jovial face, beamed at me in a manner to make me think again of the grinning, big-nosed Punches I had so often watched on the streets of Nantes, strutting on little shut-in stages and blithely whacking friends and enemies alike with great clubs.

"Hah!" he said, moving his head forward and back and lifting his shoulders at the same time, as vain men so often do to improve the set of their coats, "so you've come back to us! Good! Good! I almost like to have my boys try it, out in the great world; for they all come back—ah, most of them: hah, hah!—to more permanent quarters!"

"Do you mean the Cachot?" I asked, knowing only too well the Black Hole was the penalty for those caught in serious crimes and attempts to escape.

He smiled, a pleasant, regretful smile. "Yes," he said, "the Cachot." He picked up some papers from his desk. "This is a rather serious business, you know. Not the usual case! No, indeed: not the usual case! One thing on top of another!"

I waited for him to say what he had to say, thinking helplessly, as I had thought from dawn to dark during the past weeks in Exeter jail, of Emily Ransome.

"At all events," he went on, "you'll have company. Four other Americans. They tried to burn a prize; so we were forced to give them duration."

"You were forced to *what?*"

"Duration. Serious offenses, you know! Not as serious as yours, but serious enough."

"Do you mean you're putting me in the Cachot for the duration of this war?"

"That's it! I knew you'd be sensible about it."

"Wait a minute," I said. My brain was in a muddle. There was no escaping from the Cachot, I knew. It was a stone coffin. There would be no way in which I could get word from Emily; no way in which I could get word to her; and God alone knew when the war would be over.

"This Sir Arthur Ransome——" I said.

"You've got it!" Shortland smiled. "There was the burning of the *Lively Lady,* and the escape by impersonating a Frenchman—of course, you'd only get ten days in the Cachot for attempting to escape; but you see there was also breaking and entering and the destruction of property at Ransome Hall. Ransome's laid information against you for the whole affair. Nothing else to do, you know." He cleared his throat. "I'll send you in."

"Just a minute," I begged him. "Give me a hearing on this. I haven't had a trial."

"Why *should* you have a trial?" he asked. "We have Ransome's word—and Ransome's a gentleman, you see."

"Oh, my God!" I said, "there isn't a Negro in Number Four whose word wouldn't be honester! The man's working out a personal spite on me! I claim a right to be heard!"

"I've heard enough!" he said, and the geniality vanished from his face.

"No," I said. "Wait! There was no breaking or entering at Ransome Hall. And since when has it been a crime to escape from a war prison? I gave you no parole! Nobody asked me for a parole! I was captain of a privateer of eighteen guns and entitled to parole, but I asked for none. Why shouldn't I try to escape if I get the chance? Wouldn't you?"

He stuck out his jaw and blinked his eyes, and all at once the dangerous temper of the man was on his face. Captain Shortland had the record of an officer brave to rashness, a hot fighter; but his nature was brittle, and never was more than a thin cracking lacquer over the anger that seemed always smoldering underneath. "Look here," he said, "your second officer escaped with you—Tucker. Where is he?"

"How should I know where he is?"

"Well, somebody helped you get away, and when you went, Tucker went too. Now you tell us where you last saw Tucker, and who helped you, and I'll see what can be done."

"Why, then, you *can* see what can be done, can't you! My God, Captain, get me a hearing, will you? You can't put me in the Cachot like this!"

Shortland's face turned wine color. "You damned Yankees," he said, lowering his head like a bull and half whispering the words, "you think you own the whole damned earth! You keep this place in a mess with your damned screaming and complaining and bellowing for your rights, until ten of you are worse than a million Frenchmen. Let me tell you, you haven't *got* any rights here! And you're no judge of what I *can* do and what I *can't* do! I've got orders from the Transport Office to put you in the Cachot for duration, and that's where you go!" He raised his voice to a bellow. "Mitchell! Mitchell!"

The chief clerk popped in at the doorway.

"Oh, for God's sake!" I said. "Let me write Pellew! Let me write the American agent again—Reuben Beasley! I wrote him twice from Exeter, but he may have been away. Let me try once more!"

Shortland shouted with mirthless laughter. "Beasley! If you wait for an answer from Beasley you'll stay in the Cachot forever! He never answers letters! Not from Americans! Wouldn't you like to write the prince regent? Take him out, Mitchell!"

He left the room, slamming the door behind him. Mitchell gave me a blanket and a truss of straw, and turned me over to a sentry, who led me down across the empty market place, dismal in the light of flickering lanterns. The dim, ogre-like face of Number Four glowered at us as we came to the barred gate that cut off its yard from the market. The sentry drew his bayonet along the bars with a clatter and turned to look appraisingly at me.

"We'm a-gettin' all the 'Merricans this side o' hell," he said. "Won't be none o' 'ee left to foight, soon, I'm a-thinkin'."

A turnkey came in answer to the racket of the bayonet against the bars, and the two of them led me to the left, along the covered walk, and finally out into the space between the circular inner wall and the high fence of iron bars. The Cachot stood snugly between the inner wall and the iron fence, looking, because of its granite sides and arched roof, unpleasantly like a tomb. As we approached, a squat figure came out from behind it and peered inquiringly at us.

"Here's another, Carley," the turnkey said. "Duration for this one, too."

The squat man came close up to me. "Duration, hey? Holy bones, you must be bad! You must 'a' spit on an admiral!"

The sentry and the turnkey laughed and left us. Carley took a key from his pocket: a huge key fastened to him by a chain. "Anyways, 'twon't be as if yez were alone, with four in for duration a'ready, and ivery wan av ye'er four thousand felly citizens fixin' to git throwed in with yez for attimptin' to brek out av the dippo. Mary help us all if thim four thousand divvles iver gits over the fince!"

A hoarse voice hailed us from the Cachot. "Mike!" the voice said, "let that poor boy come to bed! He'll be gettin' his death o' cold, standin' on that damp grass!"

Carley turned the key in the lock, dragged the iron door outward, pushed me in with a sweep of his arm, and swung the door shut with a clang.

I was in a dark room, smelling powerfully of damp straw, latrines and dirty bodies. There was a slit of dim twilight in the door, where the wicket was half open; and high up, on opposite sides of the room, were two other small openings into the dusk of that August day: openings smaller than my hand. There was no other light in the room, and the darkness was like dark wool against the eyes.

The hoarse voice spoke up. "I don't seem to recall your face, though you have a kind of familiar look."

There was a spatter of laughter from the interior of the room.

"Jesse Smith of Stonington, Connecticut," the hoarse voice went on. "That's me! A reformed Federalist that's seen the error of his ways. Who might you be?"

"Richard Nason," I told him. "Arundel."

When Smith spoke again his voice seemed almost respectful. "Got your straw with you?"

I said I had, and immediately felt him take me by the arm.

"We got a few choice positions vacant," he told me, urging me forward. "Being last in, I took the one farthest away from the door. That's the nicest when you're last in, because it's the only one you'll get. How'd you like a nice empty space next to me, only a little further removed from the door?"

"Fine!" I told him, heartened by his folly.

He pulled the truss of straw from my shoulder, and I could hear him breaking it open. "You want to take your bearings damned careful if you have to get out of bed in the dark," he warned me, "because this is an awful easy place to get turned around in. If you get lost, you might be five or six months finding your bed again."

The other men snickered. It seemed strange to hear their laughter coming up from the floor. Being unseen and unidentified, they were unreal, like ghosts.

"Wasn't you in command of the *Lively Lady* when she sunk the *Gorgon?*" Smith asked.

"It was the *Chasseur's* fight," I told him. "We only got there at the end."

Smith rustled my straw. "There you go!" he said at length. "All smooth and soft, like corn stubble after a frost. Lay down a minute before supper and let these other jailbirds do some warbling for you."

I followed his advice, grateful to him for his flow of talk. One of the other men coughed and cleared his throat.

"Simeon Hays: Baltimoe," he said softly. "Privateer *Surprise* of

Baltimoe. We-all heard about the *Gorgon*. That must 'a' been a right amusing lobster-boiling. Jim Rickor, of 'Nappolis, he's over beside the doe. Next him is 'Lisha Whitten of Newburyport, and across from Jim is John Miller. All *Surprises*. John, he used to be an Englishman, but he don't like 'em no moe, so he's an American."

"Strange he don't like 'em!" a new voice said.

Smith spoke up again. "Meet Obed Hussey," he said. "Another of them Maine Federalists."

"Jesse," the new voice protested, "that ain't right, not even in fun. I'd ruther you called me what you call the lobster-backs than be called a snivelin', English-lovin' Federalist!"

"Well," Smith said to me, "you prob'ly get the general idee."

"Supper!" a voice near the door said suddenly. The wicket slid wide open.

Smith took me by the arm and led me to the door, where each of us received a tin cup of cocoa and a quarter loaf apiece.

"Drink it where you are," Smith said. "If you try to walk round with it you might drop it, and you wouldn't get no more."

When we had given our cups to Carley and gone back to our straw again, I knew I could have eaten five loaves of bread instead of a quarter loaf, and topped off with something substantial like a sizeable platter of salt fish and pork scraps and one of my aunt Cynthy's lemon pies as a sort of stopper on it.

"Can't we get more than that?" I asked.

"That's more'n we're supposed to get," Hays said. "The bread, that's fixed up for us by the prison committees. They give the money to Carley, and he buys the bread. We ain't supposed to have that much to eat. You get kind of used to it, though. Your stomach shrinks."

"Your brain don't shrink, that's the hell of it!" Jesse Smith said. "You get to thinking about baked beans and brown bread, or a nice clam chowder with sliced potatoes and onions in it and pork scraps floating around on top." I could hear him swallow hard.

"Or hash," said another voice.

"There goes 'Lisha Whitten with his hash!" Smith said bitterly. "Can't you talk about *nothin'* but hash?"

"I like hash," Whitten said. "You take a nice hash chopped up plenty fine with boiled potatoes and raw onions, and brown her——"

"Listen," Smith said harshly, "do you s'pose anybody in this Cachot don't know as much about hash as you do? We never mention food in here without you have to go to work and drag in that hash of yours. Hash, hash, hash, hash, hash! That's all you can think about: just hash!"

My mind seemed like a pond that is, as our Maine people are given to saying, working. The consciousness of Emily Ransome completely filled my head, yet other thoughts seemed to rise through that consciousness as air bubbles rise from the bottom of a working pond. They rose and vanished, leaving behind the deep and unchangeable consciousness that occupied me. I could hear Jesse Smith telling about the new tunnels the Americans were digging—tunnels large enough to let all of the five thousand American prisoners escape at one time; and simultaneously I could wonder and wonder unceasingly what in God's name had happened to Emily: where she had gone and with whom; and whether she was comfortable, with enough to eat.

"They're going down twenty feet," Jesse said, "straight down from the floors of Number Four, Number Five, and Number Six! Then they're going to level out, bring 'em together, and dig for the wall."

He told how every American in the prison had been sworn to secrecy; how an arrangement of lamps and small wooden windmills, revolved by hand, had been invented to keep the air pure in the tunnels; how the excavated dirt was concealed from Shortland and the turnkeys by being fed, handful by handful, into the streams that run through each prison yard for washing.

"They're down there now," he said, "pecking at that damned yeller gravel an' bringing it up in their pockets and shirt tails." He stopped suddenly, and I knew he had remembered some of us were in the Cachot for duration; so that no tunnel could lighten our troubles.

One of the men near the door burst into a racking, interminable fit of coughing. Another went to snoring lightly.

There was this much to be said for the Cachot, along with the many things to be said against it: it seemed to act like a drug on most of us, so that we slept easily and heavily in it, despite the roughness of its granite floor and the brutal chill that fingered at our bones both night and day.

* * *

I had my first look, the next morning, at our tomb and those who shared it with me. By the faint light that filtered through the two hand-sized slits I could see that our granite box measured six paces by six paces, and maybe fifteen feet high. The floor was made of enormous blocks: the walls of smaller ones down which there was a perpetual trickle of moisture. There was a small pile of straw for each man, and at the end opposite the door a wooden bucket for a latrine. To one side of the iron door was a shelf, and on it a bucket of drinking water. Attached to the shelf by a piece of spun yarn was a half gourd for a drinking cup. We had the clothes we lay in, and our coarse prison blanket for a wrapping and a couch. In the room there was nothing else.

The door was of iron, with an eight-inch wicket in it. Toward night Carley would open the wicket a little, so we could look out without standing on each other's shoulders. At eight in the morning Carley came in with our breakfast: a cup of hot cocoa for each of us, and a quarter loaf of bread apiece, though the bread was not supplied by the British. Seemingly the smuggling of it to us was known and winked at. At the same time Carley would carry out and empty the bucket, renew our drinking water and look at us to see whether we were sick. At noon he brought us a bucket of soup. At night he brought us cocoa and bread again. Usually he brought it at six o'clock in summer and at four in winter, though he made the supper-hour later on days when other prisoners were sent to the Cachot. He did this so the new men wouldn't have to go supperless to bed. He was a kind-hearted man; and while he could do little because he had been threatened with punishment if he was caught smuggling food or liquor or newspapers to us, he did whatever he could.

Smith explained the workings of the place to me when we had heaped our straw in piles after breakfast and covered them with our folded blankets. He was a studious-looking young man with a long mop of straight black hair that came back over his ears and hung to his coat collar behind. If it had not been for his manner of closing his eyes after saying something particularly grave, and then opening them slowly and rolling them at his hearers with an air of simulated intolerance, he would often have been suspected of being serious, which he seldom was in my hearing.

"You got to keep busy in this place," he said, "and you can't keep 'em busy unless you drive 'em. They'd rather lay and brood. On account of that, we elect a captain and a first mate every week. Me, I'm captain this week, and Obed Hussey, he's first mate. Obed ain't a bad first mate."

Obed Hussey, I saw, was tall and broad shouldered: as fine looking a boy as would be encountered in a month of Sundays, except for the beard on his face and the raggedness of his clothes.

"Mr. Hussey, prepare the race track for the first race!"

Jesse explained while Obed Hussey busied himself in spreading his blanket in the middle of the Cachot floor. "We run a series of louse races. That's one way to keep 'em busy. Every man supplies his own louse; and anybody that claims not to have one is supplied by the nearest contestant. That prevents shirking. The winner gets held up to the window to report on what's going on outside. Losers have to let the winners stand on their shoulders. It's a good idea to have your races early and late, before and after market, when there's plenty in the yard to report. Between times you got to make 'em take exercise. They don't let us out of the Cachot to exercise; don't let us out for nothing except sickness, and you got to be awful sick to be took to the hospital. If you catch jail fever, they won't let you be took to the hospital till you're mottled with it, and that's pretty late. In fact, it's too late."

"Race track prepared, Captain Smith," Obed said.

The men rose reluctantly from their piles of straw, spectral gray figures in that dim tomb, and approached the blanket, on which Obed, with a bit of lime, had drawn seven narrow alleyways.

"You got yourself a louse?" Jesse asked me.

I told him I had come in clean.

"We'll fix that," Jesse said. "Rickor, give Cap'n Nason one of your best bugs. Don't give him none of them half-growed ones, neither! Give him a good big one, so's he'll have a chance with the rest of us."

Rickor, a tired-looking, stoop-shouldered man, searched himself carefully: then handed me an active gray insect.

The men knelt in a circle around the blanket, holding their entries at one end of the alleyways.

"Are you ready?" Jesse asked.

The others growled expectantly.

"Go!" Jesse shouted.

The seven entrants were dropped on the starting line. They moved jerkily and indecisively on the rough surface of the blanket.

"I snum!" Hussey said. "I got another putterer! I ain't had a fast one in a week!" He poked at his entrant with a straw, baulking him in his effort to go in the wrong direction.

"Whitten!" Jesse shouted angrily, "you're blowing on yours!"

"I ain't neither!" Whitten protested. "I got to breathe, ain't I? I wasn't doing nothin' but breathing."

"Breathe through your nose, then," Jesse said.

My entrant tacked first to starboard, then to larboard, as if in search of a safe haven; then stood still.

"What do you do when they stop?" I asked Jesse.

"Hope and pray," he replied. "They can't be touched when resting."

My insect conquered his suspicions and moved rapidly ahead.

Simeon Hays set up a shouting and snapped his fingers furiously.

"Move yo' laigs, Gray Ghost!" he cried. "Come on, you li'l' gray rascal!"

His louse, a long slender one, forged across the finish line.

"That's the fifth time in three days you came in first, Sim," Jesse Smith said sourly. "Either you're tempting that insect with some kind of food, or you're holding him over on us. Lemme see you execute him right now."

Simeon obligingly cracked him between his thumb nails.

Last of all Obed Hussey glumly herded his entry across the finish line with a straw, picked him up and examined him carefully; then destroyed him.

"I declare," he said, "there's something plumb contrary about these animals of mine! If I could do it, I'd be almost tempted to clean 'em out, lock, stock, and barrel. Come on, Sim!"

Simeon Hays mounted easily to Obed's shoulders, hooked his fingers over the sill of the small slit near the ceiling, and peered out through it. The rest of us went back to our blankets.

"It's kind of foggy up back," Simeon reported, "but you can see the hills the other side of Princetown. They's a man on a donkey on the long road, 'bout two mile away, heading north by east. Looks like a flea carryin' a littler flea. They's four Rough Alleys huntin' in the swill box back of Number One cookhouse. One of 'em's found something. Looks like a turnip! They's about two hundred men in sight. They got a Keno table pitched between Number One and Number Two. They's seven fellers playin' ketch with a ball made out of spun yarn . . ."

The rest of us lay back on our blankets in the gray gloom, striving to see into the prison yards with the eyes of Simeon Hays. It seemed to me that the world of which he spoke was a foggy, unreal world of specters and pixies. I took my miniature from my pocket and unwrapped it, holding it in the crook of my arm so I could study it unseen. The lips, I thought, moved as if to whisper to me; but in the Cachot there was no sound save the slurred Baltimore speech of Simeon Hays, telling us the few things he could see and understand of the infinitesimal happenings behind Prison Number One.

XXVIII

In the Cachot every man, I think, found his sharpest suffering from a different source. My own was the intolerable pressure of my incessant wondering: where had Emily gone, and how were things with her? What did she suffer, and what did she suffer for me? I think mine was the sharpest mental anguish there. For most of the other men, what they bore physically was enough to be busy over. Added to their special ills, we had a common bitterness in the scantiness of our food and light. Perhaps the darkness was the hardest to bear for most of us; there was never any light in that place save what filtered through the two small barred windows. Yet there were some among us who seemed most discomfortable because of the skimpiness of the rags they wore. One man would talk whimperingly an hour at a time of a fine suit of clothes he had once worn. Another bragged over and over of a beaver coat his father had given him on his fourteenth birthday; and there were others whose speech dwelt eternally on the diseases to which the Cachot, as well as the whole prison, exposed us. They would shiver and pretend to knock on wood as they spoke of jail fever, smallpox, and a violent pneumonia that set the lungs to crackling. Some found it most horrid—and indeed this was a thing oppressive to the soul—that for weeks on end we might have no more news of the world and of the movement of life upon our planet than did the very dead in the churchyard. The earth seemed to have closed over our heads and to lie heavily there.

It was not until October that we had word of how the war went, and then what we heard was horrible. Carley told us, doubtless not realizing what he added to our sorrows; for, as I have said, he was as kind as he dared be. He told us how the British had landed from their fleet in the Chesapeake and marched up to Washington, with Mr. Jefferson's militiamen running before them like frightened rabbits; and how they had put the torch to the library in Washington, to the Capitol, to the President's House, and to many public offices, as well as to the navy yard.

There was no racing on the blanket, and not even any looking out through the slit in the wall on the day after we heard that.

Perhaps it was a month after this when a New Bedford man, consigned to the Cachot for ten days, came in with news he had from a fresh draft of prisoners just brought to Dartmoor from the sea. Thus we learned how American privateers were being built in ever greater numbers and destroying more British commerce than at any time since the first two months of the war; and how British merchants were demanding the war be stopped before they were ruined. Even a hoarse and racking cheer went up from that dismal place when we thus heard of the greatest of all the privateering feats of the war: how the American privateer brig *General Armstrong* lay in Fayal harbor, neutral waters, and how she was unrightfully beset by a British sloop-of-war, a frigate and a ship-of-the-line, and fought off four hundred men, who came in boats to take her, destroyed most of them, and then was sunk by her own captain, who reached the shore safe with all but two of his men.

Through that chill autumn we gradually hardened to the increasing cold and dampness and so kept our health. Those who came in for ten-day stretches, however, having been accustomed to the use of hammocks and to better food and to exercise, developed troubles in their lungs from sleeping on the cold granite and quickly became fit subjects for the hospital.

The chief surgeon was a man named William Dykar, who had served in America with the British in our war for independence. He was an old man, violent tempered and opinionated, like so many officers who reach high positions in every army and navy; and he would visit no sick man in the Cachot because it was his belief that Americans could never be trusted to speak the truth and claimed always to be sick so to escape. Therefore sick men could get no treatment in the Cachot; though if one of them, on being released, was unable to stand, Carley would call a sentry and take him to the hospital, where too often he died. Therefore I say, after due thought and consideration, that this William Dykar, chief surgeon of the depot at Dartmoor from 1809 to 1814, was a deliberate and cold-blooded murderer.

It was toward the end of October that a seaman from Townsend, Maine, one Jesse Field, was put in among us. Beyond the fact that he had attempted to escape, and in so doing had lain full length in freezing mud against the wall of Number Seven Prison for a matter of six hours before being discovered, we could find out nothing from him, for he was weak and shaken with violent chills. He lay all that day on the straw we gave him, since he had been sent in without any; and on the following morning we saw there was a sort of brown crust on his lips and teeth. It looked to us like typhus. When Carley came with the breakfast, therefore, I told him to go again to Dr. Dykar and ask him for the love of God to give an order for this man to be taken to the hospital before all of us came down with the disease.

"I been meanin' to tell yez," Carley said. "Dykar's out! They t'run him out!"

"Who's the new man?" I asked. "Is he a real doctor, or a murderer, like the other?"

"Yez'll soon know!" Carley said. "His name's Magrath, and he's one of the salt of the earth—a descendant of the Irish kings."

We went back to watching Field and to cursing our jailers for their heartlessness. Before we knew it, almost, there was a rattling at the door, which swung back and revealed Carley standing at the side of a tall, thin, one-eyed man. He stood staring in at us, his mouth pursed up and pushed to one side and his left hand feeling at his face as if he sought a beard that wasn't there.

"How many of you in here?" he asked suddenly. His voice was deep and pleasant, with none of the snarl in it we were accustomed to hear from Dartmoor officials.

I came to the door and told him.

He looked me up and down. "Anything wrong with you?" he asked.

I told him there wasn't. "It's a man that came in yesterday: Jesse Field. He looks like jail fever."

"Hm," he said. "I'll trouble you to wrap him in his blanket and bring him out where I can see him."

Hays and I made a blanket snug around Field and brought him out. It was the first time we had been in the open air since August. The sky seemed huge and brilliant, even though heavy with gray clouds; and the air had a queer, piercing smell to it, as if drugged.

We put Field on the ground. The new doctor pulled down his eyelid and looked into his eye, then peered into his mouth.

"Call four sentries," he said to Carley. "This man goes to the hospital at once."

"Sor!" Carley said, "I'll have to be havin' an order. I'll run to the office and ask kin I have wan."

"No, you won't!" Magrath said. "You'll run to the nearest sentry! Who are you to talk about the office when I can see with half an eye you have a decent heart in you? Get along!"

He turned back to us. "Let's see this hole you live in." He walked into the Cachot, lowering his head as he passed through the door. We stayed behind, eager to have the air as long as we could.

He was pale when he came out, and there were beads of perspiration on his upper lip. "How are the vermin in there?" he asked.

"The fleas are bad," I told him, "but we keep the lice pretty well under control."

"We could do better with 'em if we had some light," Hays said.

"You have no light?" Magrath asked incredulously. "You mean you spend your lives in the dark?" The other men in the Cachot came to the door one by one, then edged, blinking, into the open, staring up at the sky and at their own raggedness.

"We're not allowed to have candles," I told him. "This is pretty brutal treatment, Doctor. If I'd ever caught one of my men treating a dog like this, I'd have knocked him into the scuppers."

Four sentries, militiamen, warmly dressed in long hooded overcoats, came up and looked wonderingly at us. I would have paid well for one of their overcoats if I had had the money, but Exeter jail had left me with only seven dollars.

"Take this man to the hospital on your muskets," Magrath said. They stood there for a second, uncertain. Magrath snapped his fingers, and they moved, then, to obey, though they were clearly reluctant.

"What are you in for?" he asked me.

"Four of these men are in on a false charge," I told him. "They're in for duration. So am I. There's more reason to what they charge me with, but I'm guilty of no crime. I'm guilty of nothing but trying to escape."

There was a commotion in the prison yard on the other side of the tall iron fence that separated the Cachot enclosure from the prisons. Prisoners shouted and ran toward the pickets. We saw Captain Shortland, followed by a militia officer, hastening toward us.

We watched him coming, stocky and strong; and the prisoners in the yard shouted in time with his footsteps, "LOB ster, LOB ster, LOB ster!" By the time he reached us he was red and angry.

"Good-morning to you, Captain," Dr. Magrath said.

"Who let these men out?" Shortland demanded. "Carley! Carley! What in hell do you mean? Put these men where they belong!"

"My fault, Captain," Dr. Magrath said. "I had a report: a case of jail fever. These men, if you'll permit me to say so, Captain, should be looked after more carefully."

"*Looked* after!" Shortland said. "What in God's name do you mean? I was told to put 'em in close confinement. Should I button 'em into lace nightgowns and send 'em to bed in my guest chamber?"

"Indeed and indeed, Captain," Magrath said, "you've little leeway in carrying out your orders! Aye! What I have in mind, Captain, is that these men, after all, are prisoners of war, and I have a fixed conception of a prisoner of war. He's a man held in trust: a man for whom an accounting must be rendered when the war's over."

Shortland laughed, a sharp, mirthless bark. "Good God, Doctor," he said, "let's not have trouble at the very beginning! You know what orders are! These men are where they belong! What good is close confinement if you make it a damned lawn party, eh? These men get exactly what they deserve! Here, you, Carley! Push 'em back in the Cachot!"

Carley fussed around us like a kindly old woman, saying, "Now, byes! Now, byes!"

Magrath went on talking to Shortland in his deep, soothing voice, and we hung back against Carley's insistent pushing so we might hear as much as we could.

"Quite so, Captain," he said, "but we don't have to change close confinement to something worse, eh, Captain? Sleeping on granite, now, in this climate! There's nothing like this in all England. Did you ever try sleeping on granite, Captain?"

"No, by God!" Shortland shouted, "and until I do what these men have done I never expect to!"

"Not that, Captain!" Magrath protested: "You don't mean that! These men served their country, as I understand it. Nothing about that to deserve granite beds in winter, eh? I doubt you'd have been pleased, Captain, when you were first lieutenant of the *Melpomene* —hah, hah! There's a many of us remember that cutting-out party of yours, Captain! Suppose, instead of cutting out the *Avanturier* and winning the rank of commander you'd fallen into the hands of the French and they'd clapped you into a black hole? Left you there with no light, and wet granite for a bed, eh?"

Shortland made a contemptuous sound in his throat. "Punishment's not punishment unless a man knows he's being punished!" he said.

"Every damned one of these Americans is determined to get free! If we don't punish 'em we'll have 'em all breaking out and terrorizing the country."

"Ah," Magrath said, "I had Americans at Mill Prison before I came here. There isn't one of 'em that'll give up trying to get free because you put 'em in the Cachot when they fail. No, no! Nothing gets anywhere with 'em but kindness! The harder you are on 'em, the worse you'll find 'em. They're not Frenchmen, Captain."

"You're wasting your breath, Doctor," Shortland snapped. "I know how to handle my men!"

Magrath twisted his mouth and fingered his chin. "Yes," he said mildly. "That must be true. But let's look at the medical end of it, eh? I tell you, Captain, I don't like this African smallpox that runs about here, nor this violent pneumonia. They're like deadly poisons if not treated quickly and treated well. I must ask to be allowed to keep my eye on these men, or the guard may slip the wicket some fine morning and find all of 'em stiff as a sternpost."

They turned toward the Cachot, as if already it had become a charnel house; and when Shortland saw us still crowded in the doorway, holding it open against Carley's efforts to push us in, his face took on the look of badly cooked beef.

Before he could speak Simeon Hays shouted to Magrath: "Feed him some calomel, Doctor! His liver ain't what it ought to be!"

With that, not wishing to cause trouble for Carley, we gave ground, and the door clanged shut on us once more.

Now, whether the doctor's suggestions had some effect on Shortland, or whether the doctor himself was responsible, I don't know; but one November evening—a cold, dark twilight, when we were lying silently on our piles of straw, which had grown so shredded and mouldy that they were less like straw than like dusty chaff—Carley rattled the door and pushed open the wicket.

"Here, byes!" he said. There was exultation in his voice. "I got a present for yez!"

I got up quickly, stumbling over Hays, and went to him.

"Don't nivver say I ain't give yez nothin'!" he said, handing me a piece of candle, an acid bottle, and a bundle of sulphur-tipped spunks for dipping in the bottle.

"Who are they from?" I asked.

"I dunno nawthin' about it," he said. "When yez finish with that, I'll get yez more; but pay attention to this, for the love av Mary! Whenivver yez use it, stuff the windys full of straw so the light won't show."

I doubt there are many folk, barring the blind, who know what it is to spend the greater part of their time in the thick dark. There is little I can say about it save that all of us dreaded the coming of night more than we had ever dreaded anything. Miller, the Englishman who had turned American, got the horrors one November evening. He burst out snuffling and groaning and hiccupping like a child, declaring he couldn't live another day in the place, and saying there were bells ringing in his ears, piercing his brain like knives. He carried on to such a degree that Hays and I crawled over and got our hands on him, lest he knock out his brains against the floor.

That one small point of yellow flame, almost absorbed by the dark walls of the Cachot, turned our misery into what, by comparison, seemed gaiety; for when the candle was kindled, our minds took fire from it as well, so we were able to speak, instead of lying silent and helpless. If we wished to move we could do so without stumbling over a man's legs—which was a serious business, because our legs were thin-skinned from scanty food, close confinement and perpetual dampness. Above all we could occupy ourselves by lying around the candle as the spokes of a wheel radiate from the hub and engage in the making of hair bracelets, this being an art in which Jim Rickor had perfected himself when he should doubtless have been working at something that is known as "more useful." Because of this I have ever since been loth to say what is useful and what isn't.

Since our hair had not been cut for months—nor our beards shaved, for that matter, nor our clothes washed, nor clothes or shoes given to us to replace the rags in which we lay—we were able to pull long hairs aplenty from our own heads for the making of bracelets. These, we hoped, would serve a double purpose; for not only did they occupy our hands, but Rickor claimed they were sovereign remedies against rheumatism. Therefore we made them prodigally; and each one of us had hair bracelets on his wrists and ankles, and hair rings on his fingers, while Rickor made himself a collar, an inch and a half wide, with a neat cravat, all woven out of hair.

With the coming of December we had a fruitful subject for conversation. The month had no sooner started than Carley told us there was a rumor through the prison that American commissioners and British commissioners had met in Ghent, in Holland, to discuss peace, and were close to arriving at a decision. Thus, suddenly, we began to hope. For months we had thought of nothing in the morning except how to get through the day, and at evening how to bear one more night. But now we had rosy and heart-stirring dreams that Peace might come at any moment to free us from cold and filth and aching bones, as it had come to free the Frenchmen. Every visit of Carley's was an adventure: he might, we thought, have news; and whenever he came to the wicket we held our breaths for fear we might lose a word.

Our hopes rose and fell like a fire. Jesse Smith came back to us on the ninth, swearing that if he hadn't known us in the early days of our imprisonment, he'd have taken us for haystacks because of the length of our hair and beards. He had been caught trying to scale the wall, he said; and when we asked him why he had tried to escape with Peace imminent, he laughed sardonically.

"Peace!" he said. "If there's to be Peace, why are the British fitting out an expedition to capture New Orleans? They don't know when they're licked! They don't know yet that we licked 'em in the Revolution! You got to lick 'em three times before it counts, and we've only licked 'em twice, so far!"

Sick at heart, we told him to hold his tongue, and set him to making a hair bracelet, loaning him our own hair for it. I can hear him now, commenting on his first bracelet.

"Hair bracelets!" he said. "My God! If the folks at home could only see me now! What if this should ever get to be known in Stonington, Connecticut! I can hear 'em, pointing at me and saying, 'There goes Jesse Smith, that was captured by the British in the war and suffered horribly, making hair bracelets! Wounded, too, he was: cut his finger on a hair!'"

But rumors of peace persisted, and so, too, did the attempts to escape, as we knew from men who were daily thrown in the Cachot.

A part of the fever to escape, it seemed to me, was due to the approach of Christmas; for Christmas is made much of in our province of Maine as well as in all New England; and as December dragged by, on snow-laden wings, our thoughts and our speech turned continually to our homes, so that we were filled with a powerful longing for them. There were times when it seemed to me I could smell, even through and above the stench of the Cachot, the odor of roasting goose, the sweet scent of spices on apple sauce, the faint mellow perfume of cider, the fragrance of mince pie. In my imagination I could see the frost figures on the windows of our large front room and catch the smell of the house: a scent of dry pine wood and cinnamon and soap and smoke, mixed with a faint trace of hay and sea air.

Christmas was a dark day, and we burned our candle all the morning so we could see to work on our hair bracelets; and Carley, instead of opening the wicket to give us our soup, unlocked the door and swung it open. Behind him we saw the doctor, tall and thin and one-eyed, wrapped in a heavy brown overcoat dusted with fine snow. From under his coat he drew a small bundle.

"Well, gentlemen," he said in his deep pleasant voice, and he wasn't being sarcastic, either, though we were the wildest and raggedest looking men, I do believe, that ever in the history of the world had been called "gentlemen," "well, gentlemen, I wish you many, many merry Christmases—in your own country."

"We wish you the same, Doctor," said Simeon Hays. "We wish you the same, in this country or any other."

"Yes," the doctor said, clearing his throat, "yes. I appreciate that very much. Are you gentlemen quite well?"

"Why," Simeon Hays said, "considering the amount of wine we drink and the number of rich seegars we smoke, we're tollable, Doctor—tollable. Our appetite ain't too good: probably there ain't one of us could eat more than one cow, unless it was an awful small one."

"I see," the doctor said. "I wished very much to bring you something to read, gentlemen, but like most other things, that seems to be forbidden. I've brought you a small plum pudding, and Carley has a full ration for you today instead of the regular two-thirds ration. I deeply regret the plum pudding is so small, but I'm forced to say that gentlemen who've been on two-thirds rations for months are almost better off with no plum pudding at all."

He gave the bundle to Simeon Hays. Carley, overcome with emotion, rattled our bowls against his pail of soup with as much noise as though building a new wing on the Cachot.

I fished two clusters of hair bracelets from behind my pile of straw and handed one of them to the doctor. "Doctor," I told him, "we couldn't figure what to give you for a little remembrance, so we left it to each man. Oddly enough each man decided that the most useful thing would be a hair bracelet. We want you to take them as meaning we're grateful."

The doctor took the lot and examined them, smiling queerly. When he spoke, he seemed to find difficulty in expressing himself. "Why, gentlemen," he said, "this is a—this is a—I'm sure I shall never—this is a most unexpected——"

"From his childhood he's always hankered for nothing on earth so much as a hair bracelet," Simeon Hays enlightened us in a hoarse whisper.

Seeing the doctor had no desire to make a longer speech, I handed the other cluster of bracelets to Carley.

"Timothy Carley," I said, "these are for you, with thanks for past kindnesses."

"Oh, holy Mary!" Carley said, snuffling childishly, "I'm as proud of 'em as I'd be of the Garter!"

"Why, you wicked, blasphemious old man!" Simeon expostulated, very ladylike; "*whose* garter?" With that, being half starved as usual, we went for our soup.

Dr. Magrath cleared his throat. "I have one other little gift for you, gentlemen. It's only a bit of hope, so to speak; but there's worse gifts than hope. You may be quite certain that before this month is over there'll be a peace treaty signed between England and America."

We stared at him. I know that I, for one, had such a pounding in my throat that I had trouble in downing my soup; for the face of Emily Ransome came so suddenly into my mind that an enormous hand seemed to clutch at my heart and squeeze it.

Magrath smiled a lopsided smile at us, blinking his one blue eye; then the iron door clanged shut behind him.

"Well," said Simeon Hays, holding up a spoonful of soup. "Here's to Christmas and freedom!"

* * *

Magrath had been right, for on the twenty-ninth day of December word was cried through the prison that on December 24th, in Ghent, the commissioners of England and America had signed a treaty. The war was over!

Peace! Nothing to do but for everybody to go home, kiss his wife and family or his sweetheart, and go back to the counting house, or begin milking the cow or hauling the nets again.

Peace! Nothing to do but throw the prison gates open. Nothing to do but open the door of our hell, the Cachot, and let us walk forth free men.

No, it was not like that. It was with the very signing of peace that the climax and worst of our Calvary began.

All the world knows that the St. Bartholomew of Dartmoor Prison came after the Peace had been signed.

XXIX

In the Cachot we innocently thought night after night that with the coming dawn Shortland would throw open the iron door; yet the days and the weeks went by, leaving us no better off than we had been before the Peace. January came down on us with a howling blizzard, and the short, bitter cold days dragged so slowly that we came to seem to ourselves like old, old men. Things that had happened a week before were lost, almost, in the dust of distant ages.

From overmuch lying on the granite floor we had sores on our legs and hips and shoulders. Some of our sorry company were given to periods of moaning and sobbing that made me shiver and retch. For days on end Simeon Hays sat huddled in his blanket, hugging his knees, staring at nothing out of hollow eyes, making no sound except to grind his teeth. I turned more and more to my small picture of Emily Ransome, to look at it and stay my spirit with its loveliness; and when I did, my fingers shook and seemed to me more like claws than the fingers of a human hand.

Magrath came frequently to see us, but his visits were short because, apparently, the sight of us distressed him and he could do nothing to help us. Whenever he came we always asked about the Peace; but he could tell us nothing except that it could not be genuinely regarded as a peace until the sloop-of-war *Favorite* had carried a copy of the treaty to America, and until it had been ratified by President Madison and brought back again to England.

"Look here," I said to him one morning, late in January, "these men are losing hope. I can't make 'em work any more."

"Why not?" he asked.

"Well," I said, "I can handle one of 'em easily, but together they can beat me. I no longer have the heart to hit 'em."

He nodded and left us. That afternoon he returned with Shortland; and the five of us who were for duration were brought from the Cachot and lined up before the commandant and the doctor.

I was blinded by the glare of the open sky reflected from the snowy ground, and it was a little while before I was able to see the true fearsomeness of Hays and Rickor and Whitten and Miller, who were emaciated and horrible-looking.

Shortland and Magrath stood and eyed us silently, Magrath tall and pale and one-eyed, and Shortland broad shouldered and curly haired and red-faced, looking like Punch and smelling so strongly of rum that he made my mouth water. Shortland looked inquiringly at Magrath. "Well, what's wrong with 'em? They look like any of these damned tricky Yankees, so far as I can see."

Magrath stepped up to me and felt my upper arm. "Would you mind holding out your hand?"

I held out my hand. It seemed almost transparent.

Magrath thanked me: then stepped back beside Captain Shortland. "Captain, these men must be clothed. They must have fresh air each day. They've got to have half an hour of exercise in the open. I'll help you do your duty, but I won't connive at murder."

Shortland's face grew purple. "Why, by God, Magrath, what do you mean!"

"What I mean," Magrath said, and he spoke as pleasantly as though offering an opinion on the weather, "what I mean is that these men are sick. Hope deferred maketh the heart sick, Captain. They're not only sick; they're being starved to death. Surely your eyes are as good as mine."

Shortland dug his heel in the ground angrily. "These men are criminals!"

I heard Simeon Hays, beside me, mumbling in his unkempt beard, and took him by the wrist to keep him quiet.

Shortland took a quick step toward him. "What's that you say?"

"You're a hell of a captain," Simeon said dispassionately.

Magrath moved between Shortland and us. "Captain," he said, "these men are unstrung from cold and poor food and living in the dark. They feel an injustice has been done them, and I must confess to having the same feeling myself. They've been brooding over it. You must make allowances for them."

"I'll show 'em——" Shortland began savagely.

"I beg of you!" Magrath protested. "This is all beside the point! I've made up my mind. What I ask is little enough. If you find it impossible to agree, I shall be obliged to pursue the matter through other channels—at once."

"Of course," Shortland said sourly, "of course, if they'd give their paroles not to——"

"Just a moment, Captain!" Magrath broke in. "My opinion is not contingent on these men's paroles. They've got to be clothed and have exercise, whether they give paroles or not."

Shortland glowered, his lips pressed tight together so that he looked more than ever like Punch. Then he turned to Magrath with a frank and pleasant smile. "Well, well!" he said, "we mustn't be too hasty. I think I see your point of view—yes, indeed! I'll give it careful consideration, Doctor: careful consideration."

"That's a very generous spirit, Captain," Magrath said. "Under the circumstances, any undue amount of consideration would be inadvisable. Ah—you'll let me know to-morrow morning, eh?"

Shortland whirled to look for Carley. "Put 'em back!" he snapped, jerking his thumb at us. And off he stamped through the snow without another word to Magrath, while the prisoners behind Prison Number One, gathered at the iron picket fence that separated us from the yards, began to chant, in time to his footsteps, "LOB ster! LOB ster! LOB ster!"

* * *

Four days later Carley brought us five prison suits of coarse blue cloth, and new prison shoes made of felt with wooden soles. In the middle of the morning of that same day Carley unlocked the iron door and called the five of us into the narrow enclosure between the inner stone wall and the iron picket fence. There were five sentries drawn up in a line, waiting. At a word from Carley they went to pacing along the enclosure, twenty-five yards one way; then twenty-five yards back to the Cachot again; and we, like five sheep, or like five merchantmen under the convoy of five sloops-of-war, paced beside them.

The Americans came running from the yard of Prison Number One when they saw us, whereupon Carley warned us that if we attempted to talk with any other prisoners our exercise would be immediately stopped. With that he went over and stood by the iron picket fence to speak to the constantly growing crowd.

"Yez'll have to spread the word," he shouted to them. "Any attempt to talk to these byes in here and they'll get no more exercise. Look at 'em all yez want to, but don't say nawthin' to 'em!"

They liked Carley, we could see; they must have known he would do whatever he could for us; so they said never a word to him or to us: only stood pressed against the iron bars, looking and looking at us; and above their ceaseless gabbling we could hear other prisoners running across the cobbles of the prison yard to see this strange new spectacle: men who had been buried alive since midsummer.

Up and down we paced by the side of the sentries, and it was hard to tell which helped us most: the stretching of our legs in the open air, or the sympathy we could feel coming out to us from the restless, silent, strangely dressed crowd of men beyond the iron pickets.

Every day thereafter we were taken out and marched up and down by the side of the sentries for half an hour; and every day the men came from all the yards to watch us. King Dick was there on the second day, his bearskin hat towering above the men beside him. His black face was expressionless; but whenever I looked at him I could see his enormous white eyes, round as china doorknobs, rolling from side to side, and from the ground to the top of the twelve-foot iron pickets and back again: examining, I knew; estimating; calculating.

Because of the walks and the warmer clothes, and the decent feel of them against our bodies, we got back our self-respect and went to making hair bracelets again, and to holding our races, which we had given up.

It was on the morning of February 6th, a Monday, that we heard Carley gabbling to someone outside, very amiable and friendly.

When the door opened, Jesse Smith stood there, his hands on his hips, grinning down recklessly at Carley; and with him was another figure, a smaller one. Behind Jesse, a rolled blanket on his shoulder, peering and peering in an effort to penetrate the darkness of the Cachot, was Tommy Bickford—pink-cheeked, smiling, brown-eyed Tommy Bickford, whose father had taken my father on his shoulder when the Congress galley fought the whole British fleet at the Battle of Valcour Island and carried him wounded but safe to shore.

Carley pushed them in, looking hard at Smith before he swung the door shut. "Holy Mary!" he said. "Don't yez nivver do nawthin' but try to escape? There ain't nobody can say yez don't know what yez want! Yez'll be a great man, Mr. Smith!"

Jesse ignored him and pushed Tommy Bickford toward me. "There he is," he said. "Your eyes'll get used to it in a minute. Edge over."

I caught Tommy's wrist and drew him down on my heap of matted straw.

"Cap'n Dick," he said, "Cap'n Dick——" His voice broke.

"That's all right, Tommy," I told him. "I'm glad to see you; awful glad! What on earth have you been doing, Tommy, to get yourself put in this place?"

"Nothing, Cap'n Dick," he said. "Honest, I didn't do nothing! Only made out to escape."

"Well, you must be a born fool, Tommy, with good clothes and good food and good treatment, trying to——" I stopped. It came to me, suddenly, that he had made the attempt so he could be put in the Cachot with me.

"I only made out to, Cap'n Dick," he said, grinning at me.

"Who put you up to it? King Dick?"

"No, sir. King Dick, he thought mebbe he hadn't ought to let me do it on account of the way you might talk to him when you got out. He said you'd make a turrible yukkus, but I told him you wouldn't."

"When I get out?" I asked.

"Yes, sir. King Dick, he said if he could get word to you about getting out, you could probably get out."

The mere thought of escaping from the Cachot brought a moisture into the palms of my hands and a trembling into my knees. "The trouble with that, Tommy, is that if I should try it, the others wouldn't be allowed to take exercise any more."

"No, he meant all of you, Cap'n Dick, he meant you and the other four gentlemen."

Simeon Hays crawled over beside me and leaned on his elbow, staring at Tommy. Elisha Whitten and Jim Rickor and John Miller sat up on their blankets as if pins had been thrust in them.

"Go ahead, Tommy," I told him. I was proud to have the others see him sitting there, neat and pleasant and smiling, and to have them know our town of Arundel could produce a boy like Tommy Bickford.

"Cap'n Dick," Tommy said, and it was easy to see he was as excited over what he had to tell us as we were to hear it, "King Dick says these militia soldiers are turrible thick-headed: thicker-headed than any of the colored gentlemen in Number Four. He says they come from Somerset, up north of here, and he says a donkey's awful intelligent and thoughtful compared to Somerset militia. He says he's watched their eyes when they do sentry-go with you gentlemen, and every time they turn round, their brains keep right on travelin' for as much as a minute almost."

"He's right, by Jiminy!" Simeon said. "They're thick, and they're mean."

"Yes, sir," Tommy said. "And King Dick says any folks that have been treated the way you gentlemen have been treated can pull themselves up to the top of that iron fence; and he says the time to do it is when these Somerset lobsters turn around on their beat. He says they ain't thinking of nothing when they turn around, and it's awful hard for 'em to start thinking."

"Tommy," I said, "that fence is twelve feet high."

"Yes, Cap'n Dick," Tommy said. "That's what King Dick figured. But the cross bar between the pickets is only ten. King Dick says you can get your hands on the cross bar; then he and the others can push their hands through and shove you up."

I looked at Simeon Hays. He nodded. We looked at the others. They sat silent and motionless, staring at Tommy.

"You can do it, can't you, Cap'n Dick?" Tommy asked. It was less a question than a proud statement of fact, delivered by way of setting all doubts at rest.

"Yes, I can," I told him, not wishing to disappoint him, and wishing, also, to give the others as much confidence as possible. "Of course I can get over—of course we can get over; but when we get over, what do you think Shortland will be doing?"

"King Dick says for you not to worry about nothing but getting over," Tommy said. "King Dick says you'll be looked after. He says if you get out of here they'll never get you back in again."

Simeon Hays wiped the palms of his hands on his jacket. "When did he think?" he asked. "What day was he thinking of?"

"Why, to-day," Tommy said. "He'll be waiting there, to-day, right where they turn, down at the bend." He pointed at the door of the Cachot, and it seemed to me, as I turned my head to look where his finger was pointing, that I could see open country: the marshland along the creek behind our gray house in Arundel; the silvery-green pines that rise beyond it in unbroken ranks.

"Tommy," I said, "we can't do it to-day. Carley's responsible for us, and he'd get the blame. Carley's been pretty good to us, Tommy

—the only one that has, barring the doctor. Shortland would have him flogged, and it might kill him."

Tommy's under lip sagged.

"Carley goes to mass on Sunday," I told him. "He's a papist, and he has to go to mass; but that's six days off."

"It don't make a mite of difference," Tommy said, smiling and eager again. "King Dick said he'd wait there every day until something happened. He'll be there Sunday. He'll be there, Cap'n Dick! All you got to do, the day you want to try it, is to kneel down on one knee and tie your shoe when you come out of the Cachot."

"Tommy," I said, "you're a good boy."

* * *

Every day our exercising was watched by a larger and larger crowd, until it seemed to us there must be a thousand men crammed into the little piece of yard behind the tall stone haunches of Prison Number One, all of them following our every move as we marched up and down, up and down, beside the sentries. Every day King Dick was there, pressed tight against the iron railings, but behaving in a casual manner, as though he had more interest in the weather or in the tall Negroes who accompanied him than in any of us.

It was best, it seemed to me, to have the thing over as soon as possible; and so we planned, on Saturday, that when we came out on the following morning, we would walk to the end of the beat with the sentries, walk back to the Cachot, then go to the end once more and take an extra two steps when the sentries turned. With the second step we were to break for the picket fence, a matter of eight paces from our line of march.

It was chill that Sunday morning. When we heard the rattle of the key at the door Jesse Smith slapped each one of us on the back, saying, "Don't never let me see none of you again!" Tommy Bickford, who was hoarse with a cough, touched me on the arm and said, "Good-bye, Cap'n Dick. I'll be out on Wednesday with Mr. Smith."

A sour turnkey named Parker unlocked the door for us, and we went out, blinking, into the cold February air. The prisoners were close against the iron pickets, watching for us. When we appeared they murmured among themselves, sounding like a calm sea fingering and lapping at a seaweed-covered ledge.

I went down on my knee and fumbled with my shoe. It seemed to me the murmuring stopped.

"What you come out here for?" Parker roared at me. "Exercise or not?"

I jumped to my feet and fell in behind Miller. In front of him was Hays. In front of Hays were Whitten and thin Jim Rickor.

I was chary of looking straight at the silent crowd that stood behind the pickets, for fear Parker might see guilt written on my face; but I snatched a hasty glance at their watchful ranks and caught sight of King Dick, fixing his tall bearskin hat more tightly on his head and working his arms somewhat, as though to free them of pressure. His head was thrust forward, and his eyes, which ordinarily had the look of china doorknobs, were small white slits in his black face.

Parker, lounging against the corner of the Cachot, jingled his keys and stared lackadaisically at the silent crowd of prisoners watching us. I could see we had nothing to fear from him; for whatever was to happen would be finished before he knew it had begun.

I looked at the heavy-lipped, heavy-eyed face of the militiaman beside me and saw he was indeed as slow witted as King Dick had said. He was the very man, I hoped and believed, to stand stock-still with his musket on his shoulder and just stare at me for some precious seconds when he saw me run.

When we were abreast of King Dick we turned and marched again toward the Cachot. There was a slight swaying motion among the men near our huge black friend. I breathed deep, to ease the thumping of my heart. From the tail of my eye I saw King Dick shouldering himself free of those beside him. We turned at the Cachot and trudged back again.

I looked at the top of the pickets. The cross bar, high on the fence, was higher by two feet—by three feet—than the crown of King Dick's enormous bearskin hat.

I heard Hays clear his throat and knew how he felt, stuffed full and blown up with waiting.

My head was rigid on my neck, like the ball on a newel-post. I should, I felt, have set the attempt for later, when we had become more limber. My knees were stiff; my legs seemed like bean poles— thin and brittle and quite useless.

The sentries turned. The bright bayonet on the musket barrel of the man beside me swung slowly as he wheeled. I looked away from it: fixed my eyes fiercely on the ground. I took one more step, listening. There was nothing. I took another, turned sharp to the left and moved somehow toward a wild roaring that seemed to hold me up and engulf me. There was a vague, tossing movement before me, and I was conscious of a whining close by my shoulder, a whining I knew was made by Hays, straining to reach his goal. Yet I could see nothing with clearness except the towering pickets rising from a turbulent human sea and bound top and bottom by endless cross-pieces of iron.

I felt myself leaping at the upper cross-piece—leaping and reaching. I could see my fingers rise toward it, slowly, as a gull's beak rises toward a fragment of biscuit tossed from the stern of a vessel. They caught it and clung.

I could feel the hands of prisoners lifting my legs and feet. I was pushed up and up, though how I got over the top of the pickets I don't know. I only know I did, and then pitched forward and down into a turmoil of struggling, squirming men.

Hands clutched me anew. I was dragged rapidly through the crowd. I struggled for a footing and got one at last; and as I ran, I saw King Dick had me by the shoulder of my jacket with a huge black paw. He was clinging to his bearskin hat with one hand and whisking me along with the other. There were prisoners running ahead of us and on each side. We were the center of a rapidly moving mass of men in which it was almost impossible to distinguish individuals.

This throng surged abruptly against the rear of Prison Number One and swirled around it, leaving a narrow alleyway. I went up the steps and through the door behind King Dick. The crowd poured in behind us, quiet no longer, but shouting and cursing with excitement.

I was in a chair, then, and a man was daubing lather into my beard. In front of me towered King Dick, huge and black in his woolly suit, staring watchfully from one end of the building to the other.

I drew a deep breath. "Whew!" I said, "that was close! Did they get out? Did all of them get out?"

King Dick laughed a sudden nervous laugh, but instantly fell serious. "Nemmine 'at!" he said. "Keep yo' pan quiet till 'at beard gits shaved! Mah lan', Ah never see so much haiah, not on nuffin' seppen a goat!"

The barber's razor dragged at my tender skin as though it had the teeth of a cross-cut saw.

"Ah doan' want no cuts on 'at pan," King Dick warned him. "'Member what Ah tole you!" He looked around at the prisoners who filled the alleyway, gabbling and laughing. "Whah's 'at artis'?" he demanded.

"Right here, King," a voice said. I looked under the barber's elbow and saw a slender man crouched on the floor beside King Dick, a box held tenderly against his breast. The beard at length was gone. The barber passed a towel hurriedly over my face, and immediately the slender man opened his box and went at me with breathless care. I could see that the box contained a black powder, and that he was applying it with a rabbit's foot.

"We's raidy!" King Dick told the watchers. "Git away to bofe ends."

They hurried off, part of them to the front of the building and part to the rear. The slender man rubbed my neck and chest with the rabbit's foot.

"'At's enough!" King Dick said. "Cain't be too pinnicky, not 'is minute! You come on ovah to Number Foh."

He took me by the arm and hurried me to the back door. "Doan bovver wiv no one," he said. "Keep a-lookin' down, like you's a mad nigrah!" Fifteen or twenty prisoners sauntered out ahead of us. Others came out beside us, and still others in our rear. Surrounded by these stragglers we wandered to the covered way connecting the yards. There was a commotion among the sentries. The prison yards were filled with Americans, packed around the gates, moving aimlessly in excited clumps, hooting at the soldiers. We came safely to Prison Number Four and sedately mounted the stairs leading to King Dick's domain.

King Dick pushed me into his throne room, dropped heavily on his red plush throne, and eyed me thoughtfully.

"Namiah," he said to his seckatary, who stood waiting the royal orders, "go git a basket o' plum gudgeons an' foh mugs of beer, wivout no foam on 'em. 'Ey's goin' to be a war roun' heah, an' we better git ouahse'fs raidy."

XXX

Rᴉᴄᴋᴏʀ, Whitten and Miller had not attempted the barrier. Hays had got over, and within half an hour was as well swallowed in the crowd as I was myself. Captain Shortland, raging, had promised heavy punishments to the guards if we got clear of Dartmoor: not only that, but he swore to have us back in the Cachot and see us rot there.

There have certainly been larger wars than this war of six thousand unarmed, imprisoned Americans against red-faced Thomas Shortland and his regiment of thick-witted Somersetshire militia, but I doubt that there have been stranger ones.

The prison houses buzzed like beehives after our escape, and acquaintances came hurrying to see me on the second floor of Number Four to tell me how the governing committees of the prisons had refused to deal with Shortland and had ignored demands that we be given up; how even the Rough Alleys, headed by men we knew only as Sodom and Gomorrah, were fighting him and the militiamen with all the obscenities to which they could lay tongue; and how the bulk of the prisoners, simple seamen from New England and New York and the Chesapeake, were determined to give him no satisfaction.

It was on the day after our escape that King Dick came to me, chuckling. "'At ole Shoatland," he said, "he's goin' bus' his bazoo effen he gits much moh lip offen 'ese white boys. Mm, mm! 'At ole Shoatland, he's pow'ful mad!"

He had, King Dick said, closed the market, thinking to bring the prisoners to terms.

"Mah lan'l" the big Negro exclaimed, "what 'ose white boys call him an' call 'ose Som'set m'litia—ooh! Meks yo' yahs bu'n when you heahs it."

I could hear a derisive howling from the yard outside and from the lower floor of the prison house: the howling of hundreds of men; but King Dick would not let me go to a window to see what it was.

"Rest yo'se'f right yah," he said. "'At old Shoatland, li'l' buhd tol' him 'at one of you's hidin' in 'is prison, 'an he's goin' drive ev'ybody out so's he kin suhch it!"

"Maybe I'd better get in the hole?" I said, for King Dick had a movable slab in his throne room, and underneath it a royal store-house for his money bags and private rum supply; and this was my hiding place when searchers were near.

King Dick shook his head. "Ain't nobody goin' out, not till 'ey gits raidy," he said.

The howling grew louder; and as we watched the staircase at the rear of the long hall, a mass of shouting, laughing prisoners came pouring up onto our floor. Hard on their heels was a squad of Somersetshire militia, pursuing them with bayoneted muskets at the charge.

The prisoners came past us, leaping, whistling, turning hand-springs, roaring with laughter; and behind the angry, red-faced militiamen pressed another howling, capering mob. Thus escorted, front and rear, the militiamen shambled the length of the alley and vanished down the stairs at the far end, only to reappear immediately up the stairs opposite those which they had descended. At the top they turned in seeming desperation on those who followed them; their march reversed itself, the pursued becoming the pursuers. The place, it seemed to me, was full of squads of frantic militiamen, all of them preceded and followed and hindered and jostled by contemptuous prisoners.

Eventually King Dick tucked me snugly under the slab; the militiamen were left in possession of the building and allowed to search, while the prisoners packed the yard outside and cursed them for bloody library-burning lobsters and worse.

Later that day, when the black paint on my face had been renewed, we watched from a window to see the rioting in the yard.

There were men employed to light the lamps in the yards and market place, and when these men came in among the prisoners, they were promptly seized. Thereupon a company of militiamen was sent to the yard of Number Four Prison to push the prisoners into the prison house at the points of bayonets; and I truly believe any old woman would have known more than to send a small body of troops among reckless men at such a time. Resentful of the bayonets, the prisoners sought to pry up paving stones to use as weapons. We could see the soldiers cocking their muskets; and at this the militia officers came out in front of their men and ordered them back to the market place, in spite of the shouts of Shortland, who stood on the covered walk overlooking the yard, bawling God knows what to prisoners and soldiers alike. Thus the prisoners were conscious of defying Shortland successfully, and the Somersetshire militia could see they had been flouted by unarmed men.

*   *   *

I was in a fever to be free of the prison. To find myself out of the Cachot, rightfully a free man, since the war was over, and with every right to go in search of Emily, yet to be held here and to be a fugitive within the walls, was sheerly maddening. I was troubled, as well, by the news Jesse Smith brought when he was released from the Cachot and hurried to King Dick's domain in Number Four.

"By God!" he said, when he had looked hard at me and made sure it was I beneath the black paint, "I damn near died that morning, waiting to see if you'd get over!"

"Where's Tommy?" I asked him.

"Well," he said, "I was coming to that. I been kind of dreading this. That's an awful nice boy, Cap'n Dick! Gosh! Seemed as if he wouldn't talk about *nothing* but Cap'n Dick!"

"Say what you mean," I told him. "Are you trying to tell me Tommy's sick? What's the—— He hasn't got the smallpox?"

"No, it ain't the smallpox. He—by gracious, I never *seen* a nicer boy!"

I waited for him to go on. He cleared his throat and ran his fingers through his hair, matted from his ten days in the Cachot. I could smell the stench of the place, as if a gargantuan polecat had bedded down with him; and the sweat came out on me at the thought that violent, worthless Shortland could have sent a boy like Tommy Bickford, worth a million Shortlands, into that terrible granite box.

"That night," Jesse went on, "after you'd broke out, he had a little cough, and a chill that wouldn't let up. He shook and he shook, and he couldn't get to sleep. First we thought he was excited on account of you, because he kept talking about Cap'n Dick. Cap'n Dick this and Cap'n Dick that, and some lady or other!" He coughed and cleared his throat and looked at me apologetically. "No offense," he added.

"No," I said.

"We—well, we fixed him up with extra blankets, but when he went out of his head and began thinking you were back with us, along toward morning, we suspicioned what it was."

"Did you send for Magrath, Jesse?"

"We sent for him when Carley brought breakfast."

"Did Magrath say it was jail fever?"

"He didn't say anything," Jesse said uncomfortably. "Just picked him up in his arms and walked off with him."

"Well, Jesse," I said, "he's a good boy. There never was a better. I'd like you to get cleaned up and find out about him. I'd like you to go just as quick as you can. His father saved my father at the Battle of Valcour Island."

"Sho!" Jesse exclaimed. "Did he, now!"

"Yes," I said. "Go see Magrath. Tell him I'll come over any time it'll help Tommy. You tell Tommy he needn't worry: I'll wait for him."

We waited for tidings of Tommy in the midst of a turmoil such as I had never heard or seen before; for Shortland sent message after message into the prisons, demanding this and demanding that, so that the criers were forever crying this madman's proposals up and down the aisles, and the prisoners were perpetually howling their hatred and contempt for what he proposed; and the yards outside the prison were in a tumult all through the day because the sentries and wardens were being mocked by every prisoner in sight.

At the end of a week this violent and foolish man, finding the prisoners determined to defy him, opened the market once more. Thereupon the prisoners, realizing they had beaten Shortland, celebrated their victory.

Instead of stopping their gambling at a reasonable hour, they kept it up all night; and there was riotous drunkenness and uproar on all sides, in spite of the efforts of the cooler-headed to keep order.

It was early on a March evening that King Dick came hurriedly to his throne room to stand between the stanchions, his melon-shaped head tilted over on his huge shoulder as if listening to the shrill clamor that rose from the bottom floor of the prison.

"Here!" I said. "What's the matter? Tommy isn't worse, is he?"

King Dick took off his bearskin cap and ran his huge, banana-like fingers across his forehead.

"Mah lan'!" he said. "Mah lan'! 'At's too close for mah pleasure! 'At ole ship *Favorite,* she better git in here wiff 'ose raffication papers, showin' we's free men, else 'ey git 'eirseffs jibbited up wiff bayonets!"

"What happened?"

"'Ose sentries was fixin' to lock 'em dohs when Ah come back fum 'at ole hospital," he said, "an' one of 'ose Som'set m'litia, he up an' jibbits his bayonet into one of 'ose white folks—jibbits him in his laigs an' in his back an' in his rump, so's he's all bloodied up! Mm, mm!

Mah lan', 'at ain't no way to ack! Ah doan' lak 'ose ole bayonets, no SUH!"

"What was he jabbed for?"

"Not for nuffin'," he said. "He hadn't done nuffin' nor said nuffin'."

"I don't believe it," I told him. "An armed man wouldn't bayonet a prisoner without reason."

"Ah heahs you," King Dick said calmly. "'Ese Som'set m'litia boys, 'ey bayonet 'em wiffout no reason, 'cause Ah seen it! Mm, mm! 'Ose white folks is mad! Me too! Ah's mad; on'y Ah wants sompin to fight wiff, effen 'ere's goin' to be jibbitin' wiff bayonets. Effen Ah ain't got nuffin' to fight wiff, Ah moves out. Lissen 'ose white boys! Mah lan'! Lissen now: wha's goin' on now? Lissen to——" He broke off, for in the yard outside was suddenly set up a wild yelling. We could see prisoners at the far end of our floor pushing against the windows to look down at the tumult.

"Lissen! Lissen to——" King Dick began again, but he never finished, for the prisoners at the windows broke away and ran for the staircases, shouting, "*Favorite! Favorite!*" At the same time the staircases leading down from the cock loft were filled with men, all racing for the open air.

I saw Jesse Smith free himself from the scrambling throng and swing his arms at me. "*Favorite!*" he bawled. "She's in! When you going back to Arundel?"

* * *

In that very moment the hopes of six thousand men, legally entitled to freedom, rose to a happy height. Jesse Smith was laughing deliriously. He actually began to dance, and hugged me like a bear, trying to make me dance with him. "Old Stonington, Connecticut!" he shouted, when I had pushed him off. And for half an hour thereafter he seemed unable to do more than splutter with delight and shout the three words over and over: "Old Stonington! Old Stonington, Connecticut!"

To have told any of these six thousand men then that he would be in Dartmoor more than seven days longer would have brought on an immediate fight, I think. Not one of the six thousand could have dreamed that Reuben Beasley, the American agent in England, would not have ships to carry them home in a week's time.

That night I washed the black from my face, and the next day went boldly and openly to the hospital to see Tommy Bickford. His curly brown hair had been cut close to his head; and he looked shriveled into himself from the burning of the fever, so that he seemed like a skeleton beneath the bedclothes.

"Well," I said, "how you feel, Tommy?"

"Good," he said, and moved his lips a little, as if he tried to say my name, but hadn't the strength.

"Well, Tommy," I said, "you're a good boy. I wouldn't have let you go into that Cachot, Tommy. Don't you ever do anything like that again."

"No, sir," he said.

"You hurry up and get fat and strong," I told him, "so we can start together when the time comes."

He nodded, fixing his eyes on my face as if to see whether I had any plans I was keeping from him. "That lady come back?" he asked.

"No," I said. "I've had no means to hear from her or from Jeddy Tucker."

I took her picture from my pocket, unwrapped it, and held it up for him to see, thinking it might do him good to look at a face not covered with stubble, or grooved from starvation, or gray from being penned inside dripping stone walls. His eyes fastened to it and clung; so I propped it against a fold in his blanket.

"Tommy," I said, "I want you to put some flesh on your bones. We're liable to be out of here almost any hour, but now I won't go till you go with me."

I felt a hand on my shoulder and looked up to see tall, thin, one-eyed Dr. Magrath.

"Well, well!" he said. "This is an unexpected pleasure!" He stooped over and picked up Tommy's wrist, seeming not to notice the miniature of Lady Ransome.

"Time for a little sleep, Tommy," he said. He lifted an eyebrow in my direction, so I got up to go.

"Eat your soup and get fat," I told Tommy again.

I took back the miniature and went out with Magrath. There was a strange, unpleasant, unclean smell in the stone-walled corridor.

"Can't you get him out of here, Doctor?" I asked.

Magrath drew his fingers down the blind side of his face, as if to free himself of a cobweb.

"Look here, Captain," he said, "do you think it's quite safe for you to be out in the open like this?"

"But we're at peace!"

"Yes," he said, "but you're still in prison, and some people can't distinguish between a man who happens to be in a prison and a criminal. I'm having hard work to get your friends released from the Cachot."

That was the truth of it: the war was over, yet from morning to night the Somerset militiamen glowered at us over the walls; their bayonets winked at us in the watery sun that occasionally peeped through the rain clouds and fog banks of late March. The war was over, yet the bells still hung on the wires; and each night, at sundown, sentries manned the fire steps while turnkeys herded us into our prison houses and locked the doors on us. We were at peace with the English, yet the criers cried through the prisons a notice from red-faced, hook-nosed Thomas Shortland that any man caught attempting to escape from the depot would be punished by being locked in the Cachot for ten days.

Thus the deferred hope of these six thousand penniless and half-starved men threw them into a desperate rage that grew deeper and more bitter from day to day; and after a week had gone by with no prospect of relief or release for any man there began to be talk of how we could overpower the guards, break the gates, and march in a body to Tor Bay or Teignmouth. This talk, we learned, was carried somehow into the market place and spread among the farmers and merchants of Princetown and Tavistock and Moreton-

Hampstead. Men from those towns moved their families into Plymouth for fear the country would be overrun by six thousand angry Americans. The guards on the walls were doubled.

I think I alone had cause for gratitude; for Tommy Bickford was gaining weight; his talk was beginning to sound as though there might be a trace of blood and muscle in him after all, and I made trip after trip to the hospital without being discovered by Shortland.

"Be careful, Cap'n Dick," Tommy warned me after one of my visits. "I'd feel safer about you if you'd kept on your paint, I think. Maybe you'd better turn blackamoor again."

I laughed at him then; but half an hour later I had a shock and thought for a moment that perhaps he had been right.

"You go on up to Cap'n Shoatland's office," King Dick said, meeting me at the top of the second-floor stairway in Number Four. "You go on right up there. King Dick and Shoatland, 'ey bofe say so."

"What!" I gasped. "What!"

But the big black man laughed and reassured me—though he mystified me too. Visitors for me waited in the office; the commandant himself had agreed to let me go and come, and he had added the words "in spite of past offenses."

"Who is it?" I asked.

"Ah doan know," King Dick said and giggled. "Whyn't you go fine out yo'se'f? Sooner you hurry, sooner you'll know. Ain't Ah tole you——"

So far as I know he may have finished his question. If he did, it reached only the empty air where I had stood when he began it, for I took his advice and hurried.

From the door of Shortland's office I stood and looked back, down the hill and across the market place to the seven prison buildings crouching at the bottom of the slope, like seven cats watching me patiently, as if secure in the knowledge that still I could not escape them. Then I knocked on the door and went in.

Shortland, red-faced and hook-nosed, was crouched behind his desk. Opposite him sat a slender gentleman in blue broadcloth, accompanied by a fashionably-dressed lady, plump and pretty and fair-haired. The man jumped up when I came in, and looked hard at me; and I remembered his eyes. Like those of Emily Ransome, they were the color of smoke in the swamps of Maryland.

"Why—" he said—"why—the man I wanted—why, what's happened to you? I mean, you may not remember me: Sanderson, my name is."

"Yes," I said, "I remember Mrs. Sanderson and you very well—very pleasantly." I licked my lips to take the dryness from them and steadied myself. "Your sister," I said, "your sister——"

"Yes," he said. "Where is she?"

"Where is she?" I asked. "Where is she? Don't you know where she is?"

"No," he said. There was a look in his smoke-colored eyes that wrung my heart with the memory of how Emily had put her hand to her throat when Sir Arthur had offered to buy my dog Pinky.

"Wait," I said, "wait a minute. You've heard from her, or you'd never have come to me."

"She wrote and told us," Mrs. Sanderson said. "We came home as soon as we had the letter."

"Yes," Sanderson added, "but in the letter she said you would know everything."

I turned from them and looked at Shortland. He stared back at me with hard, round eyes; and his thoughts were easily read. He would have taken infinite pleasure in having me triced up and catted.

"Letters and messages have come for me in the past seven months," I said. "Where are they?"

He answered as quickly as if I had asked him the number of guns on Nelson's *Victory*. "There's nothing for you. No letters or messages." His hawk-like glare was fixed on my face; his barrel of a chest stuck out like a pigeon's.

"No letters or messages in these seven months? Did you say there have been no letters for me, Captain?"

"That's right!" he said, "that's right! You understand me now."

He turned to Mrs. Sanderson. "These Americans give us a deal of trouble," he said, seeming to speak merrily and confidentially. "It appears we can't do anything to suit 'em."

I looked at the knuckles of my right hand and wondered at the whiteness of them; at the way these long months of darkness and dampness and bad food had made knuckles and joints stand out like knobs. What Shortland told me was impossible; but there was no way of knowing whether the letters had been appropriated by prison officials, or whether they had been sent to Sir Arthur Ransome, or what had happened to them. I knew the man was lying: I could see it in the defiance of his eye and catch it in his overready answers. Yet there was nothing to be gained by bandying words, and I told myself I must go easy, take it gently.

"Seven months!" Sanderson said. "Where have you been for seven months that you couldn't ask about letters?"

"Buried alive," I said, "but that's over now. Your sister: she wrote you a letter. Where did she write it from?"

"There was no way of telling. It was handed to the captain of a 74 in a Portsmouth gambling club."

"In a gambling club!" I said. "Who—not by——"

"No," he interrupted, "by a gentleman: a gentleman who had won money from the captain. When the captain was stripped clean, the gentleman gave back his money and the letter with it, asking that it be delivered; and in the course of time I received it."

"Well," I said, "she must have been afraid Sir Arthur might find her, I think." I looked at Shortland, sitting puffed up and angry behind his desk, eyeing me closely as though wishful of snatching the thoughts from my brain; and I made up my mind I had said almost enough.

"I think so," Sanderson said. "Aye, I think so."

Mrs. Sanderson snuffled suddenly, then dabbed at her eyes with a wisp of a handkerchief and smiled up at me mistily.

Sanderson coughed. "It took us aback at first, the things she wrote about you. Excited—a little wild—but under the circumstances—ah —I dare say quite genuine—ah—her happiness and all that! Ah—we're here because we'd like to be friendly."

Mrs. Sanderson nodded in agreement. "We'd like you to know it's understood," she said gently. "We're taking her side, of course. Yours too, Captain."

"We've come to you first," Sanderson said, "because we couldn't find her in the three days since we landed. Unhappily she hasn't any relatives but me, and no family friends to turn to. It might be you could help us find her, and, at any rate, we've come to take you out of prison. We'd like to do that for your own sake, Captain. We found out we can free you; and we'll sign the papers now if you're ready to go with us."

I looked from him to Shortland, doubting I had heard correctly.

"Yes," Sanderson said, "it's a new ruling of the War Office. Any American prisoner must be released at the request of a British subject, or of the captain of an American merchant ship; and at his release he receives a passport from Captain Shortland."

"Nothing has been said to the prisoners about this," I said to Shortland.

"I dare say," he returned coolly. "It's quite possible there's been an oversight on the part of one of the clerks."

I looked at him for a time, wondering whether his cruelty to helpless people was due to a poison in his veins.

"Well," I said after a little, "I dare say it's an oversight you can easily correct. I hope there's been no such oversight about my letters."

He started up behind his desk, his face fixed in the same queer, hook-nosed grin that Punch affects when about to thump his friends to death with his great club. "You—you damned—you presume——" He stopped, suddenly conscious of the intensity of our scrutiny, and sat behind his desk again, breathing heavily. "These Americans!" he said to Mrs. Sanderson, with that same pretense of confidential amusement. "There isn't one who doesn't feel competent to govern this prison."

Sanderson turned to me. "We'll take you out now?"

"I'm sorry," I said. "I can't tell you how happy I'd be to leave this place."

"You mean there's some reason you can't leave?"

"Because of a boy from my town," I told him. "He's a good boy— the best boy I ever knew. He almost sacrificed his life to help me, once; and many years ago his father saved my father at the Battle of Valcour Island. I promised him I'd not go away without him."

"Bring him with you," Mrs. Sanderson said eagerly. "We'll be happy to have him. There are two of us, and we're allowed one prisoner apiece."

"He's in the hospital," I explained. "He's had typhus. The doctor says he's to rest quiet for two weeks more."

"Two weeks?" Sanderson said. "That's the eighth of April. Then we'll come back for you and your friend on the eighth of April."

"Thank you," I said. "His name's Tommy Bickford. When you see him, I think you'll be glad you're taking him away from such a place as this."

"We will indeed," Sanderson assured me. "We will indeed! I wish we could take all of you!"

Shortland laughed. "You don't know 'em as I do! If you did I doubt if you'd let 'em within pistol shot of you or your wife."

The Sandersons ignored him. "The eighth of April, Captain Nason," Mrs. Sanderson said as she gave me her hand. "God send we have good news for you, too, on the day we take you and your friend out of Dartmoor."

XXXI

THE effigy of Reuben Beasley had been hanged, torn down, and kicked into the gutter by the furious men who were still prisoners because of his laziness and inability. No longer did these men in patience toil over their ship models of bone, or weave hats and boxes of straw; they drank and howled and sang desperately.

The night of the fifth of April was the worst of all, because of a sudden whim of the officials to offer us for rations the stale hard biscuits saved through the winter to guard against famine. The Rough Alleys set up an eery yelling at sundown, broke open the gates into the market, and charged up the market slope, howling for bread. There they stayed for hours, in the dim light of the market lamps, their clamor dying to confused rumbles and rising to angry roars.

By morning we heard that all the towns on the moor were in a panic over the ferocity of the Americans. It was a morning strange and memorable for its warmth and sunniness—two things I had seen so seldom on Dartmoor as to count them miracles. So began the blackest day that I have ever known.

*   *   *

I did not think it a black day as I walked slowly along the front of the market place in the early afternoon with Tommy Bickford. "One more day," we both said, time and again. "One more day, and then it's the eighth!"

Tommy was neat as a pin in a natty blue seckatary's suit presented to him by King Dick. Dr. Magrath had given him his discharge from hospital care two days before, telling me to keep him in the sun and walk him a little at discreet intervals, and with that had coughed, stroked his cheek, bidden us good-bye, and stalked away, as good a gentleman as I ever saw.

"One more day and then it's the eighth," I said, for the hundredth time, I think, as we walked along the front of the market.

Tommy touched me on the arm with a thin hand to which the life was returning. "One more day, and then it's the eighth, Cap'n Dick!"

After a time we strolled into the yard that held Prisons Five, Six, and Seven. Here we lounged, following the sun around the buildings, and we sat on the warm ground while Tommy half dozed, roused himself to murmur, "One more day," and half dozed again.

When the chill of sundown settled on us I roused him for a final walk before we should go in, and as we stood up, he murmured, "One more day," and his face wore his old-time look of seeming pleased with everything and everybody.

The yard in which we walked—that of Prisons Seven, Six, and Five —was shaped like a segment of pie. The curved crust of the pie was formed by the two outer walls and the inner barricade of iron pickets; one edge was the wall that divided us from our own prison house, Number Four; and the other edge was the wall, part masonry and part iron fence, that separated us from the barracks and the market place. We walked, therefore, along the curved iron pickets from the barracks walls to the Number Four wall, then back again, taking it slowly and having a care not to be bumped by ball players and skylarkers.

The sky was taking on the pale green color that I have seen only on Dartmoor on the few clear evenings I knew in that dismaying country: a green color that throws a strange illumination on the swarthy hills. The militiamen detailed to light the lamps in the yards were making ready, I saw, to come through the gates.

There were four sailors tossing a ball near the barracks wall as we came down to it. While we watched them, the ball struck one man's finger tips and flew over the wall into the barracks yard. The men stood there shouting for their ball like four dogs barking at a squirrel up a tree; but no ball came back to them, and one of the men pried at the stones of the wall with a sharp stick. As we looked, two of the stones fell out. The man stooped down and picked at the opening; then peered into the hole and again bellowed for the ball.

From the direction of the market place I heard a shouting no different from what we had heard a score of times every day. Then, from the sentry walk at our left, a Somerset militiaman bawled words I couldn't distinguish; words that he repeated and repeated, and that other sentries along the wall picked up and repeated as well.

It sounded like, "Ear coamin droo! Ear coamin droo!" and it dawned on me suddenly they were shouting "They're coming through!" The voices sounded panicky. I began to fear the sentries were imagining we had begun at last the attempt they had so often heard we planned.

"A little more," I said to Tommy, "and those fools'll think it's come —think we're all going to make a breach in the wall and escape in a body."

I had no more than spoken when a sentry's alarm bell clanged; then another and another. In the distance, among the buildings at the prison entrance, the big alarm bell set up a clamor, spilling brazen notes in nervous, irregular, rapid bursts, as if it, too, were stricken with senseless panic.

The Americans near us were doing nothing—not even those ball-players who had picked at the wall: they stood where they were, staring about them in the gathering greenish dusk as if to discover the reason for all this bell ringing.

I took Tommy by the arm, and we moved along the covered walk toward the yard of Number Four. The big alarm bell clanged as if a dozen men were hauling at the rope; and all the other bells in the world seemed to be jangling from the walls. The shouting I had heard from the direction of the market place was echoed in other sections of the yards; the air was filled with the sound of bells and the ragged, excited outcrying of human voices. I could see prisoners running behind us from Number Seven and Six and Five: running toward the covered walk, I knew, to see why the alarm was ringing.

"How do you feel, Tommy?" I asked.

"Good, Cap'n Dick," he said. "What they doing, do you suppose?"

I swung him along, not daring to urge him too much, but eager to get into our own yard and into Number Four, where we would be away from all this running and yelling and bell ringing.

We came to the end of the masonry wall at last and could look through the iron pickets into the market place. What I saw I didn't like. Militiamen were tumbling through the gate at the upper end; and close to us, not ten paces from the iron fence, a file had already formed: a close-packed, red-coated line of men whose faces seemed to me to have caught some of the sickly greenish light that filled the western sky.

What was worse, the gates broken two days before were broken again; and there were prisoners in the market place: a hundred, maybe; maybe a hundred and fifty. Hundreds more were crowding up to the shattered gates, so that those who were already in the market were pinned where they were—in the front by the Somerset-shire militia, and in the rear by a constantly increasing crowd of hooting, yelling prisoners.

Worst of all, I could see the stocky, broad-shouldered figure of Thomas Shortland standing at the end of the file of militiamen: standing there, sword in hand, signaling to other militiamen who were spilling through the upper gate and running down across the market square.

Knowing what I knew about Thomas Shortland, I stooped and took Tommy Bickford in my arms, swung him up against my chest, and ran for the yard of Number Four. When we reached it, it seemed full of prisoners clattering up the slope toward the market gates, all strangely pallid in the greenish twilight, and shouting to know what was happening.

Behind me I heard Dr. Magrath's voice, deep and soothing, urging the prisoners back into their yards.

"Now, gentlemen!" I heard him say. "Now, gentlemen! None of us wants trouble! Just drop back in the yards, gentlemen, so there'll be no chance for misunderstanding!"

With Magrath among the men, I thought, there would be no violence if it could be averted; so I set Tommy on his feet and looked back at the market place. I could see Magrath's head above the prisoners and above the militia. I could see, too, what Magrath could not see: that the prisoners in the market were being pressed harder and harder by those striving to be a part of a confusion that must have been as unfathomable to them as it was to me.

"Keno!" someone shouted. The cry was taken up by others. "Keno! Keno!" It was the battle-cry of the Rough Alleys.

"Now, Tommy," I said, "there's Rough Alleys mixing in it. We'll keep on going."

He smiled, though I knew he had no wish to go, and he limped down the slope beside me, dragging his leg. The men, still running toward us, dodged around us and kept on running.

"Come on and fight, you lousy lobster-backs!" someone shouted.

"Lobster-backs! Lobster-backs!" they howled. A roar went up behind us.

I heard Shortland's voice—a voice I could never mistake, because of the rasping, hurried, overwrought tone that came into it when he was excited and angry, and unbalanced because of his anger. "Get back!" he shouted. "Get back there! Push 'em back! Charge! Charge!"

A shrill cry went up, a pallid, discordant cry that blended, somehow, with the green light in which it seemed to me we moved, all of us, like shadows on a Stygian shore. I knew, on the instant, we had come to the end of all the misunderstanding and mistreatment

heaped on us; knew the hatred which had smoldered for so long had
burst at last into hot flames.

Knowing Tommy could move no faster, I picked him up again,
casting a look over my shoulder as I did so. The close-packed prisoners were struggling to escape from the market place into the
security of the prison yards. From the outcries that pierced the com-
parative silence which followed the first discordant howl it was clear
enough that the Somersetshire militiamen were paying with bayonet
thrusts for the insults they had received.

"Please not to bother about me, Cap'n Dick," Tommy said. "I can
make out all right." He was a good boy, always. I made what speed
I could toward the lowering face of Number Four.

I heard, then, what I had been waiting for—Shortland's bullying,
raging voice. "Damned Yankee rascals!" he shouted. "Fire!"

Then, for a moment, there was no sound except that of scrambling
and scuttling and running. There was a curious fearfulness to the
sound, as to the frightened rush of mice in the walls of a house.

"Fire!" Shortland shouted again, more loudly. "Fire, God damn it!
Fire!"

Then came a single musket shot, and after it a shrill tumult of yelling. The next instant the green twilight was ripped and slashed by
a musketry volley: a ragged volley that echoed and roared among
those gray stone walls and tall prison houses as though it had come
from carronades.

The shrillness of hundreds of voices suddenly became piercing. Everywhere there were men running as fast as they could; and I ran
too, but heavily and slowly, because of the weight of Tommy
Bickford.

There was another volley of musketry fire, and another and another; then, horribly, firing came from the encircling walls. Spurts
of flame stabbed the dusk all along the great ring about us. We
seemed to be the center of a whirling confusion, a crashing, screaming dizziness, almost as though this great granite millstone of ours,

in a final convulsion of cruelty, had come alive to whirl us down the barren slopes of Dartmoor to destruction.

A black man, running close beside me, tripped, staggered, and regained his feet. When he started forward once more his leg bent at the thigh like a piece of rope, and he fell on his face, struggling to drag himself forward with hands like black claws.

The reports of the muskets seemed in our very ears, as though the soldiers had come out of the market place into the yards to pursue us fleeing, unarmed people.

"What they shooting for, Cap'n Dick?" Tommy asked me. "Isn't the war over?"

We had come close up to the front of Number Four. All around us were running prisoners, converging on the entrances. Dimly I could see that those around the doors were jammed, tossing their arms and shouting. Figures burst from among them as if popped out by the press. "Locked!" I heard them screaming. "The door's locked!"

I saw Jesse Smith come out of the jam. He stopped and motioned; then ran forward and got his hands on me, pulling me to the ground. A musket exploded almost in my ear. Men ran past and over us, yelling. They had muskets, and one of them laughed wildly, stabbing at Jesse's prostrate form with his bayonet.

They were Somersetshire militia, all of them. Beyond us they halted and fired into the mass of men who still struggled before the locked doors. Two of the prisoners pitched downward and lay still. The others broke and ran, leaving some who limped and crawled away. Jesse was digging at the cobblestones with his fingers: but the stones were immovable, cemented in place by the black Dartmoor muck.

Against the end of the prison sat a man holding his shoulder, his hand a smear of blood. One of the militiamen stopped before him, loading his musket, whereupon the man, John Washington, a prize master from the Baltimore privateer *Rolla* and a peaceable good fellow, held out his bloody hand to him as if to show he was hurt. At this the militiaman dropped the ramrod back in its socket, cocked his piece, held the muzzle against Washington's face and fired.

"Oh, God!" Jesse said. "Oh, my God!" We tore and tore at the cobbles with our fingers, but could do nothing with them.

One of King Dick's seckataries, a fine-looking boy named Jackson, fourteen years old or thereabouts, who had been impressed aboard the British cruiser *Pontes* but had given himself up rather than serve against his own country, ran out from the shelter of the doorway of Number Four and raced around the corner of the building, evidently making for the rear door. He was an easy mark in his neat white trousers and short blue jacket. Four muskets spat at him as he rounded the corner. He rolled over and over, like a shot rabbit: then sprawled on his face.

More soldiers were coming from the market place. Behind us I heard Shortland's voice, yelling words I couldn't distinguish. "Quick, Jesse!" I said. "Get Jackson before they load again." Jesse ran for the small sprawling form at the corner of the building; while I got my arms under Tommy, swung him up against my breast and followed. I set off down the cruel long length of Number Four, expecting each moment to hear the crash of muskets at my back.

Jesse Smith was ahead of me. Beyond him, now that we were unprotected by the towering front of Number Four, were the points and slashes of light made by the muskets of the sentries on the walls as they sniped at the defenseless men beneath.

We turned the lower corner at last, so close to the walls that I could feel, I thought, the heat of the musketry fire blazing in our faces. Yet we were fortunate and escaped the bullets, which we heard flirting past us and smacking against the rear of the prison.

The door stood open, by the grace of God. I followed Jesse Smith up the steps and into the prison, my legs like lead and my lungs aflame.

I set Tommy on his feet and looked about me. There were no lights in the prison, but in the darkness I could make out that the floor was covered with men, lying full length with their faces turned toward the entrance.

There was a clatter of feet outside. Two more prisoners raced up the steps and threw themselves, panting, on the floor.

"Look out!" one of them said. "They're a-comin'!"

The door moved to close, but before it did a group of militiamen stood enframed against the outer green light. With no word of warning they threw their muskets to their shoulders and fired among us. The door slammed shut, leaving the militiamen outside upon the steps.

I heard Tommy cough, a distressed, bubbly cough; and I felt his hands slide down me as he slipped to his knees. "They shot me, Cap'n Dick," he said in a faint, surprised voice.

"Hold on, Tommy," I said. "Nothing'll hurt you with me here."

There was the sound of a long breath from him—a difficult breath, as if a pillow was pressed to his face.

"Tommy!" I said, so frightened that I felt close to suffocation from the pounding of my heart. "Where did it hit you, Tommy?"

There was no answer from him. "Tommy!" I said, louder; then I shouted his name and got my hands on him. I found the hole. It was under his left shoulder. My hands came away sticky. He was dead.

When the candles were lighted there was a Somersetshire militiaman pressed into the corner of that crowded room. He had come in the yard at dusk to light the lamps and had been carried into the prison with the first rush. We sat with our dead and wounded and watched him for two hours before Magrath came to take the hurt to the hospital. With them the doctor sent the militiaman, for though no man had touched him, he was mouthing and tittering like an idiot.

XXXII

Thus I lost my dearest friend and came alive myself out of the massacre in Dartmoor Prison. America bears the pain of April the 6th, 1815, and England bears the shame of that day. To my mind what Britain did less than three months later at Waterloo loses its glory because of the red smear she put upon her flags so short a time before at Dartmoor.

There were Englishmen who knew and bitterly rued the crime of Shortland. The kindly Sanderson was one of these. When he came to take me away on the day after the "one day more" that Tommy and I had talked of so happily, Emily's brother shook my hand but said not a word to me until we were beyond the walls. Then he cursed Shortland and Dartmoor and the government, and his wife cried.

"My dead friend and those others," I said, "are part of history now. May justice be done to their memory there, though justice be unknown in the land where they suffered. The Peace has reached them at last."

Mrs. Sanderson cried harder at this, and to regain my own composure I had to comfort her.

"You brought me news?" I asked a little later, as the carriage took us easily toward Plymouth, down those long, desolate hills up which had toiled thousands of leaden-hearted Americans. "You've learned what has become of Emily? You can put me on my way to her?"

Sanderson set his lips together in a tight line and stared off across the fortress-like hedgerows that guard the roads of Devon.

"Let's have the worst of it," I told him when I saw the look on his face. "I'd like to get it over with. Is she—is she——"

"I think the worst of it, Captain Nason," Mrs. Sanderson told me, "is that we can get no trace of where she went after she left Portsmouth. She vanished into thin air."

"We could have told you more, two weeks ago," Sanderson said. "When we first came to take you out of prison we didn't tell you because it seemed you were bearing all a man could, and we decided not to add to the burden upon you—not to tell you all we knew until you were out and free to move. Captain Nason, there was a good reason for my sister to vanish."

I drew a deep breath. "By vanish you mean hide—you're telling me she had to hide from someone who followed her?"

"From more than one who followed her," Sanderson said bitterly. "No, it's not what you're thinking, Captain. We'd been to Exeter before we saw you, and the place was all too busy mouthing the pitiful story."

"Sir Arthur Ransome——" I began.

"Sir Arthur Brute!" Mrs. Sanderson interrupted. "Sir Arthur Beast!"

"I suppose he thought he was within his rights," Sanderson said. "I suppose he fooled himself into thinking his revenge was 'justice.' The man is of a petty but viciously vindictive nature. We heard he spoke of 'avenging outraged honor' and of being an Aristides for law and justice. Ah, well, his vanity was on the raw!"

"What did he do?" I asked huskily.

"You see," Sanderson explained, "you see——" He coughed and tried again. "There's nobody who'd believe any of it—we knew it was only vindictiveness. Ah—he charged Emily, you know—an ugly fellow at bottom, I really think—he brought charges the authorities had to take cognizance of, whether or no. I assure you, Captain Nason—ah, that is, we don't want you to think——"

"Why, sir," I said, "I think you and Mrs. Sanderson are the kindest of people."

"Well," Sanderson went on, "he charged her with—he charged her with—he charged he found her with you."

"I hated him, always," Mrs. Sanderson assured me.

"Even more desperate in the eyes of the law than his charge on the personal account," Sanderson continued, "he laid an information against her for aiding and abetting the escape of an enemy prisoner; and there, of course, he had her; for she was trying to help you, and was caught in the act, as you remember he had witnesses to prove. If she'd been taken on that information there'd have been no possible defense, nor any way for her to save herself from a term of imprisonment."

"Well," I said, after a few moments, "God knows I was sure there was good reason why I'd heard nothing from her."

"Yes," Sanderson agreed, "it was as good a reason for lying hid as you could find; though I think that if we could get word to her that we're in England she might come out of hiding."

I wrestled with the matter for a time. "Portsmouth," I said at length. "You spoke of Portsmouth?"

"Yes, she had a small white dog when she left Ransome Hall; and it was through the dog that the police traced her to Portsmouth."

"Of course!" I said, brooding over it. "Of course; and it was from a gambling club in Portsmouth that the message came to you!"

"Yes," Sanderson said, frowning in puzzlement. "There's a strange thing, now, isn't it!" He looked thoughtfully at the neat thatched cottages that lie along the green hill slopes behind Plymouth, into which our carriage was clattering. "When the police went to her lodgings to arrest her, she was gone, and her dog too. The police learned then that her lodgings had been taken and paid for by a gentleman known as her brother; and all of them—the man, his servant, Emily and her dog—departed together as suddenly as they had come. The police investigated further and found that the man calling himself her brother had opened a small gaming club. On the eve-

THE LIVELY LADY

ning before he disappeared from Portsmouth with Emily he fought
an English naval officer and hurt him badly."

"So," I said, "they fled together from Portsmouth?"

"Yes—they did," Sanderson replied uneasily. He frowned more
deeply. Discomforting embarrassment seemed added to his distress,
and he evaded my eye. Then he looked up at me plaintively, and
his expression became one of amazement; for by the grace of heaven
I had suddenly found the courage to laugh.

"Over what had the gambler and the British naval officer fought?"
I asked.

Sanderson stared at me. "Why, I ascertained that the officer had
referred slightingly to the Scotch renegade, John Paul, who fought
in your navy under the name of Jones. The officer spoke of him as
a traitor and pirate; and with no word of warning this small impostor,
whoever he was, slapped the officer's face, then seized him by the
ears and pounded his head on a Wheel-of-Fortune table with such
force as to ruin it."

"Are you sure of that?" I asked, puzzled. "Are you sure the officer
didn't speak flatteringly of Jones?"

"We read the information laid against the man," Mrs. Sanderson
said. "It was sworn that the officer referred to Jones most disparag-
ingly. I recall he used the words 'renegade Scotch toad' and 'murder-
ing Judas' just before the man claiming to be Emily's brother
attacked him so violently."

Her husband continued to stare at me; so I said to him, putting
my hand on his knee: "Give me a little while to think, and I'll tell
you why I laughed, my dear good friend."

So they were quiet, and I *did* think. By the time we had arrived
at the Duke of Cornwall hostelry, on the high land looking out over
Mill Bay to the main harbor of Plymouth, I was satisfied I knew a
part of what had happened.

"It *is* good news you brought me, after all," I told them, when the
porter had left us alone in the Sandersons' big room, from the windows of which we could look across to Drake's Island and Mount

Batten. "All the while that I spoke with Emily in the front room of
Mark Tate's cottage there was a good comrade of mine lying in the
room behind us: Jeddy Tucker, a man she knew; and he wisely
stayed hidden while I was taken away to Exeter jail. I was sure that
if he could find means to be of service to her, he would. He's a shrewd
fellow and a true good heart. Now I know what he did. He was
quick at cards and all kinds of gambling; and it had to be by gambling that he put money into their pockets—his and Emily's and Mark
Tate's, who must have acted as his servant. Well, now what hinders
us from following them?"

I went to the window and looked out at the blue salt water. It
had been more than a year since I had felt it under me, or seen it
even; and the year had seemed longer than all the other years of
my life. There were war craft at anchor in this safe, cup-shaped
haven, and merchantmen moving in and out. I longed to be among
them with the quarter-deck of a stout vessel beneath my feet and a
fair wind filling my topgallant sails.

"Following them!" Mrs. Sanderson echoed. "How can we follow
them when none of us knows where they are?"

Before I could answer, my eye caught sight of a brigantine riding
at anchor off Eastern King Point—riding as gracefully, among the
squat, heavy merchantmen and war craft, as a slim sheldrake among
a host of clumsy gulls. She was drying her sails, from which I knew
she was newly arrived in port. There was such a rake to her tapering
sticks that she had something of the look, even at rest, of a slender
girl straining eagerly forward, running, her head tilted back and her
stomach thrust out ahead of her upper body; and I stared at her,
forgetful of my friends for the moment.

Mrs. Sanderson touched my arm. "Did you mean what you said?"
she asked. "You know the man who took her away—you think you
know where he'd go?"

I turned from my study of the brig. "I think so," I said. "Before
I was taken prisoner I sent a prize into Nantes: a fine West Indiaman, the *Pembroke*. She was in charge of Cephas Cluff, my first

officer; and my orders to Cephas were to lie in Nantes until I should come there myself to get the ship and our prize money from my agents. If Jeddy took Emily from Portsmouth to escape the police, there's only one guess as to what he would have done. He'd never have let her come near Dartmoor, for fear she'd be taken; nor would there have been any safe place in England, after that, for either of them. But it was easy enough to go to France; for then Bonaparte was still in Elba, and France and England were at peace; and to France they'd have gone: to France and to Nantes and to the *Pembroke*, where they'd be among friends."

Sanderson laughed abruptly and huskily.

"If they're anywhere," I said, "they're in Nantes. They're in Nantes, and it's to Nantes that we'll go!"

With that I laughed too, clapped Sanderson on the shoulder, took him by the arm and pulled him from his chair. "How soon can you be ready?" I cried. "How soon?"

"My dear captain!" he protested, "how can we do any such thing? No English vessels can be found to carry us into a French port, now that we're at war again! What's more, even if you yourself have means to sail for a French port and arrive there, my wife and I are English and couldn't accompany you while our country's at war with France. But I see no means for you to go yourself, Captain Nason. I fear we must wait until Boney is cornered once more and put where he'll no longer torture all the world."

What he said was true; the wind dropped out of my sails, and I stood staring dismally from the window. "Another war!" I groaned. "We must wait for the end of another war!" Then for a time we three were quiet, cogitating gloomily.

A murmurous sound intruded on our silence. At first I thought it came from out of doors; but presently I recognized it as the voice of a man talking in the next room. I listened idly: it became more audible—a gentle, winning voice that seemed to have in it a note of deference and yet a tone of assurance.

"Why," I said, "why who——" and with that I went near the closed door that shut off our room from the next. The voice became distinct to my ear. "Oh, do you think so?" it said, "do you really think so! That is very kind and thoughtful of you, sir: very gracious and very handsomely said!"

I turned to look again at the brig lying off Eastern King Point. A faint breeze caught her shivered sails, bellying them a little and dimly revealing, on her mainsail, the patches where the passage of a bushel of grapeshot had been repaired. At her mainpeak a flag stirred idly. I saw it to be the Stars and Stripes. "The *Chasseur!*" I cried. "The *Chasseur!*"

And with no more explanation than that to my two friends, I hurried from the room, ran to the door of the adjoining chamber, and went in. At the far end of the room was a table. At one side of it sat a red-faced, fat Englishman; and at the other a gentleman, neat and handsome in a brown broadcloth coat and pale-colored trousers buckled under his boots. On the table between them was a gold-headed cane and a gray beaver hat apparently in no respect different from the one that had been shot from the head of a warm friend of mine upon a certain conspicuous occasion. I saw the gentleman stroke his small black mustache and heard him say to the red-faced Englishman, "But it's *not* extravagance, if you'll permit me the correction, sir—not at all! If we're free with our money we'll find it easier when we wish other prisoners released; and after all, my dear sir, we can't even be sure of civility from most of your compatriots unless we—I hope you don't mind my mentioning it—unless we pay well for it."

I cleared my throat, for the sight of him moved me.

Captain Boyle rose to his feet and raised his eyebrows, striving to see me clearly in the dimness. "Whom have I the pleasure——" he asked politely, and I saw him dart a suspicious glance at the red-faced Englishman.

"A passenger for your packet boat," I said, with a gruffness in my voice that was due to no desire to disguise it.

"My packet boat!" he exclaimed. "You've been misinformed, I fear! I'm not in the passenger-carrying business, sir."

I cleared my throat again. "I think you might be," I said. "I think you *would* be, if——"

He came forward quickly; stopped; then stepped close up to me and dropped his hand on my shoulder. "Why—" he said, and there was a thickness in his speech that somehow brought moisture into my own eyes—"why, I've been planning—I came here to ask for your —why, yes! I think I *would* take a passenger for any port this side of hell, or the other side, for that matter, if Captain Nason wished to go there!"

*　.*　　*

It was not until the *Chasseur* was at sea that I told this gallant friend of mine why I had asked him to carry me to Nantes. Then, in his pleasant cabin and across his damask tablecloth, I told him everything, even why the *Lively Lady*, lying deep within the closure of the waters we traversed, bore upon her prow a figurehead—now, alas! encrusted—that when he saw it had hair the color of rubbed copper and was gowned in shimmering green. I told him, too, how Jeddy Tucker, who had so often fought upon our native shores and upon shipboard, enraged by any word of admiration for John Paul Jones, had contrarily fought the British naval officer in Portsmouth for referring slightingly to that same John Paul Jones.

When I had finished speaking of this strange action of Jeddy's, Captain Boyle's eyes danced; then he became graver, looking at me intently. "Splendid!" he said in a low voice. "I think it's a sign. I think it's one of the many signs—signs that the great thing is done."

"What great thing?" I asked.

"The greatest thing in the world for your country and mine," he answered. "Before we fought England this second time we were not a nation. We were a few millions of individuals, scattered into arguing, backbiting groups—towns and communities and separated jealous states; every man for his own section; every section for itself.

Now your Jeddy Tucker fights for the good name of an American hero because he can bear no tarnish put upon a national brightness; and that spirit is everywhere among us, because we've found out that we're America. Not many men know better than you what suffering the war has brought, Captain Nason; but history must say it has done a great task, and that Dartmoor was worth the price. We're a nation at last."

XXXIII

THE *Pembroke* lay at a dock on the lower end of the Isle Feydou, huge and towering in the pale night mist that drifted down the Loire from the vine-clad hills above it; and I, standing close under her high sides, called softly up to the watch on deck to know whether Cephas Cluff was aboard.

"He might be, an' again he mightn't," the watch drawled. "Depends on who wants him."

Cephas himself spared me the trouble of answering by appearing above the taffrail, broad of beam against the starlight beyond.

"Come down here," I said to him. "I want a word with you where we won't be heard."

"Land o' Goshen!" Cephas whispered, staring fixedly at me. "My land o' Goshen!" He moved quickly and lightly to the companionway and came over the side; then held to my hand with his great rough fist and breathed heavily. "It's you!" he said. "Where's the others, Cap'n? Gorry, we been afraid you wouldn't never come! Aye, we mighty near believed you wouldn't never come!"

I stood and looked at him, afraid, almost, to ask the questions that boiled in my mind.

He nodded at me. "They're aboard," he said. "They been living there. She's in the captain's quarters. Jeddy said you'd want it that way."

"Is she—how is she——"

"Good!" Cephas assured me emphatically. "Food's a thousand percent better since she came aboard. Ain't nothing gets by her!"

"Well," I said, "as soon as we settle with the Latours we'll clear for Plymouth and pick up the rest of the crew. Captain Boyle's tending to it for me."

I ran up the companionway, leaving Cephas breathing heavily behind me, and went aft to the cabin. The door to the captain's quarters stood ajar, and beyond it I heard voices. I listened, my heart thumping fit to burst.

I recognized Jeddy's impudent tones. "Box-hauling," he was saying, "is a piece of seamanship you use to claw off a lee shore, provided you got plenty of hands aboard. Say you've reached for a point in a heavy gale and find you ain't going to make it, account of wind and sea and currents; there ain't time or room to tack, so you box-haul her. Here she is, coming into this point here. The spoon's the point and the fork's the wind."

"I can see it quite plainly," a voice said—a soft and husky voice that set the blood to pounding in my head, "and it's not necessary for you to tip her like that. You know how I'd feel if she were broken."

"I'll thank you not to tell me that again, ma'am," Jeddy replied brusquely. "Now, ma'am, having her in that position, you got to turn quick—turn her on her heel. All right: you clap your helm a-lee, haul up your mainsail, brail up your mizzen and mizzen staysail, square the after yards, let go the fore tack, sheet, bowlines and lee braces— be so kind as to point 'em out, ma'am."

"Here and here and here," said the soft and husky voice.

"Correct, ma'am," Jeddy said. "Then you brace the head yards sharp aback, haul over the weather jib and foretopmast staysail sheets, and she pays round off on her heel—and there you are, ma'am, free of your lee shore and headed for open water. Now, what was it she done to get there, ma'am?"

The soft voice answered him in the tone of an obedient child saying her lessons. "The main and mizzen topsails lying aback gave her sternway, and when the larboard side of her rudder pressed against the water in backing, it helped her head to cast to larboard."

I opened the door softly and went in. At the long gold-covered table beneath the silver lamps sat Emily and Jeddy, their backs to me and their heads close together over the small bone frigate I had last seen in the dreary market place of Dartmoor Prison. Beyond them rose the rudder case, carved and colored to represent a close-packed stand of bamboos; and because of the swirling in my head at the sight of Emily, the carved green fronds that branched above her seemed to sway and flutter in a silent breeze.

"So there we are," she said, looking at Jeddy, "free of our lee shore and headed for open water." Then her eyes descended to the little frigate; her head bowed and her figure drooped. "Headed for clear and open water," she said sadly. "Ah, if we were! Do you think we ever will be, Jeddy?"

There was a faint growl, and my little white dog Pinky came out from behind the rudder case, walking importantly on his toes, to stand peering doubtfully at me. Emily, seeing him staring beyond her, looked up into one of the paneled mirrors. Her widening eyes met mine. With a fluttering hand she set down the frigate, and even before she turned to me I could see in those dazed, widening eyes of hers all I had ever hoped to have of life.

"Free of our lee shore," I said unsteadily. "Free of our lee shore, my dear, and headed for clear and open water."

AUTHORITIES

On privateering, seamanship, and the War of 1812: ABBOT, WILLIS J., *American Merchant Ships & Sailors*; BOWDITCH, NATHANIEL, *New American Practical Navigator*; CHAPELLE, HOWARD IRVING, *The Baltimore Clipper*; CHAPIN, HOWARD M., *Privateer Ships & Sailors*; CHATTERTON, E. KEBLE, *Sailing Ships & Their Story*; CHATTERTON, E. KEBLE, *Ships & Ways of Other Days*; COGGESHALL, GEORGE, *History of the American Privateers*; DAVIS, CHARLES G., *Ships of the Past*; ESSEX INSTITUTE, COLLECTIONS OF THE, Vol. II, No. 2, *Private Armed Vessels Belonging to Salem During the War of 1812*; ESSEX INSTITUTE, COLLECTIONS OF THE, Jan. 1901, *Account of the Private Armed Ship "America" of Salem*; JAMESON, JOHN F., *Privateering & Piracy in the Colonial Period*; JOHNSON, CHARLES H. L., *Famous Privateersmen & Adventurers of the Sea*; LEVER, DARCY, *The Young Sea Officer's Sheet Anchor*; MACLAY, EDGAR S., *History of American Privateers*; MAHAN, *Sea Power in Its Relations to the War of 1812*; PEABODY, ROBERT E., *The Log of the Grand Turks*; ROBBINS, ARCHIBALD, *Journal of the Loss of the Brig "Commerce"*; ROOSEVELT, THEODORE, *Naval War of 1812*; SCOTT, MICHAEL, *Tom Cringle's Log*; SHERBURNE, ANDREW, *Memoirs*; STATHAM, COMMANDER E. P., R.N., *Privateers & Privateering*.

On Dartmoor Prison, and on conditions in England and France at the end of the Napoleonic Wars: ABELL, FRANCIS, *Prisoners of War in Britain, 1756–1815*; ANDREWS, CHARLES, *The Prisoner's Memoirs, or Dartmoor Prison*; BROEMEL, P. R., *Paris & London in 1815*; COBB, JOSIAH, *A Green Hand's First Cruise, & Five Months in Dartmoor Prison*; HAWTHORNE, NATHANIEL (edited by), *Yarn of a Yankee Privateer*; LOLIEE, FREDERIC, *Prince Talleyrand & His Times*; PALMER, BENJAMIN F., *Diary of (at Melville Island & Dartmoor)*; RECORDS OF ARUNDEL PRISONERS, *Registry of Prisoners of War (Dartmoor Section)*, Public Record Office, London; THOMSON, BASIL, *The Story of Dartmoor Prison*; VALPEY, JOSEPH, JR., *Journal of (in Dartmoor Prison)*; WATERHOUSE, BENJAMIN, *Journal of a Young Man of Massachusetts . . . at Dartmoor*.

❈ ❈ ❈

The descriptions of the *Chasseur* and the second *Lively Lady* are based on Model 986 in the Louvre Marine Museum—that of the brigantine *La Gazelle*, 18 guns, built at Bayonne on the plans of M. Marestier and launched in 1822. Marestier studied Baltimore clippers in America for the French navy; and *La Gazelle* is believed to be the only existing model that accurately reveals the lines of the best Baltimore clipper privateers of the War of 1812.

❈ ❈ ❈

The author gratefully acknowledges the generous assistance of Mr. Booth Tarkington, Mr. Howard Irving Chapelle, Commandant Edward Hubert of the Louvre Marine Museum, Mr. Henry Dawes, secretary to the American Ambassador to the Court of St. James, Mrs. Marion Cobb Fuller of the Maine State Library, Captain William H. Gould of Kennebunkport, Me., Mr. J. Templeman Coolidge, Mr. Irving R. Wiles, and the Library of Congress.

TRENDING INTO MAINE (published Little Brown, 1938: Double-day, 1944)
"Kenneth Roberts takes you into the kitchen, sits you down by the stove, hands you a doughnut, and stuffs you full of Arundel, Maine traditions, Maine smells, Maine people, the hardships of soldiering, the pleasures of ducks' breasts, the bravery of sea captains' daughters."
—E. B. WHITE, *Saturday Review of Literature*

MARCH TO QUEBEC (published 1938: revised 1940)
"Bringing together, in *March to Quebec,* the journals of the Quebec Expedition is an exceedingly valuable contribution to the Americana of the Revolution. . . . Many have been practically inaccessible. . . . Only a few libraries in the country have them all, and he who would buy them for himself would be obliged to spend a large sum of money and wait for a year or so before some dealer in rare books could accumulate all of them." —*Boston Evening Transcript*

MOREAU DE ST. MÉRY'S AMERICAN JOURNEY (1793–1798)
(published 1947: a translation by Kenneth and Anna Roberts)
"Here is a cross-section of a nation in the process, to use Moreau's apt phrase, of being born." —*New York Times*

I WANTED TO WRITE (published 1949)
"The record of the reading, the assimilation, the eternal tracking down of details, the enormous correspondence, and the starts and stops of a historical novel in progress. Here is the reason why it took three years to write *Oliver Wiswell* and five years to complete *Lydia Bailey.* Here is what you go on doing, once you have learned to write."
—*Atlantic Monthly*

HENRY GROSS AND HIS DOWSING ROD (published 1951)
"In October, 1949, Henry Gross dowsed a fresh-water dome at Clayhouse on a map of Bermuda, an island on which no potable spring water supposedly existed. The Clayhouse well was drilled and, on April 27, 1950, flowed 44 gallons a minute, a daily 63,360 gallons 'wasting its sweetness on the desert air.' . . . It is the greatest Bermuda story ever told." —PARK BRECK, *Mid-Ocean (Bermuda) News*

THE SEVENTH SENSE (published 1953)
"*The Seventh Sense* is Roberts' answer to the volleys of his critics —the account of the first year's operation of Water Unlimited Inc., whose aims are to insure an adequate supply of water for the world's people, and to obtain for Henry Gross a steady income."
—ALAN NASH, *Rochester Times-Union*

WATER UNLIMITED (published 1957)
"The earlier books [*Henry Gross and His Dowsing Rod* and *The Seventh Sense*] convinced me of the authenticity of Roberts' reports, and of his theories about the circulation of subterranean water. . . . I recommend this volume and the two earlier ones to any person not blinded by unshakable prejudgments as offering a major contribution to the world's vital need for water resources."
—EDMUND FULLER, *Chicago Tribune*